Praise for the Novels of National Bestselling Author Susan Bowden

Forget Me Not

"In this pleasant read, Bowden ably depicts the life of a family—and a town—twisted by secrets, guilt, and suspicion."
—*Publishers Weekly*

"A terrific story liberally laced with romance and suspense. . . . Susan Bowden just gets better and better."
—*Romantic Times*

"Haunting . . . entertaining . . . multilayered. . . . Another character-driven hit that will immensely please her fans."
—*Painted Rock Reviews*

"Satisfying . . . sharply drawn characters, uncluttered and efficient dialogue, and a genuinely intriguing mystery."
—*Winnipeg Free Press*

"Bowden spins a captivating work of suspense, underscored by an element of romance."
—*Prairie*

Continued on

Family Secrets

"Readers looking for a compelling drama and dynamic family relationships will be thrilled with Ms Bowden's newest offering."   —*Romantic Times*

"A riveting plot . . . draws readers in from its opening page . . . craftily building suspense."
—*Winnipeg Free Press*

"An intriguing plot filled with a collection of interesting characters. Bowden drops the clues one by one, keeping interest constantly burning."
—*Affaire de Coeur*

Homecoming

"The very talented Susan Bowden consistently demonstrates her special ability to peer deep into the hearts and souls of her all-too-human characters. The complex family relationships and conflicting emotions of this novel make for compelling reading."
—*Romantic Times*

"A long, leisurely read with finely crafted, memorable characters."   —*I'll Take Romance*

Also by Susan Bowden

BITTER HARVEST

Susan Bowden

A SIGNET BOOK

SIGNET
Published by New American Library, a division of
Penguin Putnam Inc., 375 Hudson Street,
New York, New York 10014, U.S.A.
Penguin Books Ltd, 27 Wrights Lane,
London W8 5TZ, England
Penguin Books Australia Ltd, Ringwood,
Victoria, Australia
Penguin Books Canada Ltd, 10 Alcorn Avenue,
Toronto, Ontario, Canada M4V 3B2
Penguin Books (N.Z.) Ltd, 182–190 Wairau Road,
Auckland 10, New Zealand

Penguin Books Ltd, Registered Offices:
Harmondsworth, Middlesex, England

First published by Signet, an imprint of New American Library,
a division of Penguin Putnam Inc.

First Printing, February 2001
10 9 8 7 6 5 4 3

 REGISTERED TRADEMARK—MARCA REGISTRADA

Printed in the United States of America

PUBLISHER'S NOTE
This is a work of fiction. Names, characters, places, and incidents either
are the product of the author's imagination or are used fictitiously,
and any resemblance to actual persons, living or dead, business establish-
ments, events, or locales is entirely coincidental.

BOOKS ARE AVAILABLE AT QUANTITY DISCOUNTS WHEN USED TO PROMOTE
PRODUCTS OR SERVICES. FOR INFORMATION PLEASE WRITE TO PREMIUM
MARKETING DIVISION, PENGUIN PUTNAM INC., 375 HUDSON STREET, NEW
YORK, NEW YORK 10014.

This book, which is set in the Maritime Province of New Brunswick, is dedicated to Jacqui Good and Leon Cole, dear friends and Maritimers, with gratitude for all their support over the years and, particularly, for their research assistance with this book. They are not, however, responsible for any errors I may have made in my descriptions of this beautiful province, which completely captivated me on my very first visit.

Chapter 1

Eleanor Tyler halted when she reached the top of the stairs. As she stood in the shadows, gasping for breath, leaning heavily on her ebony cane, she hoped that no one in the hall below could see her. She'd had more than enough talk from them about installing an elevator or a stairlift. Damn their interference! If she decided she needed an elevator she'd order it for herself. Stupid people! Didn't they realize that the more they suggested it, the more determined she was not to get one?

As she set off down the carpeted corridor to her room, she felt the floor rise and fall beneath her feet. She had to admit that the stairs were starting to get to her. She was positively light-headed. For one head-spinning moment she thought she might have to sit down on one of the Sheraton chairs to catch her breath. She clearly recalled buying the set of four chairs at Sotheby's in London when she and Ramsey visited Europe to celebrate their thirtieth anniversary. Or was it their twenty-fifth? Frowning, she trailed thin arthritic fingers across her forehead. She wasn't sure. A long time ago, anyway. A time when her legs didn't give out on her after a few steps.

Digging her cane harder into the carpet, she slowly and painfully made her way to her bedroom and opened the door. The curtains had been drawn around the large bay window. Only the small crystal lamps had been switched on, casting two pools of light onto her dressing table. The rest of the room was in shadow.

She took two steps into the room and then froze. Instinctively, she knew that something was out of place. There. On her bed. A small mound in the center. She limped across to the bed and stared down at it. Her heart leapt. "Oh, Griffon," she whispered, smiling down at her little dog. "You came back. I knew you would." She stretched out her hand to pat his golden fur, then snatched it back. Griffon lay there, stiff, unmoving, his head at an unnatural angle to the rest of his body.

Eleanor pressed her hand to her mouth to stifle the scream that rose from her throat. Heart racing, she sank into the chair beside the bed. She wanted to rush to the bedroom door, to scream to those who were still gathered in the hall to come to her aid. But there was no aiding her little Griffon, her one true friend, whose body lay spread out on the patchwork quilt that her own great-grandmother had made a century ago. That, in itself, was a monstrous sacrilege: she had *never* permitted Griffon to jump on her bed—or any of the beds or chairs, for that matter. Everyone knew how much she cherished those precious ancient relics that had belonged to the two families, hers and her husband's, some of them dating as far back as the eighteenth century when the two loyalist families had escaped from Boston during the perils of the Revolution.

Eleanor put a trembling hand to her head. Why in the name of heaven was she worrying about her family history and a stupid quilt when Griffon was lying there, dead? It wasn't an accident, that was certain. Griffon had been missing for two days. Now someone had laid his body out on her bed, for her to find. Who could have done this? None of the disturbing things that had happened to her recently could prepare her for this horror.

But the greatest horror of all was knowing that the only people to enter the house since she'd left her bedroom this afternoon had been the various members of her own family. And Janet, of course, but Janet had been her loyal and efficient housekeeper for almost forty years. Oh, and Andrew Lenzie had visited her yesterday, but Andrew had been their family physician ever since his father had died.

Douglas Bradford had also visited her yesterday. She'd called him in again to discuss her will. She was never quite sure which side her lawyer was on. No doubt Douglas told Norman that she'd been talking about changing the will again, but that was all right. She liked to keep them all guessing.

What was the matter with her? Her mind kept turning to unimportant matters when she should be dealing with this abomination. *Concentrate, woman, concentrate,* she told herself.

She braced her hands on the arms of the chair and slowly got to her feet. Averting her eyes from the bed, she drew a lace-edged handkerchief from her sleeve, pressing it over her eyes and mouth. Slowly, she moved to the door. Forcing herself to breathe evenly, she straightened her shoulders, opened the door, and went out into the upper hall.

She halted at the head of the stairs. Her fingers grasping the polished wooden post, she peered down into the hall below, but although she could hear muffled voices, she could see nothing. "Janet!" she called sharply.

The voices quieted and then faded to silence. Her eldest son, Norman, came into the well of light at the foot of the staircase. He lifted his dark head to stare up at her. "She's not here, Mother. Anything I can do?"

"Where's Janet?" she demanded. "I want her. Now."

"I'll get her for you." That was Lauren speaking, Norman's second—and much younger—wife. No doubt his reason for getting that ridiculous hair transplant.

"Thank you."

Grace appeared beside him. "Is something wrong?"

"Yes," Eleanor snapped at her daughter.

Grace started up the stairs.

"No!" Eleanor said. "Don't come up yet. I want Janet first. Where the blazes is she?"

"I'm coming, I'm coming," Janet said as she suddenly appeared behind Grace.

Relief swept over Eleanor. "I want you to come up, Janet. But no one else until I call, understand?"

Eleanor could hear Grace's impatient sigh and saw Norman shrug and shake his head. *They think I'm going crazy,* she said to herself. But this time they would see for themselves that she wasn't imagining things.

When Janet had hauled herself up to the top of the stairs, Eleanor gripped her arm. "I warn you, it's going to upset you," she told her.

"What is?"

Eleanor's lips trembled. "Someone's killed Griffon."

Janet's mouth formed an O of horror. "Oh, no!" She peered over her glasses at Eleanor. "Are you sure?" she asked, frowning. "I know he's been missing since Thursday, but—"

"He's dead. And he's lying on my bed." Eleanor turned on her heel and led the way into the bedroom. She paused only to turn on the main light from the switch by the doorway. "See?" she said, steeling herself as she turned, dreading having to look at the bed in the full light.

There was nothing there. The ancient, faded quilt lay there, unruffled, with no sign whatsoever that Griffon's inert little body had lain there only a few minutes before.

Janet approached the bed. "There's nothing here, Mrs. Tyler."

Eleanor's hand went to her throat. "Griffon was there, on the bed. I saw him. I touched him." Her voice cracked. "He was cold and stiff."

She joined Janet at the side of the bed and ran her hands over the quilt where Griffon had lain, searching for some sign—a few hairs from his coat, perhaps—

that Griffon had been there. The quilt was pristine, its faded blue-and-cream cotton soft beneath her fingers.

She flung down her cane and turned back the heavy quilt, to see if Griffon's body lay beneath. Nothing. "Oh, God," Eleanor breathed. She sank down into the wing chair beside the bed and looked up at Janet. "He was here," she whispered. "You must believe me. He was lying on the bed. I saw him."

Before Janet could reply, Norman came into the room, followed by Grace and Lauren. "What's happened?" he asked.

"Your mother thought . . . " Janet began. She stopped, her round face flushing with embarrassment.

"Where's Stewart?" Eleanor demanded.

Norman gave her one of his odd frowning looks. "He left last week, Mother," he said. "Don't you remember? He had to fly to London."

Of course. Her younger son had promised to bring her back some Scottish smoked salmon from Harrods. Maybe she *was* getting a little forgetful.

"What's wrong?" Grace asked impatiently.

Eleanor gripped her hands together to try to hide their trembling. "Griffon was lying dead on the bed. I saw him."

Norman's frown deepened. "Which bed?"

"This one, of course," Eleanor said impatiently. "On top of the quilt your McLeod grandmother made."

Norman glanced at his sister and shook his head. He went to examine the quilt. "There's no dog here, Mother."

"He was there, I tell you." Eleanor's voice rose. "He was stiff and cold."

Grace and Lauren went to join him by the bed. "Turn on the lamp at the other side of the bed," Grace said. Lauren went to turn it on. All three peered at the quilt, turning it over, while Eleanor avoided meeting Janet's eyes. She knew only too well what she'd see in them.

"There's nothing at all here," Norman said in a flat voice. "No dog. Nothing."

"It's another one of your spells, Mother," Grace said. "Just like the last one, when you said you'd found weevils in your bread. Or the time before, when you saw cockroaches in your bed."

Norman sighed. "Maybe you've taken too many of your blood-pressure pills again. I'm going to call Andrew."

"You'll do no such thing." Leaning heavily on the arms of the chair, Eleanor stood up, wincing at the pain in her knees. "I don't need any doctors. I feel perfectly well, apart from having seen my dog lying dead on my bed. That would shock anyone, I should think, even someone half my age."

"But your dog isn't on your bed," Norman said.

"Then where is he?" Eleanor demanded. "Tell me that."

"He's not here, Mother," Lauren said. "I've checked the room."

Eleanor swung around on her daughter-in-law. "Who asked you? Why don't you mind your own business, young woman? Go paint your toenails emerald green or something else productive."

Lauren blinked her long black eyelashes.

"Leave my wife alone," Norman said. "I've asked you before, Mother, not to vent your spleen on her."

"And I have told you countless times not to bring her here when we are having business meetings, meetings that are no concern of hers."

"Lauren is my wife. I am the CEO of the company. She has every right—"

"She has no rights. While I am the majority shareholder, I call the tune at Tyler Foods. I thought I made that perfectly clear last week. That's how your father wanted it, and don't you ever forget it, Norman Tyler." Eleanor's breathing came hard and shallow, so that she felt close to choking again.

"No one's forgetting anything," Janet said. "Except that you should not be upsetting yourself like this."

She gave Norman and Grace a warning glance. "Whatever your mother thought she saw this evening," she said in a soothing voice, "must have really upset her."

"I didn't *think* I saw anything," Eleanor told her. "I keep telling you, Griffon was on my bed."

"Maybe we should let your mother rest," Lauren suggested to Norman in her soft little-girl voice.

"Good idea," he said.

Lauren gave Eleanor one of her insipid smiles. "Good night, Mother. I hope you feel better in the morning."

Eleanor made a growling sound low in her throat. She felt Norman's cool lips on her forehead. "Janet's right," he said. "Get lots of rest. It's time you took that cruise you keep putting off."

She hated cruises. A lot of stupid people dressing up in beads and sequins, comparing tans and face-lifts. Besides, what fun was a cruise if you went by yourself? What she needed was a close friend . . . or maybe a lover. She laughed inwardly at the thought. She could just imagine their faces if their seventy-eight-year-old mother suddenly produced a boy toy. No, what she really needed was an ally. Someone unattached to the family whom she could trust absolutely.

Suddenly she wanted to be left alone. "Get out, the lot of you," she shouted. "I need my sleep."

Another cool kiss, this time from Grace, her heavy scent overpowering.

"You smell like a high-priced whore," Eleanor muttered.

Grace laughed. "I'd have to be a high-priced one to pay for this perfume," was all she said.

"Where was your gorgeous husband tonight?"

"Larry's in New York. I'll call you tomorrow, Mother, to see how you are."

"I'm perfectly fine, thank you. I just want to know why all these things are happening to me."

"Of course you do," Grace said in that infuriatingly

patronizing tone of hers. "Now you sleep well and stop worrying."

Eleanor was relieved when she heard the front door slam behind them. Apart from Janet, she was alone.

Or was she?

In the few minutes she'd been out in the hall, someone had managed to get into her room and remove Griffon's body. Maybe that same person was lying in wait for her somewhere in the house? Waiting until she and Janet were in their beds, fast asleep.

Waiting to strangle her or break her neck or poison her, as they'd no doubt done to Griffon.

Sickening shivers ran down her spine. She hobbled as fast as she could to the window and lifted her cane to sweep back the curtains. Her heartbeat settled down. There was no one there.

She drew the curtains closed again. Although no one would believe her, not even Janet, she was certain she hadn't imagined her dog lying on the bed. She desperately needed someone to confide in. Janet was intensely loyal, she knew that, but Norman and Grace had far too much influence on her. "Despite the fact that it's I, not them, who pays her wages," Eleanor muttered to herself.

What she needed was an outsider, yet not an outsider. Someone she could trust. Someone who would care about her, not for the stock she held in one of the largest grocery store companies in North America, but for herself.

Someone who hadn't yet learned to hate her because of the power she wielded.

Her heart started pumping hard again, this time with excitement, not fear. She sat down at the mahogany desk that she'd brought to Tyler House when she married. It had been in her family for two centuries; one of the few pieces of furniture her loyalist ancestor, a lawyer, had managed to save from the mob that had burned down his house in Boston. He and his family had escaped to build a new life in Canada. Eleanor knew the story well. Many people in New Brunswick were descended from those loyalist settlers and the stories were handed down from generation to generation. She ran her fingers over the desk, its satin surface and gleaming wood giving her much-needed solace. Ramsey had loved this desk so much that he'd insisted they put it in their bedroom. "That way," he'd said, "I can work late into the night and yet not be separated from you."

Eleanor kept a small portable computer on the desk, which she used for all her business correspondence and most of her personal letters, but this letter was so important it must be written by hand. Opening the center drawer, she took out three sheets of heavy linen paper headed with her name embossed in gold.

She'd put off writing this letter for far too long. Now was the time. As she poised her pen above the first sheet of paper, she prayed that she hadn't left it too late.

Chapter 2

The letter from Eleanor Tyler dropped into the apartment mailbox marked NORTON & TYLER along with the September bills and several flyers.

At exactly the same time, the telephone rang in Apartment 720.

Michelle Tyler was drying her hair when the call came through. "Could you get that?" she yelled to Brian.

He already had it. Through the whine of the hair dryer she could hear his voice from the bedroom. Although she couldn't hear what he was saying, she sensed that it was something important. He was asking questions, followed by long pauses while he was presumably getting answers. Her stomach clenched into a knot. After four years of being married to Brian she could read all the signs.

She met her own eyes in the steamy mirror. "Here we go again," she mouthed. But this time she was determined not to accept it. This time there was too much at stake.

She brushed her dark hair forward, the new gamin haircut framing her face, and then turned off the hair dryer. When she went back into the bedroom, Brian was standing by the window, gazing out across the Assiniboine River to the horizon, but she sensed that he wasn't really seeing what was there. She came to stand behind him, sliding her arms about his waist. He smelled of soap and herbal shampoo. But when she pressed her breasts against his bare back, she felt his body tense and draw away from her.

His rebuff sent a surge of anger through her. She recognized the symptoms. He was already setting distance between them, making it less difficult for him to leave. The angrier she became, the easier it was for him to go. And she fell for it every time, so that she ended up feeling that *she* was the unreasonable one, the miserable witch stopping him from a vital assignment to wherever the current war or disaster zone was. This time, however, she was determined to remain calm, dig her heels in, not break down and cry or yell.

This time could be their last chance.

She sat down on the end of their bed and pulled on her bra, reaching behind to hook it up. "Who was on the phone?"

He was dragging on a T-shirt, his back still turned to her. "The network's Asian section."

"Oh?"

Brian turned around. His face looked drawn beneath his summer tan. "They want me to go to Indonesia."

She stood up and pulled on her black panties, then a yellow cotton top with thin straps. "Indonesia?" she repeated with an upward inflection.

"They want me to do a special. Cover the riots in Jakarta, investigate the unrest elsewhere. Get into East Timor, if I can. A kind of overview of the upheaval in the country."

"There must be someone else who could go." Her tone was eminently reasonable.

"They want me."

"I'm sure they do. After all, you're the best foreign correspondent they have, aren't you?" Now her voice was heavy with sarcasm. She pulled on her shorts and fastened them, then turned to face him. "But you gave me your word when you got back from Moscow that it was going to be your last foreign assignment."

He tilted his head to one side, his mouth sliding

into a smile. "Come on, Mish," he said in a coaxing tone. "Sure, you wouldn't be keeping a fella from his work, would you?"

She didn't respond to the smile. "You can cut out the phony blarney. You promised me you wouldn't be taking any more foreign correspondent jobs. You told me you'd spoken to Sam about it."

His smile faded. "I told you before, I did speak to him."

"Right. And he just laughed and said, 'Michelle will understand you're the best man for the job.' I know that, but you told me you wouldn't go when the next foreign job came up. So, basically you lied to me, right?"

He grimaced. "I wouldn't exactly call it lying. Maybe wishful thinking." He put his arm around her, trying to draw her close. "Come on, sweetheart. Let's not spoil our time together. We've got three whole days before I have to leave. Let's make the best of it."

She pushed him away, feeling like she'd been punched hard in the stomach. "You mean you have to leave on Monday?"

"Sorry. I have to spend a week with the crew. Lots of intensive preparation, research . . ."

"Will you be back in time for Thanksgiving?"

He avoided eye contact. "Could be. But I have to tell you, it doesn't look like it. They want an in-depth coverage thing."

"So I get to spend yet another Canadian Thanksgiving on my own." She hated to hear herself whining this way, but her disappointment was tangible, like a searing pain inside her.

"What date is it again?"

Michelle sighed heavily. "You should know by now. The second Monday in October."

"No way I'd be back. Couldn't you get together with Joanna and her family?"

"I'm sure I can. They must be used to having me for Thanksgiving dinner every year."

"And I should be back by the end of October,"

he said, ignoring her sarcasm, "so we can celebrate American Thanksgiving together."

Michelle drew in a long, deep breath. "Have you completely forgotten what we talked about last time this happened? Having a family, buying a house? You said you might even get a dog, remember?" She was trying hard to keep it light, but her stock of patience was getting pretty low.

"Look, it's a glorious day. Let's not waste it. Why don't we go get some fresh air? Maybe grab something to eat at McNally Robinson's café? Read *The New York Times*—"

"No, Brian. I want to discuss this *now*, not later. And I certainly don't want to talk about it in a public place." She was starting to lose it. She drew all five feet three of her up, glaring up at him. "I told you two months ago that I want to start a family soon. I want to be young enough to enjoy my kids through their teens, not be going through menopause when they're ten years old." She ran her hands through her hair. "Shit, Brian! Why do I have to go through all this again?" she yelled at him. "I thought we'd settled it for good."

She was about to tell him she'd stopped taking the pill two months ago, but decided against it, knowing that this wasn't the right time.

He stood there, his mouth set in a grim line. Then he shrugged. "What can I say? Sam told me he wanted me to keep doing foreign assignments. We've got a great team. We're used to working together in difficult circumstances, covering each other's butts. They don't want to have to bring someone else in."

"If you refused to do it, they'd have to get someone else, wouldn't they?"

"And maybe I'd lose my job in the process." He dragged his fingers through his thick, dark hair. "Hell, Mish, you know how much I love this work. I've tried to explain how much working on North American assignments bores me, but you won't listen."

"I'm not the one who won't listen. Before we got

married, I told you how important having kids was to me. Mom was all the family I had. Once she went, I didn't have a single, solitary relative."

"You do so. What about your mother's family in—"

"You can't count them."

He grinned. "Don't worry, sweetheart. I've got enough relatives for the two of us."

She felt like hitting him. "It's not a joke, Brian. I thought we got married for the whole bit: kids and house *and* dog. It seems I was wrong."

"Couldn't we give it another year?" he pleaded. "You'll still have plenty of time to have a family. Lots of women have babies in their mid-thirties, even later, nowadays."

She threw up her arms. "Let's forget it. Forget the whole thing. Go to goddamned Indonesia." She strode past him into the living room. "But don't expect to find me here when you get back," she yelled.

He followed her. "Now you know you don't mean that." He tried to put his arms around her, but she shook him off.

"Wanna bet?" She opened the sliding door to the balcony and stepped outside. She expected Brian to follow her, but he didn't. She lifted her face to the sun, hoping its warmth might ease her tension, then she leaned her arms on the balcony railing. Brian was right. It was a perfect fall day. A gentle breeze stirred the trees that lined the riverbanks. They still had their leaves, although some were starting to turn to russet and gold, and the red geraniums in the window box were still flourishing. The first killer frost was late in coming this year.

But ice was forming around her heart and in her veins.

"I'll go get the mail," Brian announced to her back. Michelle didn't reply.

She heard the front door close behind him. Was this how it was always going to be? Her pleading and yelling; him dancing around the issue and trying to kiss it away? She'd soon discovered he was a quintessential

Irish rover when she'd met him at a friend's party in Minneapolis six years ago. "Don't get too attached," Barb had warned her later, when she knew that Michelle was falling for him. "Brian's a rolling stone. He'll never settle down."

But they'd surprised everyone—especially Brian's friends—when, a few months later, they'd announced they were getting married. Michelle loved him so much that she'd told him she'd be able to live with the fact that he had to take foreign assignments for his job with Minneapolis-based JNN, as long as they could continue to live in Winnipeg. "That's only fair," she'd told him, seeing his hesitation. "If you're going to be away a lot, I don't want to give up my business and my friends to move to Minneapolis. And there are daily flights to Minneapolis from Winnipeg."

Reluctantly, he'd agreed, staying with his sister, Rosie, whenever he had to spend extended time in Minneapolis.

"That sounds like trouble," some of her friends said, but it wasn't other women she was afraid of. It hadn't taken long to discover that her only rival was Brian's passion for his work—and his itchy feet, which couldn't bear to stay in one place for any length of time.

For the first three years she'd been willing to wait, immersing herself in her own work to avoid the loneliness when Brian was away for weeks at a time, in Belfast or Moscow or Kosovo . . . After all, she kept telling herself, she was still young, they had lots of time. But then their arguments about his foreign assignments began to grow more bitter on her part, more evasive on his, until she got his promise—so she thought—and decided to stop taking the pill. She knew she should have discussed it with him first, but . . .

"Damn him," she yelled into the air, scaring off a pigeon that was about to alight on her neighbor's balcony railing.

She heard the apartment front door open and

tensed herself to turn and face into the living room as
Brian reappeared. He tossed a couple of flyers and
some mail on the coffee table, but held on to one
envelope. There was a strange expression on his face,
a sort of repressed excitement.

"You've got a letter," he told her when she stepped
into the room. His cobalt-blue eyes danced.

"Who from?"

He hid the letter behind his back. "You don't get
it until you come here and give me a kiss."

She sighed. "I'm not in the mood for games." She
held out her hand. "Give me my letter."

His expression grew serious. "I think I should prepare you for it first."

"What is it?" she asked, her voice sharp.

"It's from New Brunswick. Fredericton."

Michelle felt the blood drain from her face. "Fredericton?" she repeated in a whisper. She crossed her
hands over her fast-beating heart. "My mother's—my
grandmother must have died. That would be the only
reason I could think of for them to write to me."

"I don't think so." He handed her the letter. She
took it reluctantly, as if it were burning hot. "It says
it's from Mrs. Ramsey Tyler. Isn't that your grandmother's name?"

Michelle gave a wry smile. "Her name's Eleanor,
not Ramsey."

"Yeah, yeah, I know, but she must be pretty old,
your grandmother. She'd be used to the old ways. I
guess she thinks it's more prestigious to be Mrs. Ramsey than Mrs. Eleanor."

Michelle held the cream-colored envelope in her
hand, staring down at her name and address written
in thick black strokes. Somehow this didn't look like
the writing of a woman who needed prestige from her
dead husband's name. Of course, someone else could
have written it for her.

"Open it," Brian said.

She stared at him, her eyes wide. "I'm scared to."

"Why?"

"This is the first letter I've ever had from her . . . from my grandmother."

"Be a devil. Open it."

Michelle swallowed hard, then ripped open the envelope. There were three sheets of heavy, cream-colored paper inside, all covered with the same black writing as the envelope.

"Want to read it on your own?" Brian asked. "I can go make some fresh coffee."

"Good idea." Her face felt as if it were on fire. "I'll read it outside." She went back out onto the balcony, sliding the glass door closed, shutting herself away from him.

She'd read the letter three times and was still staring down at it when Brian rapped on the glass and held up the coffeepot. She slid open the balcony door.

"Everything okay?" Brian asked anxiously.

"I don't know. I'm in shock." She looked down at the pages in her hand. "She's asking me to come to New Brunswick in October to celebrate Thanksgiving with her and the family."

Brian's face lit up. "That's great."

"Is it? I'm not so sure." Michelle frowned. "Mom always warned me to steer clear of her family."

"I know they treated your mother badly, but perhaps they regret it now and want to make amends."

"It's too late. After all, she didn't even send a card, never mind flowers, when my mother died. Read it." She handed him the letter. Taking the coffeepot from his hand, she walked past him into the kitchen.

When she'd poured herself another mug of coffee and cut a slice of the banana bread she'd made last night, she sat down beside him on the couch, watching him as he read the letter, his long legs stretched out in front of him, heels on the coffee table. Breathing in the comforting aroma of coffee, she squeezed her eyes shut, her mind swirling with both the contents of the letter and the realization that, whatever she said to Brian, he was going away from her yet again.

"Wow!" he said when he'd finished reading.

"I know. Talk about soap opera, eh?"

"That's heavy-duty stuff . . . losing her youngest daughter, searching for her after she'd left home."

"Yeah, well . . . that's her version of the story."

"She says she sent your mother checks and letters, only to have her letters returned unopened. Is that really what happened?"

"Not exactly. She makes it all sound like she and the family were loving and supportive, which isn't the way I heard it. Mom was sixteen when she got pregnant. My father was her first lover. She told me she got pregnant after they'd made love only twice. But Mike Gaudry was a lumberman. Highly unsuitable for the daughter of a wealthy grocery tycoon. You'll notice that Mrs. Ramsey Tyler says that my father wasn't from their background at all. Which means that he was not only a lowly lumberman, but also a French-speaking Acadian."

"So your mother ran off with him?"

"Yes." Michelle's lips tightened. "Unfortunately, Mom's family was right about him. He abandoned her a couple of months after I was born. That was probably the hardest part of it for her: having the family proved right." A shiver ran down her spine. "But, in the end, I'm the one to blame. I was the cause of my mother's pain, the split with her family, the hard life that followed."

Brian reached out to squeeze her hand. "Don't be stupid. You weren't even born at the time. Besides, you've told me how close you and your mother were."

"I know. We were more like sisters than mother and daughter." Michelle's eyes filled with tears. "God, how I miss her, even now, after all this time! I thought it would get easier, but it doesn't."

His hand squeezed harder. "I know. But you've got me, babe."

She looked up. "Have I?"

He blinked and turned to pick up his coffee mug.

"Wherever I go, you're always on my mind. You know that."

"That's nice." The acid in her tone could have corroded steel.

Brian picked up the letter again. "She says here that her informant—I guess she must have hired a private detective to find you—told her you own a small gift store in Winnipeg and are married to an American."

"Big strike against me, I'm sure, knowing the family's strong loyalist background."

"Oh, come on, you've got to be kidding. All that stuff happened more than two centuries ago. Besides, she talks about still having cousins in Boston and New York, descendants of both sides of the family. Sounds quite proud of it."

"Who cares? Apart from Mrs. Ramsey Tyler."

"She's your grandmother, Mish. Sounds as if now she's nearly eighty she wants to get to know you before it's too late."

Michelle took the letter from him and read the last few lines over again.

I sincerely hope that you will be willing to end the long separation between us by accepting my invitation to join us for our Thanksgiving celebration over the weekend of October 8–11, enabling you to be reunited with your mother's family. Perhaps, as I said, you might come earlier in the week, so that I could have more time with my granddaughter.

The letter was signed *Affectionately yours, Eleanor Tyler (your grandmother).*

Michelle stared down at the pages in her lap. Arriving, as the letter had, on the heels of the phone call for Brian, she had a sense of fate or karma . . . whatever. *What should I do, Mom?* She still talked to her mother in her mind. *Why did you return those letters and checks from your mother when you so desperately needed their help?*

Was it pride or obstinacy that had made her mother cut herself off from her family? Or something more sinister?

"So, what's the verdict?" Brian asked.

Michelle jumped, the pages sliding from her lap onto the couch. "Sorry, I was miles away."

"I think you should go."

"Sure you do. After all, that would make you feel better about not spending Thanksgiving with me, wouldn't it?"

"You're right, it would," he said with a faint smile, "but that's not the reason for saying you should go. This invitation is pretty important to you. It's ten years since your mother died. You've always said how much you miss having your own family. Here's your chance to get one." He grinned. "Even if she does sound a bit formidable, your grandma."

She had to smile. "She sure does. Wow! Talk about a set regime: formal dinner Saturday, church service in the cathedral Sunday . . ."

"Reads like a royal command. From the sound of it, she has everyone there right under her thumb."

"That's probably why my mother ran away. She was pretty independent, you know, sometimes to the point of being pigheaded."

Brian's arm reached out to squeeze her against his side. "Sounds like someone I know."

Michelle swatted him with the letter, but this time she didn't pull away from him.

"I wish I'd known your mother," Brian said.

"I wish you had, too."

"But I could get to know your family . . . if you decide to go meet them."

Michelle drew away from him to study his face. "You really think I should go, don't you?"

"That's what I said."

She sprang up to pace to the window and back again. "You're definitely going to Indonesia?"

Their eyes met, locked for a moment, and then he glanced away. "I gave Sam my word."

"You gave *me* your word two months ago." She wasn't angry anymore, merely resigned. The letter had diffused her anger—for now.

"Let's discuss it later, when you've decided how to reply to your grandmother's letter. One important thing at a time."

How like a man, Michelle thought. Couldn't he see how inextricably entwined the two things were? They were both about family and her need for one, either her own or her mother's. Or both.

A wave of heat surged through her. If she had a baby, she would need to give her child roots, a family. What better reason to get in touch with her mother's family than that? For the first time since she'd read the letter, she felt a stirring of excitement.

"If they're the family from hell," Brian said, "you can tell them, 'I'm outta here,' and get the next flight back home."

"But then you wouldn't be here. I'd have to spend Thanksgiving on my own." She said it in a matter-of-fact tone. "I could spend it with Becca for a change," she added quickly, before he said it. "But she doesn't bother with Thanksgiving, so it's not the same."

He rubbed the bridge of his nose. "Let's face it, this would be a great time to visit your grandmother and the family. It's obvious she really wants you to come. She sounds a bit pompous, but that's okay. You can cope with that."

Michelle stared down at her coffee mug and sighed.

"If you turn her down," Brian said, "I don't think she'd ask you again."

"I suppose. I just wish you could come with me for the first visit."

He pulled her down on his knee. She no longer felt like resisting him. "Tell you what. If you find they're not so bad, we could go visit your folks for Christmas."

Your folks. It sounded so strange. She'd never had someone talk about *your folks* before. Somehow the homey phrase didn't go with the formal tone of her grandmother's letter.

"They make such a thing of Thanksgiving—dinner and church and a barbecue in their summer home—

just think what they'd do with Christmas." Brian laughed. "Maybe they rent a palace or something and have two separate balls, one for the upper crust and one for the servants, like they did in *Gone with the Wind*—or was it *Rebecca*?"

Michelle buried her head in his neck. "You're nuts, that's what you are, Brian Norton," she said, giggling. She began to kiss the side of his neck, sliding her lips to his ear.

His arms tightened around her. "I've got a better idea than going out for brunch," he whispered, his hands warm on the bare skin beneath her cotton top. She jumped up and pulled him to his feet. Their bodies instinctively pressed against each other, his hands behind her, sliding inside her shorts, drawing her even closer. The knowledge that he was going on a dangerous mission again fueled the heat spreading through her.

He lifted his mouth from hers. "Bedroom or rug?"

Her response was to draw him down with her onto the handwoven rug in front of the fireplace.

Later, much later, she felt the breeze from the open balcony window cool on her bare skin. Brian was still asleep, lying on his stomach, his arm heavy across her.

She suddenly realized she was ravenously hungry. She leaned over Brian and tousled his hair. "Wake up, lazy. I'm starving. Let's go get a pizza."

He was awake in an instant. An ability, she'd long ago decided, he must have learned on the job. He sat up, yawning. "Sounds good." His mouth slid into a slow, languorous smile. "And you look good." He reached for her again.

"You can forget that. For now, at least." She scrambled to her feet. "I'm going for a quick shower. Give me fifteen minutes and I'll be ready."

"I'll believe that when I see it."

He stretched his tanned arms above his head, the muscles taut. Her heart and body responded. *God,* she thought, *he's gorgeous* . . . and he was good to her and for her. Apart from the one vital thing that separated them: his work. Yet how could she live without him? She couldn't. They'd just have to work things out, that was all.

She walked across the room and then turned at the door. "I've decided to go to New Brunswick for Thanksgiving."

"That was sudden."

"My mind is clear now."

"Ah, there you go." He gave her his slow grin. "We'll just have to make sure your mind gets cleared more often."

"Be serious. This is important."

"I know that. Sorry."

"I think it's the right thing to do."

"I think so too. It's time you met your family." He tilted his head at her. "Just look at it this way—what have you got to lose?"

Chapter 3

By the time she'd clambered onto the small prop plane for the last leg of her journey east—from Montreal to Fredericton, New Brunswick—and had had to give up her small carry-on bag because there wasn't enough room for it at her feet, Michelle began to wish that she'd accepted her grandmother's offer of an executive-class ticket. That way she could have taken the jet flight instead of this sardine can. Unfortunately, there hadn't been any economy seats left on the jet.

Unlike Brian, who was just as comfortable getting on a plane as taking a bus, Michelle was a nervous flyer. She'd already had to endure two flights today, but at least they'd been jets. As she stepped into the cabin of the plane, she tensed when she saw how small it was. Squeezing past the smiling flight attendant, she walked down the narrow aisle to find her seat nine rows back, the last in the line of single seats. Thank heaven this wasn't a long flight.

Although her stomach had been queasy since she'd left Winnipeg, she took the attendant's offer of a snack to help pass the time. When she'd finished the cheese roll and the plastic cup of apple juice, plus a mini Mars bar, she took her grandmother's letter from her bag to read it again. *We usually congregate at the family home in Fredericton on Friday evening,* Eleanor had written, *and have our Thanksgiving dinner on Sat-*

urday, but why don't you come on Thursday so that we can become acquainted before everyone else arrives?

Michelle had chosen not to arrive until Friday evening, preferring to keep this first visit to her mother's family as short as possible. Although her grandmother had begged her to stay on, Michelle had insisted that she must leave on Monday, so that she'd be home in time to open up her gift store first thing Tuesday morning.

That meant she had to endure almost three days in the company of people she knew only through her mother's naturally biased vision.

Michelle folded the letter, put it away in her bag, and stared at the back of the seat ahead of her. She was more apprehensive than excited about this visit. Her mother had rarely spoken to her about her family, but when she did talk about them her bitterness was like vitriolic acid. "All they cared about was money," she'd told Michelle. "That's all I ever heard: Tyler Foods for breakfast, the state of Tyler's shares for lunch, Tyler's latest sales figures for dinner. And they all sucked it up, Norman and Grace—even easy-going Stewart—and Mother. Especially Mother. Although it was my father's family business, my mother was the brains behind its development into a national foodstore chain. Stewart was a bit of a black sheep, but he liked the money too much not to toe the line. I was the outcast, the one who didn't give a piss for the family business."

"But you were only a kid," Michelle had protested. "Why would you care about it when you were a teenager?"

"You think that made a difference? Although he went on to get his master's degree in business admin, my brother Norman was put to work stocking shelves for his pocket money when he was twelve. It was always taken for granted that he'd go into the family business once he graduated, and he did. The same went for Stewart and my darling sister, Grace."

Michelle had always wondered what it must be like

to be cut off forever from the family you'd grown up with, never to see your parents or sister and brothers again. Yet her mother had never shown any desire to return to New Brunswick. "I'm better off without them," she'd said curtly, when Michelle had tentatively asked her why she never went back to visit her family.

Now here she was, doing exactly what her mother had vowed never to do. She closed her eyes. *Is this a big mistake, Mom?* The only answer was the heavy drone of the plane's engines drumming in her ears. Her stomach clenched. Eating had been a mistake. She suddenly felt such an acute stab of longing for Brian that it brought tears to her eyes, but Brian was several thousand miles away, in Indonesia. She was on her own.

When the plane landed, she walked through to the arrivals hall, looking around to see if any of the few people there might be waiting for her. "Someone will be at the airport to meet you," Eleanor had said when Michelle had called her to say she was coming. Michelle had told her that she'd be wearing a dark green jacket and that her suitcase would have a purple ribbon on it, but no one came forward to greet her.

She had just retrieved her case from the baggage carousel when a man's voice from behind her said, "Sorry I'm late. You must be my niece." He sounded breathless, as if he'd been running.

Michelle turned around to face him.

"I'm your Uncle Stewart," he said, his mouth sliding into a charming, lopsided grin. He had dark, wavy hair liberally flecked with gray, but his boyish, Mel Gibson–type face made him look much younger than his actual age.

"Hi." Michelle was about to hold out her hand, but he took her arm and bent to kiss her cheek. She could smell liquor on his breath.

"Uncle's prerogative." He went to grab the case, but Michelle kept her grip on the handle.

"It has wheels."

"Ah, just as independent as your mother, I see."

Michelle lifted her chin, challenging him with her eyes.

"My God, you look just like her," he said softly. "You're smaller than she was, but she could devastate you with one of those looks, too. Let's go," he said before Michelle had time to reply. "This all your luggage?"

"Yes."

"Okay. Let's get out of here before I get a ticket."

Stewart had parked the car directly outside the airport with the hazard lights flashing. "Thanks, Harry," he shouted to the security officer, who was hovering by the curb. He threw Michelle's bags into the trunk and opened the passenger door for her, then dashed around to jump into the driver's seat. He reminded Michelle of someone she'd dated when she was at university. Charming, but immature. Except that her Uncle Stewart, as she knew from the family tree she'd worked out before she'd left home, must be at least fifty.

As he sped along the rural road in his racing green Jaguar convertible, Stewart cast a look at her profile. "You've caused quite an uproar in the old Tyler homestead."

"I have? Why?"

"Suddenly turning up after all these years."

Turning up? Michelle frowned. Hadn't her grandmother told her family she'd sent her an invitation? Well, she wasn't about to play games with them. "I'd hardly call it turning up. Your mother invited me."

"Oh, I know all about that. But what I don't understand is why you'd write to her in the first place, after all this time."

Michelle was about to deny that she'd written, but something told her to be careful. She didn't want to cause trouble between her grandmother and the family. "Oh, I see," she said in a noncommittal tone. "I suppose I thought it was time for me to meet my mother's family. After all, they are the only family I have."

He glanced at her again. "I suppose that's true. Do you know much about your father's family?"

"No." She didn't want to talk about her father.

"I take it you knew he was dead."

"Yes, his wife wrote to my mother when it happened. She said he'd been killed in a traffic accident in Maine."

"He tried to outrun a train at a crossing with his pickup. The train won. He had a couple of kids . . . besides you, I mean. Two boys. Did you know that?"

"No." She wished he'd stop talking about it. She didn't want to hear any more about the father she'd never known. Or his family.

"Sorry," Stewart said. "I just thought you'd like to know."

"Not really," she said lightly. "I never knew him. He left when I was two months old." She'd seen just one picture of him. A slim man with black hair and a dazzling smile, his baby daughter cradled awkwardly in the crook of his arm.

"He was a good-looking guy. The kind that teenage girls go for. My father did his best to—"

"Tell me about the family," Michelle interrupted, desperate to stop him. "Are you married? Have you got any children?"

"I've been married twice. All I have to show for it is a sadly depleted bank account and one daughter, Jennifer, who lives in London."

"So you're divorced?" It felt weird to be asking a stranger such personal questions.

"Only once. You'll meet my wife, Anna, tomorrow."

"Oh, good. What about my aunt?"

"Grace? What about her?"

"Married? Any children? I'm not trying to be nosy," Michelle added hastily. "It's just easier for me to know ahead of time." She grinned in the darkness. "Saves me from making any big mistakes."

"You feeling nervous?"

"A bit," she admitted.

"Can't say I blame you. We Tylers are rather overwhelming en masse." He reached out a hand to pat hers. "You've got your mother's spunk. You'll be fine."

"I hope so. I wish Brian had been able to come with me."

"Brian's your husband?"

"Yes. I told your mother about him."

"Ah, yes." He hesitated. "You must understand that my mother is seventy-eight now. Her faculties are . . . are not as good as they used to be. She forgets a lot of things. For instance, she told us you were single."

"That's strange. She asked me quite a few questions about Brian on the phone."

"Did she, really?" Stewart looked surprised.

"Brian's a foreign correspondent for JNN, the American television network. He's on a special assignment in Indonesia. That's why he couldn't come with me." Michelle hesitated, frowning. "I still don't understand. Your mother said in her letter that she knew I was married to an American."

Stewart sighed. "That's the problem. Her memory comes and goes. Sometimes she's fine. Other times she can't remember anything, or she imagines strange things that haven't really happened. Poor Mother. It's hard to see her deteriorate like this when she was once so active, mentally and physically."

Michelle was alarmed. "Is it Alzheimer's?"

"We hope not. Her doctor's recommended tests and he's trying some new medication, but so far nothing seems to work."

"I'm sorry." Michelle felt a surge of disappointment—and guilt. She should have made this journey a long time ago.

Stewart slapped his hands on the leather steering wheel. "But let's not spoil your first visit to New Brunswick with all this gloomy talk. It is your first visit, isn't it?"

"Yes."

"Can't see much of it tonight, of course. Too dark and wet, but the forecast is good for the weekend."

"That's great."

"The trees are at their best this week. Wait till you

drive down to our summer house in St. Andrews.
You'll be able to see the fall colors in all their glory
then. That's the St. John River on your right, by the
way." He nodded toward her window. Michelle caught
glimpses of the wide stretch of water beyond the trees
that lined the road. "Won't be long before we're at
the Tyler residence, so I'll fill you in quickly on the
rest of the family. Your Aunt Grace is still on her first
husband, poor guy. His name is Larry Anderson and
he's English. Bit of a jet-setter, Larry was. At first he
was like a fish out of water in Canada, but he's okay
now. He was some sort of bigwig financier in London,
so my father put him in charge of our international
holdings. Larry jets around the world and comes home
every now and then. Grace flies off to join him whenever she can. Strange sort of marriage, but they seem
very happy, so who am I to question it?"

"Any children?"

"One daughter, Sophie, a brainy girl. She's a computer engineer at Nortel. And a son, Jamie, who's a
bit of a disaster, I'm afraid. Your Uncle Norman has
two sons, both in the business."

Michelle shook her head. "I'm never going to remember all these people."

"Don't bother yourself about it. We'll all be far too
busy talking about ourselves to notice."

Soon the rural area became more built up, signaling
their entry into the outskirts of the small city. They
passed several large houses, which were set well back
from the road, fronted by stretches of lawn and shaded
by old trees.

"What lovely houses!" Michelle exclaimed.

"Fredericton prides itself on its old clapboard
houses. I'm so used to them I suppose I get a bit
blasé." He glanced sideways at her and gave her a
wry smile. "Give me a Manhattan apartment anytime."

"You were telling me about your brother, Norman.
Two sons, you said?"

Stewart braked hard, the tires squealing on the wet

road, as they came to a red traffic light beside an Irving gas station. "Oh, yes. Norman has assured the bloody dynasty."

Michelle stole a glance at him and saw, in the reflected light from the dashboard, that his handsome face was grim.

"One son, Ramsey, named after my father, is his grandmother's favorite. The other son, Eric, is a brain, with a capital B. He's the technology expert. Your Uncle Norman is also onto his second wife, by the way. The beautiful Lauren. Delicious body, few brains. That's the way our Norman likes 'em. Makes sure they don't interfere in his business affairs." He revved the engine and raced away from the other traffic as the lights changed to green. "Unlike our darling mother."

"Did she interfere in your father's business?"

"Interfere?" Stewart laughed. "My mother *was* the bloody business." He continued driving in silence for a while, almost as if he'd forgotten she was there. Then he slowed the car. "Here we are: Waterloo Row, the Park Avenue of Fredericton."

Michelle peered out as he turned into a curving driveway leading to a large mansion. Her heart was beating fast. She had time only to catch a glimpse of white pillars and a black-roofed turret before they drew up beside the flight of stone steps leading up to the imposing old clapboard house. "It's beautiful," she breathed.

"Is it?" Stewart turned off the ignition. "I suppose it would be to an outsider. For me it holds too many wretched memories."

Michelle was surprised by the bitterness in his voice.

Stewart gazed up at his childhood home, as if he were trying to see it through her eyes. "Count yourself lucky that you didn't grow up in it. If you ask me, my little sister did you a big favor by getting out of here before you were born."

Chapter 4

B eyond the tall white pillars, the front door opened. In the light flooding from the interior of the house Michelle saw an elderly woman in the doorway, dressed in a navy-blue dress with a white lace collar. She was stocky but not overweight, and her round face was beaming a welcome. Relief flooded over Michelle. This wasn't at all the formidable woman she'd expected. She opened the car door and started up the wide flight of steps.

"Janet Marlow, your grandmother's housekeeper," she heard Stewart say from behind her as he opened the trunk to get out her bags.

Michelle halted on the top step. Of course. How could she have been so stupid? This woman couldn't possibly be the tyrant her mother had described.

"Welcome to Tyler House, Miss Tyler. I hope you had a good journey."

Michelle was tempted to tell her it had been a long and uncomfortable journey, but knowing that the question was just part of the greeting she merely said, "It's good to be here," which was also far from the truth. Her uncle's remark about the house had left her feeling uneasy.

"Your grandmother is waiting for you in the heritage room. Would you like Bob to park your car, Mr. Stewart?"

"No, thanks. I'll do it myself. But you can get him to carry in the bags."

"I'll tell him as soon as I take Miss Tyler—"

"Please call me Michelle," Michelle interrupted.

Janet paused, her hand on the inner door. "Miss Michelle?"

"No. Just Michelle."

"I'm not sure Mrs. Tyler would like that."

"But I like it. *Michelle*, please."

Janet's shoulders rose and fell in a slight movement of resignation. "Right. But I know you'll understand if I call you Miss Tyler in front of Mrs. Tyler."

"Okay." They exchanged smiles. Janet led the way across the hall, oriental rugs on the gleaming wood floor, and into what she'd called the heritage room. It was an unusual shape, six-sided, with a large bay window. Michelle realized that the room must be part of the turret with the black roof that she'd seen from the car.

An archway divided the room into two halves. The four people standing nearest her turned to look at her as she came in, but said nothing. Beyond the archway was a long couch covered in burgundy velvet. Beside it, seated in a high-backed wing chair, was a white-haired woman she knew must be her grandmother, Eleanor Tyler. She was every inch the queen on her throne waiting to give an audience.

As soon as she saw Michelle, Eleanor stood up, tall and imperious, one white hand grasping her black cane. "Michelle Tyler," she said, making it sound like a pronouncement. "So you've come to see us at last. Have you met your uncle and aunt yet?"

"Give her a chance, Mother," said the tall woman who was a younger version of Eleanor. She turned to Michelle. "I'm your Aunt Grace." She bent to brush cheeks with Michelle, emitting a strong smell of expensive perfume. "Welcome to Tyler House." But there was no hint of welcome in the cold gray eyes that examined her.

Michelle felt like a specimen on a slide.

Now the large man with the gleaming black hair moved forward, holding out his hand. "Norman

Tyler," he said, squeezing her hand and then abruptly
releasing it. "Had a good journey?" Michelle could
tell he couldn't give a damn about her journey—or
her, for that matter.

"Not bad. I had to take three planes and—"

"How about something to drink? White wine?"

"I'll have a mineral water, thank you," Michelle
said, trying to hide her annoyance. He could at least
have waited for her answer to his question. Thank
God she'd met Stewart first or she might well have
got on the next flight back to Winnipeg and never
made it to Tyler House. In two minutes she'd decided
the Tylers were thoroughly dislikable, overbearing—
and overpowering. Of course, it didn't help that they
were all tall and she was five feet three. Tall people
always made her feel defensive.

"I imagine you must be hungry, knowing how appalling the food is on planes nowadays," Eleanor said.
She slowly lowered herself into her chair again. "Can
you prepare something for her, Janet?"

"I've made a chicken salad, Mrs. Tyler. Would that
be all right for you, Miss Tyler?"

Michelle turned to smile at Janet. "That sounds perfect," she said, although the last thing she wanted was
more food. "But first I'd like to freshen up a bit after
the journey."

"Of course," Eleanor said. "And you'll want to
change, I imagine."

Michelle felt everyone looking at her faded jeans
and comfortable tunic sweater. She was about to
agree, but then stopped herself. If she was going to
spend three days in this place, she'd better establish
right now that she wasn't taking any orders from them.

"You probably won't want to stay up too long, as
it's late," she said to Eleanor, "so I'll just have a quick
wash and be down again in a few minutes."

She caught a gleam in Eleanor's eyes. "That's fine.
However, we do usually dress for dinner at Tyler
House."

"But I guess you've had dinner already," Michelle said. "Right?"

"We have." Eleanor glanced at the gold watch that hung loosely on her thin wrist. "It is now ten-thirty-five Atlantic time."

Michelle smiled. "I must change my watch. Mine is still on central time: eight-thirty-five."

Eleanor's high forehead wrinkled beneath the snow-white hair. "I don't understand. I thought you were two hours behind us."

"That's right. It's eight thirty-five in Winnipeg at the moment."

"No, no. That's not right," Eleanor protested, her voice growing querulous. "It must be *twelve* thirty-five in Winnipeg."

"It doesn't matter," Grace said hurriedly. "As long as we know what time it is right here in New Brunswick, we don't have to bother about anywhere else, do we?"

"I don't understand," Eleanor said again in an agitated voice.

Grace glared at Michelle, her eyes issuing a warning not to pursue the subject of time zones.

"Could you show me where to go?" Michelle asked Janet in a low voice, and followed her from the room. Stewart had warned her about Eleanor, but seeing the sudden change from a woman in complete control of the situation to someone picking nervously at the arm of her chair was deeply disturbing.

They mounted the carpeted stairs in silence until they reached the upstairs hall. "Mrs. Tyler sometimes gets a little muddled," Janet said in a low voice. "We find it best to agree with whatever she says to avoid upsetting her."

"Okay." Again, Michelle felt that spasm of disappointment. "Has she been like this for long?"

"She'd been getting a little forgetful this year, but recently it seems to have grown much worse."

"That's sad."

Janet sighed heavily. "It is, indeed. Mrs. Tyler has—

at least, she had—a wonderful brain. Sharp as a tack she was where business was concerned." She climbed the second flight of stairs, halting halfway to catch her breath. "These stairs are a bit much for me nowadays."

"I could have found my own way up."

"With Miss Grace and her family staying here for the holiday, we had to put you on the top floor. But I'm sure you won't mind, being young and agile. Here we are. This is the room above your grandmother's. It gets a little warm in the summer, being just under the roof, but it shouldn't be a problem now."

The room was low-ceilinged with a bay containing three small windows. When Michelle went to look out, she could see nothing but trees.

"You'll be able to see the river in the morning," Janet told her. "You have a lovely view of it from here. That's why your grandmother prefers a room at the back of the house. It's also quieter, away from any traffic."

"This is fine."

"The bathroom's next door. You'll have to share it with Sophie when she arrives tomorrow, but for tonight it's yours. Towels on the rail there." Janet nodded to the old-fashioned wooden towel rack. "I've given you a kettle and some tea and coffee. There's a little fridge in the cupboard here with fresh milk and cream." She opened the door in the wall. "Homebaked cookies in the tin."

"Yours?" Michelle asked. Janet nodded. "That's great. Thank you." Michelle suddenly wished that Janet would go. She desperately needed time to herself, to prepare for another session with her relatives downstairs. Her energy level seemed to be at zero after the long journey.

"I'll let you be, then." Janet peered at her. "You look tired. It's probably been a long day for you."

"It has," Michelle had to admit. "I left home about twelve hours ago."

"Take a few minutes to rest, then. But don't leave

it too late. Mrs. Tyler is usually in her bed by ten. She stayed up especially to be able to greet you." Janet hesitated, her hand on the door. "She's been very excited about your coming."

She certainly hadn't shown it, Michelle thought.

"They're not a very demonstrative family," Janet said, reading her mind.

"You can say that again."

"Your mother was different."

Michelle's face flushed with excitement. "You knew my mother?"

"Oh, yes. She was three years old when I started working for the Tyler family. I was just a part-time nursery maid here then, if you can believe it."

"That's wonderful. You can tell me all about her, what she was like when she was growing up."

A blind seemed to come down on Janet's friendly face. "Didn't she talk to you about her childhood?"

"Not very much. She said it was all too painful to remember."

Janet opened her mouth . . . and then turned away. "Well, I must be going down or Mrs. Tyler will wonder where I've got to." She paused at the door. "Please let me know if there's anything else you need."

Before Michelle had time to thank her again, Janet had gone, closing the door behind her. Michelle was left feeling rebuffed, her excitement at meeting someone friendly who could tell her about her mother's childhood here ebbed away.

Deciding it really wasn't such a great idea to antagonize her grandmother on their first evening together, she hurriedly washed and changed into black silk dress pants to replace the jeans, and then went downstairs again.

She was almost at the foot of the top flight of stairs when she heard a voice. Grace was standing in a doorway of one of the bedrooms, a cell phone to her ear. She looked up and saw Michelle standing there. Immediately, Grace stopped talking, switched off the phone and without saying a word to her, followed Michelle downstairs.

Michelle drew in a deep breath. *Only three days*, she told herself. She had the feeling they were going to be the longest three days of her life.

Chapter 5

Michelle found Eleanor Tyler on her feet in the heritage room, leaning both hands on her ebony cane. As soon as she saw Michelle, she glanced pointedly at her watch. "It is way past my usual bedtime, young woman."

"I'm sorry. I took a few extra minutes to change."

The glacial blue eyes swept over her. "I don't see any change."

Michelle bit back a heated response. "I was wearing jeans for the journey." She saw Grace raise her eyebrows at her brother Norman, whose face remained devoid of expression. *What the hell am I doing here with these people*? Michelle asked herself. It wasn't as if this visit had been her idea in the first place.

Eleanor released a theatrical sigh. "You had better come up to my room when I'm in bed. I'll send Janet for you."

"I don't think's that a good idea, Mother," Grace said.

"Oh? Why not?" her mother demanded.

"You know what Andrew says about making sure you relax before you go to sleep, to avoid unpleasant dreams."

"Andrew!" Eleanor made a derogatory sound. "Fat lot Andrew knows. He's a quack."

"We have all day to talk tomorrow," Michelle said. She wasn't in the mood for a long interrogation tonight.

Eleanor turned her piercing gaze on her and then, to Michelle's surprise, agreed. "You're right. Better to talk in the morning when we're both feeling brighter." She said good night to her daughter and two sons, accepting their dutiful kisses on her cheek without any sign of emotion, and then turned to Michelle. "Walk with me to the stairs."

Michelle felt the pressure of her grandmother's hand beneath her arm. Matching her slow pace, she walked with her from the room, feeling Grace's gaze like sharpened darts in her back.

Eleanor halted at the foot of the stairs. "I don't give anything away where they're concerned," she said in a half whisper. "It's safer that way."

Surprised by her air of conspiracy, Michelle didn't know what to say, so she merely smiled and nodded.

For the first time since they'd met, she saw her grandmother smile. It was little more than a wrinkle of the lips, but it warmed her eyes. "You are so very like your mother," she said softly. "Smaller, of course. Most of the Tylers are as tall as redwoods, but you have her features. And I may say you seem to be every bit as stubborn as she was."

Michelle grinned. "That's what Brian tells me."

"Brian? Oh, yes. Your husband. He's an American, isn't he? We have all kinds of American cousins in New England. I must show you the family tree our genealogist is working on for us. It goes back to the days when my family first came from England to settle in Boston."

"How interesting."

"Do you mean that, or are you merely being polite?"

"No," Michelle said, laughing, "I mean it."

"Good. I must try to remember to show it to you tomorrow. Where's Janet?" Eleanor asked abruptly.

"Right here." Janet appeared from the room across the hall. Michelle had the feeling she'd been listening in to every word they'd been saying.

"Time for bed." Eleanor extended her cheek to Michelle for what seemed to be the Tyler ritual nighttime kiss, but Michelle put her arms around her grandmother and gently hugged her. She felt the thin body stiffen against hers—and then relax. As Michelle reached up to kiss the powdery cheek, she felt her grandmother's hand press against her waist.

"Good night, Grandmother."

"Good night, child." Eleanor turned away, but not before Michelle had seen the trace of moisture in her eyes. "Come along, Janet. Help me up these confounded stairs. Everyone keeps nagging me to get an elevator put in," she told Michelle, "but when they told me they'd have to spoil my lovely dining room to build one, I said definitely not."

"How about one of those staircase chairlifts instead," Michelle suggested. "They'd be fun to use."

Eleanor's eyes widened. "Would they? I must admit I've never thought of a stairlift as being fun."

"You should. It's just the sort of thing I would have loved as a child." Too late, Michelle saw a look of pain come into the older woman's eyes and winced inwardly. How tactless of her to remind her grandmother that she'd never known her as a child.

"An aid to climbing stairs is not a plaything," Eleanor said, her expression severe again. As she slowly mounted the stairs, Michelle stood there, wondering what to do next.

She turned around . . . to find Grace so close behind her that she jumped. "Oh!" She gave her aunt a half smile. "You scared me."

"Did I?" Grace jerked her head in the direction of another door farther down the hall. "Follow me." It was an order, not a request. Turning sharply, she led Michelle to a room on the right-hand side of the house, which appeared to be a library or study. It was furnished in a heavy Victorian style, with two large polished mahogany desks and shelves lined with books. In the fireplace was an old-fashioned black grate. A set of brass fire implements gleamed on one side of the fireplace, a wood box filled with logs on the other. A large oil portrait of a strikingly handsome man of about forty hung above the mantelpiece, his piercing eyes watching them. Michelle guessed that this must be Ramsey Tyler, her grandfather.

"Sit down," Grace said.

"I'd rather stand," Michelle said, preferring not to give her aunt the advantage of her height. Grace wore a simple but beautifully cut black silk-crepe dress that screamed *expensive* and fitted her willowy form perfectly.

She opened her black silk purse and took a cigarette from a gold cigarette case, lighting it with a matching lighter. She inhaled as if she'd badly needed a cigarette and then blew smoke out again. "Exactly what the hell are you doing here?"

Michelle looked at her with a little half smile. "I didn't think they still made cigarette cases. Especially gold ones. Is it real?"

Grace threw her purse down on a table. "What's that got to do with anything?"

Michelle shrugged. "Nothing. I just wondered, that's all."

Grace folded her arms, holding the cigarette between two fingers. "I repeat, why are you here?"

"I heard you the first time. I'm here because my grandmother invited me."

"After you'd written to her first."

Michelle frowned. "No, that's not the way it was. Your mother wrote to me."

"I'm sorry, but I know for a fact that was not the way it happened. You wrote to her first, asking if you could come to see her."

Michelle shrugged again. "Suit yourself."

"Why, after all these years, did you want to come and see her?"

Michelle stared at her aunt. "God knows," she said, smiling again.

"Your manners are deplorable."

"Are they?" Michelle drew in a long breath. "Yours aren't that hot, either. I'm amazed at your reception of your dead sister's daughter on her first visit to what I understand to be the family home. You and Uncle Norman seem determined to make me feel unwelcome. I'm glad it was Stewart who picked me up or I might never have made it here."

"Which wouldn't have been a bad thing." This came from Norman Tyler, who had just entered the room. Despite his size, he walked as stealthily as a cat. Michelle hadn't realized he was there until she heard his voice. "My mother's mental health is in a very precarious condition. The least little upset could tip her over."

"I don't intend to upset her."

"I'm sure you don't, but nevertheless she must be kept on a strictly controlled regime to maintain a delicate balance. No excitement, no emotional upset. If you don't believe us, you can speak to her doctor tomorrow."

"Andrew the quack?"

"I beg your pardon."

"That's what your mother called him, didn't she?"

"I find your attitude offensive."

Michelle gripped her hands together. "Not half as offensive as you're being, Mr. Tyler. I was invited here by your mother for a family Thanksgiving celebration. Despite the many reservations I had about coming, I accepted her invitation, thinking it was time I met my mother's family. But now I'm beginning to understand why my mother never came home again."

"Your mother never came home again," Grace said, two spots of color flaring on her cheekbones, "because she knew she wouldn't be welcome. Not by any of us, but particularly not by her mother. She broke her heart by sleeping with a low-life lumberman, who got her pregnant and—"

"Excuse me," Michelle broke in, "this is my father you're talking about. I don't remember him but—"

"That was your one piece of good fortune. He molested your mother—"

"That's not the way she told it."

"Naturally not," Grace said scornfully. "She'd want you to think the best about your father. Besides, she led him on and then was surprised when she couldn't get rid of him."

"Make up your mind. First he molested her. Now she led him on." Michelle stared at her aunt. "What on earth did my mother do to you to make you hate her so much?"

"I don't hate your mother."

"You must have, to speak about her this way when she's dead."

Norman looked uncomfortable. "Let's deal with this more calmly, shall we?"

"Suits me." Michelle sat down on one of the swivel chairs. She tried to appear nonchalant, but she was feeling desperately tired.

Norman sat down in another chair and leaned toward Michelle. "I'm sorry. We've started this all the wrong way. The bottom line is that we're deeply concerned about our mother. She's been acting very strangely recently, imagining all kinds of weird things. She didn't tell us you were coming here until Wednesday. We thought of calling you to tell you our concerns, but we were afraid she'd be even more upset if you didn't turn up."

Grace glared at her brother. "That was *your* worry, not mine. As far as I'm concerned the contact should never have been made in the first place." She took in another long drag of her cigarette. "Which brings me back to my first question. Why are you here? Do you need money?"

Michelle smiled. Rebecca, her friend and partner in the gift store, would have said that you should watch out when Michelle smiled that way, with her eyes almost shut. "I have my own business," she told Grace. "My husband is one of the best and highest paid foreign correspondents in American television."

Grace blew smoke in her direction. "No one ever has enough money."

Michelle stood up and stretched. "Excuse me, fam-

ily, but it's been a long day. It's time I went to bed."
She went to the door. "Thanks for the great
welcome."

Norman followed her into the hall. "Wait, Michelle.
We don't want you to feel unwelcome. You have to
understand that our main concern is our mother's
health."

"So you said. I just don't like being told point blank
that I'm likely to cause trouble because I've come
here."

"Grace is upset."

"Oh?" Michelle looked past him at her aunt, who
was glaring at her over her brother's broad shoulder.

Norman held out his hand. "A truce?" He smiled
and Michelle saw how this man might charm his opposition while he ruthlessly rammed through a corporate takeover.

She shook his hand. "Okay. See you in the
morning."

"You'll meet my wife Lauren tomorrow. And my
sons." His dark eyes warmed. "You'll like Lauren."
It seemed an odd thing to say, as if he wanted to
reassure her before she met his wife.

"Great."

"Anything you need? Another drink, perhaps?"

"No, thanks. Janet has left drinks and stuff in my
room for me. I'll be fine. Good night."

"Good night, Michelle. Sleep well. And in case nobody has said it before now, welcome to Tyler House
and to New Brunswick."

"Janet said it, but thanks, anyway." Michelle peered
around him, to raise her hand to the figure in the
study. "Good night, Aunt Grace."

Her aunt muttered some response and turned away.

When she reached her room, Michelle found the
bedside lamps with fringed shades switched on and
her bedcover turned down at a precise angle. A robe
had been taken from her suitcase and laid out at the
foot of the bed. On the little table was a tray with a
white cloth over it. No doubt the chicken salad Janet

had promised her. It was a relief to be able to close the door and turn the key in the lock, shutting herself away for a few hours.

An intense longing for Brian swept over her. She glanced around for a phone, then opened a couple of cupboards, but couldn't find a telephone anywhere in the room. She had her cell phone, but she knew from experience that she wasn't likely to get through to Indonesia with it. Besides, Brian had told her she'd have to leave a message for him at their main base in Jakarta, as he'd be away on location much of the time. He intended to visit the more remote regions of the vast country, and would sometimes be inaccessible for days. If she couldn't speak to him, hear the warmth of his voice, what was the point of calling?

She suddenly felt very cold. The thought of not being able to reach him if she needed him chilled her. Then she shook her head. "Idiot," she murmured. She'd managed fine without Brian before. Sometimes for two or three months. Why should this time be any different?

But this time *was* different. She hugged herself, her arms clasped around her abdomen. She was extremely tired, that was all. She'd feel a hundred times better in the morning.

She tossed her bag onto the bed, unpacked, and then opened the door of the wardrobe that dominated the room. As she hung some clothes in its dark interior that smelled of mothballs, it loomed over her, making her feel it would topple onto her if she were to give it the slightest push. "You'd think they could afford to install one miserable built-in closet," she muttered.

She put her favorite photograph of Brian on the bedside table and sat on the edge of the bed, looking at him, wondering what he was doing right now.

A shiver ran across her shoulders. Didn't these people believe in turning on the heat in October? No wonder they had so much money. She looked around and found a supplementary electric baseboard heater, which she turned onto the low setting. She'd soon warm up once she got into bed.

She took the cloth off the tray, to find not only the chicken salad, but also rolls and butter, and a small basket filled with fruit. The thought of food of any kind made her stomach churn. She'd have to get rid of the salad somehow, to avoid hurting Janet's feelings. Having made herself a mug of hot chocolate, she changed into her pajamas and climbed into bed. At least they'd invested in a comfortable, modern bed.

When she'd finished half the hot chocolate, she kissed her fingers and leaned over to press them to the cold glass of the framed photograph, over Brian's lips. "Good night, sweetie," she whispered. Picking up the collection of Alice Munro's short stories she'd been reading on the plane, she snuggled down beneath the covers, but she was asleep before the end of the page.

Lying beneath his mosquito net on the evil-smelling bed in the seedy hotel, Brian lit a cigarette and flung himself on his back to stare up at the ceiling. He always traveled with his own mosquito net and the sleeping bag that Michelle had made for him from cotton sheets, but after only a few minutes it was already sticking to him, soaked with his sweat. Above him, the desultory ceiling fan cranked and squeaked, noisy enough to keep him from sleeping, but offering little release from the cloying heat. He and the crew usually got up well before dawn to catch the cooler part of the day, then took a couple of hours of rest in the hottest part of the afternoon.

As he lay there, certain that he was being bitten by every kind of bug imaginable, his mind turned, as it always did at such times, to thoughts of Michelle. It would be the middle of the night for her now.

God, how he missed her! Why hadn't he listened to her and stayed home? He must be out of his mind to choose this stinking hole over Michelle. That was the trouble, though, wasn't it? He was bored when he was in North America, but when he was away he longed for home—meaning Michelle.

What the hell was the matter with him? A case of arrested development? Was he doomed to be one of those guys who had to climb mountains or sail solo around the world until death—or old age—got them by the balls and finished them off?

He hated hurting Michelle. In the darkness of his soul he loathed himself. Saying good-bye to her in Winnipeg had been the worst time ever. He could see her now, her small, perfect face paler than usual, laughing a little too loud, telling him she was glad to be visiting her family at last, that next time they'd go to New Brunswick together. He'd even managed to convince himself that it was better for her to go alone for the first visit.

But now, as he lay staring up at the circles of smoke rising to the ceiling, with its mildewed, peeling paint and darting geckos, he began to worry about her, remembering the stories she'd told him of her mother's childhood.

Tomorrow, he decided, he'd call her, find out how she was getting on. But deep down he knew that this was only a ploy to make himself feel better. He'd tried for two days to get through to Minneapolis, with no success. Half the time the lines were dead. The few times he was able to get a line, he could hear heavy breathing. They didn't even do their eavesdropping subtly here. He and his crew were tolerated only as long as they toed the line, played the game. Only a few days ago, they'd had several hours of footage destroyed on the whim of the local police chief. There was no use protesting.

Persuasion and tact—and a bagful of U.S. dollars—was what they used. And lots of patience.

Brian stirred restlessly and stubbed out his cigarette on the empty Bintang beer can. He popped open another can. Despite being warm, it tasted good. The quicker they got this special on Indonesia wrapped up, the faster he'd be back with Michelle. There was something about her recently, especially on the day he'd left, that had been bugging him ever since, like a wood tick beneath the skin. She was holding something back from him, which wasn't like her. Michelle could be impulsive, she could be annoying and argumentative, but rarely could she keep a secret from him.

As he lay there, sweltering in the heat, he knew that sleep would be a long time coming, if he slept at all. He reached for his tape recorder and started to record his recollections of yet another grueling day, but found it hard to concentrate, his concern about Michelle continually niggling in a corner of his mind.

Chapter 6

Once she was sure that neither Janet nor Michelle was hovering around upstairs, Grace went down to the study again.

"Okay?" Norman asked as she softly closed the door behind her.

"Yes. Mother's settled for the night and there's no sound from either Janet's room or the top floor." Grace sat down on the footstool, carefully avoiding her father's old leather chair. "Get me a brandy, would you? I need one badly."

"I already did." Norman picked up the balloon glass from the table and handed it to her.

"Thanks." Grace took a sip and swirled the cognac in her mouth before swallowing it. "So . . . what do you think?"

Norman's dark browns lowered. "About Michelle? I think she could be a major source of trouble."

Grace nodded. "Despite what she said, do you think she is here for money? I just called Larry. That's what he thought."

"If she is, we'll give her money. That's easy."

"Larry said the same thing. Pay her off and get rid of her."

"My concern is that she's legit. That she genuinely wants a relationship with Mother, if not the entire family."

"Ha! She can forget that. We don't want anything to do with Carolyn's bastard."

"You may not want to, but Mother probably will."
Norman drew in a breath and let it out slowly. "I
think she took to the girl."

"She's no girl, Norman. She must be at least thirty,
thirty-one."

He gave a sour smile. "That's young to me. She's
very attractive. When I first saw her it was a shock. I
thought Carolyn had walked into the room."

"She's smaller than Carolyn. But you're right. I
think Mother liked her." Their eyes met. "Bloody
hell! The timing couldn't be worse."

"You're right. We have to agree to the merger with
Bruneau by the twenty-second of this month or they'll
go elsewhere."

"Did you speak to Mother about it today?"

"Of course. I speak to her about it every day."

"And?"

Norman shook his head. "The usual response." He
mimicked Eleanor's autocratic voice. " 'Ours is a family firm. Your father would turn in his grave if he
knew you were wanting to merge with another company, especially one with Quebec connections.' "

"So her answer is still no."

"Right." Norman drained his glass of cognac and
set it down on the desk. "She's losing her touch, you
know. That's what bothers me. Five years ago I would
have listened to her opinion, but not anymore." He
rubbed his fingers across his forehead. "She's getting
less sure of herself, too. You saw her tonight, falling
apart because she couldn't work out the difference
between Atlantic and central time."

"I know. I hate to see her like this." Grace drummed
restless fingers on the table. "She seems to be losing
her concentration. You'll be talking to her about
something and suddenly she's off on a tangent about
something totally unconnected. That's not like her at
all. I'm trying to persuade her to take those new tests
Andrew suggested."

"For Alzheimer's?"

"Right. But she's adamant there's nothing wrong with her."

"That's ridiculous. There's obviously something wrong. In the past few weeks alone there's been a marked deterioration."

"I'll speak to Andrew again tomorrow. He's already concerned about these hallucinatory episodes she's had. And the paranoia. He's changed her medication to see if that will help." Grace's eyes met Norman's again and immediately glanced away. "As I've said before, what we need—especially now with Carolyn's daughter landed on us—is for one of us to get Mother's power of attorney."

Norman slammed his fist down on the desktop. "Don't I know it, but she won't hear of it. Goes berserk every time I even mention it."

"There must be some other way to get her to agree to the merger. Why not let Stewart take a try at persuading her?"

Norman stared at her. "Stewart? If I can't get through to her, Stewart certainly couldn't."

"Oh, I don't know. Stewart has always managed to wheedle his way with her." Grace gave a laugh that was brittle as glass. "Far better than you could."

"Stewart could charm money out of her purse, but I doubt he could manage to change Mother's mind on a vitally important business matter like this. We're talking a major upheaval here."

"If you remind Stewart that there's a lot of money in it for him as well, maybe he'll make an effort."

"Make an effort? Stewart? He's never been anything but a lazy bum, sucking all he can from the business and never putting anything back into it."

The door opened. "Talking about me again?" Stewart drawled as he sauntered into the room.

"Were you listening outside the door?"

"Got it in one, brother."

Grace couldn't help laughing. "As long as you were the only one listening, that's okay."

Stewart sat down in his father's old desk chair. He

nodded toward Grace's brandy. "Pour me one of those, would you?"

"You look as if you've had more than enough already. I take it you were over at the hotel bar?"

"How did you guess?" Stewart accepted the glass of cognac Norman poured for him. "So how did the family reunion go tonight? Did Mother take to her new granddaughter?"

"Unfortunately, yes," Grace said.

Stewart looked at her and then Norman. His smile faded. "This isn't good, is it?"

"You can say that again."

"Carolyn was always Mother's favorite."

Grace darted a venomous look at him.

"No point in glaring at me, Gracie. You know it's true."

"You could have fooled me. She practically threw Carolyn out of the house when she found out she was pregnant."

"The poor kid. That was because of good old Dad. But even he couldn't stop her from sending Carolyn money."

Grace stared at Stewart. "How do you know that?"

"Mother told me years ago, when Carolyn died and Father forbade her to go to the funeral. She was so upset that I guess she had to talk to someone about her. She said she'd been sending Carolyn checks, but she kept returning them."

"That, I don't believe," Grace said. "I mean the part about Carolyn returning them."

Stewart shrugged. "That's what Mother said." He turned to Norman. "What's the news with the merger?"

"It's still a go, but we have exactly fourteen days left before we have to give them our answer, and Mother's still adamant that she won't agree to it."

"And now a new granddaughter arrives. Someone who's untainted by our desire to get hold of Mother's shares—"

"I'm not trying to get Mother's shares for myself,"

Norman protested, his face reddening. "I want them for the good of the firm. Let's be brutally honest. We may be doing well at the moment, but we could do a great deal better if we accepted this merger. At present we're viewed as a good but old-fashioned family firm mired in the past."

Grace's heart pounded. "And once news got out that we wanted to merge, but couldn't because of Mother, our stock could plummet. We could even find our personal assets involved as well."

Stewart whistled. "So we've got to persuade Mother to agree to the merger or else somehow get her shares away from her, right?"

"Right," Norman said. "And make sure she doesn't give those shares, or even a small part of them, away to someone else."

"Like Michelle?" Stewart said.

"Exactly. And all this must be achieved within two weeks or we're all in trouble."

"Good luck."

Norman rounded on Stewart. "This includes you, brother. You do nothing to earn your generous salary except sit on your fat fanny—"

"I can deal with clients better than either of you two."

"Right. Playing golf and boozing," Norman said.

"That's all part of it."

"Well, it won't be with the new merger. We'll be a lean and mean machine. At least that's what Martin Grostig told me."

Stewart laughed but there was a hint of nervousness in his laughter.

"We're in deep trouble," Norman told him. "The era of family business is dead. Look at Eaton's, for God's sake. You want to be a dead dynasty like the Eaton family? Mother's grip on the firm has meant that it isn't prepared for the twenty-first century. There are too many colossal, cut-price merchants out there now. We're too small. Either we merge with Bruneau's or we go under." He fixed Stewart with his slightly protuberant eyes. "And you'll go under with us," he reminded him. "Which could mean no Jag convertible. So you'd better join us in thinking of some way we can get those shares from Mother *and* insure that she doesn't give any of them to Carolyn's daughter. Otherwise, you could be looking for another job very soon. One where you'll actually have to work."

Chapter 7

Michelle awoke to the sound of her doorknob being turned, followed by a discreet knock and a loud whisper. "Miss Tyler! Miss Tyler, are you awake?"

She forced herself awake, trying to peer at her watch in the subdued light coming through the drawn curtains. "Hang on a minute." Blinking, she sat up. A wave of spinning nausea struck her. "Oh, God," she groaned. She pulled on her robe and fumbled her way to the door. She turned the key and opened it.

Janet was standing there, a tray in her hands. "I hope I didn't wake you," she said anxiously.

"Not at all." Michelle stifled a yawn. "Come on in. What is the time, anyway?"

"Seven-thirty," Janet said in a bright, wide-awake voice.

Seven-thirty! Michelle wanted to yell. That was only five-thirty central time. No wonder she felt as if her mouth had been scoured with Drano. "Sorry, but it's a bit early for me." She tried not to sound too irritated.

"I thought you'd like some fresh tea and toast." Janet set the tray down with a decided snap on the round table by the window, so that the spoon clinked against the cup and saucer.

The thought of putting anything in her mouth was disgusting. "Thanks. That's very kind, but you shouldn't be carrying that heavy tray up two flights of stairs." Janet's face was red and shining, and her breathing labored.

"No problem. I'm used to it."

"Give me a moment, Janet," Michelle said, edging to the door. "Don't go away. I'll be right back."

"Are you okay?"

"Fine," Michelle shouted as she dashed for the bathroom and slammed the door. The toilet seat felt icy cold when she sat on it. She quickly stood up and bent over, hands pressed to her stomach, trying to cover the sound of the miserable retching by pretending to cough. Beads of perspiration sprang out on her forehead. But beneath the wretched physical feeling, she felt a huge surge of excitement at this further verification of her suspicions.

After a few minutes she flushed the toilet and went back into the bedroom, hoping she didn't look as unsteady as she felt.

"Are you sure you're feeling okay?" Janet peered at her. "You're very pale."

"That's just my early morning complexion," Michelle said with a laugh. "I'm fine."

Janet moved to the window bay. "I've put your tray here," she said, indicating the circular table covered with a floral cloth. "Sit down and have your tea and toast before it gets cold. Mrs. Tyler's outside, taking her morning walk."

"Outside?"

"She never misses a morning walk by the river, unless it's winter and we've had a heavy snowfall. Even then I've known her to put on her boots and parka and go out first thing."

"I'm surprised. I didn't think she was able to get around that well."

"She never gives in. Her arthritis is very bad, but she says she refuses to pander to herself." Janet's hand hovered over the white china teapot with little blue flowers on it. "Shall I pour for you?"

"No, thanks." Michelle wished Janet would go so

that she could grab another hour of sleep, but Janet seemed in the mood to chat.

"Of course she got into the habit of walking in the early morning because of her dog."

"I didn't see a dog last night."

Janet shook her head. "No. He disappeared a few weeks ago. They never found him, even though they advertised and offered a large reward. He must have been run over."

"That's awful."

"It certainly is. Mrs. Tyler was very fond of her little dog. She was devastated. Would you like me to open the window a bit?"

Michelle gave an involuntary shiver. "Go ahead," she said, resigning herself to the fact that she wasn't going to be able to go back to bed again. "Some fresh air might help to wake me up."

Janet pushed open one of the windows. "See. There she is now, walking down to the river." She gave a little gasp. "Oh, dear, I hope she's careful on that muddy slope. Those fallen leaves are sopping wet. She might slip. Bob should have gathered them up before she came out."

Michelle came to stand beside her, seeing the slightly stooped but still tall figure dressed in a long suede leather coat with a fur-trimmed hood. "Should she be out on her own like that?"

"She's not on her own. Bob will be nearby in case she needs help, but of course she won't let him walk with her."

Suddenly Eleanor looked around and they heard her voice calling a name. Then she stopped abruptly, her left hand pressed to her mouth. Leaning heavily on her cane, she turned and slowly made her way back to the house.

Janet stepped back from the window. "Don't let her see you watching her," she whispered. She stood there, unmoving, her face distressed.

Michelle sat down at the round table, unsure if she should say something or not. Then, when Janet still didn't move, she said, "She was calling her dog, wasn't she?"

Janet nodded, her mouth quivering. "She does that sometimes. Then she remembers. It's so sad. That little dog was like a child to her."

"She should get another one."

"She won't. Mr. Stewart told her the same thing, but she said that Griffon was irreplaceable." Janet opened her mouth as if she wanted to add something, but then closed it again. "I must be going. She'll be needing her breakfast." She eyed Michelle's tray. "I think she'd like you to join her in her room for breakfast."

"Milk and toast is enough for me." And a bit more sleep would be nice, Michelle wanted to add.

"Oh, you need more than that in the morning to get you going. I'll be making fresh porridge and bacon and eggs for the family."

The thought turned Michelle's stomach even more. "I never eat a cooked breakfast." That wasn't exactly true, but it saved any explanations.

"Mrs. Tyler suggested you come to her room at eight o'clock."

Another royal summons. There went the idea of more sleep, for sure. "Okay," Michelle said, sighing. "I'll do my best to be there by eight."

"What would you like for your breakfast?"

"Bran flakes would be fine. And a glass of milk."

"Certainly." Janet smiled, having achieved her mission. "Miss Grace likes strong coffee in the morning. But Mrs. Tyler is strictly a tea drinker."

"Just milk, thanks. This must be a very busy time for you. A lot of extra work."

Janet's face brightened. "I love it when the family's home, under one roof. It's like old times. Besides, they don't all sleep here at Thanksgiving, you know. Only Miss Grace moves in to help out—and the rest of her family, when they arrive. And I have lots of help. I don't have to do the Thanksgiving dinner by myself."

"Glad to hear it. You can count on me, you know. I can peel veggies and stuff."

Janet laughed. "Oh no, that wouldn't do at all. Mrs. Tyler engages a chef from the club and I have my daughter in to help. She lives on Mitchell, just a few minutes away. So I don't need help from anyone else. Thank you, though, for offering," she added as she opened the door. She went out, closing it softly behind her.

The Tyler family appeared to have been the center of Janet Marlow's life for a very long time. They still were, apparently. She seemed so dedicated to them that Michelle was quite surprised to hear that she had taken time off to have her own family.

She mentioned this later, when she joined her grandmother for breakfast. This time Eleanor made no comment about her being late. Which was good, considering it had been quite a scramble for Michelle to shower and dress and report to Eleanor's room at ten past eight. "Janet seems devoted to you and the family. Oh, no tea for me, thanks," she added hurriedly. "I prefer milk." Her grandmother had been about to pour tea from the bone-china teapot for her.

Eleanor looked surprised, but merely set the heavy pot down on the table. "Janet is like my own right hand. I can't think how I'd manage without her. Of course it wouldn't be wise to tell her so."

"Why not?"

Eleanor's steel-gray eyebrows shot up. "Why not? Because it doesn't do to praise people too much. They become complacent. It's important to keep employees on their toes."

"She must be more than a mere employee, surely, after all this time with you?"

"Janet is paid extremely well," was all Eleanor said. She reached with a shaking hand for the dish of breakfast rolls and held it out to Michelle.

Michelle took one of the warm, flaky croissants and spread butter on it. "Mmm, these are delicious," she said, as she bit into it.

"Our own bakery delivers them to me fresh every morning."

"Lucky you. About Janet. I find that praising people makes them work even harder. It's always nice to be told that you've done well."

"Well, you have your ways and I have mine. Tell me, Michelle," her grandmother said, abruptly changing the subject, "what kind of education did your mother give you?"

"I'm not sure about her *giving* me an education. Somehow, with the help of student loans and scholarships, I managed to get a BA in Fine Arts. I'm a potter, you know."

Her grandmother looked puzzled. "A potter?" she repeated.

"Yes. I make pots. Ceramic dishes and mugs, that sort of thing. I also teach classes."

"Is there any money in pottery?"

"If you sell it in your own store, as I do, there is. You get the benefit of the markup. Well, Becca and I do."

"Who is Becca?"

"Rebecca Horowitz. She and I have been buddies since sixth grade."

"That sounds like a Jewish name."

"It is."

If her grandmother made the smallest derogatory remark, Michelle told herself, that would be her cue to be long gone from Tyler House, but Eleanor said, "I had a Jewish friend at school. We lost touch when I married Ramsey."

"Becca's great with the business's side of retailing. I do the buying. Our store's called Simple Pleasures."

"Hmm," was all her grandmother said.

"We sell all sorts of gifts, of course," Michelle said, eager to defend her store, "not just my pots. It's a great outlet for local craftspeople. We even have a wedding registry now, so that people can have fun choosing different things, instead of the usual boring towels and place settings. That way, they also support the local arts and crafts as well." Michelle grimaced. "Sorry, I tend to get overenthusiastic about our store."

"It's vitally important that you be enthusiastic about your own business. If you're not enthusiastic, why should anyone else be?"

"True."

"Your little store sounds very nice," her grandmother said wistfully, "I wish I could see it."

"Maybe you will one day."

"I doubt it. I don't travel much nowadays."

"You should. There's lots of wonderful places to visit."

"My family wants me to take a cruise."

"Sounds like a good idea."

"I loathe cruises. Boring and stupid. And I dislike the kind of people who go on cruises. They're boring and stupid, too."

"I've never been on one, so I wouldn't know. There are other ways to travel, you know."

"Alas, I don't have the legs for it anymore. Where's your husband at present?" Frowning, Eleanor shook her head impatiently. "What's his name? Bill, Ian . . . ? You must excuse me. I'm not very good with names lately."

"Brian. He's in Indonesia."

"Is he, indeed? Dangerous place to be at the moment, Indonesia. You must worry about him."

Michelle's throat constricted. "Yes, I do, but he's doing what he's good at, what he wants to do." She sighed. "I asked him to stay home," she confided, "but he gets bored."

"That's men for you." Her grandmother shook her head.

"Not just men. There are lots of women in the foreign correspondent field now. You see them on CBC news all the time, reporting from Russia or Kosovo or . . ."

"Terrible job for a woman," her grandmother said. Then a spark came into her eyes. "I must say, though, I wouldn't have minded it when I was younger."

"Bet you wouldn't." Michelle grinned.

"Now you must please feel free to call your husband from here whenever you want to talk to him."

"Thank you, but I leave the calling to him. It's too tough to get hold of him. He has enough trouble getting through to his television station, never mind me trying to get him. He might be able to take a break in Bali for a few days. We'll be able to chat then."

"Bali is one of those places I've always wanted to see, but Ramsey had no interest in going there." Again, there was a wistful tone in Eleanor's voice.

"You'd love it. The rice paddies are brilliant green and there are bright-colored flowers everywhere. And the people are beautiful, too. Always smiling."

"Is this based on information from your husband or have you been there yourself?"

"Brian took me there for our honeymoon."

"Better than Niagara Falls?"

Michelle laughed. "I should think so. Is that where you went for your honeymoon?"

"Good Lord, no." Eleanor gave a rueful smile. "We were married just after the war started. Ramsey had joined the RCAF and was posted to England, so we had only two days together at the Algonquin Hotel in St. Andrews before he left."

"How sad."

Eleanor's blue eyes shone. "Not sad at all. Knowing that you had such a short time left together added a certain zest, you might say."

Michelle laughed out loud. "I can imagine," she said, remembering that last weekend before Brian had left for Indonesia. "What made you write that letter?"

"What letter?"

"Your letter to me."

"What on earth has that got to do with honeymoons?"

"Sorry. My mind jumped. I do that all the time. It drives Brian nuts."

"It would drive me nuts, too," her grandmother said dryly. "Don't forget the mind doesn't stay quite as keen when you get older. You'll need to signal when you're turning to another subject, if you don't mind."

"Okay. I'll try."

"Now you've made me forget what you were asking me. Oh, yes. My letter."

"Yes. Why did you write to me after all these years?"

"Well, I should have thought that was obvious," her grandmother said. "I wrote in response to the letter you sent me."

Michelle held her breath for a moment, then released it. "But I didn't write to you."

"You most certainly did. I have the letter in my desk."

"The only letter I wrote was a little note confirming my arrival times." Recalling Norman's warning, Michelle chose her words carefully. "You'll remember that I called you after I received your invitation. I told you I'd love to come for Thanksgiving."

"My dear Michelle. I may be a little less clear in my mind than I used to be, but I can assure you that you *did* write me a letter, asking if you could come and visit me. How else would I have known that you were married to an American and had a gift store in Winnipeg? Tell me that." Eleanor rapped her hand on the table to emphasize her point.

Michelle was about to keep up the argument, to challenge her by asking to see this letter, but something stopped her. It was as if Eleanor Tyler *needed* to think that her letter had been in response to one Michelle had written to her.

Or she needed someone else to think that this was the case.

But surely she didn't require permission to write to her own granddaughter, did she? Then Michelle recalled Grace's venom the previous night . . . and wondered.

"Taking you a long time to answer me."

"Sorry." Michelle shook her head. "I guess . . . If

you've got my letter, I must have forgotten I wrote to you."

"Now who's losing their mind?" Eleanor said with an air of triumph.

Michelle grinned. "Me, for sure. I suppose I felt guilty for not having written earlier."

"So you should. But never mind. I'm just glad you got around to it eventually, before it was too late and you'd be coming to put flowers on my grave."

Michelle was about to make a laughing protest, but her grandmother's expression stopped her. There was no laughter in those blue eyes. She really meant it.

Eleanor leaned forward and grasped her arm. "I am so grateful you came, Michelle." Her fingers tightened. "I feel so much safer now that you're here."

She was about to say more, but was interrupted by Janet knocking on the door and then peering in to ask, "Do you need anything more?" She came further into the room. "More tea, perhaps? I've brought you some more hot toast." She put the toast down on the table.

"I asked that we be left alone," Eleanor said, her voice sharp. "And we have plenty of toast and rolls."

Janet's smile faded. "I am sorry. I thought you might need some more toast. There's nothing worse than cold toast, is there?"

"There certainly is! Being interrupted by someone dithering around when I've expressly asked that we be left alone. That's worse than cold toast!"

Janet's mouth quivered, then she smiled. "I'll leave you alone, then." She walked to the door and was about to go out, but then spun around. "Oh, I almost forgot. Mr. Deloraine called from the club. He said he needs to talk to you about tomorrow's dinner. Something about not being able to get raspberries for the Pavlova."

"Damn the man! I knew he'd forget to order them. I should have done it myself. Bring me the portable phone," Eleanor ordered Janet. She turned to Michelle. "I'm sorry, but this just can't wait."

"That's okay. I'll go for a walk by the river. Maybe take a look at the town."

Eleanor's forehead creased in a frown. "There was something important I wanted to talk to you about, but it will have to wait," she said in a low voice. She glanced at Janet. "You can clear this away now, Janet."

Michelle started to help Janet pile the breakfast dishes on her tray.

"That's not your job," Eleanor said.

"I want to help." Michelle's eyes clashed with her grandmother's for a moment. Then her grandmother shrugged and, taking up her cane, limped to her desk to call the unfortunate chef.

Chapter 8

Michelle followed Janet from her grandmother's bedroom, feeling both frustrated and uneasy. Eleanor's mood swings from forceful and positive to morbid and forgetful were troubling. Again, she felt sorry that she hadn't come for a visit before now. Yet her grandmother seemed genuinely pleased to have her there. Michelle paused for a moment on the stairs and frowned. Not just pleased. Relieved. And what exactly had she meant when she said that she felt safer with Michelle there?

"When is the rest of the family arriving?" she asked Janet, after she'd helped her load the dishes into the dishwasher. Although the kitchen was old-fashioned, with wooden plate racks and a huge pinewood cupboard, it was also equipped with state-of-the-art appliances, which Janet proudly showed her.

"Mr. Norman's boys are already in town, of course. Mr. Anderson arrives this morning from New York."

"Mr. Anderson?"

"Your aunt's husband. Larry Anderson."

"Oh, of course. I'm not too good with names. They have a daughter, right?"

"Yes, Sophie. She's coming from Toronto and is bringing a friend. Their son, Jamie, is here already."

Michelle picked up the pieces of uneaten toast and opened the garbage bin.

"Don't throw that out," Janet shouted.

"Why not?"

"Mrs. Tyler doesn't like waste. I'll eat it."

"Cold buttered toast? Don't be silly." Michelle let the toast drop into the bin.

Janet's face flushed.

"Waste not, want not."

"Somehow I don't think that throwing out a few slices of toast is going to bankrupt this family."

Janet bit her lip, but said no more.

"If everyone's arriving this morning, I think I'll go out and explore the town until they're all settled in."

"You should see the art gallery today. It's well worth seeing and everything will be closed for the rest of the weekend and on Monday, of course."

"Can I walk there from here?"

"You surely can, if you don't mind a good walk. Just keep going along this road. You'll reach the park. Keep going, past the bridge. Then keep walking and you'll come to the Beaverbrook Art Gallery. It's opposite the old Legislative Assembly Building."

"Beaverbrook?"

"Named after Lord Beaverbrook, the famous newspaper magnate. He was raised in New Brunswick and made his first million by the time he was twenty-six. Lord Beaverbrook was very good to Fredericton, especially the university. He also gave us an art gallery and a theater." Janet glanced at her watch. "I must get on. The others will be here soon."

"I'm going."

"Are you sure you don't want to be here when they arrive?"

"Very sure." Michelle walked to the front door.

"And where are you going, Miss Tyler?" Stewart's voice boomed down the hall.

Michelle spun around. "Out for a walk."

Stewart came to join her by the door. "You look more like someone breaking out of jail." His lips quirked into a smile.

"Janet said I should see the art gallery today, or I won't see it at all."

He frowned. "That's right. I'd forgotten. You're leaving on Monday, aren't you?"

Michelle nodded.

"What a shame. There's so much to see in this part of the province alone. Our famous covered bridges, the port of Saint John . . . Well, at least you'll see more of the countryside and the coast when we drive to St. Andrews tomorrow, after church."

"That's good."

"I hope you didn't miss me too much last night."

"Let's say it might have been a little more relaxed had you been there."

"Wasn't the company of my beloved sister and brother entertaining enough for you?"

"Of course. I just wondered where you were, that's all."

"So you did miss me, eh?"

Michelle gave him one of her daunting looks, frowning up at him.

"Okay, okay, don't remind me of your mother, please. I was over at the Beaverbrook Hotel. The company and music were a lot more lively there." He grinned. "Sorry. I should have taken you with me. It must have been pretty bad to make you miss me."

Michelle edged nearer the door. This type of humor was just a little too close to coming on to her for her liking. "Let's say I wasn't made to feel very welcome, particularly by your sister."

"Grace can be pretty bitchy, but she's also very loyal to the family. I imagine she'd defend you like a lioness with a cub if some outsider attacked you."

"You could have fooled me." Michelle put her hand on the door. "I must go or I won't have much time. I've been given strict instructions to be back for lunch, so that I can meet everyone then."

Stewart grasped her arm. "A word of advice."

"Yes?"

"Well, two pieces of advice, actually. Get carried away seeing the great art and the graves in the loyalist cemetery and the lovely clapboard houses, and don't come home until after lunch."

"Why?"

"Because the Tylers are easier taken in small doses."

Michelle smiled, shaking her head at him. "What's the second bit of advice?"

"Take an umbrella. Looks like more rain." He pulled a black umbrella from the stand by the door and handed it to her.

"Thanks."

"Want me to drive you?"

"No, thanks. I feel like a good walk."

"Okay. Watch out for that gallery," he shouted after her as she made her way carefully down the rain-slicked steps. "It's got dirty pictures in it."

Ignoring him, she started off down the driveway and was soon walking on the path that ran parallel to the St. John River. White clouds scudded across the sky, blown by a fresh wind, leaving stretches of clear blue in their wake. The rich brilliance of the trees that lined both sides of the broad river was breathtaking. Gold and russet, crimson and dark green, the tapestry colors of maple and sumac and pine contrasted with the reflected fresh blue of the river.

On her left, she saw a Gothic-style church set in the middle of a large stretch of green that reminded her of England. This was probably the cathedral her grandmother had mentioned in her letter. No need to stop to see it now. They'd be going there tomorrow.

The old houses she passed were all large and detached, standing in their own grounds, like Tyler House. Some had imposing bay windows and filigree wrought-iron railings; others had pillared porches. Their clapboard sidings and contrasting shutters were painted in vibrant colors: royal blue and cream, lemon and black, russet and French gray. These old, beautifully preserved houses spoke of people's pride in their heritage. They gave the small city a sense of history and solidity, of roots going down deep into the damp earth.

Michelle halted abruptly on the path and gazed around her with eyes that were suddenly more aware. Although she'd never been to New Brunswick before, this was where her own roots were. The place that had nurtured her mother and *her* mother before her. The line stretched back on both sides for two centuries. This realization gave her a strange yet exciting feeling of belonging. Something she'd never felt before.

She started walking again, kicking her feet through the fallen wet leaves as if she were a kid. Her mother had probably walked this very same path when she was young, wading through the leaves that had fallen from the same trees.

A shiver rippled across Michelle's shoulders. She was being morbidly sentimental. How could you belong to a place you'd never seen before? A place where your mother had been so unhappy she'd been forced to run away?

She came to a modern building with two contemporary sculptures on the slope of green outside, one of which—two figures of stark white marble on a plinth— was in the style of Henry Moore. This was obviously the art gallery. She ran up the steps and went inside.

As soon as she'd paid her entrance fee, her eye was caught by the two massive paintings that faced each other across a sunken floor. One, she knew, was the famous Dalí painting, *Santiago El Grande*. The gallery's pride and joy. The other, she realized immediately, was the source of Stewart's remark. A huge depiction of a group of naked, coal-streaked miners, filled with anger and defiance.

"It's a Lukacs," said a voice from behind her.

She turned and saw that the speaker was an older man, one of the gallery's guides. "It's very powerful," she said.

"Not part of our permanent collection. More's the pity."

"Why?"

"Very controversial. We get more comments about that picture, for and against, than we've ever had before. But that's what art's all about, isn't it? To make people think and talk about it."

"You're right. It is." She smiled at the guide, before he moved away.

The little exchange gave her hope. Fredericton wasn't just a stuffy old historic city living in its past. It was feisty enough to show a controversial painting—and be proud of it.

There was plenty of traditional stuff there as well, including some delightful little Krieghoff winter scenes, but when she'd seen the entire collection in the main galleries, she spent several minutes looking at the painting by Lukacs again, taking in its raw energy. Then she bought several postcards and went outside.

For a moment, she stood at the foot of the gallery steps, uncertain what to do next. Ahead of her was the street that led to the heart of the small downtown area. Across the road was the stone legislative building, five flags flying from its roof. She stared up at them, trying to discern which flags they were, as they flapped in the strong breeze. She could see a couple of Canadian Maple Leaf flags, the provincial flag, and a Union Jack. The fifth flag looked like the French tricolor, but with a golden star. She guessed it must be the Acadian flag.

The thought gave her a jolt. Wallowing in all the pretty Britishness of Fredericton she'd quite forgotten that part of her own inheritance was French Acadian. The flag reminded her that in her veins ran the blood of those people who'd been ousted from this very area two centuries ago and forced to settle elsewhere.

"Your father had two sons," Stewart had told her last night. She'd shown no interest. She'd learned from an early age, by intuition rather than actual words, that her father was a no-good loser who'd seduced her mother and then abandoned her and her baby. But somehow the sight of the flag flying above the legislature, where a French Acadian had been, until recently, the premier of the province, made her feel she should be proud of her Acadian heritage, in spite of her father.

She was suddenly overcome by an attack of giddiness and nausea, so that she had to sit down on the wooden bench outside the gallery. She'd been looking up at those stupid flags for too long. This was the worst she'd felt, so far. She hoped that it wasn't going to get any worse than this.

After a few minutes rest, she forced herself to stand up again and began to walk in the direction of the downtown area. Next to the gallery, past a narrow path down to the river, was a hotel. She hadn't been able to eat much breakfast. Maybe she should go in and get a sandwich and a glass of milk. She'd found that eating a small meal helped to ease the nausea.

She stood outside the hotel, overcome by a desire to have Brian beside her. What the hell was she doing here, all by herself, two thousand miles from home . . . and three or more weeks pregnant? She'd done it all wrong. She should have told Brian outright that she was going off the pill, but she'd thought that you didn't get pregnant right away when you'd been on the pill for a long time. She'd expected to have plenty of time to plan everything with him when he got back from Indonesia. She'd been wrong.

She pushed open the door and went into the hotel's bright foyer. The woman at the desk pointed out the way to the restaurant and the rest room. Michelle wasn't sure which she needed more, but, taking a deep breath, decided she'd try some food first and see what happened.

The restaurant was just what she needed. Pretty, almost quirky, the white-painted trellised gazebo in the center of the large room emphasized its fresh, summery theme. She was given a table by the window. As she looked out over the river, she recalled Stewart's remark about breaking out of jail. The atmosphere in Tyler House was oppressive. There was an uneasiness lurking in the heavy furniture and opulent furnishings that disturbed her.

Don't be so ridiculous, she told herself. It was sad that her grandmother was getting forgetful, but that was all it was. She was letting her imagination run away with her.

When she scanned the menu, she was tempted to order a bowl of seafood chowder, but decided against it. That could be asking for trouble. She ordered a glass of milk, some French toast with real maple syrup, and herbal tea—no more coffee for her. She then decided that she'd call Rebecca as soon as she'd finished. Becca would soon bring her down to earth.

The light meal made her feel a hundred percent better. She made a mental note to buy a couple of packets of plain cookies before she went back to Tyler House so that she always had something to nibble on. The cookies Janet had left in a tin for her were made with butter and far too rich.

When she dialed the number, the sound of Becca's voice brought a sudden rush of tears to her eyes. "You okay?" Becca asked.

"I am now."

"Don't tell me New Brunswick's that bad."

Michelle sniffed and blew her nose. "Not really. I'm just homesick, I suppose."

"And missing Brian."

"You can say that again."

"Honestly, that guy . . . " Becca's voice trailed away. She'd said it all before. "So what's your millionaire family like?"

"A bit overwhelming. My grandmother's rather like Ethel Barrymore, but she has a strangely youthful face. She must have been very beautiful when she was young. But she's very forgetful. I'm afraid she may be getting Alzheimer's. For instance, she insists I wrote to her first, not the other way around."

"Older people get like that, Michelle. You're just

not used to them, that's all." Becca was eminently practical.

"I know. It's just a bit disappointing. I should have come here ages ago."

"Why? They never asked you before, did they?"

"I suppose not."

"And all the things your mom told you were enough to put anyone off going to visit her family."

"You're right."

"What about the rest of them? Your aunt and uncles, their kids."

"I haven't met the younger generation yet. My uncle Stewart picked me up. He's okay, I suppose. Like's to think he's still young and dashing. Drives a Jaguar convertible. You know the type."

"Yeah. Better keep your distance, uncle or not. And your aunt?"

"Grace is a bitch. Obviously hated my mother. I don't know why."

"Probably your mom was the favorite. Youngest kids usually are."

"How wise you are, O Ancient One," Michelle intoned.

"Oh, shut up!" They both laughed.

Michelle felt much better already. Becca was making her feel centered again.

"And the other uncle . . . what's his name?"

"Norman. I'm not sure about him. I imagine he calls the shots, but he's diplomatic about it. I only met them last night, so it's hard to tell. All I know is that you can almost smell the money as soon as you step inside Tyler House. Everything is the best—Turkish carpets, gleaming old Victorian furniture—and it's all immaculately kept. The house is really beautiful, but it's like a—a museum."

"Yikes! Sounds awful."

"It's not awful. It's just not a place I'd like to live in, that's all. I can see why my mother wanted to leave."

"Poor you. Still, you're only there for three days. Then you can come home to dear old Winnipeg."

"You're right. Any snow yet?"

"Nope. It's been lovely and warm again today."

"Becca." Michelle hesitated, not quite knowing how to begin.

"Yeah. What?"

"I've got something to tell you. I was going to wait until I got home, but . . . I want you to know now. I'm pregnant." The word seemed to reverberate around the foyer. She glanced around to see if anyone was close enough to have heard her.

"I guessed as much."

Michelle sighed. "Thought you might. It's hard to hide it from you when I'm rushing to the back of the store to throw up every morning."

"Does Brian know?"

"Not yet. You're the only one. I want to keep it that way till he gets home, okay? If he happens to call you, please don't say anything about it to him."

"You should have told him," Becca said flatly.

"I didn't know I was pregnant until after he'd gone."

"I mean you should have told him you weren't taking the pill."

"I know that now. This isn't something I wanted to keep from him. It was an impulse thing. It's all your fault, Rebecca Horowitz."

"Me?" screeched Becca down the line. "How come?"

"You told me it could take ages to get pregnant once I came off the pill. I thought I'd have plenty of time. I just wish I hadn't done it without discussing it with Brian first."

"Stop worrying. He'll be over the moon when he hears. You wait."

"You think so?" Michelle's voice was filled with doubt.

"I know so."

Michelle released a sigh of relief. "Thanks. You've made me feel a whole heap better."

"You poor old thing. Newly pregnant, throwing up,

and having to stay with the millionaire Munsters. No wonder you're homesick."

"It could be worse."

"You come home Monday evening, right?"

"Yep."

"I'll pick you up at the airport."

"I should get in at seven. Thanks, Becca. It'll be good to see a friendly face when I get off the plane."

"Hang in there. Maybe Grandma will give you and her great-grandbaby one of her millions."

"That'll be the day. I don't suppose she has any say in all that money, not with Grace and Norman around. And I should think that Stewart would be a big-time spender, too. Besides, there are all sorts of other grandchildren, as well."

"Would this be her first great-grandchild?"

"I hadn't thought of it, but I think it might be. When Stewart told me all about the family it was just a lot of names, but I don't recall him mentioning another generation."

"If that's the case, your baby will be special, won't she—or he? I mean special to your grandmother."

"I suppose so," Michelle said slowly, her mouth suddenly very dry.

"Will you tell them about the baby?"

"No, I won't. And I want you to promise me you won't mention this to anyone else. No one!" Michelle's heart was beating fast.

"Okay, okay. Don't get so excited. What on earth did I say to get you all jumpy?"

"Nothing. I guess that's just the way I am at the moment. I'm sure I'll be fine once Brian knows."

"Okay. Go relax. Take a walk by the river. If there is a river."

"There is. It's massive. Makes our two rivers look like little streams. And you should see the trees, Becca. The fall colors are glorious. If I weren't such a third-rate painter, I'd want to paint lots of pictures."

"Take lots of photographs instead. Now go for a long walk and calm down. Getting excited won't help your baby. Remember, even at this early time in your pregnancy, it's essential to think positive thoughts. No negative thoughts, no booze. Don't forget, every-thing—and I mean *everything*—gets passed onto your baby."

They said their good-byes. *Your baby*. Smiling, Mi-chelle repeated Becca's words to herself, her left hand going instinctively to her stomach in a protective ges-ture. Telling Becca had somehow made it more real for her.

But, a few hours later, when she reluctantly made her way back to Tyler House in the early afternoon, she was even more convinced that it was essential to keep her pregnancy a secret from the Tyler family.

Chapter 9

As soon as the breakfast dishes were cleared away, Tyler House became a hive of activity. The doorbell and telephone seemed to be ringing constantly. Fresh flowers were delivered and put in pails of water in the sun room until Eleanor had time to arrange them. People kept coming and going: the hairdresser to do Eleanor's hair and manicure; deliveries from the bakery and the delicatessen. Bob fetched Larry, Grace's husband, from the airport, so that Grace could stay and help her mother. Although she'd be staying at Tyler House with her family, the others would be sleeping in their own homes in Fredericton. Tyler House was large, but there wasn't enough room there for the entire family. Besides, Eleanor preferred not to have a lot of people around her. In the old days she used to thrive on visitors and family parties, but now any disruption to her daily routine made her anxious.

Having given orders to Janet and the cook and extra kitchen staff, Eleanor retreated to her bedroom suite and had a light lunch there, eating only half of one of Janet's delicious seafood crepes.

She continued to try to direct operations from her bedroom desk. "What about the wine?" she asked Grace.

"Norman and Ramsey are looking after that. Ramsey will bring the bottles up from the wine cellar later."

"That boy gets more like his grandfather every day," Eleanor said with a satisfied smile.

Grace looked down at the list she was making. She knew that Norman's eldest son was Eleanor's favorite. If she hadn't been so worried about the current situation she'd quite enjoy seeing that pompous young know-it-all's position usurped by Michelle.

"I saw your Jamie earlier," Eleanor said, her mouth pursing like a prune. "He was as uncouth as ever; just grinned at me when I spoke to him. He's a mess, Grace."

Grace's lips tightened, but she said nothing. It was no use reminding Eleanor about her son's good points—his affection for his mother, his quirky sense of humor . . .

"Has Michelle come home yet?" Eleanor asked for about the tenth time. "I'm worried about her."

"I told you, Mother, she'll be fine."

"Have Larry and Sophie arrived yet?"

"Yes, Mother. I told you. Bob picked Larry up at the airport and Sophie drove in with her boyfriend, Joel."

"*Another* one? It's hard to keep up with them." Before Grace could reply, Eleanor said, "I take it you've put Jamie in the small room next to yours, as I asked?"

"Yes, Mother." Jamie hadn't wanted to stay in his grandmother's house at all. It had taken all Grace's resources of tact to persuade him to move there for the one night. She sincerely hoped they'd get through the weekend without any trouble from him.

"And Sophie is in the room on the top floor, next to Michelle?" her mother was saying.

Grace drew in a deep breath, praying for patience. "That's right."

"I thought it would be best to have the two girls next door to each other, so that they can get to know one another better."

Grace doubted very much whether her daughter would have the slightest interest in getting to know her cousin better. Much as she loved her daughter, there was no escaping the fact that Sophie was monumentally selfish. She also had her new man in tow, so probably her only interest would be having sex with him in his room at the hotel, to relieve the usual monotony of the Tyler Thanksgiving celebrations.

"Oh, God, do I really have to come this year?" she'd whined when Grace had reminded her about Thanksgiving. She'd sounded more like a ten-year-old brat than a grown woman of twenty-nine with an excellent brain. Grace had had to bribe her with a promise of a winter cruise to get her to come.

It was going to be the family holiday from hell. Grace could feel it in her bones.

"Now, there was something else I wanted to discuss with you," Eleanor said. "What was it? Something about the dinner." Muttering beneath her breath, she started searching through the papers on her desk.

Grace could feel one of her migraines coming on. She hardly slept at all after the discussion with her brothers, but she knew she'd have to keep going, whatever happened.

The surprise arrival of Carolyn's daughter had compounded their problems. Heaven alone knew what Eleanor had in mind for her. Although Carolyn had been headstrong, she'd always been Eleanor's favorite. Probably *because* of her rebellious nature. Their parents—particularly their father—had demanded absolute obedience, but then admired those who had what her mother called "an independent spirit."

"I can't find it," Eleanor said. Defeated, she came around the desk to sit in her armchair, holding a pile of papers on her lap.

Grace gritted her teeth as she waited for her mother's next question.

"Has Michelle come back yet?"

"No, Mother, she hasn't," Grace said with a sigh. A hammer inside her head seemed to be striking stunning blows against her temples.

"I'm worried about her. She might be lost."

"In Fredericton?" This time, Grace couldn't hide her exasperation. "For God's sake, Mother. It's not exactly London or New York, is it?"

"There is no need to use that tone of voice with me, Grace. This is her first time here. I asked her to return for lunch." Eleanor peered at her watch. "It's now almost two o'clock."

"You told me yourself that Stewart said she was going to the gallery and the old loyalist burial ground. That would take her a couple of hours, at least, wouldn't it? Never mind any shopping she might want to do. Today's the only chance she'll have. Stop worrying. She'll be fine."

Her mother fidgeted with the papers, aimlessly shuffling them. "I do hope so. So many things have been happening recently . . . you never know."

Grace sighed. "I'll go down again and check," she said, grasping the chance to escape and spend some precious time with Larry. "I promise I'll let you know as soon as she comes in, okay?"

"Thank you, Grace. And thank you, too, for all your help." Eleanor rubbed her fingers wearily across her high forehead. "I still have the flowers to do. I don't seem to be able to do as much as I used to."

"You do far too much as it is. That's the problem. You do so much you exhaust yourself. You know what Andrew says."

"Oh, damn Andrew. What does he know? He's not much older than my grandsons. Is he coming to dinner tonight?"

"Yes. He said he was so used to coming here with his parents, it wouldn't seem like Thanksgiving without our dinner."

Eleanor's face softened. "He must miss his father and mother. Dear Fran. What a good friend she was! She's the main reason I've kept Andrew as my doctor since his father died."

"He also happens to be a good doctor."

"He's far too young. And I don't approve of him separating from his wife, either."

"She was the one who left him, not the other way around."

"I don't care," Eleanor said. "She was a lovely girl. Andrew should have made sure to hang on to her. What about Douglas?"

"What about him?" Grace frequently found it difficult to follow her mother's train of thought.

"Is he coming to dinner?" Eleanor said impatiently.

"No. His sister's family is in town, but he said he'd drop in for a drink later on in the evening."

"I wanted to see him before then." Eleanor's fingers became agitated. "I left a message for him at his office, but he didn't call me back. Be sure to let me know the moment he arrives. Please don't forget."

Grace's heart sank. What did her mother want with her lawyer this time? It was like living on the edge of a precipice these days. She'd have to warn Larry—and Norman—that her mother wanted to talk to Douglas Bradford. Coming so soon after Michelle's arrival, this was certainly something to be concerned about.

Almost at the very moment Michelle rang the bell, the front door was flung open. "Where on earth have you been?" Her aunt's greeting came at her like pitched stones.

"Exploring the town, shopping . . . Why?"

"My mother has been going wild with worry about you. How could you be so thoughtless!"

"I'm so sorry," Michelle said with heavy sarcasm. "I hadn't realized I have to clock in and out while I'm here. Can I come in?" Grace was still blocking the doorway, with Janet hovering nervously behind her.

Grace stepped back and motioned to Michelle to come in. "You might have picked up a phone and given us a call to let us know you weren't coming back for lunch."

Michelle was about to make another sarcastic remark, but thought better of it. "You're right." She set down her shopping bags. "I should have called. It was just that I realized everything would be closed after today, so I thought I'd better do some shopping. I found this marvelous pewter gift store—"

"Aitken's Pewter."

"Right. I bought a couple of gifts, really pretty things, and then thought I might see about doing business with them, selling some of their stuff in my store. That took a lot of extra time."

"Oh, well. That's different." Grace's severe expression relaxed a little.

"Of course it is," said a young woman who was coming down the stairs. She was dressed in a tight black turtleneck and even tighter jeans that accentuated her thin body. "If it's business you're doing, Mom doesn't mind, but if you're having fun, shopping for yourself, forget it."

"My daughter, Sophie," Grace said to Michelle. "This is Michelle," she told her daughter.

Sophie gave Michelle a disdainful glance and an unfriendly "Hi," showing no interest whatsoever in meeting her cousin. "I'll be over at the hotel with Joel," she said to her mother, pushing past Michelle and opening the door.

"Have you seen Jamie?" Grace asked her.

"Last time I saw my little brother he was smoking a joint in the garden." She gave her mother a malicious smile.

Grace's face flushed. "Make sure you're back before five. I take it you'll be changing?"

"Could be." Sophie went out and crashed the door behind her.

Michelle saw the anger in Grace's eyes before she turned away.

"Should I go and explain to . . . " Michelle hesitated, not quite sure what she should call her grandmother to this woman whose resentment of her was tangible.

"Mother's resting at the moment. I'll let her know you came back."

"Please tell her I'm sorry I didn't call."

Grace gave her a faint half smile, then went upstairs, leaving Michelle with the feeling that the next couple of days were going to seem like constantly walking on eggshells.

She suddenly felt very tired. Her feet were sore from walking and her stomach was acting up again. She should have stopped for another snack before she came back. Still, at least she had her packets of cookies. She started up the stairs, only to find someone else crashing down them. She flattened herself against the wall as a young man with dark, shoulder-length hair falling over his eyes raced past her. "Hi, I'm Jamie," he shouted as he ran to the door and went out. The door slammed behind him.

"Bedlam, eh?" Stewart sidled into the hall. "It's always like this when the extended Tyler family get together. That's why my wife refuses to come until the last minute."

"Can't say I blame her." Michelle grinned at him. "But I suppose that's not very polite."

"Maybe not, but it's true. You'll have gathered that there's no love lost between Sophie and Jamie. Sophie's the brains of the family. Takes after her mother."

"Is your daughter coming?" Michelle asked, tactfully changing the subject.

"Jennifer? Not her. She hasn't been home for years."

"But you still live here, in Fredericton, don't you?"

"I do." He gave her a twisted smile. "Here in the prissiest goddamned town ever known."

Michelle sat down on the stairs. "Why do you stay if you dislike the place so much?"

"This is the center of Tyler Foods' operations. The main plant and warehouses and head office are just outside the city." He smiled wryly. "This is where I work. Although we have branches all over North America and now in Europe as well, Norman and I run the operation from here."

"I see." She also gathered from the lack of enthusiasm in his voice how much he hated the work he did.

She wondered what it must be like to work with—or for—your elder brother. Particularly when he was a controlling, manipulative man like Norman.

Stewart leaned against the wall, looking up at her. "You took my advice," he said in a low voice.

"What was that?"

"To stay away for as long as possible."

Michelle held up her bags. "I did some shopping."

"Amazed you could find anything decent in this place."

"I certainly could—and did. Fredericton not only has beautiful houses, it also has lots of interesting places to see and to shop. Even in the short time I had, I got some great ideas."

"Ideas? Oh, yes. I forgot you have a little business of your own."

It was obvious from Stewart's tone that her "little business" wasn't worth talking about. How monumentally self-centered they all were, Michelle thought. "I'm going to go and have a rest," she said, pulling herself up. "My feet are killing me."

"Michelle, can you come up, please?" Grace called, her voice sharp with annoyance. "My mother wants to see you."

Stewart pushed himself away from the wall. "You have been summoned. The royal command." He walked away, stumbling slightly. Obviously he'd started celebrating early. Michelle wondered what state he'd be in by dinnertime.

"Michelle! Did you hear me?"

"Yes, I'm coming."

Grace stood outside her mother's bedroom door, her arms folded across her chest. Her carefully coiffed hair looked a little awry, tendrils escaping from the smooth French pleat at the back and straggling down her neck, as if she'd pushed her hands through it. "Be careful what you say. She's very upset."

"Because I was late?"

"Probably, but who knows?" Grace held the door open for her. "Go on in." Michelle was close enough to hear her aunt draw in a long breath and release it before she spoke, like an actor preparing for an entrance. "Here she is," she said in a cheerful voice. "Safe and sound. Home from her shopping expedition."

Eleanor was sitting in a high-backed chair by the large bay window. Michelle set down her shopping bags by the door and walked in, feeling like a child being summoned to the principal's office. The room reeked of Grace's heavy scent. She must have bathed in the stuff, probably in preparation for her husband's homecoming.

"Sit down, Michelle." Eleanor indicated the small love seat covered in a rose-patterned fabric that faced her chair.

Michelle did as she was told. Grace was about to sit in another chair, but her mother stopped her. "I want to speak to Michelle."

Grace smiled brightly. "I know you do, Mother. I thought I'd—"

"Alone. I'm sure there's a great deal to be done before the evening," Eleanor added pointedly.

For a moment, Michelle felt sorry for her aunt.

Grace's smile didn't waver. "There certainly is."

"Has Celia arrived yet?"

"You mean Anna. Celia was Stewart's first wife."

"I liked Celia far better than the one he has now."

"I'm sure you did, but there's nothing we can do about it now."

"She never comes to visit."

Grace's smile started to slip a little. "Are you talking about Celia?"

"Of course I am."

"Celia went back to London long before the divorce."

"And that's why I never see Jennifer, either?"

"I suppose so."

"She was such a nice girl."

"I expect she still is. Are you sure you wouldn't like me to stay for a while?"

"No. Michelle and I are going to spend a little time together before everyone arrives. Where's that wretched daughter of yours?"

Grace's attempt at a smile completely disappeared. "If you're talking about Sophie—"

"Of course I am. She's a disgrace. You tell me she has a good job at Nortel. High time she bought some decent clothes."

"Sophie likes to relax when she comes home." Grace flashed a look of venom at Michelle, who pretended to be gazing out the window.

Don't blame me, Michelle thought. *I'm not responsible for what your mother says.*

"I'll go and see if the desserts have arrived yet." Grace turned abruptly and left the room.

"Please shut the door," Eleanor asked Michelle in a carrying voice. "My daughter has a habit of leaving it open, so that she can listen in to all my conversations."

"Now," Eleanor said when Michelle had closed the door, "what were you doing that kept you away so long?"

Michelle told her about her visit to the art gallery and had to list all the stores she'd been into, receiving a nod of approval or a word of criticism on her choices.

"Where did you eat?"

"At the hotel."

"The Lord Beaverbrook, I trust. I hope you told them who you were."

"No, why should I?" Michelle asked, surprised.

Eleanor smiled and then her mouth quivered. "You remind me so much of your mother. She had the same attitude. 'We're no one special, Mom,' she'd say. 'Just people who've made a lot of money, that's all.' "

Michelle had to smile, too. It sounded so much like her mother. "She was right."

"Are you saying you don't want to make money in your business?"

"Of course I do. But it doesn't make me a better or more special person if I do, does it?"

"Money buys respect and prestige."

"Who on earth said that?"

Eleanor drew herself up. "Your grandfather, Ramsey Tyler, said it."

"Well, I'm sorry, but that's a load of garbage. How you behave with your money is what gets you respect, not the money itself."

Eleanor leaned forward. "That was what I used to say to my husband when I was your age."

"And?"

"He'd laugh and tell me I was naive." Eleanor glanced at the portrait of her husband on the far wall, a smaller version of the one in the study. "Ramsey could be rather patronizing at times."

"Sounds like it."

Eleanor frowned over her glasses at Michelle. "Your grandfather was a great man," she said severely. "He was revered and respected by all who knew him."

"I'm sure he was." Michelle thought it best to leave it at that.

"But that's not what I want to talk to you about."

Eleanor's long fingers began plucking nervously at the mohair shawl over her knees. Then she threw it off, letting it fall to the ground. "I wish Grace wouldn't wrap me up like a senile old woman," she muttered.

"Can I help?"

"You most certainly can: by not interrupting me again. There is something I need to tell you before one of them comes back to spy on me."

Michelle could see that her grandmother's head tremor had grown more pronounced, reminding her of Katherine Hepburn in her later movies. "Would you be more comfortable lying down on your bed? I could sit down beside you."

"No!" The sharp response startled Michelle. "I don't like lying down in the daytime." Her grand-

mother glanced fearfully at the bed and then averted
her eyes, as if she couldn't bear to look at it. "I can
take sleeping pills at night," she said, "but I refuse to
take them during the day." She pointed a twisted finger in the direction of the bed, without turning to look
at it. "That's where I saw him," she whispered.

"Who?"

"Griffon. My little dog. He was lying on my bed,
right in the middle of the quilt. His neck had been
broken."

Michelle felt as if she'd suddenly been immersed in
an icy lake in the dead of winter. "Are you sure?"

"Oh, yes."

"How could you tell?"

"His head was at an odd angle to his body."

"But . . . I thought your dog had been run over by
a car." Suddenly Michelle wanted to escape from this
dark, overpowering room. She was sure this creepy
conversation wasn't good for her baby—or her grandmother, for that matter.

"That's what we thought must have happened, but
they never found his body." Eleanor glanced at the
door, as if she expected it to open at any minute.
"That's not all. After I'd seen Griffon, I went out to
the landing and called down to them all to come up."
Eleanor's breath came faster and she raised her hand
to her throat, as if she was choking. "By the time we
all came back into the room, my Griffon was gone.
There wasn't even one hair from his coat on the bed."

Michelle felt relieved. The dead dog had all been
in her grandmother's imagination. A shadow on the
bed. Perhaps the quilt had been ruffled, creating a
lump that might look, to a sight-impaired person, like
a beloved dog.

"I ordered everyone to make an immediate
search, but Griffon's body was never found. It had
disappeared completely." Sighing, Eleanor sank back
into her chair, her head tremor even more pronounced.

"I'm sorry." Michelle wanted to console her in some way, but she wasn't sure if she'd be rebuffed or not. "And that's why you don't like sleeping in your bed?"

"Yes." For a moment Eleanor sat in silent thought. "I take sleeping pills at night, which makes it a little easier."

The thought of her grandmother dreading going to bed, for whatever reason—imagined or otherwise—disturbed Michelle. "Why don't you move to another room, sleep in another bed?"

"Oh, I couldn't possibly do that. Apart from our summer home and our travels away this has been my room, mine and Ramsey's, ever since he brought me here after our marriage nearly sixty years ago."

"I can understand that." What else could Michelle say? That her grandmother shouldn't worry because the body of her dog had never been there? That it was all in her overactive imagination?

"That wasn't the first strange thing that happened. It was the worst, of course, but the cockroaches were pretty nasty, too."

"Cockroaches?" Michelle repeated, squirming as if something were running over her skin. She didn't want to hear this, real or otherwise.

"A few weeks ago, when I went to bed, I put my feet down and felt something moving against them. I threw back the bedclothes and found six large cockroaches lying there on the sheet, where my feet had been."

Michelle shuddered. "Oh, my God. Were they alive?"

"Oh, they were alive all right. My feet had touched them. That's the fastest I've moved in years." Eleanor's grim humor seemed to bring veracity to her story.

A wave of nausea passed over Michelle. And then another. The room undulated before her eyes.

Eleanor leaned forward. "Then there was the—"

Michelle stood up. "I'm sorry. I don't feel well. I must have eaten too much at lunch. Excuse me."

She rushed from the room, pausing only to grab her shopping bags, then raced upstairs, dumped the bags on the carpeted landing, and dashed into the bathroom.

Several minutes later, she came out, her legs weak and her body clammy. She went into her room, locked the door, and stretched out on the bed, with a damp washcloth on her forehead. Whatever her grandmother thought of her, she was definitely not going to go back to that room. At least, not until she'd had a break from the entire Tyler family for a while.

As she was on the edge of falling asleep, the sound of a telephone ringing somewhere in the house filtered through to her. Leaning up on her elbow, she waited to see if someone might call up the stairs to say it was for her, but all she could hear was the muted rumble of traffic from the street and the hum of the gas furnace blowing warm air into the room.

She sank back onto her pillow, her heart heavy with disappointment. Brian had promised he would call her as soon as possible after she arrived in Fredericton. Never before had she missed him so much or felt quite so alone. This visit to her mother's family had been a huge mistake. With their baby growing inside her, she needed to be secure in her own home, surrounded by the things that she and Brian shared. To see constant reminders of his place in her life, even when he was away from her. Without them, she needed desperately to speak to him, to hear his voice.

Brian let the phone drop with a crash into its cradle. The man who'd answered the phone had told him that Michelle was sleeping and asked him to call back later. When Brian had tried to explain, the guy had cut him short, saying he couldn't hear him. Either the idiot didn't want to hear or the line genuinely wasn't clear—although it seemed fine from his end. He left a message for Michelle, telling whoever it was to be sure to give it to her when she woke up. "Wish her a happy Thanksgiving from me and tell her I'll call her from Bali next week, when she gets home."

He was left feeling angry and frustrated as hell. It had taken him almost two days to arrange a reasonably good line. He'd had to trek across town to get to the telephone on a night when he had to get up at three in the morning to fly back to Jakarta. Now, he was feeling so goddamned mad, he was sure he'd never get back to sleep. Michelle would be furious, as well, when she found out that he'd called her from Indonesia and they hadn't even bothered to call her to the phone.

That was another thing that disturbed him. He'd never known Michelle to take a nap in the afternoon—except to go to bed with him, or on a very rare occasion when she had the flu. Was she sick? Or was she just trying to get away from the family? Either way, it meant she was having a rotten time.

Usually, on these foreign assignments, whenever he managed to get a telephone line, he could get through directly to Michelle, or at least leave a message on her answering machine if she wasn't at work or at home when he called.

The fact that he hadn't been able to do even that, after managing to get a line out, left him feeling not only mad, but also anxious. The quicker he had this project in the can and got home to Michelle, the better.

Chapter 10

The table in the dining room at Tyler House gleamed, its polished wood surface reflecting the silverware and crystal glasses. The centerpiece of bronze and gold chrysanthemums with autumn leaves was set on a delicate lace cloth. The table itself was so large, with its extension panels added, that there was barely room to pull out the matching chairs that lined both sides of the table, with two armchairs, one at each end. Their crimson damask seat-cushions had gently faded to a soft rose.

Against the long wall, parallel to the table, was a mahogany sideboard set with electric warmers to keep the tureens of vegetables and gravy and sauces hot. The various aromas of the festive meal—a mixture of roast turkey, spicy dressings, and onions—had been permeating the house for several hours.

Not sure where she should sit, Michelle waited in a corner of the dining room, the younger Tylers—her cousins—walking past her to take their assigned places.

When they'd all gathered earlier for pre-dinner drinks in the heritage room she'd been introduced to the rest of the clan. Grace's son and daughter had pointedly ignored her. Norman's sons had politely welcomed her, and Penny, Ramsey Tyler's wife, had tried to draw her into the conversation, but the rest did nothing to make her feel more at home.

As Michelle stood there, reflecting on how this must

be the most self-absorbed family ever, Norman's wife, Lauren, approached her. "I'm sorry. You seem to have been abandoned," she said in her girlish voice. When Michelle had met her earlier, her first reaction had been that the black dress glittering with sequins was a little over the top for a family gathering. Her second, that Lauren was nervous, as if she, too, felt herself to be an outsider. Michelle wondered how long she and Norman had been married. She looked at least twenty years younger than he, possibly five or six years older than Michelle. With her long blond hair and svelte figure she was definitely what some people might call a trophy bride.

"Norman says that Mother Tyler wants you to sit next to her," Lauren said.

"Where's that?"

"I'll show you." Lauren smoothed back her fall of blond hair with crimson-tipped fingers, reminding Michelle even more forcibly of her namesake, Lauren Bacall. It remained to be seen if she also had Bacall's brains. "The Tylers are a teensy bit overwhelming when they all get together, aren't they?" she said with a little giggle. She led the way to the place on the left of the head of the table. "There you are. This is where you're to sit."

Michelle thanked her and sat down. She turned to her right, to find herself beside Grace's husband. He was a handsome Englishman, tall and lean, with gray-blue eyes and fair hair turning to silver.

He smiled. "I don't think we've met," he said, holding out his hand. "I'm Larry Anderson, your aunt's husband. Which, I suppose, makes me your uncle by marriage," he added with a wry grin.

They had been introduced, but he'd been so engrossed in his conversation about business with Norman that he'd barely glanced at her at the time. "Michelle Tyler," she said.

He gave her a sharp glance. "Ah, so you've retained the family name."

"My mother's name. Yes."

"Grace tells me this is your first visit to Tyler House."

Michelle nodded, waiting for him to say something about her mother, but he was intent on being polite it seemed, nothing more. "It's a lovely old house, isn't it?" he said, looking around the room.

"Yes, it is."

"It's Eleanor's pride and joy. You should ask her about the family history. She's made a lifelong study of it. She loves to talk about how her family escaped the mob at Boston with only two trunks of possessions. How her husband's ancestor, Oliver Tyler, was tarred and feathered, and his house torched. Sometimes she can make you think she was actually there and—"

He was interrupted by a burst of clapping, as Eleanor, dressed in a long sapphire gown, diamonds glistening around her throat, entered the room on Norman's arm. She looked so regal with her upswept silver-white hair and her serene smile that Michelle experienced an unexpected surge of pride that this woman was her own grandmother. She found herself joining in the rhythmical clapping as Eleanor took her place at the head of the table, with Norman at the other end.

"We shall now say grace," Eleanor said, and everyone bowed their heads.

"Bless, O Lord, these gifts on our table. We thank thee for thy great bounty and ask that you help us to share what we have with others who are less fortunate. We also give thanks to thee for this family gathering." She paused and then, glancing sideways at Michelle, added, "And I wish to give thanks to the Lord for His answer to my prayers that the daughter I lost would one day return to her home. At last she has done so, in the form of *her* daughter, Michelle. Amen." Eleanor held up her glass. "Before we start our meal, I ask you all to welcome Michelle and to continue to make her feel welcome throughout her stay. To Michelle!"

Eleanor's toast was received with a subdued murmur and a second round of far less enthusiastic applause. Michelle acknowledged it with a smile. "Thank you. I'm really glad to be here with my mother's family."

It didn't feel like her own family. She felt as if she were an extra in a play or pageant, where all she had to do was nod and smile and make sure she didn't get in the way.

As she started in on her lobster bisque, Michelle saw that Grace was seated across the table from her. Next to her sat Dr. Andrew Lenzie. A man of about forty, he was of medium height, with an engaging smile and warm brown eyes. He was listening intently to Grace, who was speaking to him in low, earnest tones, while trying to finish his soup at the same time. The doctor had particularly attractive hands with tapering fingers that reminded her of Dürer's bronze.

Although Grace had turned away from her mother's direction, as she spoke with Dr. Lenzie he was giving Eleanor occasional glances. Michelle guessed that her grandmother was probably the main topic of their conversation. She wished she could hear what they were saying. She was increasingly concerned about her grandmother's mental health. She shuddered involuntarily, recalling their conversation this afternoon, and Eleanor's bizarre stories of dead dogs and cockroaches.

"Are you cold, my dear?" her grandmother asked.

"No, not at all. Just someone walking over my grave."

The old saying came out before she could stop it. She wished it hadn't.

Eleanor smiled. "I suppose your mother used to say that to you." She leaned forward across her barely touched bowl of soup. "Tell me about her," she said eagerly.

Michelle looked around. "I'm not sure this is a good time."

"Perhaps not. Did you bring some photographs of her with you?"

"Yes. We can look at them later, when we have some time to ourselves." She was aware of the lull in the buzz of conversation and that Grace had turned to look at them.

"They'll never allow us to have time to ourselves," Eleanor complained in a carrying voice. "They never let me alone. If it's not Grace or Norman or Stewart coming by every day, as if they didn't have enough to do with their own work, it's Janet coming in every other minute to check on me."

"You're lucky to have Janet," Dr. Lenzie said. "She looks after you well."

Eleanor looked startled, as if she hadn't realized that her remarks could be overheard. "Too well," she muttered. She gave Michelle a secretive little smile. "You're right," she said in an undertone. "We must talk later. I still have a great deal to discuss with you. You dashed off before I could tell you . . ." She looked up and her voice trailed away as she became aware of being watched. She lifted her chin. "Finish your soup, everyone," she said in an imperious voice. "Janet is standing in the doorway, waiting to announce the bringing in of the turkey. Am I right, Janet?"

"You are, Mrs. Tyler."

The turkey and all its accompaniments were carried in by the chef and Janet and the younger Tylers. It was like a scene from a Charles Dickens book, *Pickwick Papers* or *A Christmas Carol*. All Michelle wished was that she'd be able to get through this evening without making a fool of herself. She was already regretting the lobster bisque, and the mere thought of having to wade through a loaded plate of turkey and chestnut and sausage stuffings and various vegetables was making her queasy. Why did she have to have morning, noon, and night sickness, rather than just morning sickness? she wondered ruefully.

She toyed with her meal while Larry or Eleanor engaged her in conversation. Eleanor kept her topics to general questions about her work or where she'd traveled, now carefully avoiding anything personal.

But all the time Michelle sensed that her grandmother was on edge. She was merely picking at her food and when her hands were not engaged, they roamed restlessly, fingers nervously dusting bread roll crumbs off the table or fiddling with spoons and forks.

This was not a woman at peace, Michelle thought. Something was disturbing her deeply. She thought of speaking to one of the family about her concerns, but then, recalling Eleanor's anxiety to get rid of Grace earlier that afternoon, she rejected the idea. Besides, the family seemed well aware of Eleanor's problems. Norman himself had warned her last night of her grandmother's precarious mental health.

She wondered if she might have the chance to speak to Dr. Lenzie. She glanced up, to find those brown eyes dwelling on her. He grinned at her when he saw she'd caught him out, and then turned away to answer a question from Ramsey, who sat on his other side.

Yes, Michelle thought. Her grandmother's doctor might well be someone she could ask about Eleanor.

"Grace tells me you're leaving on Monday morning," Larry said in his distinctive upper-class voice when Eleanor had finished speaking to him. "Not a very long visit."

"I thought it might be better not to overstay my welcome on my first visit."

"Good idea." He took a drink from his glass of burgundy. "Eleanor's growing very frail." He glanced at Eleanor, who was now talking in a low voice to Janet. The housekeeper was bending close to hear her.

"Has she been this way for a long time?" Michelle asked Larry.

Larry frowned. "What way?"

"Worried, edgy. She seems very . . . nervous all the time." Michelle swallowed hard, the image of the pet dog's body lying on the bed in which Eleanor had slept for decades coming unwanted to her mind. Although it had obviously never happened, the fact that Eleanor thought it was real must be like an ongoing nightmare for her.

For a moment she was so encouraged by Larry's friendliness she thought of asking him about that episode, but then decided against it. Eleanor's doctor was definitely the best person to talk to. If she could ever get him away from Grace, who seemed to have commandeered him.

"Have you spoken to your husband since you arrived?"

Grace's question came across the table like a sudden bolt from a cannon.

Michelle managed to smile. "No. I wasn't expecting to hear from him."

"Why not?" demanded Grace. "Surely he'll phone you sometime over the Thanksgiving weekend, won't he?"

"He's traveling in some of the more remote areas of Indonesia, as well as the main cities, so access to a reliable phone line isn't always possible. If he doesn't call me here, I'm sure to hear from him sometime next week, when I get home."

"It sounds like more than your regular foreign news reporting," Larry said.

"He's working on a special hour-long program about all the upheaval throughout Indonesia, including East Timor and Aceh."

"A major undertaking, I should think. Will he be away long?"

Too long, Michelle thought. "He's been away for three weeks already. I should think it would be at least another couple of weeks before he gets back to North America. I'll probably fly down to Minneapolis to join him while he's working on the editing process at the network."

"Is he directing the project or is he just the front man, so to speak?"

"Both. He started as a news reader, but he loves working in the foreign field, so he quit the more lucrative position and became a freelance foreign correspondent."

"But he's attached to a network now."

"Yes, JNN in Minneapolis."

Eleanor was listening in. "Then why do you still live in Winnipeg?"

It was a good question. One that a lot of people asked her. Michelle usually evaded it somehow or, as she did now, used her business as an excuse. "I don't want to give up my own business. It's going well and I'm not sure I'd want to start it up somewhere else. Besides, I couldn't work if I went to the U.S. At least, not until I got a green card and that can take a very long time, even when you're married to an American." But she knew that there was more to her wish to stay in Winnipeg than just her business.

"I can understand your wanting to stay in your own home," Eleanor said, "considering your husband is away so much. I was more fortunate. Although my husband traveled, it was only for short periods of time. But I, too, would want to stay in the place where I was born and grew up if my husband was away a great deal."

Michelle gave her grandmother a warm smile, grateful for her endorsement of what was often a hotly argued source of dissension between her and Brian.

"Eat up. You haven't touched your fiddleheads," Eleanor said sternly. "Fiddlehead greens are a New Brunswick delicacy, you know."

Michelle knew, but not even for her grandmother could she eat anything more. "I'm sorry. I'm not very hungry."

"What nonsense." Eleanor peered at her. "I hope you're not on some special diet, are you? You're far too thin as it is."

"No, I don't have to diet."

"Lucky you," Lauren said, her hands instinctively smoothing down her dress over her hips. Norman bent to whisper something in her ear and she gave him a seductive smile in return.

"Well, there's to be no dieting in this house," Eleanor pronounced. "Not this weekend, anyway. And once these plates are cleared away, we shall have the desserts brought in, please, Janet. Spiced pumpkin pie, of course, sherry trifle, and Ramsey's favorite, maple sugar pie." She beamed at her grandson as he thanked her.

Michelle's eyes closed for a moment. She silently offered a prayer that she might get through this meal without having to bolt from the room. To her relief, her dinner plate was taken away without any further comment from Eleanor.

As the meal wore on, Eleanor grew more fractious, picking on individual members of her family with snide little comments. Michelle was free to observe the family dynamics around the happy Thanksgiving table. Ramsey was obviously the favorite grandchild. He looked slightly embarrassed when his grandmother praised him, as she frequently did. His wife, Penny, was a lawyer. She was dressed in a severely cut black suit with a white blouse, as if she were about to appear in court. She had clasped Michelle's hand so tightly when they'd been introduced that Michelle was sure her knuckles would turn purple.

Norman's second son, Eric, was a more stocky version of his father, but without his confidence. He wore wire-rimmed glasses and rarely smiled. Michelle had not been surprised to hear that he was a computer systems expert and ran the technical side of the company.

Grace's daughter, Sophie, sat at the other end of the table with her boyfriend, Joel. Beside them was Grace's son, Jamie. All three sat slumped at the table, not even trying to hide their boredom. Throughout the meal, Sophie talked solely to Joel. Jamie talked to no one, but while everyone was eating dessert he took one long call on his cell phone, turning his chair around, with his back to the table, until he was ordered from the room by Eleanor.

"Those machines are an abomination and you, Jamie, are an antisocial misfit," she told him. "Go climb some rocks, or whatever it is you like to do. And take your little toy with you."

Jamie seemed amused at his dismissal. Grinning, he shoved his chair under the table, muttering, "Thank God for that," in an audible voice, and left the room. Michelle, glancing at Grace, saw her dart a resentful look at her mother, her lips compressed.

Larry leaned over to speak in Michelle's ear. "Family celebrations can be such fun, can't they?" he drawled.

She gave him a wry smile. She had known nothing of this kind of family gathering until she'd married Brian. His was a large, outgoing family, typically Irish in its exuberance and noise and love of such get-togethers. When she spent Christmas or a special family party at his parents' home in Chicago, Michelle had always felt like an outsider, as she did here, but Brian's family gatherings were a lively exchange of loving banter that released your inhibitions and swept you up in their enthusiasm. Whereas here she could feel the uncomfortable frisson of animosity between family members.

Jamie's exit seemed to signal a general exodus, despite Eleanor's protests. "You can't leave yet. We haven't had the Thanksgiving toast."

"We'll be back, Gran," Sophie said. She came to kiss her grandmother's cheek. "Just going out for some air." Her friend with the gelled hair laughed at this and followed her from the room.

A sudden wave of nausea swept over Michelle. She could feel beads of sweat forming on her forehead and trickling between her breasts. "Excuse me," she murmured and hurriedly left the room, trying not to run as she'd had to do this afternoon from her grandmother's room. She raced up the two flights of stairs, praying that she'd make it in time.

Several minutes later, having dashed cold water on her face, Michelle went into her room to lie down on the bed. She felt an overwhelming desire to sleep, but she knew that her grandmother was waiting. She swung her feet over the side of the bed and stood up.

The room swung around her. Groaning, she sat down hurriedly on the bed again.

"Oh, Mom!" she whispered. "Now I know why you never wanted to come back here." She squeezed back tears. "What the hell am I doing here?" she asked Brian's picture. "And why aren't you here with me?" Having asked these unanswerable questions, she stood up, reapplied her lipstick, and went downstairs again. Apart from the servers clearing away the debris of the meal, the dining room was empty. Even her grandmother was nowhere to be seen. Everyone was taking a much-needed break.

Michelle went out into the rear garden and inhaled the damp, chilly air, forcing down the nausea. Then she heard a rustling. Eyes adjusting to the darkness beyond the pool of light cast by the lamp over the door, she saw two people entwined on a wooden bench. She turned away, too intent on her own discomfort to care about anyone else. Above her, wisps of gray cloud drifted in the darkened sky. The thought that several thousand miles away Brian might be looking up into this same sky was strangely comforting. "Hi, Brian," she whispered.

She was rudely brought down to earth when Sophie and Joel suddenly loomed out of the darkness. They crunched across the gravel and walked right up to her, standing so close that she instinctively took a step backward.

"Were you spying on us?" Sophie asked belligerently, her words slurred.

"Maybe she'd like to join in?" the creepy Joel said.

They were obviously high on something. Michelle's newly heightened sense of self-preservation told her to turn her back on them both and go inside, but she stood her ground. "What's your problem?" she asked Sophie.

Sophie's eyes narrowed. "My problem? I don't have one, apart from wondering what you're doing here. Why don't you leave my grandmother alone and go back to the boonies where you belong?"

Joel gave a yelp of laughter.

Michelle's heartbeat quickened and her hands balled into fists at her sides, but she turned away and walked across the terrace and into the house with even strides. She almost collided with Stewart, who was standing just inside the door.

"Are you okay?" Stewart asked her. "You look as if you've just seen a ghost."

"I'm fine."

"Mother's gone upstairs to freshen up. When you left, everyone else seemed to think it was a good idea to take a break as well. She's asked me to gather everyone together again in the heritage room so she can make her annual Thanksgiving toast."

"I don't think I'm in the mood, thanks." Michelle walked past him down the hall.

"Please, Michelle. It means a great deal to her."

Michelle halted at the foot of the stairs, but didn't turn around.

Stewart went to her. "I don't know what Sophie said to you, but you're too mature to take any notice of a spoiled brat."

She squeezed her eyes and blinked. "I'm tired. It's been a long day. But most of all, I'm fed up with being constantly sandbagged by members of this family."

"I know the feeling."

He was about to say something else when his wife Anna came downstairs. She'd been a surprise to Michelle, who'd expected Stewart's wife to have been more like Lauren. Solidly built and slightly taller than her husband, Anna was simply dressed in a plain black dress that did nothing for her sallow complexion.

"Is everyone in the heritage room?" she asked abruptly. "She's about to make her entrance again."

"Okay. We're coming." Stewart gave Michelle another pleading look.

As they were about to go into the heritage room, the front doorbell rang. Stewart went to answer it. "Ah, Douglas," he said, and stood back. The small, balding man stepped inside. "You're just in time for the toast."

"Too bad," the man said dryly. "I hoped I'd miss it. She's running late this year."

"Probably because of me," Michelle said.

The man turned to look at her with shrewd gray eyes. "You must be Michelle, Carolyn's daughter."

"That's right. And you must be my grandmother's lawyer, Mr. . . . "

"Bradford. Douglas Bradford." The lawyer held out his hand. He had small, neat hands. "Happy Thanksgiving, Miss Tyler."

When they'd shaken hands and the lawyer had removed his raincoat, he turned back to Stewart. "What's your mother's problem this time, do you know? She's been leaving urgent messages for me at the office and at home."

Michelle saw Stewart's eyes flicker to his wife. "You'll have to ask her that, Douglas. You know Eleanor, she tells us nothing about her private business," he said, just a little too heartily. "Come on in. Let's get this toast over with, so we can get on to the hard stuff."

From the heritage room came the murmur of conversation. The door leading to the kitchen opened and Sophie came into the hall, crashing the door closed behind her. Grace and Dr. Lenzie appeared from the study, so that Sophie almost collided with them.

"Watch where you're going," Grace snapped. "You almost—"

A scream cut through what she was saying, like an alarm bell at close quarters. The screaming continued. For an instant they all froze . . . then everyone rushed for the stairs. Sophie was first, dragging up her long tight skirt in one hand and leaping up the stairs, two at a time.

Michelle knew, instinctively, that the terrified screams were coming from her grandmother's room.

Chapter 11

❧

Eleanor could hear herself screaming, but at the same time the noise seemed to be coming from someone else. She cowered in her chair, the piercing screams issuing from the back of her throat, hurting her ears. Although she couldn't see the figure anymore, the memory of its ravaged face remained imprinted on her mind.

A group of people burst into her bedroom, led by her granddaughter, Sophie.

"What is it, Gran? What's happened?"

Someone switched on the central light, making the shadows disappear.

The screams changed to a wailing. "He's there. Behind the curtain." Eleanor saw someone go to the curtain. "No," she cried, "don't open them. I don't want to see him." She covered her eyes with her hands, drawing in painful, shuddering breaths as she struggled to regain her self-control.

She heard the swish of the pulley as the curtains opened. "There's no one here," Grace's voice said calmly and clearly. "Nothing. The windows are tightly shut. Everything's fine."

Oh, God! It was happening again. Just when she thought it had ended, it was starting up again. She was breathing fast—short, shallow breaths—and her heart was galloping in her chest. *Easy. Take it easy*, she told herself.

Norman came to stand in front of her, blocking out the light. "What did you think you saw, Mother?"

She couldn't stop shaking. "I saw him, I tell you. He was as clear as could be, standing there." She lifted her hand and pointed to the window.

"Who?"

"Ramsey," she whispered. "Your father. His face was all . . . all crushed and torn." A long shudder vibrated through her. "It looked as if it wasn't all there, as if he'd come from the grave."

She could hear Grace's impatient sigh. "It was your imagination, Mother. That was all." She turned to someone standing beside her. "See what I mean?"

"Yes, I do. Excuse me. I'd like to examine her." Andrew Lenzie's voice this time. Calm, infinitely reasonable. A typical doctor's voice.

Damn the man! As always, he spoke as if she weren't there, either physically or mentally. Eleanor sat up straight in the chair. "I don't need to be examined."

"You're very upset," Andrew said soothingly. "You've been badly scared."

"I certainly have . . . and I did not imagine what I saw."

He made suitably understanding noises, which annoyed Eleanor even more. Although she was still shaking, she objected to being treated like a child who'd merely had a bad nightmare—especially by someone almost as young as her grandchildren.

"It would be best if you all go downstairs," Andrew said, raising his voice. "I'm sure it won't be long before Eleanor's fully recovered and back with you for this year's Thanksgiving toast."

They began to slip away. Although none of them had been much help to her, Eleanor felt terror wash over her again as the room emptied. "Michelle. I want Michelle to stay."

"I'll stay with you, Mother," Grace said.

"No, I want Michelle."

Grace's lips pressed into a thin line. *Too bad*,

thought Eleanor. Michelle came forward as the others retreated. Eleanor could sense the family's animosity to Carolyn's daughter.

"Close the door," she told Michelle when everyone had gone. "It's a good thick door. Not easy to eavesdrop once it's shut. Have you two met?" she asked, nodding to Andrew and Michelle.

"Yes," Michelle said.

"I'm going to check your grandmother's responses, to find what her present state is," he told Michelle.

"No need to tell her that," Eleanor snapped. "She's not a fool. She can see what you're doing."

"I wanted to explain."

"Forget the explanations. Just do it. Get it over with. I warn you, it won't tell you a thing about what happened to me."

He took her pulse and blood pressure and listened to her heart. Then he checked her eyes.

"Well?" Eleanor demanded as he neatly folded his stethoscope and put it in his leather bag.

"Your blood pressure is far too high."

"Of course it is. I just had a terrible scare. What do you expect?"

"You're right. As always," he added with a slight grin at Michelle. "We'll need to check her medication."

"Don't tell *her* that, you fool. She's leaving here on Monday. What does she care about my medication?"

"You asked your granddaughter to be here while I examined you. Naturally, I thought you wanted her to know what I've found."

Eleanor subsided. "I'm sorry. But you know, Andrew, you have a most annoying habit of speaking about me to other people as if I didn't exist, particularly if Janet or Grace is there."

Andrew stiffened. "Forgive me. It's certainly not my intention to ignore you."

"I should sincerely hope not, considering I'm the one whose body you're examining." She gripped the arms of her chair, forcing herself to breathe more easily. "If there's something seriously wrong with me I want to know now. You are not to hide it from me. Is it Alzheimer's?"

He glanced first at Michelle and then looked directly at Eleanor. "It could be."

It was what she had most feared. That all these things that had been happening to her were not real. That the horrible things she'd seen were hallucinations conjured up by a brain that was deteriorating. *Her* brain.

She felt a hand clasp hers gently. She looked up through tear-filled eyes and saw Michelle's face, filled with compassion.

"You came too late," Eleanor whispered.

Michelle shook her head. "You're still here, aren't you? That's what matters."

"We need to run some tests," Andrew said. "There's new medication and excellent programs to help."

Eleanor suddenly rallied. "I don't give a damn for your programs. Even if I have got whatsit, I still say that I saw Ramsey—or someone dressed up to look like him."

Andrew bent to do up his bag. Eleanor intercepted the look he gave Michelle. "I know you don't believe me," she said. "That's why I think you're a quack. In fact, I've a good mind to get a new doctor."

Andrew shrugged. "Do as you please." His voice was cool. "You asked me to give you my honest opinion. I have done so."

"Someone's doing this. Someone's after my money."

"Oh, Eleanor." He sighed and shook his head. "We've been through all this before. You really should try to trust your family a little more."

"Oh, I trust 'em all right, as long as I hold the reins." Eyes gleaming, she smiled at Michelle. "I'm going to do something about that right now. Has my lawyer arrived yet?"

"Mr. Bradford?" Michelle asked. "He arrived a few minutes ago. Just as . . ." She faltered.

"Just as I was seeing my husband's poor torn face," Eleanor whispered. Her eyes closed for a moment, but the image was still there, hovering in the darkness of her mind. She quickly opened her eyes again. "I think God sent you to me in the nick of time," she told Michelle. Eleanor lifted her hand to touch her grand-daughter's hand. "How soft your skin is. Mine is so dry and harsh."

Michelle bent to kiss her cheek. Her lips, too, were soft. "You're going to be fine," she said firmly. Her eyes, so like Carolyn's, were shining.

Eleanor felt a sudden rush of adrenaline. "With your help I believe I am. I want you to go downstairs and ask Douglas Bradford to come up here."

"I'll speak to Douglas," Andrew said.

"Very well, but then I want Michelle to leave us."

"Couldn't this wait?" Andrew protested. "You've had a nasty shock. You should rest."

"I can rest later. Please get Douglas for me. I want to do this *now*."

Chapter 12

❧

As they waited in the heritage room, the mood was subdued. Unable to curb his impatience, Norman went out into the hall and was about to go and check on his mother when Andrew came down. "What's going on up there?"

Andrew shook his head. "That's a very good question. She's hypertensive. Pupils are dilated, but—"

Grace joined them. "Is she okay?" she asked in a low voice.

Andrew gave a noncommittal grunt. "I was just telling Norman. Everything indicates she's had some sort of shock, but who knows what brought it on."

"She's not on her own up there, is she?" Grace asked.

"No, Michelle is with her."

Grace's lips tightened. "Of course, she would be."

"Eleanor has sent me down here to fetch Douglas."

Norman's heartbeat went into overdrive. He exchanged glances with Grace. "Thanksgiving or no Thanksgiving, we've got to speak to you and Douglas in private," he told Andrew.

"I'd better fetch Stewart, as well," Grace said.

"I suppose so." Norman was unable to hide his reluctance to involve Stewart, but he realized he had no choice.

He went back into the heritage room. "I'm sorry," he announced, "but Grandmother won't be down for a while. She's going to be fine," he added in response to questions from the family, "but she needs to take a rest. We're going to speak to Andrew for a few minutes. Please party on, but keep the music down, okay?"

Lauren came to him, teetering on her three-inch-high heels. He could see she'd already had too much to drink. His heart sank. "Is your mother all right?" she asked anxiously. "Did she think she saw her little dog again?"

"Who knows what the hell she thought she saw," Norman said wearily. "I have to find Doug Bradford. Do you know where he went?"

"The last time I saw him he was talking to Janet in the dining room."

"Thanks." He turned to leave, then turned back and ran his thumb beneath her left eye. "Your mascara's running."

"Oh, no." She made it sound like the end of the world. "Don't worry, honey. I'll fix it."

He gave her a perfunctory smile and went out into the hall again. "Douglas is in the dining room with Janet," Grace told him. Her eyes narrowed. "I wonder what they're talking about."

"God knows. Did you find Stewart?"

"Not yet. I've sent Larry to look for him."

Norman frowned at her. "Larry can't be included in this."

"What the hell do you mean?" Grace demanded. "Larry's a partner in the company."

"This is a family problem. No spouses involved. Unless you want me to bring Lauren in on it." He cast a warning glance at Andrew's back. He was talking to Ramsey, who was asking him about his grandmother. "The fewer the better," he said beneath his breath. "And make sure you don't say anything about the merger to either Andrew or Douglas, okay?"

"Of course not," Grace said scornfully. "What sort of idiot do you think I am?"

"Sorry." Norman heaved a sigh. "I'm worried about Stewart. He's been on the booze since this morning.

He's quite likely to blurt out something he shouldn't. I wish to hell we could keep him out of it."

Norman's wish was granted when Larry returned to say that he'd been unable to find Stewart in the house or the garden. Grace opened her mouth, probably to suggest calling the bar in the Lord Beaverbrook Hotel, but Norman nudged her and she said nothing.

"Excuse us, Larry," Norman said, "but we want to discuss Mother's health with her doctor, okay? It won't take long."

Larry hid his reaction to being excluded very well. "Fine," he said. He glanced at Grace and winked at her. "See you later, darling."

When Norman walked into the dining room he saw the lawyer and Janet, their heads close together in earnest discussion. They moved apart, almost guiltily, Norman thought, as if they didn't want their conversation to be overheard.

"Can you come into the study for a moment, Douglas?" Norman asked. "Excuse us, Janet." He gave her no explanation.

"Is Mrs. Tyler all right?" she asked, anxiety creasing her forehead.

"She's much calmer now," the doctor told her.

Janet stood up, wincing from the pain in her arthritic knees. "I'll go up to her."

Andrew held up his hand. "No hurry. Michelle is with her."

Janet's face flushed. "That's good. As long as she's not alone."

"She's not," Andrew confirmed.

"We'll go into the study." Norman led the way down the hall and, once everyone was inside, shut the door.

Douglas Bradford sat, as if by habit, in the chair at the desk. He leaned back and rubbed his hands together. "Why the sudden meeting?" he asked, directing his question to Norman.

"I think I can answer that," Andrew said. "Eleanor's asking to see you."

"So?"

"We think she's about to change her will again," Grace said.

"Surely that's between your mother and her lawyer," Douglas said, sounding even more pompous than usual.

"Normally, that would be the case, of course. But, to be brutally honest, Douglas, we're very much afraid that Eleanor is becoming more and more incapable of rational thought." Norman looked at Andrew.

"Is it that bad?" Douglas directed his question directly at Andrew.

Andrew frowned. "I'm not sure, but . . . it could be. It depends if these . . . hallucinations are products of her imagination or the result of some chemical imbalance caused by her medication. It's hard to tell."

"Can you get another medical opinion?"

Andrew glanced at Grace. "We've talked about Alzheimer's tests, but Eleanor hasn't been keen. However, to speed things up you might prefer to have her go to Boston or the Mayo Clinic. That way she wouldn't have to wait so long."

"I'm not sure she'd agree to that." Grace shook her head. "You know Mother. Although she could afford any medical attention money can buy, she has this bee in her bonnet about waiting her turn in Canada."

"Have you any idea why she wants to change her will?" Douglas asked.

Grace looked at Norman. He gave her a slight nod. "She probably wants to add Michelle to her list of legacies," she said.

"What's wrong with that?" Douglas Bradford took off his glasses, polished them with his large, white handkerchief, and then put them on again. "I would have thought it would be perfectly natural for her to add a legacy to her youngest daughter's only child. I don't think I'm betraying a confidence when I tell you that she often speaks to me of her regret that she was unable to help Carolyn."

Andrew cleared his throat. "I think Norman's and

Grace's concern is that Eleanor may not be considered capable of making a will."

"You mean you think she's not of sound mind?" Douglas demanded. "Legally as well as medically speaking, I mean."

"It's possible."

"Damn it, Andrew. You're more cagey than a bloody lawyer."

"I'm trying to protect my patient's best interests."

Douglas gave a faint smile. "Is that what you're doing?" He sat at the desk, frowning as he doodled on the lined pad in front of him. When Norman tried to read the notes he'd written there, Douglas turned over the page.

"I agree that it is absolutely reasonable for my mother to add Michelle to her list of legatees. We were all very upset when Carolyn ran away from home. Right, Grace?"

"Oh . . . certainly. Terribly upset."

"However, I would hate to see this family dragged through the courts in a challenge to the legality of Eleanor's will," Norman said, carefully choosing his words.

Douglas met his eyes, glanced at Grace, and then back at Norman again. "Is that what it could come to?"

"It's possible."

Douglas chewed on his lip and then threw down the pen. "I agree with you. It is possible. In fact, it's more than possible. It's very likely that any change to Eleanor's current will might be challenged by a member of the family, after what we've all seen happen tonight."

"That's what we thought," Norman said, trying hard not to show his elation at Douglas's sudden capitulation. "You know how devastating it could be to the family, as well as the business, if that were to happen in the future. We all know how family squabbles can destroy a business, even without a challenge to a will to complicate matters. Is there anything you can do?"

Douglas tilted the swivel chair back so that it almost

touched the wall. He sat there in silence, frowning, until Norman felt like throttling him.

At last he brought the chair upright again and spoke. "Here's what I propose, with Andrew's agreement, of course. Whatever it is that Eleanor wants changed in her will, I will tell her that she should wait until she has finished all her medical tests and received the results."

"You mean you'll suggest that to her?" Grace asked.

"No. I will tell her."

"She'll ignore you. She'll say she's perfectly capable of making decisions. That there's absolutely nothing wrong with her mind. That all these things she saw actually happened." Grace blinked away tears. "Poor Mother. How I hate to see her like this!"

Douglas leaned forward. "I will tell your mother that until she receives a clean bill of health, any changes she makes to her will could be subject to a challenge from the legatees. I will also remind her that such a challenge could not only tie up her will for a very long time, but would be extremely costly to the family members involved."

"I agree with Douglas," Andrew said. "That sounds the ideal solution. Just tell her to postpone any changes until she has undergone tests and we have the results. I'll see what I can do about getting her tests done more quickly. Once they're done, we should have the results within two, three weeks at the most. I'm sure she won't mind postponing any changes to her will for such a short time."

Norman felt as if he'd been holding his breath for several minutes. Now he released it slowly, letting it seep out unnoticed by the others. The sense of relief made him feel almost giddy. He didn't dare even glance at Grace, but he guessed she must be feeling the same way.

He was less worried about his mother's will than he was about the possibility of her transferring some of her stock to Michelle before the merger went through.

If his mother agreed to Douglas's advice, she would probably hold off on all business changes for a while. They had thirteen days in which to persuade her to agree to the merger. He was sure that the three of them could wear down her opposition in that time. One way or another.

The one big fly in the ointment was Michelle.

Chapter 13

Not long after Andrew had gone downstairs, Janet came up to see how Eleanor was. Then Norman and Grace, followed by the doctor and lawyer, trooped into Eleanor's room.

"What's this?" Eleanor asked, her eyes narrowing. "A delegation?"

"We have important matters to discuss with you, Mother," Norman said. "Private matters." His dark eyes locked with Michelle's. "Would you mind leaving, Michelle? This won't take long."

Eleanor felt red-hot anger boiling up inside her. She struggled to her feet to confront them. "This is my home, my bedroom. I am the only one who gives orders around here."

Grace intervened. "Norman wasn't giving orders, Mother. He was merely asking Michelle to leave us together for a short time."

"Tell me why my granddaughter has to leave when Andrew can stay?"

"It's a medical matter," Grace replied.

Eleanor looked a question at Andrew, but he avoided it by turning away.

"And Douglas?" Eleanor demanded. "If this is a medical matter in what way is Douglas involved?"

"It is also a legal matter," the lawyer replied. He gave Eleanor an encouraging smile. "It shouldn't take long."

Eleanor felt the pressure of Michelle's hand on hers.

"I'll see you later, when you come down to give the Thanksgiving toast," Michelle said. Her warm smile reminded Eleanor so forcibly of Carolyn that she felt tears forming behind her eyes.

Proudly, she watched Michelle as she walked from the room, her head high. Not even these vultures seemed to daunt her. Yes, this was Carolyn's girl, all right.

Grace murmured something to Janet, who then followed Michelle from the room. As she was leaving, Stewart appeared in the doorway. He came into the room. "Something going on I should know about?" he asked. His tone was casual, but Eleanor could hear the anger in his voice. Stewart always hated being left out.

"You might as well come in and join us," Eleanor said. A spasm of fear caught her breath as Stewart closed the door on Janet. She was on her own, without allies, it seemed. So be it. "Well?" she said.

"Sit down, Mother," Norman said, trying to ease her into her armchair, but she flung him off. The others drew chairs into a semicircle around her. She felt like a lamb surrounded by a pack of wolves.

She kept them waiting, knowing that none of them would sit until she did. It gave her a sense of power, but standing without support was hell on her knees. Eventually she gave in and lowered herself into her chair. Folding her hands over the gilt handle of her cane, she kept her spine as straight as possible, concentrating hard on trying to keep her head still. That damned head tremor made her look like a querulous old crone. Her stomach roiled. It felt crampy and queasy. *Too much rich food,* she told herself. *I really must remember not to eat so much when Christmas comes.*

"I'm waiting," she said when no one spoke.

Norman cleared his throat. "We believe you're about to change . . . to make an addition to your will."

Eleanor stared at him. "And what business is that of yours? Of any of you, for that matter." Her gaze

swept around the four of them. "Other than Douglas."
She frowned. "Did you tell them I wanted to change
my will?" she demanded of the lawyer.

"How could I?" he asked. "I knew only that you
wanted to see me as soon as possible. That's why I'm
here, instead of enjoying the evening with my sister's
family."

"You're paid exceptionally well to come when I
ask," Eleanor said coldly.

Douglas glanced at her with something like loathing
in his expression and then looked down at the hands
clasped in his lap. With his Burgundy velvet vest and
small, neat hands, he reminded her of the mole in *The
Wind in the Willows*. Eleanor fixed her eyes on the
top of his bald head, noticing how the light shone on
it, as if it were polished. "It is my understanding that
a will concerns nobody but the testator and his or her
lawyer." Her mouth tilted into a caustic smile. "Or has
something changed that no one has told me about?"

"Are you wanting to change your will?" Douglas
asked her bluntly.

"Are you asking me to discuss the matter with my
family looming over me like vultures?"

"That's most unfair, Mother," Grace protested.
"We're concerned only for your welfare."

"Yes, I'm sure you are." Eleanor's tone was etched
with acid. "My welfare and also what you can get out
of me."

Norman's face reddened. "This is not the time to
be discussing business matters." His eyes flashed a
warning at Eleanor.

Eleanor smiled sweetly back at him. If they all
thought she was going gaga, there was no harm in
playing with Norman and Grace, pretending she'd
blow the whistle on their ridiculous talk of a merger.
In fact, if they pressured her much more about it, she
might very well do that. Call the *Globe and Mail* and
spill the beans. That would serve them right! Her
smile broadened as she thought about how Norman
must be squirming inside.

But, of course, she'd never do anything that might harm the company. Didn't they realize that? Tyler Foods was *her* baby, hers and Ramsey's. Did they really expect her to abandon it to some uncaring conglomerate that might shut it down and get rid of half the workers who depended on it for their livelihood?

"Yes," she said suddenly. "I do want to change my will. If you must know I want to add a bequest to Michelle." *And also arrange to transfer some of my shares to her right away,* she added to herself, but she wasn't going to tell them that.

She saw Grace glance at Stewart. "Don't you think it might be better to wait a little before you make any changes, Mother?" he said in that annoyingly syrupy tone that he often used when he wanted to get his own way.

"Why?"

Norman answered for Stewart. "It would give you the chance to get to know Michelle a little better. For all you know—"

"She's Carolyn's child. That's all that matters to me."

"She's also the daughter of a—"

"That's enough!" Eleanor's voice shot out like a whip. "None of this is your business. Now get out of my room and leave me alone with my lawyer."

Douglas folded his little paws together. "There's a problem, Eleanor. These . . . episodes of yours."

Eleanor felt a chill run over her. "What episodes?"

Douglas ran his tongue over his bottom lip. "Your dog. The other things you think you've seen."

Eleanor felt her head start to shake again and couldn't stop it. "Are you saying I imagined them all, including tonight?"

Douglas glanced at the others, but they kept quiet, happy to leave this to him. "We're saying that there was no evidence of these things you saw actually happening, that's all."

"So I'm going insane." Eleanor's voice rose. "Is that what you're all here to tell me?"

Andrew leaned forward. "You are not going insane. But I, for one, am very concerned about your health. It could be a strong reaction to your medication or a sign of the onset of some physical disability."

"Whatever it is," Grace said impatiently, "it's impairing your ability to think straight."

Andrew pressed his lips together and shook his head slightly in annoyance.

"Well, that's true, isn't it?" Grace insisted. "Let's call a spade a spade, for God's sake."

"I wouldn't have put it quite like that, but yes, it's true."

Douglas cleared his throat and they all looked at him. "You're a sensible woman, Eleanor—"

"That's not exactly what you're telling me, is it?" she said with a bitter laugh.

"What we are trying to tell you is that any change that you make in your will at this time could be questioned down the line."

"By 'down the line' you mean when I'm dead, right?"

"Exactly."

She looked at her children. They had adult faces, but they were still children to her. "You mean you'd challenge my will on the grounds of mental incompetence?" she asked in a low voice.

"Not us, in particular," Norman said. "But anyone involved in the will might have a good case, armed with the evidence to back him or her up."

Eleanor looked back at Douglas. "And what would that mean?"

He sighed and shook his head. "It could tie up the settlement of your estate for a very long time."

"Indeed?" A hint of a smile hovered around her mouth. "And the company? How would it be affected?"

"That would depend on how you left your shares in the company. It could cause a great many problems."

She looked at Norman. "That's what you were saying about the problems of keeping the firm in the family, wasn't it, Norman dear?"

He glared at her, but didn't dare respond in case she retaliated by saying more.

"What were those figures you gave me?" Eleanor said. "Only one in ten family businesses survive to the third generation?"

"Something like that," he murmured.

"Well, let's hope for your boys' sake ours is one of the lucky ones." She stood up. "I thank you all for your concern, but I think I'll take the risk of being found incompetent." She gave a wry smile. "After all, by then I won't be here to worry about it, will I?"

Grace's face looked as if it were bleached white, despite the perfect makeup. "Don't rush into this, Mother. After all, you've known Michelle for only one day. How can you possibly tell what she's like in such a short time?"

Eleanor studied Grace for a long time. She looked defiantly back at her mother. "I can tell," Eleanor said softly. "Besides, for many years you and Norman and Stewart have benefited from all the hard work your father and I put into Tyler Foods. The company pays for Larry's Porsche and your villa in Tuscany, doesn't it? I think it's time that Carolyn got her share, don't you?"

"But this isn't Carolyn," Grace protested. "It's her illegitimate daughter by an Acadian lumber worker."

Eleanor was gratified to see the disgust on Andrew's face. "Very nice, Grace dear. You show your prejudices quite clearly to us all."

"Prejudices I learned at my parents' knee," Grace replied, breathing fast.

"We've all changed since those days. I'd hoped you had as well. It seems I was wrong." Eleanor turned to Douglas. "I wish to add something to my will," she said firmly.

"Very well. But, because of the holiday, I won't be able to get it typed up, ready for your signature and those of your witnesses, until Tuesday."

"That's fine. As long as I can get it off my mind now. Please excuse us," she said to the others.

"I'll just get my briefcase," Douglas said. "It's downstairs."

Eleanor sat down again and watched them as they silently left her room. She was sure they'd be having a hurried conference as soon as they got downstairs. She didn't care. She wanted to get this done. When her will was read, Michelle would discover she was a very wealthy woman. Meanwhile, she would make sure that Michelle would never want for anything. The desire for outside help had driven her to contact Michelle, but now that Carolyn's daughter was here, she fully intended to do her best to make up for those lost years. God willing, they'd have plenty of quality time together.

Her heartbeat quickened. Surely whoever was doing these terrifying things to her wouldn't actually kill her, would they? She shrank back in her chair, her eyes widening with fear as she watched the open doorway.

"What the hell are you playing at, Douglas?" Norman demanded as soon as they reached the study. "I thought we'd agreed that she must not be allowed to make any codicils to her will."

Douglas drew himself up. "I can't refuse to allow your mother to add something to her will. That would be unethical."

"But she's not mentally competent." Grace looked around. "Where the hell is Andrew?"

"He said something about going to his car," Douglas said. "And we don't know that she's not mentally competent." His smile was grim. "There are times when I think Eleanor Tyler is far more competent than all of us put together."

"Oh, for God's sake." Grace paced to the window and back again, her silk skirt whipping about her legs.

"I am not questioning your motives in wanting your mother to give careful consideration to this matter before she comes to a final decision." Douglas looked over his glasses at Grace. "On the other hand, I believe she has every right to make a change to her will, if that is her wish. I would have preferred to wait until the medical tests were completed. That way no one could have been accused of undue duress either way."

Stewart frowned. "Duress?"

"On the part of your niece, Michelle . . . or of you and Grace and Norman."

"That's the point, surely?" Grace said, eager to grasp it. "Obviously Michelle is leaning on Mother, telling her a hard luck story. That's why Mother's wanting to give her money."

Douglas smiled. "But your mother has every right to do what she pleases with her own money. Her will concerns me far more than what she does while she lives. What I want to avoid, if possible, are any legal difficulties and challenges to her will in the future. I shall advise her accordingly."

"What the hell does that mean?" Grace demanded.

"I'm sorry, but that has to be between Eleanor and me."

"But she won't be signing the will until Tuesday, at least," Norman said slowly.

"That's right. I felt that that would give her some time to think things through before she made a commitment." Douglas picked up his battered black briefcase. "Excuse me. I must go back to her before she starts to think I've abandoned her."

He left them there, in the study. Stewart standing by his father's old desk, his face more florid than usual, Norman and Grace in the center of the room, staring at each other.

Chapter 14

—⁓—

They all gathered in the heritage room for the Thanksgiving toast, raising crystal glasses filled with the finest vintage champagne. But it was Norman, not Eleanor, who proposed the toast, after he'd announced that his mother wasn't well enough to come down again.

As everyone in the room exchanged hugs and kisses, Michelle set down her untouched glass on a small table and backed into the hall, intense loneliness washing over her.

Norman had used the same traditional toast her mother had used at every one of their simple Thanksgiving meals. Now Michelle realized that despite her negative feelings about her family her mother had never forgotten her background. And she also understood for the first time how difficult it must have been for her mother to adjust to living in small, cheap apartments after living here, in this mansion, with everything she needed. Everything except love. On special occasions, like this holiday, her mother's mind had always seemed to be somewhere else. Michelle now understood that despite all her protests that she couldn't care less, her mother had missed her home and her family.

As Michelle missed hers. Her longing for Brian was like a gnawing pain beneath her heart. She turned to go up to her room . . . and almost collided with Andrew Lenzie.

"Sorry," he said, stepping back.

"My fault. I wasn't looking." She blinked rapidly, to hide her moist eyes from him.

"You okay?" he asked, frowning.

"I'm fine. How's my grandmother?"

"She's resting. I gave her a sedative. She should sleep well tonight."

"I'm really worried about her," she said impulsively.

"Are you?" He gave her a quizzical half smile.

"I know that sounds a bit weird, considering I've only just met her, but . . ." Michelle shrugged, unable to put her feelings about Eleanor into words.

"It can't be easy for you, coming into a family gathering like this, meeting your relatives for the first time."

"You're right, it's not easy." It was a relief to find someone who understood how she felt. "I was just thinking about my mother living here. She used to say the same Thanksgiving toast as Norman did."

People were pushing past them to move into the less formal family room at the back of the house, which was part library, part den.

"It's a pleasant evening," Andrew said. "A bit damp, but not that cold. Fancy a walk?"

"Now?"

"Why not?"

Michelle glanced around her. Chairs were being pushed back, folding tables set up. She gave him a wry smile. " 'Why not' is right! I don't think I'll be missed, do you?" She liked the fact that he didn't try to make some polite rebuttal. "I'll go get my coat."

She ran upstairs to her room and took off her heels to change into walking shoes. As she pulled on her raincoat and buttoned it up, she could feel Brian's eyes boring into her back. She spun around. "No use looking at me like that," she told his photograph. "He's a friendly, good-looking guy and I'm bloody lonely. And we both know whose fault that is, don't we?"

She was tempted to slam the photo down on its

face. Instead, she turned her back on it, grabbed her wallet from her bag, and left the room without a backward glance.

As she passed her grandmother's room, Janet came out, carrying an empty cup and saucer. "How is she?" Michelle whispered.

"Sleeping," Janet said, her voice curt.

"That's good." Michelle waited for the normally loquacious Janet to say more, but it seemed she was not in a talking mood. Her glance took in the coat Michelle was wearing. "I'm going out for some fresh air," Michelle explained.

"The family usually plays games after the Thanksgiving dinner." It sounded like a reproach.

"I'm not much into games," Michelle said, and walked past her, down the stairs, to join Andrew in the hall.

As she walked with him down the front steps, Michelle consciously lowered her shoulders, aware that they had been tensed for a very long time. The smell of fecund wet earth and leaves permeated the moist air. She breathed it in, catching the aroma of wood smoke, which no doubt came from the log fire that was burning in the family room.

They walked down the driveway and along the road in companionable silence, sunk into their own thoughts, their feet scuffing the leaves piled along the side of the road.

"I love the fall, don't you?" Michelle said at last as they came to the stretch of parkland by the St. John River.

"You've chosen the best week to come, if only the rain would stop. The leaves are at their finest. I hope you'll have time to see some of the countryside while you're here."

"I think the plan is to drive to the cottage tomorrow, after the church service in the cathedral."

Andrew laughed. His laughter had an edge to it.

"What's so funny?" Michelle asked.

"Sorry. It was hearing you call the Tyler summer home a cottage."

"Oh! Well, that's what Eleanor called it."

"I'm sure she did. Eleanor is a little blinkered about life at times."

"I take it that it's a bit more than the sort of cottage I'm used to in Manitoba: a log cabin with one sitting room and a couple of small bedrooms."

"Just a bit."

"Not that we could afford even that, of course. Lots of my friends had family cottages at the lake, but my mother couldn't afford a holiday, never mind a cottage." Now it was her turn to sound bitter.

"Not fair, is it? Even less fair when you see what the rest of your family has." Andrew kicked at a pile of leaves, sending them into the air. "What did your mother tell you about her family?"

"She hardly ever talked about them. It hurt too much. I suppose you know what happened to her."

He nodded. "I didn't know her personally, of course. She left here when I was still a small kid. But I knew all about her. This is a fairly tight-knit town," he explained apologetically. "Besides, I'm the last of a line of Lenzie doctors. My father and grandfather were the Tyler family physicians."

"So they would have known my mother when she was living here," Michelle said eagerly. "I'd love to meet someone who knew her." She grimaced. "As you can imagine, the family's a bit biased, both for and against her. I'd love to hear about her when she was a kid, before her world exploded."

"Sorry. I can't help you there. My grandfather and both my parents are dead. My dad died last year."

"Oh! I'm sorry."

"Don't be. He died on the golf course, with a club in his hand. It was the way he'd have chosen to go." Andrew hesitated. "He didn't have much ambition, my father. A small family practice and time for his golf, that was all he asked for in life."

"And you?"

"Oh, I'm much the same, I suppose. A chip off the old block."

Somehow his response didn't ring true. "You never wanted to get away, to explore?"

"Certainly. Didn't we all? I did a bit of backpacking in Europe before I went to medical school. I'd hoped to do a specialty, but my father got sick and I had to take over his practice, so that was that. How about you?"

"No, I never traveled much when I was young. Couldn't afford it. Then my mother got sick and I had to stay home to help out."

"Seems we have a lot in common."

"Sounds like it. But I've made up for it since I got married. Brian likes to be on the move all the time, even when he's not working, so I've been able to see places like London and Paris and Rome and parts of Asia . . ."

"Lucky you."

"Yes, I suppose I am. But I'm always glad to get home."

"And home has always been Winnipeg?"

"Yes. Brian wanted me to move to the States, but I—I just couldn't." It felt weird talking about something so personal to a virtual stranger, but the feeling that Andrew was a kindred spirit kept her talking. "From a practical viewpoint it would have meant I couldn't work, of course, and I would have hated that, but there were other reasons."

The wet leaves on the sidewalk were slippery. She didn't want to fall. Without thinking, she slid her hand into his arm and felt a spark of electricity jump between them. They walked close together, matching steps. The night was so quiet, with only an occasional car passing them, that she could hear Andrew's steady breathing.

"My mother's buried in Winnipeg," she continued. "We'd looked out for each other since I was born. I just couldn't go away and leave her alone." She gave an embarrassed laugh. "Sounds stupid, doesn't it?"

"Not at all. Your mother had no one else in her life. You'd feel you were abandoning her if you left the place you'd lived together."

She stopped and turned to him. "You do understand. You should have been a psychiatrist or analyst or something."

"Should I?" he said lightly.

"Brian doesn't understand at all. Oh, he tries to, but . . . he has a large family and feels very secure with them."

"You have quite a large family, too."

"I don't feel any affinity to them. Apart from Eleanor, perhaps."

"That's not surprising, considering you've only just met them. Give it time."

"Do you really think I'll ever fit in? The daughter of a lumber worker who seduced the Tylers' daughter?"

"You've left out the worst part," Andrew said. "A *French-speaking* Acadian lumber worker." They both broke into laughter at the same time.

"These things used to really matter to people, didn't they?"

"Don't kid yourself, to some people they still do, unfortunately. How's your French, by the way?"

"It's quite good. When I found out that my father had been Acadian, I thought it was terribly romantic. I always hoped that he'd turn up at the door one day, and when that happened, I wanted to be able to speak to him in his own language. Of course he never did come," she added lightly. "And now he never will. Anyway, I asked my mother if I could take French lessons in Saint Boniface. That's the French part of Winnipeg," she explained.

"It would be a different French though. Acadian French is unique."

"I know that now, but I didn't then. My mother let me take lessons, although money was always tight in our house."

"Your mother must have been a very special person."

Michelle swallowed. "She was."

Almost imperceptibly, she felt his arm press hers against his side.

She was relieved when the streetlights of the town loomed ahead and they came to the art gallery. Walking in the darkness with this man had been just a little too intimate for her liking. Yet when she drew her hand away from his arm, the loneliness she'd felt before welled up again.

"You should go here," Andrew said, nodding up at the stone building. "For a small gallery it has some exciting exhibits."

"I know. I was here this morning."

"You were?"

"You forget. I'm leaving here on Monday, so I had to do my sightseeing today or not at all."

"Monday?" He sounded disappointed.

"I have a business to run. Besides, I didn't want to stay too long on my first visit. Just in case I couldn't stand it."

"And?"

"And what?"

"What's your opinion of the Tyler family? Or is that too personal a question?"

"Not at all. You must know them all much better than I do."

He gave her a quirky smile. "I guess I do. Want a drink?" he asked suddenly.

They were outside the Lord Beaverbrook Hotel. She was reminded of her call to Becca from here earlier. Thank God, the queasiness she'd felt at lunchtime had dissipated. "I'd love some tea."

"Okay." He held the heavy glass door open for her.

The dining room was busy, but the server managed to find them a table in a quiet corner. Andrew ordered her tea and a New Brunswick ale called Moosehead for himself.

"So what do you think of them?"

"Who?"

They both laughed.

"Sorry," Andrew said. "Your Tyler relatives."

Michelle sat back, frowning, thinking about these new relatives of hers. She watched Andrew pick up his beer. Again, she silently admired his hands, the tapering fingers with short, well-kept nails. The hands of a sensitive man, she thought. He waited patiently for her answer. "The Tylers? I'm not sure, really. It's hard to have them all thrown at me at once, if you know what I mean."

Andrew nodded.

Michelle thought for a moment. "Stewart picked me up at the airport, so I had some time alone with him. He seems friendly, at least, which is more than I can say for Aunt Grace and my other uncle. Is he the black sheep of the family?"

"Who, Norman?"

"No," she said laughing. "Stewart. He seems a bit . . . I don't know. He drinks more than he should. And he strikes me as someone who likes the good life without having to work hard for it."

"Very astute."

"Am I right?"

"I'm the family physician. I can't really comment."

"Oh, come on. You can't ask me what I think of them all and then clam up when I ask about them."

He smiled his warm, attractive smile. "I said you were astute. That should be enough."

"Okay, Dr. Lenzie. I'll accept that you don't think it right to talk about your patients, but surely not all of them are yours."

"Let's say that my main patient is your grandmother. Unfortunately, she thinks I'm far too young to be her doctor. She only keeps me on because of my father. *And* my mother."

"What connection was there between your mother and my grandmother?"

"My mother and Eleanor were best friends. I was an only child, born when my mother was in her late thirties," he explained.

"I see. So you and the Tyler family go way back. I mean, on both sides, your mother and your father."

"Yes." He didn't expand. "What do you think of Norman?"

"He's more difficult to read. Tough, I imagine, but good at negotiating, getting what he wants. A good businessman."

"And Grace?"

Michelle rolled her eyes. "Grace is like Eleanor. Direct. Tough like Norman, but she doesn't have his corporate charm. I imagine my grandmother might have been like her when she was young, but old age has softened her a bit."

Andrew chuckled at that. "So you don't like your Aunt Grace?"

"Not really, but . . . there's something about her. She seems to adore her husband. And occasionally she reminds me of my mother. They didn't get along."

"Grace and your mother?"

"Right."

"Apparently, Carolyn was Eleanor's favorite child," Andrew told her.

"Oh! That would explain why Grace doesn't like me. And also why losing Carolyn must have been really hard for Eleanor. Still, I don't think parents should have favorite children."

"People are only human."

"It must be devastating to know that you come second in your parents' eyes. I was *numero uno* in my mother's life."

"You were very fortunate."

"Do you have any children?"

A shadow crossed his eyes. "One daughter."

"What's her name?"

"Cassie."

"Have you any pictures of her?"

With surprising reluctance, he drew out a photograph from his wallet. It was creased. "Oh, she's beautiful," Michelle said, gazing at a girl of about twelve.

"Yes, she is."

Suddenly she remembered that Eleanor had said he was divorced from his wife. "Does she live here?"

"No. In California. My ex-wife's married to an American. I see Cassie in the summer. That's all." He shoved the photograph back in the wallet and slid it into his pocket.

"That's rough."

He sat there, absentmindedly staring at his beer, obviously not wanting to discuss his daughter. She hurriedly changed the subject and asked him about something safe and dear to the hearts of all Canadians. "How severe are your winters here?"

As he launched into a description of winter in New Brunswick, Michelle sat back and allowed herself to enjoy the relaxed atmosphere in the bar and the warm companionship of Andrew Lenzie.

Pierre Gaudry heard about Michelle's visit to Tyler House from a friend who lived in Fredericton. She called him Saturday evening and said, "You'll never guess what. Your dad's daughter's in town visiting her family."

For a moment Pierre hadn't a clue what she was talking about. Then it sunk in. "Michelle? You're kidding!"

"Nope. She's there for Thanksgiving. Their housekeeper's granddaughter's a friend of mine. She just finished helping in the kitchen at Tyler House, and she called to tell me. Thought you'd like to know."

Pierre thought for a moment. "Did she say what she was like?"

"Said she was quite small . . . dark hair, like your dad. She also said her grandmother—the housekeeper—was worried Michelle might be after Tyler money."

"Wouldn't blame her if she was. There's lots of it to go around, that's for sure."

"I called you now, as she's going back to Winnipeg

on Monday. Why don't you come tomorrow, sleep in the basement? Bring a sleeping bag."

As soon as Suzanne rang off, Pierre called his brother, Marc, who lived with his girlfriend in Miramichi. Marc whistled when Pierre told him about Michelle. "Maybe we should pay our little sister a visit," he said, with a laugh. "I guess she's not so little. She's seven, eight years older than us, isn't she?"

"Suzanne said she's going back to Winnipeg Monday."

"Then we'd better drop in tomorrow, so's we don't miss her, eh? I always wanted a sister." They both laughed.

"Why don't I call the house," Pierre suggested, "to make sure she's there first, before we drive all the way to Fredericton?"

"Good idea. Call me back later."

"I wish to speak with Michelle Tyler." The man's accent was unmistakably Acadian French.

"Who is this?" Janet asked. It was hard to hear with all the background noise.

There was a moment of hesitation. "I am Pierre Gaudry."

Janet tensed. Michelle's father's name had been Michel Gaudry. "She's not here at the moment. She's just gone for a walk. She should be back soon. Can I give her a message?"

"No, *merci*. I wish only to speak with Michelle. I will try again." He rang off before Janet could stop him.

Chapter 15

⁓

Fredericton's Christ Church Cathedral stood on a great swath of green. Graced by venerable old elm trees, its weathered stone walls and green roof blended perfectly with the colorful clapboard mansions surrounding the green. With its Gothic arched windows and massive spire, it was as close as you could get to an ancient English cathedral in North America.

"It looks as if it's been here for centuries, doesn't it?" Eleanor said to Michelle as her car turned into the cathedral's driveway. "But it was completed in 1853. The church archives contain Queen Victoria's letters patent, appointing the Bishop of Fredericton and officially making Fredericton a city."

Having been greeted with deference by the ushers at the door, Eleanor moved slowly down the aisle, leaning on Stewart's arm, her cane tapping on the stone floor, acknowledging people's smiles as if she were Queen Victoria herself. Michelle followed behind her, with her cousin Ramsey, who had gone out of his way to be friendly. She couldn't help contrasting the cathedral with her own small church at home on Thanksgiving Sunday. At home, there'd be a colorful display of the abundant fruits of harvest from people's gardens set haphazardly on the altar steps: orange pumpkins, wicker baskets of red tomatoes saved from the early prairie frost, oddly shaped squash, green cucumbers that had escaped the canning jars, sheaves of wheat. Here, the only decoration consisted of two vases of tasteful bronze and yellow chrysanthemums set on both sides of the altar.

Michelle was about to sit down next to Janet, when Eleanor turned and motioned to her to come and sit with her. Michelle wished she wouldn't make such a public statement with all the family there, particularly Eleanor's other grandchildren, but there was no ignoring the peremptory index finger pointing to the space Grace had made for her.

As she passed her aunt, who had stepped into the aisle to let her through, Michelle felt as if she were walking past the open door of a freezer.

When she sat down on the cushioned bench, she caught sight of Andrew across the aisle, a row ahead of her. He was sitting with two women, whom she took to be his mother and sister until she remembered that he'd told her his mother was dead and he was an only child. As if he'd felt her gaze on him, he turned to smile at her. She smiled back, her face warming as she recalled their companionable evening together yesterday. He raised his hand in a small greeting. Not small enough, however, to be missed by Eleanor.

"You and Andrew seem to have become very friendly in a short time," she said frostily.

"I like him," Michelle replied.

Eleanor gave a grunt and then handed her a copy of the Book of Common Prayer, opened at the page for the traditional Morning Prayer service. "There's a contemporary service later," she said in a loud whisper, "but I prefer the traditional service."

That figures, thought Michelle. The cathedral was filled mainly with people dressed in their holiday best. Some of the women even wore hats. Not for them the jeans and casual clothes many people wore in her own church. Probably the more informal dressers turned up later, at the contemporary service. But as the organ boomed through the great stone church and the choristers in their red robes moved down the aisle, she couldn't help but be impressed and, yes, moved by the pomp and the grandeur.

The sermon was excellent, filled with reasons for being grateful to God, but she missed the strong emphasis she was used to of Thanksgiving also being a time to remember—and help—those who had little reason to give thanks. She also missed the stampede of excited children up to the altar, bearing plastic shopping bags filled with cans of baked beans and hams and baby food for Winnipeg Harvest, the inspired source for the food banks in her city.

As she stood to sing "Now Thank We All Our God" at the end of the service, she thought of all the things for which she had reason to be grateful: her mother who had been baptized here, in this church, and who lived on so strongly in her memory; this reunion with her mother's family though fraught with tension was also rewarding in her burgeoning relationship with her grandmother; Brian, who drove her wild with his wanderlust, but also made her feel as if she were the most beautiful and desirable woman in the world. The mere thought of him now made her body tingle. She smiled to herself. Not exactly correct feelings for church. But, then, hadn't God Himself devised lovemaking as a delicious way of procreating the species?

And that brought her to her last prayer of thanks . . . for the new life growing within her. *Please God, keep my baby safe,* she prayed. A tiny shiver rippled at the back of her neck and ran down her spine. *Must be cool in here,* she thought. A church this size was too large to heat properly.

It was a perfect fall day outside. A breeze had blown most of the clouds away and the sun warmed them as they stood outside on the edge of the green, waiting for Bob to return with the old Daimler. "Comes out three times a year," Penny whispered in Michelle's ear. "Christmas, Easter, and Thanksgiving."

Michelle smiled. *Why not?* she thought. The other members of the family had their Jags and BMWs. Why shouldn't Eleanor have her own choice of car? Andrew drove up and she almost laughed out loud. Now *that* was more her style: a Toyota Corolla with rust on the rear wheel panel.

He drew up in front of them. "Anyone need a ride? My aunt and cousin are staying on for a while to prepare for the next service, so I've got plenty of room."

Impulsively, Michelle nodded. "I'll go with Andrew," she said to Eleanor over her shoulder. Andrew leaned over to open her door and she got in.

As they moved off, Bob drew the Daimler up behind them. "Are you sure you can demean yourself to drive with me in this rust bucket?" Andrew asked, glancing in his rearview mirror.

"Don't be ridiculous. I'm happy to get away from them all for a few minutes." A sudden silence descended on them. Michelle became very aware of his arm brushing against hers as he changed gear. "The houses are so beautiful here," she said as they passed a pale blue house with royal blue shutters. The broad porch had elegant white pillars that extended to the upper balcony. "I had no idea Fredericton was such a lovely town."

"That's because everyone forgets the Maritime Provinces were thriving when much of western Canada was still being settled."

"I don't get a sense of a maritime region here. After all, the sea's about fifty miles away, isn't it?"

"We're tied to the sea by the St. John River. It was the main highway that brought most of the early settlers here, whether they came from Europe or the States. We Maritimers have roots that go down deep." Andrew glanced at her. "That includes you, too, don't forget. This is where your roots are. Your ancestors came here from Boston two centuries ago."

"What about yours? Are you from loyalist stock, too?"

"Not us. We were latecomers. Poor folk from the Scottish borders, who were brought here to do the rough work. Clearing the woods for settlements, building log cabins.''

"It's strange.''

"What?''

"The sense of history you have here. I didn't expect it.''

He grinned. "Are you saying we're old-fashioned?''

"Not really. It's just that . . . looking around at these beautifully preserved houses and churches you seem to have more reverence for the things of your past than those of us in the West.''

"I've been to Winnipeg. You've kept some of your old buildings there, too.''

"Not that many. And they're not nearly as old.''

"Nor are these houses when you compare them to the old farmhouses and homes in Quebec, for instance. Some of them were built in the seventeenth century.''

The mention of Quebec reminded Michelle that she had a French-Acadian heritage as well. "You keep talking about my loyalist background, but don't forget I'm part Acadian, too.''

He gave her a quick glance. "You sound quite proud of that.''

"As a matter of fact, I am. I wish I had time to see some of the Acadian places in New Brunswick. Next time.''

He raised his eyebrows. "Will there be a next time?''

Michelle laughed. "That's a point." Her laughter faded. "It depends, I suppose.''

"On what?''

"On how this visit ends. On how long my grandmother lasts.''

Andrew was silent as he turned into the Tyler House driveway. When he came to a halt in front of the steps, he left the engine running, but shifted to face Michelle, his arm along the back of her seat. "Your grandmother's still in good shape for her age,'' he told her.

"I know.'' Michelle twisted the strap of her bag round and round her hand. "But her mind is . . .'' She sighed. She looked up at Andrew through misty eyes. "I wish I'd come sooner."

"I wish you had, too." He spoke with such intensity that Michelle felt pleasure, at first, and then uneasiness at the feelings that hovered between them in the close proximity of the car's interior.

Andrew drew his arm away and stared out the front window, his jaw tight. "Well," he said eventually, "I don't suppose I'll see you again." He sounded almost angry. "You'll be off to St. Andrews for the family barbecue, I suppose?"

"I think that's the plan." Michelle glanced at her watch. "We're supposed to leave by noon."

He still stared out the window, his left hand clenched on the steering wheel, the knuckles white. "Are you staying down there overnight? I know they usually do, but I wondered if you were staying or coming back?"

Michelle felt that little chill down her spine again. Maybe she was getting a cold bug or something. She hoped not. Instinctively, her right hand slipped down to below her waist. She didn't want to catch anything that might hurt her baby. "Eleanor told me to pack an overnight bag, but I'd really rather not stay. I have to get a flight out early tomorrow afternoon. I can't miss it. I *have* to get back to Winnipeg tomorrow." Her heart was racing. What on earth was wrong with her? Why was she feeling so panicky about a short trip to the family cottage?

"Then tell them. Say you'd rather not stay the night."

"Eleanor would be really disappointed. She said it's a family tradition that they stay there until . . ."

"Monday evening. I know. But you can't stay until the evening. You have a plane to catch."

"I guess I'll have to take all my bags with me and go directly to the airport in the morning. Eleanor tried to persuade me to change my flight to Tuesday, but I promised Becca I'd be back in time to open up Tuesday morning."

"Becca?"

"Rebecca, my partner in our store. Also one of my best friends." Michelle moved in her seat. The tension between them was tangible. They were talking about nothing important, really, to spin out the time. Avoiding the finality of saying good-bye.

"Are you planning to see your half brothers before you leave?" The question came out of the blue.

For a moment, she wondered what he was talking about. Then she said, "No. Why?"

"I just wondered . . . as you were here. I think one of them lives in Moncton. The other one's a bit farther away, somewhere near Miramichi. That one works as a forester in Kouchibouguac National Park."

"How do you know so much about my father's sons?"

He gave her a wry grin. "Eleanor likes to be kept informed about everything concerning her family, however remote it might seem."

Michelle sighed and shook her head. "She's like an octopus, tentacles everywhere."

"Right. Anyway, I just thought I'd ask. If you were interested I'm sure I could find their phone numbers for you so you could call them."

"If I wanted to." Michelle knew her voice sounded frosty, but she didn't like talking about her father or his family. Her days of thinking of Michel Gaudry as a romantic figure were long gone. "But I don't. My biological father abandoned me and my mother thirty years ago and never bothered to make any sort of contact with us, so why should I bother to get in touch with his sons? They wouldn't have a clue who I was."

"You're right." He turned to smile at her. "You're better off without them. You never know what trouble getting in touch with them might cause. I'm afraid the family doesn't have a very good reputation." He hesitated. "If they knew you were here, they might come looking for you."

"You mean looking for money?"

He nodded. "Sorry."

"Don't be. My mother told me what it was like for

her after I was born. She said she was better off when my father left." Michelle didn't want to discuss her father anymore. Talking about him brought back the nausea she'd been holding off all morning. She put her hand on the door. "I must go. I want to get something to eat before we start off."

Andrew jumped out and came around to her as she got out of the car. They stood in awkward silence, keeping some distance between them, neither knowing quite what to say.

"Thanks for being there for me," Michelle eventually said. "It helped to make a difficult time much easier." She held out her hand to him, but he surprised her by leaning forward and kissing her on the cheek.

"Family friends," he explained with a tense smile.

"You're right."

"Enjoy the rest of your holiday." He spoke the words as if by rote, his mouth stiff, the smile fading.

"I'll try. You, too." He turned abruptly and started to walk away. "Andrew," she called after him.

He stopped as he was about to get into the driver's seat. "Yes?"

"Please look after my grandmother."

"I will."

She could feel his gaze on her as she went up the steps. When she turned he was driving off around the curve of the paved driveway and didn't respond to her wave.

Heart heavy, she went to the front door, reluctant to go inside. Although the sun was bright in the blue autumn sky she felt as if a dark cloud had descended on her, leaving her in shadow. She had lost the only ally she had, other than Eleanor. Andrew's departure also reminded her that she still hadn't heard from Brian. Things must be pretty desperate in Indonesia for him not to have called her.

Or she just wasn't high on his list of priorities, she thought bitterly.

Chapter 16

~

Michelle had always thought that fall was the best season in her own province of Manitoba, but as the car sped south to St. Andrews, the variegated colors of the trees were so vivid that when she closed her eyes they remained imprinted on her memory. The silver-green aspens and dark green pines were a more muted background to the hectic red and gold and brilliant orange mantling the deciduous trees.

Sometimes she caught a glimpse of an isolated farmhouse with black-and-white cattle in a field, small orchards of apple and plum trees, a black-roofed barn. Occasionally, they passed a small community with a few houses, each with its pile of logs stacked up against a wall, ready for the long winter. The village would have at least one, sometimes two, churches. Usually United Baptist and Anglican. Occasionally, Wesleyan.

Michelle felt as if she were visiting New England again. The rolling countryside, the brilliance of the trees, the pretty villages . . . all reminded her of the week she and Brian had spent in Connecticut, staying with an old school friend of his. But that was hardly surprising. After all, the border with Maine was only a few miles from here. Only a political boundary separated them.

Fortunately, it was a friendly separation now, considering she was married to an American. But she could imagine how difficult it must have been in those

days when brothers or fathers and sons were on op-
posing sides, both geographically as well as politically.
In the days of the American Revolution, families who
were separated would probably never see each other
again. When loyalists fled from the places that for
many of them had been their homes for all their lives,
mothers lost sons and sisters lost sisters, their conflicting beliefs slicing them apart.

"You're very quiet," Eleanor said, turning her head
to look at Michelle in the backseat of the comfortable Lexus.

"I was thinking about the people who came here
from the Revolution. What it must have been like
to leave your home and family and have to start all
over again."

Eleanor beamed at her. "Ah, yes. I must show you
the letters my great-great-grandmother wrote to her
sister in Boston. She kept a diary as well. It's absolutely fascinating."

"Don't get Grandmother started," said Eric, Norman's younger son, who was driving. "She'll never
stop."

"Don't you be rude, young man," Eleanor snapped,
but there was a twinkle in her eyes.

They passed a deserted farm, the house permanently shuttered, barn door swinging on one rusty
hinge, the neglected apple trees knee deep in weeds
and wildflowers.

"There are plenty more of those in the province,"
Eleanor said. "Young people pulling up roots and
moving away. Very sad."

"It's what young people have done for centuries,
Gran," Eric said.

"They shouldn't have to. That's why it's imperative
big companies like Tyler Foods or McCain's exist to
keep them employed locally."

Eric swiftly changed the subject to the latest news
about the Supreme Court ruling on native fishing
rights. Michelle didn't join in the conversation. She
sat, staring out the window, thinking about the past

thirty-six hours. She gathered all her memories, starting with Stewart meeting her at the airport, trying to assess all the new people she'd met, not only her various relatives but also Janet and Douglas Bradford—and Andrew.

She also wanted to make sense of her grandmother's strange behavior, her tales of dead dogs and cockroaches in the bed. At times, like now, Eleanor appeared so eminently in command of her mind, sharp, decisive, that it seemed impossible she could have such mental aberrations. Yet Michelle herself had seen her suddenly change into a woman with wide, fearful eyes, her head and hands shaking; a woman who herself questioned her own mental ability.

But slowly, as she mulled over the past two days, something told Michelle that it wasn't only Eleanor's behavior that was troubling her. Something else was going on within the family. There'd been vague undercurrents in Tyler House, muted voices behind closed doors, meaningful looks passing between people that shut her out.

And she was sure that her grandmother was anxious to tell her something, but kept holding back. Why had Eleanor written to invite her to visit at this particular time? And why had she pretended that it was Michelle who had written to her, rather than the other way around?

As the car sped farther and farther away from Fredericton, Michelle felt a creeping uneasiness. She hadn't been particularly at ease in Tyler House, but there, at least, she'd been near the town, able to get away from the house and its inhabitants when she wished. The Tyler cottage was remote, she'd been told, two miles from the small historic town of St. Andrews.

Two miles is nothing, she told herself. She could easily walk that—and would, if necessary. She kept fit with tai chi and often went running in Assiniboine Park. And she and Brian loved to cross-country ski in the winter.

So why the hell was she feeling so panicky? Perhaps

because she hadn't heard from Brian since she'd arrived. And now, unless he could get to her on her cell phone—which was unlikely—he wouldn't be able to reach her. The rule was no telephones of any kind at the cottage, Penny had told her, rolling her eyes. Recalling the debacle at the dinner table on Saturday, Michelle could understand why. But she'd hidden hers away at the bottom of her suitcase, just in case.

She wished that Andrew had been invited to the cottage. Not only for her sake but also for Eleanor's. What if she was taken ill there or had another one of her hallucinations? Michelle's heart began pounding in her chest. What on earth was wrong with her? It was so unlike her to worry herself sick about nebulous things. It must be her hormones going crazy.

Stop this right now! she told herself. *You're upsetting the baby.*

Crossing her arms over her stomach, she gazed out the window at the spectacular fall colors, taking slow, deep breaths for relaxation. Tomorrow she'd be doing this journey in reverse, en route to flying back home to the security of her own apartment and the regular routine of working in her own store. By tomorrow afternoon, she'd be on the plane from Fredericton, and her first visit to her mother's family would be over.

Chapter 17

———————

Prospect House, the Tylers' so-called cottage, was larger than the house in Fredericton. Built of sandstone quarried from the local beach, it stood high on a hill at the end of a private road lined with elm trees, its many windows on the south side overlooking Passamaquoddy Bay. Two smaller clapboard cottages stood in the grounds.

"We'll wait for the others to arrive before we go in," Eleanor said. She'd already given Michelle a brief description of the area as they were driving down the access road. "You have to drive down nearer the town to get closer to the sea. It's high tide at the moment. When the tide's low it's possible to drive out on the bar road across the mud flats to Ministers Island to visit Sir William Van Horne's summer home. But it's open only in the summer. You must come back next year so that we can go there together. And we'll also go to Campobello Island to see the Roosevelt estate."

Michelle had mixed feelings about the thought of a return visit, but she murmured something suitably optimistic to please her grandmother.

"Which room is Miss Tyler to sleep in?" Bob asked, once everyone had arrived and he was carrying in the bags.

"Miss Tyler will be in the main house," Eleanor replied firmly. "In the room next to mine."

Grace halted at the foot of the stone steps that led up to the porch and turned to stare at her mother.

"That is our room," she said flatly, her voice under tight control. "Larry and I have always slept there."

"You and Larry can take the larger room in South-cove cottage." Eleanor smiled sweetly at her. "That will give you all lots of privacy." She turned her back on Grace and slowly made her way up the steps and into the stone house.

Seeing Grace's expression, Michelle hurriedly followed her grandmother, but not before she heard Grace's daughter say, "I think we're all being usurped, don't you? Or should that be supplanted?"

"That's enough, Sophie," Larry said.

Let me out of here, Michelle said to herself. Thank heaven she was going home tomorrow.

The living room was dominated by a large picture window looking out over the gray, white-capped sea. Michelle shivered involuntarily.

"Yes, it is cold in here," Eleanor said. She sank into a maple rocking chair without taking off her coat. "Frank should have had the fire going by now. He's getting too old. That's why I bring Bob down with us. Put a match to the fire, would you, dear?"

Michelle went to the vast stone fireplace where the fire was already set with kindling and small logs. She took one of the long matches from the box on the hearth and lit the firestarter. It flared up and in a moment the logs were blazing and crackling.

"Seasoned apple," Eleanor said. "Burns well and gives off a lovely smell."

An elderly man came into the room. He was stooped and walked with a dragging gait, as if he were in constant pain.

"Ah, there you are, Frank. I was wondering where you'd got to. It's freezing in here."

"Sorry, Mrs. Tyler. I wasn't 'specting you this early. I was down at the store, getting you fresh milk."

"All right. You can go help the others bring in the food. Tell Nancy to put the steaks and fruit pies into the fridge immediately. And ask her to make us a cup of tea right away."

"Will do." He scurried away, like an awkward brown spider.

The room Michelle had been given was so obviously Grace's room that she felt guilty and embarrassed. As soon as she went in, she could smell Grace's scent, which seemed to have permeated the entire room. Curtains, carpet, even the bedspread, smelled of Grace. And when she opened the closet door, she found several pieces of clothing—a heavy sweater, an old pair of suede slippers, an old muskrat fur coat with a ripped sleeve—which were probably Grace's as well.

She was annoyed with Eleanor for having placed her in such an impossibly difficult position with her aunt. Throughout the afternoon, the tension built, with Grace making it very clear that she was furious with both her mother and Michelle. Larry tried to be the peacemaker. He was unfailingly pleasant with Michelle, even to the point of coming to talk to her at the start of their late afternoon meal of barbecued steak, chatting to her as she chose salad and accompaniments from the dozens of dishes laid out on the pinewood buffet. But however much he tried to draw Grace out of her angry mood, she continued to seethe, like a bomb threatening to explode any minute.

That evening, after the meal had been cleared away, the younger generation of Tylers decided to go to the Algonquin Hotel in St. Andrews. "Why don't you come with us?" Ramsey asked Michelle. "There's some good jazz music on there tonight."

"You must come," his wife, Penny, insisted. Dressed informally in khaki pants and a gold sweater, she had shed her uptight lawyer image. "It'll be fun."

Michelle hesitated. Eleanor had shown her the old Tudor-style red-roofed hotel when they'd driven through the little town. It had looked very inviting. She was growing to really like Ramsey and his wife and it would be great to get away from the tension in the house. On the other hand, an evening with Jamie and Sophie and her moronic boyfriend was definitely not her idea of fun. Particularly when she couldn't even have a drink. "Thanks." She smiled at Ramsey and Penny. "But I'm going to make it an early night. I have to get up at the crack of dawn tomorrow."

Stewart scrambled to his feet. "I'll come with you," he said to Ramsey.

"No, you won't," his wife snapped. "You've had quite enough to drink already. We're staying here."

He glared down at her. "Who asked you?"

"Sorry, Uncle Stewart," Ramsey interrupted before Anna could reply. "This is for the younger generation only. That's why I asked Michelle."

"Quite right," Eleanor said. "Sit down, Stewart, and stop acting the fool."

Michelle was startled to see the sudden dart of anger, almost hatred, Stewart directed at his mother. It lasted only a split second, then was gone, replaced with a shrug and a wry grin. But it made her think that something else lurked beneath the genial exterior he usually exhibited.

"How about bridge?" Grace suggested when the younger set had left. "There are eight of us. We could set up two tables."

"Sorry," Michelle said, "I don't play bridge."

"Of course she doesn't," Stewart said. "Bridge is for old people." He gave Michelle a hug, planting a whiskey-fumed kiss on her cheek, which did not endear her to his wife, who glowered at both of them.

"Then how about Trivial Pursuit?" Grace suggested.

"You can count me out," Norman said.

"Oh, don't be such a tight-assed bore," Grace said. "You don't like playing because you don't know all the answers." She gave a short bark of laughter. "They don't have a business category. But this time, none of us will know the answers, so that'll be fair."

"Why won't we?" Anna asked belligerently.

"Because I've brought the new pack of cards Ramsey gave us for Christmas." She produced them triumphantly from her leather bag. "See." She leaned over

Norman's shoulder and waved the pack of cards in front of him, almost hitting his face with them. "They've never been opened."

It occurred to Michelle that Stewart was not the only one here a little worse for drink. *My baby's turning me into a prude*, she thought. It was interesting to see how even someone as uptight as Grace could become unbuttoned after a few shots of alcohol.

Grace chose the two teams. Michelle, Lauren, Stewart, and Grace against Eleanor, Norman, Anna, and Larry.

"That way we have no married couples fighting because their spouses gave the wrong answer," Grace said.

"We wouldn't fight because of that, would we?" Larry asked, his hand slipping around his wife's trim waist.

Watching them, Michelle saw Grace's eyes glow as they rested on her husband. "We never fight," Grace said softly. "Especially about stupid things like a game."

He turned his head to kiss the back of her neck, his lips lingering there. The sexual tension between these two oddly matched people was tangible.

"Oh, get off it, you two," Anna said, frowning. "Let's get on with this stupid game if we're going to play it. Keep your personal games for the bedroom."

"My wife, the romantic," Stewart remarked to nobody in particular.

Eleanor shook her head and pursed her lips. Michelle wasn't sure if it was Anna or Grace and Larry who'd annoyed her. Probably all three. Michelle hastily set up the board, with Stewart's help, wondering what on earth had made him marry such a disagreeable woman. Where marriages were concerned there was no accounting for taste. Some of her own friends had warned her against marrying Brian, she remembered as she opened the new set of cards and put them in the boxes.

Perhaps they'd been right. She blinked rapidly,

swallowing against the sudden tightness in her throat. A bit late now to realize that, she told herself. "Okay," she announced brightly. "Everything's ready."

She'd noticed before that playing games was often a way of discovering surprising things about people. Brian had bought the *Men Are from Mars, Women Are from Venus* board game and playing it with their friends had been a revelation. Which was to be expected, she supposed, with a game like that. But this game of Trivial Pursuit also made her change some of her initial ideas about the people that constituted the only family she had.

She'd expected Norman to be quick, decisive, but he was slow and ponderous, mulling over every question he was given, until everyone groaned and Anna told him to "Get on with it, for Pete's sake." His wife Lauren, on the other hand, was a fountain of knowledge about all kinds of trivia and gave her answers quickly and with confidence. Every time she did so, Norman said, "That's my girl!" and gave her a proud smile.

"She's not on our team," Anna reminded him.

"Who cares?"

"We're very glad she's on ours," Grace said.

Michelle had the feeling Grace wasn't used to praising her sister-in-law. Grace herself was quick with her answers, but they were often the wrong ones. Whenever this happened she would swear and roll her eyes. "Trouble is I don't have time to read *Entertainment Weekly* from cover to cover."

Although Lauren knew this was directed at her, she let it ride, but Michelle, in her observer mode, saw the flicker of anger in those sapphire-blue eyes.

Larry was very laid-back with his answers, not really caring if he got them right, laughing at himself if he gave a particularly outrageous guess. Michelle felt that this probably reflected the man himself. Not too serious about life, able to laugh. He'd be a good antidote for Grace's intensity.

Stewart, on the other hand, became quite annoyed

when he didn't get the right answers, displaying a competitiveness Michelle had not expected in him. And Eleanor played the game with as much dignity as she could muster, until it became obvious to her—and to everyone else—that she was woefully incapable of answering more than one or two of the questions.

Gradually, her growing frustration threw a dark pall over the evening. The laughter became forced, the tension increased, until Eleanor suddenly leaned over and swept cards and board and player pieces from the table. She looked appalled at what she had done, as if some malevolent force had taken hold of her. Then she said, "I can't play this stupid game. It's too difficult."

The silence that had greeted her sudden action was broken by everyone talking or acting at once.

"I've had enough, too," Grace said. She bent to pick up the game board from the floor and Larry and Lauren helped to gather the cards that had been strewn across the carpet.

The others bustled around, Stewart asking if anyone wanted another drink, as he was going to have a Scotch. Michelle was the only one to go to Eleanor, who was sitting in her armchair staring at the floor, her head and hands trembling. Michelle slipped her arms around her, but Eleanor pushed her away with surprising force.

"I will not be treated like a senile old woman," she shouted.

Her face hot with embarrassment, Michelle stepped away. "She doesn't like being embraced in public," Stewart whispered to her.

"Sorry," Michelle whispered, speaking to no one in particular, but wishing she were a thousand miles from here.

"Don't worry about it. I'll get you a drink. How about a brandy?"

Michelle had turned Stewart down several times already. "Thanks. I'll have a Sprite."

"I think you need something stronger," Stewart insisted.

"I'm fine. Just a Sprite."

Eleanor's raised voice cut through the room. "You think you can all hoodwink me, but you can't. I know what you're up to."

"I think it's time you got some rest, Mother," Grace said. "It's been a long day."

Lauren hovered near her mother-in-law. "Why don't I put the kettle on and make you some hot chocolate?"

"Why don't you mind your own business?" Eleanor snapped.

"She's had too much to drink," Norman said quietly to his wife. "With her medication, she shouldn't have any alcohol. That's your fault, Stewart. You've been pushing booze on her all day."

Stewart opened his mouth, but Eleanor's voice stopped him. "That's enough, Norman. I said before and I'll repeat it now. I *will* not be treated like a senile old woman." Although Eleanor's head was shaking even more than usual, her gaze was fixed on her son. "If I want to have some wine, I will, and no one is going to stop me, least of all you, Norman Tyler. You, with your talk of mergers and selling Tyler Foods."

It was as if a sudden ice age had engulfed the room. Everyone froze. Grace was the first one to thaw. She grabbed Michelle's arm. "Excuse us, but this is a private matter."

Michelle felt herself being pushed in the direction of the door. She shook herself free and turned on her aunt. "I don't need to be shoved out of the room."

"Quite right," Eleanor said. "If anyone else dares to touch my granddaughter, they'll have to answer to me. Come here, Michelle."

Michelle walked across the room to stand beside her grandmother's chair. When she looked up she found herself the focal point for several pairs of eyes. Others, like Stewart and Lauren, looked away. Her legs were trembling and a wave of nausea threatened to sweep over her, but she forced it down. "Can I help?" she asked Eleanor, her voice low.

Eleanor grasped her hand. "You can stand by me while I tell these ungrateful children of mine exactly what I think of them. Just in case one of them tries to shoot me to keep me quiet."

"For God's sake, Mother," Norman muttered.

"Stop encouraging her," Grace said to Michelle. "She's a sick woman."

"Oh, yes, I agree with you there, Grace dear. That's what I am. A sick woman. But who has made me sick, that's what I'd like to know? Who has tried to prove me insane? Who killed my little Griffon and put those horrible things in my bed and dressed up to look like my beloved husband come from his grave to scare me to death?"

"Oh, Mother." Grace's eyes filled with tears. Shaking her head, she turned to Larry, who put his arm around her drawing her close.

"No one would want to hurt you, Mother Tyler," Lauren said in her little-girl voice.

"If that's the case, then you won't mind me explaining to my granddaughter exactly what's going on here, will you?"

Chapter 18

Norman stepped forward, breathing heavily. For a moment, Michelle was afraid he was going to attack his mother. He was a large man and she knew she hadn't much chance of being able to protect Eleanor from him, but she'd do her best. "You'd better keep quiet, Mother," he said. It was an unveiled threat.

"Or what? I'm not afraid of you, Norman Tyler. I used to change your dirty diapers, remember?"

His face flushed brick-red. "I don't want you to be afraid of me. I want you to remember what I told you, that the smallest hint of what we talked about in private could bring our company crashing down." His voice was low, but Michelle could tell he was exerting a great deal of effort to control it. "Is that what you want? To lose Tyler Foods completely to some maverick trader taking advantage of us? Or do you want us to take our rightful place in the twenty-first century and become even more successful than we are already?"

"I want Tyler Foods to remain a family firm, completely under the control of the Tyler family. But you and Grace and Stewart want to give it away to strangers, so that you can make your own personal fortunes."

The heated exchange about the family business swirled around Michelle. So electric were the anger and tension that the room felt as if it were the epicenter of a hurricane. Ever since she'd arrived at Tyler House she'd sensed that something strange was going on. Now, she was starting to understand what it was all about. Money! And lots of it, from the sound of it.

"Are you talking about a merger with another company?" she asked, seeking clarification.

Grace disengaged herself from her husband. "This is none of your business." Her glacial eyes narrowed to slits. "And you'd better keep your bloody mouth shut about it."

"I'm not likely to talk about my own family's business affairs in public, am I?" Michelle replied, her voice cold.

"You might, considering you have absolutely nothing to do with the family business."

"Well," said Eleanor, "I'm planning to do something about that as soon as possible."

Michelle felt a spasm of fear in the pit of her stomach. Eleanor's provocative statement had acted on the room like a hail of bullets.

"That's up to you, Mother," Stewart said, seeking to relieve the tension. He gulped down the liquor in his glass and, reaching for the bottle of Glenlivet that he'd set on a nearby table, filled his glass again. He held the bottle up to the others, but no one accepted his offer.

Michelle took a deep breath. "I'd like to ask one question. Then I'll leave the room, if you promise to let Eleanor rest. Is there a deadline for this merger?"

"They have twelve days before they must come to a decision," Eleanor said, before the others had a chance to reply. "The deadline is October twenty-second."

Now the spasm of fear moved up to squeeze Michelle's heart. "That soon," she said, her breath catching in her throat.

"Exactly. That soon." Eleanor caught and gripped her hand.

It all made horrible sense. They were pressuring Eleanor to agree to the merger. She was probably the

majority shareholder. Was it possible that her grandmother wasn't going senile? That she was being perse-
cuted to force her to vote for the merger?

Or even to make her appear mentally incapable?

Norman sat down on the leather chair, which emit-
ted a whoosh as his body forced air from the cushion.
His heavy sigh echoed the sound. "So now you know."

He didn't address her directly, but Michelle knew
he was talking to her. She faced them, speaking to all
of them at once. "Are you trying to force my grandmother to agree to the merger?"

Grace shook her head. "We're not forcing her in
any way. She's just being as stubborn and close-minded
as she's always been. Throughout our lives she's always put the business first. We always came second."

"Michelle doesn't want to know this, sweetheart,"
Larry said.

"She seems to want to know everything else, why
not let her know what her darling grandmother is
really like?"

Stewart glared at her. "Cut it out, Grace. This isn't
the time or the place."

"Then what is?" Grace marched over to the table
by Stewart and poured the single malt into her glass.
She sank onto the sofa again, the liquor slopping over
onto her tan suede pants. "Michelle wants to get to
know the family. Here we all are, ready to tell her
about us. Well, my dear niece, let me tell you that
contrary to our mother's paeans of praise about him,
your grandfather was an absolute bastard."

"Grace!"

Grace ignored her mother's interjection. "He
abused us all. Not sexual abuse, thank God, although
I wouldn't have put it past him to try. But physical
and, especially, mental abuse. We could never do anything right in his eyes. He never gave us praise for
anything. We all got thrashed for the smallest things.
'Builds character,' he used to tell us when he undid
the clasp on his leather belt."

Michelle was appalled. She sank onto the arm of

the chair nearest to her, her legs too unsteady to bear her up any longer.

"Only one of us escaped his sadism. Can you guess who that was? Your pretty little mother . . . the darling of their hearts. Carolyn not only escaped the beatings, but she got praised for everything she did, however minor and unimportant. 'What a lovely picture, Carolyn! Aren't you a wonderful little dancer, sweetie!' " Grace's bitterness was like acid pouring from her mouth.

"Shut up, Grace," Norman said beneath his breath. His head hung low, he turned away from his wife. Lauren's eyes were like blue saucers, wide with shock.

Grace was on a roll now. "Poor old Norman got the worst of it, being the firstborn. I didn't know why my big brother used to cry himself to sleep until I was old enough to start getting my father's brand of discipline myself."

Michelle was speechless. She didn't want to be here, listening to Grace's appalling story of her father's cruelty. But she knew it must be true. Norman's and Stewart's silence spoke more loudly than words. And when she glanced at Stewart, she saw that he was staring out the window into the darkness beyond, his mouth trembling.

She didn't dare look at Eleanor.

"So now you know about us, Michelle," Grace said after a long pause. "The laugh is that the only one who went unscathed was also the one who managed to get away: your mother." She gave a sharp crack of laughter. "Carolyn always did have the best luck."

Michelle found her voice at last. "I don't think getting pregnant and having to leave home before you've finished school could be called being lucky, do you?"

"It got her away from this family, didn't it?"

Someone in the room was weeping softly. Michelle turned and saw that Eleanor was slumped over in her chair, her face hidden in her hand. She started up, but Grace was there first. "Come on, Mother," she said in a brusque voice. "Let's get you to bed. This has been a tough night for you, hasn't it?" She put Eleanor's cane into her hand and helped her up from the chair.

"Can I help?" Michelle asked.

"I can manage." Grace hesitated. She gave Michelle an unpleasant smile. "See what happens when you interfere in something that doesn't concern you? Sometimes truth will out . . . especially when Stewart keeps pouring."

Stewart was blowing his nose loudly. "Don't blame me. You never could drink, Gracie. It always made you a blabbermouth."

Norman got up from the leather chair. "I'm going out for some fresh air," he muttered.

"I'll come with you, honey," Lauren said, her face anxious.

"I'd rather be alone, thanks."

She looked crestfallen at his rejection. "I'll go make some hot chocolate."

Only Anna and Stewart remained in the room with Michelle. "You okay?" Stewart asked her. "You look a bit shell-shocked."

"I feel it."

He gave a harsh laugh. "Not to worry. Just an average Tyler family gathering."

"Let's go back to the cottage," Anna said, her hand on Stewart's arm. "You should take it easy. Your color isn't good."

Michelle was surprised. The last person she'd expected to be compassionate was Anna.

"Anna was a nurse," Stewart explained. "She's my good angel."

Michelle felt even more bewildered. Each time she thought she had a fix on one of her relatives, they changed, like chameleons. "Can I ask you one question before you go?"

"Ask away. As long as it's not about this bloody merger. I won't discuss it." He frowned. "And you'd better not talk about it outside these walls or else . . ."

Another threat. Michelle felt like telling him to back

off, but she realized that everyone was in a state of heightened tension tonight. "Why didn't your mother intervene to stop your father hurting her children?"

"Good question," Stewart said curtly. "Why don't you ask her? I wouldn't mind hearing her answer myself."

Anna took his arm. "Come on, Stew. Let's get you to bed."

"Good idea." Stewart gave a mirthless laugh. "Cheer up, little niece. We're not as bad as we seem." He picked up the bottle of Glenlivet and then bent to kiss Michelle's cheek. "Nighty-night."

"Good night."

Anna peered at Michelle. "Will you be okay? You look very pale."

"Not surprising, is it? I'll be fine. As soon as I've said goodnight to Lauren, I'm going to bed."

"Good idea. Night."

Several minutes after Anna and Stewart left, Lauren came into the room with a tray of mugs filled with steaming hot chocolate. "Oh," she said when she saw only Michelle. "I made enough for us all." She set the heavy tray down on the coffee table.

"I'll have one. Just what I need," Michelle lied. "And I'll take one up to Eleanor."

Lauren hesitated, then said, "May I give you a little piece of advice. Leave Eleanor to Grace. She knows how to deal with her when she's upset."

Although Michelle seriously doubted that, she wanted to avoid any further trouble. She—and her baby—had had enough trauma for one night.

Lauren was peering out the window. "You haven't seen Norman, have you?" she asked.

"No. He probably needs time to himself. He must be pretty upset."

Lauren nodded. Her eyes filled with tears. "I just wish he wouldn't shut me out that way."

"Men have a way of doing that, don't they?" Michelle hesitated and then went to Lauren and gave her a little hug. "He'll be fine."

Lauren sniffed. "I know he will. Thanks, Michelle." The sound of a car engine came from beyond the house. Lauren peered out the window. "The kids must be back."

"Already?"

Lauren smiled. "Things close down early in St. Andrew's."

"I'm getting out of here. Thanks for the hot chocolate." Michelle went to the foot of the stairs and then turned back. "Did you know about this merger?"

"Oh, yes. But Norman warned me not to talk about it. He said that it would not only be good for the firm itself, but it would also make us all a heap of money. But if anyone leaked the story before the deal was signed, we could lose just about everything."

"But you need Eleanor to agree to it, right?"

"That's right. She's the only one who doesn't want the merger. They've all been working on her: Norman, Grace, Larry, even Stewart."

Bet they have, thought Michelle. As she mounted the short flight of stairs her mind was racing. There was obviously a great deal at stake for Eleanor's family in this merger. A powerful reason to terrorize an old woman into submission. Well, she thought as she walked down the corridor to her room, she was determined not to let them get away with it. Thank God she'd disobeyed the order not to bring any cell phones to the cottage.

First, she intended to call Brian's network in Minneapolis to find out if they'd heard from him. Then she'd call Andrew. If anyone could help her with Eleanor, it was Andrew.

Finding the bathroom free, she went in. When she'd finished, she returned to her bedroom, quietly closing the door. She was about to lock it, but found there was no key in the old-fashioned lock. The thought that anyone could slip into her room at any time, whether she was there or not, disturbed her. She looked around the room. If she dragged the chest across the floor to bar the door, Grace would hear her from Eleanor's room next door and probably demand to know what she was doing. She'd have to try wedging the ladder-backed chair under the doorknob.

She lifted the chair and slid the back beneath the knob. Twice, it slipped out, the second time crashing onto the floor. She held her breath for a moment, sure that Grace would knock on the door, asking what was going on in there . . . but she didn't.

The third time, once she'd added extra ballast with her suitcase, it worked. It wouldn't hold very well, but at least she'd be warned if someone came into her room.

She zipped open the case, careful not to disturb the chair. She'd wrapped the cell phone in her brushed cotton pajamas at the bottom of the case. Ah, there they were, on the left side, beneath her runners. No wonder she couldn't find them. She could have sworn she'd packed them on the other side.

As she was dragging out the pajamas, the closet door creaked behind her. She spun around. "Looking for this?" a black-clad figure said in a gruff voice through the mouthpiece of the ski mask that covered his face. He held up her cell phone, then threw it on the floor and stamped on it. Michelle opened her mouth to scream just as the light went out and a stunning blow to the side of her head sent her spinning into darkness.

Chapter 19

She was scuba diving in Palau with Brian, pink coral and bright fish exploding like fireworks into vivid colors around her. Then, all at once, she was on the ocean floor, darkness closing in, tons of water pressing down on her. Gasping for air, she watched helplessly as the oxygen tank slowly floated away from her. When she tried to scream for Brian, water filled her mouth and no sound came out.

Now she was utterly alone, fighting for breath in the inky-black water. Brian had disappeared. She struggled to reach the surface, but her hands and feet were bound. Panic surged as she fought to fill her lungs with air. *Please God, let this be a dream*, she prayed. But somehow she knew it was not.

As if someone had opened a drain and let it out, the water suddenly sucked away from her. She lay there, dry, but still struggling to breathe, like a beached whale.

She was lying on something hard. It was pitch-dark. She struggled to sit up, then groaned as a wave of nausea eddied over her. *You must not throw up!* she told herself. She tried to open her mouth, but her lips were glued together. She was gagged with some sort of tape.

Panic surged again as she fought to breathe. Then she suddenly remembered. The baby! She must calm herself for the baby's sake. Her heart banging hard in her chest, she took deep breaths through her nose.

Again she tried to move, but her hands and feet were bound. She struggled to right herself and managed to get into a sitting position. Something horribly furry brushed against her face. She let out a stifled scream, but the furry thing just hung there, lifeless. Her horror faded as she caught a whiff of scent. Grace's scent. She must be in the clothes closet with Grace's fur coat. In fact, now that her senses were slowly returning, she realized that there were other clothes hanging around her.

She edged her way back, until her spine touched the rear of the closet. Trying to keep as calm as possible, she continued to draw in slow, deep breaths through her nose, fighting to quiet her fast-pounding heart. Whatever was happening to her, she must think of the baby first.

As she breathed, she tried to recall what had happened. There had been that extraordinary scene, when Grace had poured out all that stuff about her father. Then Grace had taken a weeping Eleanor to bed. What then? It was difficult to remember with her head pounding like a jackhammer. Oh, yes, Lauren. She'd talked with Lauren, who'd told her something more about the merger. She couldn't remember exactly what it was, but she was sure it would come back to her. While they were talking Ramsey, Penny, and the others had returned from St. Andrews. Or at least she'd heard their 4x4 outside. Not wanting to encounter any more Tylers, she'd scurried off to her room, looked for her cell phone—which wasn't there—and then turned to see a tall figure clad completely in black.

That was all. She guessed from the pounding headache that she must have been knocked unconscious. But who had done this to her? She frowned, striving to recall if the black figure had moved toward her. All she could remember was that the person had stomped on her phone. Had someone else come into the room and hit her from behind? If so, there were at least two of them involved. But who were they and why had they attacked her?

More importantly, what did they intend to do to her? Perhaps they were burglars who'd been caught off guard when the family had arrived at the house, and had hidden in her room? That would make sense. If so, it wouldn't be long before some member of the family found her. But, deep down, she felt that there was something far more menacing than a break-in going on.

Was she going to be kidnapped, held for ransom? What a stupid idea! After all, she and Brian weren't that well off, were they? Fear gripped her. She and Brian might not have that much money, but the Tyler family was extremely wealthy.

If they were hoping for a huge ransom payout, they'd picked the wrong Tyler. Although her grandmother would care, she doubted that the Tyler family in general would give a damn if she lived or died.

Michelle forced away to the back of her mind the most plausible explanation for her assault. The most plausible—and the most terrifying. So terrifying that she didn't feel strong enough to deal with it right now.

How to escape? That was the most important question at present. If, as Michelle suspected, she was in the closet in her room, then there was a good chance that Eleanor, at least, would be able to hear her if she could make some sort of noise. But what could she do with her hands and feet bound and her mouth gagged?

She straightened her spine and began rocking back and forth, hoping it would make the wooden boards in the old closet squeak, but all she could hear was the blood pounding in her ears with the added exertion. She flung her head hard against the wooden panel, but that made her feel so nauseated she gave it up after the first try.

Footsteps . . . whispers outside the closet door. Her body tensed as she waited. The door opened with a squeak of hinges. Although the room was dark, she thought she could see the outline of the small bow window. Which would confirm that she was still in her bedroom in the Tyler cottage. A figure bent toward her, its face masked, and hauled her out. *Please, please, let me go,* she begged. But her words became unintelligible grunts behind the evil-smelling sticky tape over her mouth.

A woolen hood was dragged over her head and face, cutting off her vision. It felt like a ski mask.

Panic struck as she realized that now her nose would be covered, as well as her mouth. How would she be able to breathe? She struggled and yelled, but the yells came out as grunts.

Maybe they didn't even care if she couldn't breathe. If they *were* kidnappers, she'd be easier to deal with as a dead body, wouldn't she? *Oh, God, I can't breathe. My baby will die.* Tears flowed from her eyes, wetting the woolen hood.

She heard a low murmur and then, to her immense relief, she was turned around so that her back was to them—she sensed that there were two of them—and the woolen hood was dragged off. A scarf was bound around her eyes instead.

A hard object jabbed into her side. "That's a gun," one of them growled. A man's voice, guttural, harsh. "Make a sound and you'll be sorry." The gun jabbed hard. "Understand?"

She nodded.

"Not a sound."

She was picked up and flung over a shoulder like a sack of potatoes. They were going to carry her down the stairs. If only she could shout, even with the tape binding her mouth someone might hear her, but with the gun pressed hard into her side, she didn't dare make a sound.

Recently, she'd read a mystery about a woman who was kidnapped. To Michelle, the character in the book had seemed ridiculously calm about the whole episode, trying to register everything—sounds, movements, smells—as it happened. But now she understood. You had to do something to keep yourself from going totally berserk and getting yourself killed. Or, at the very least, injured. And getting injured, Michelle knew only too well, meant hurting her baby.

So she, too, began making mental notes about everything as it happened. The sound of muted footsteps and creak of floorboards in the carpeted hall. Yes, there were definitely two people involved. The opening of what she imagined was the back door and the rush of cold air about her head. It felt so good after the confines of the closet that she breathed it in deeply through her nose, able to distinguish the salty tang of the ocean. Concentrating hard, she realized, had helped to heighten her senses. At least, the two senses she had left: hearing and smell.

She counted the paces as she was carried. Twenty-seven. Then a car door was opened and she was laid on the backseat, thank God. She let out a sigh of relief. All the time she'd been counting the paces, she'd been fighting her fear that they'd put her in the trunk of a car.

It was cold in the car. She could smell cigarette smoke. The two men moved away, but not far. She could still hear their murmuring voices. She seemed to have been lying there for ages. She started counting in sections of sixty, twitching the muscles in her increasingly numb fingers, to count off the minutes. About six long minutes passed, but it seemed like an hour to her. Then, with a muttered "Shit!" someone jumped into the car, revved up the engine, and the car moved off, fast, bumping over the private road.

She wondered what time it was. Did she still have her watch on? Not that it would do her much good at present, but she hated not knowing what time it was. Certainly, it was still nighttime or before dawn. That, at least, she knew.

She smelled fresh cigarette smoke. Oh, God! That was all she needed. Then a blast of music shocked her. It sounded like some kind of techno-pop group. Despite his choice of music, the sound system was a good one. It was probably a CD player. And despite

the fairly rough road and the fast driver, the car's
suspension seemed to absorb most of the worst bumps.
So, a modern and probably expensive car. But good
as it was, Michelle began to wonder how long she
could manage to cope with the smoke, the gag, the
pounding headache, and the incipient nausea.

Don't think about it, she told herself. Thinking
about it just made it worse. If only she could have
something to eat. And what if she needed to go to
the bathroom?

Don't think about it, she repeated. *Think about the
baby.*

In her mind, she began to speak to the new life that
had only just began to blossom within her. *We're going
to be fine,* she assured her baby. *We're going to get
out of this together, without any harm. And your daddy
is going to be so thrilled when he hears about you. I'll
bet the first thing he does is call his mom and dad and
tell them.*

We're going to be fine, she repeated like a mantra.
We're going to be fine.

After a short drive down the private road, the car
moved onto a main road. Immediately, its speed accelerated. For a long time Michelle only dozed, waking
frequently to find the car still speeding along and the
music blaring. Then, exhausted, she fell into a sound
sleep.

She awoke with a start when the car came to a
sudden halt. She sensed that they'd traveled a long
way. Her mouth was parched and she was so stiff she
could barely stretch out her legs. The driver got out.
Her heart started racing again. What now? She heard
him open the trunk and take out something that rus-
tled. A bag of some kind. It sounded as if it could be
some kind of garbage bag. The trunk slammed and
then she heard soft footsteps, moving away. Oh, God
was she to be abandoned here, trussed like the
Thanksgiving turkey, to starve and rot?

A door somewhere creaked open and then slammed

shut again. He was coming back. Michelle didn't know whether she should be relieved or not. She waited for him to say something, but he opened the trunk again and lifted something else out. Something heavy, from the grunt he made as he lifted it.

The third time he returned, he opened the rear door of the car, reached in, and grabbed her feet. She started to struggle against him, but then felt the tape binding her feet being cut away. When he'd finished, he dragged her out and set her on her feet. Her knees were so stiff, she almost fell.

"What the hell's wrong with you?" he growled.

The voice was disguised, but it didn't sound like the other voice she'd heard in her room at Prospect House. And when he grabbed hold of her to help her walk, she gauged that he was shorter than the other man. Again, she breathed in the air. This time she smelled wet earth and felt the cushion of fallen leaves beneath her feet. Rain fell steadily on her, soaking her hair and face as she was guided none too gently from the car. The stillness was broken only by the steady drip of rain, the snapping of twigs and the sudden raucous cawing of a crow, all of which told her she was in a rural wood or perhaps a forest. Were there forests in New Brunswick? There were national parks, but she doubted that a kidnapper would drive his victim into a national park. *If* she was being kidnapped.

The man halted. Although she couldn't actually see anything behind the tightly bound scarf, she sensed that they'd stopped in front of a building of some kind. She heard what sounded like the scrape of metal and then a door creaking open. The same sound she'd heard before. A hand pressed against her back and shoved her across the threshold. She stumbled and almost fell over the step, but was saved by the guy grabbing her. His hand tight on her arm, he half led, half dragged her inside.

To her amazement, she felt his fingers fumble with the scarf . . . then it was gone and she was able to see. She blinked, the sudden return of her sight such a surprise that at first she couldn't distinguish anything in the darkness of the unlit room. Then, by what appeared to be a flashlight's beam, she saw that she was in the small room of a cabin built of logs.

Heat pounding, she swung around to confront her captor. He was of medium height and build, but that was all she could tell, because his face and head were covered with a black ski mask with slits for the eyes and mouth.

"I need to go to the bathroom," she said, behind the gag, but of course he couldn't understand. She started to walk away from him, but he grabbed her and swung her back.

"Where the hell do you think you're going?" He had an accent of some kind. She couldn't make out if the accent was genuine or if he was using it to disguise his voice.

She jerked her head to indicate that she needed to go somewhere.

"Oh, you need to take a leak." He laughed. His eyes glittered behind the mask. An icy chill ran over her as she realized how much at this man's mercy she was. He could do anything he liked to her. The profound silence outside had told her that no one else was nearby to help her. She was on her own. She and her baby. And, for her baby's sake, she couldn't take any physical risks. No attacking this guy by trying some of the basic self-defense moves she'd learned in school. Much as she'd like to kick-box him where it hurt or attack him unexpectedly with some kung fu move—she knew she couldn't risk getting injured, not unless she was sure she had no other choice. She would have to rely on her wits alone to get her out of this crisis.

Chapter 20

⌒

The man went to the oil lamp on the wooden packing case that served as a table and lit the wick with his lighter. The flame guttered and died down, and then took, shedding a pool of dim light in the center of the small room. He replaced the glass shade and then unzipped his parka, to reveal a leather sheath hanging from his belt. He dragged what looked like a hunting knife from it and came toward Michelle. She shrank back from him in terror. He laughed and then spun her around, so that he was behind her.

Tensed and poised to duck out of his way, she waited for his next move. Her racing heartbeat settled a little when he began to slice the tape from her hands. When he'd finished, she turned to face him and brought her hands forward to try to massage some feeling into them, but he grabbed her right hand back again. "One hand only," he growled. From his pocket he took a roll of brown duct tape and turned her around again. Michelle felt his hand on her spine and tensed at his touch. He lifted her sweater so that she could feel the cold air on her bare skin. Dragging her right arm behind her, he bound her hand to her back, winding the tape round and round her bare waist.

When he'd finished, he shoved her in front of him toward the front door. Opening it, he thrust her outside ahead of him, and then followed her, letting the door spring shut behind him. For a moment she wondered what he was going to do with her. Then, when her eyes adjusted to the darkness, she saw the pathway leading to the small outhouse.

To her immense relief, he didn't insist on standing over her, but shoved her inside the stinking outhouse—which smelled as if it had never been cleaned—and then stood guard outside until she'd finished.

When she was twelve, she'd broken her right wrist in a skating accident. She'd had to use her left hand for everything. Determined to make the best of a frustrating few weeks she'd worked on becoming ambidextrous. Now she wished she'd worked even harder at it. It was a tough job managing her clothing with only one hand, but she did what she could. When she was finished, she marched out, head in the air, determined not to show him any sign of embarrassment.

He moved like a fairly young man, perhaps her age or younger. He pushed her ahead of him down the path and back inside the cabin, the storm door crashing behind him again.

Her head was swimming from hunger. There'd been a moment in the outhouse when she was sure she was going to throw up. She *had* to get this tape off, or she might choke to death. "I'm hungry," she mumbled behind the tape.

"What?"

With her left hand, she made signs of spooning something into her mouth and drinking from a glass.

All she could see were those eyes gleaming in the flickering light, like the eyes of a feral animal in a primeval forest. He hesitated, then said, "I take the tape off, you eat and drink only, not talk." He spoke in the same bass, guttural voice as before, still with an accent. She wasn't sure what sort of accent. She knew that Maritimers spoke with quite a strong and distinctive accent, and Newfies from Newfoundland sounded Irish, but the man's voice kept changing, which made it hard to pinpoint his origin. "Okay?"

She nodded. "Okay."

"No questions. Nothing. Or else . . ." His hand went to the place where she knew the knife was. He pulled it out, but she backed away, shaking her head. He came at her, holding the knife out.

"No," she screamed. "Not the knife." Her lips were raw from rubbing against the vile-tasting tape.

He shrugged. "Okay. No food." He turned away, sliding the knife back into its sheath.

Then she remembered she had nail scissors in her bag.

But she didn't have her bag . . . or did she? She peered around the room, trying to find the plastic bag he'd carried to the cabin.

"What?"

She caught sight of the large green garbage bag by the door. She pointed to it and then to herself. "Mine?" she tried to say.

"Oh, yeah." He went to the bag and ripped it open. Then, right there by the door, he turned the bag upside down so that everything in it rolled onto the floor. Her handbag came out first, then all the things she'd left on surfaces or in drawers at the Tyler cottage—hairbrush, cosmetic bags, her books and perfume bottle—all tumbled onto the floor. The last thing to fall out was her coat and boots. Whoever had packed this bag wanted to make sure there was nothing left of hers at the Tylers' place.

Nothing except her suitcase and small carry-on bag. Where were they? she wondered. But she wouldn't worry about that now. The sight of her own things gave her a surge of hope. Killers or rapists didn't bother to bring their victims' personal belongings, did they? She went to the door to pick up her bag and scrabbled in it, producing the pair of nail scissors. His eyes watched her, right hand on the hilt of his knife, like a native warrior in an old cowboy B movie.

"Go ahead."

What the hell did he mean, *go ahead*? Did he mean cut the tape off her own mouth with her left hand in this dim light without a mirror with nail scissors; blunt ones, too, she remembered from the last time she'd used them.

She fumbled in her bag again, this time bringing out a tiny mirror, which she set up on a stack of old magazines that smelled of damp and mildew, like the rest of the cabin. The lamp on the table gave off very little light, but it would have to do. Picking and snicking at the tape—and, occasionally, her face—she managed to loosen and then cut through the tape. Then, flinching, she peeled it off centimeter by painful centimeter until only shreds were left hanging, caught in her hair at the nape of her neck. Her face burned, as if it had been flayed.

She ran her tongue over her lips to moisten them and then gagged as her tongue licked up the gum from the tape. She kept opening and shutting her mouth, trying to ease the pain and tension in her jaw. "Could I have a drink?"

His hand went to his knife. "No talking, *comprende*?"

"Sorry." When he merely stared at her, she resorted to sign language again, imitating drinking from a glass.

"Yeah, yeah," he said. He moved to the other end of the room, then turned and jerked his head at her. "You, too." He wasn't going to let her out of his sight.

There was a galley kitchen behind a plywood wall. It consisted of a filthy sink, filled with used paper cups and other debris. She began to wonder if this place was some sort of hunting or logging lodge. Somewhere basic for people to shelter when they were on the move. On the grimy countertop was a large picnic cooler, the kind you filled with ice to keep things cool. Not that that was necessary. She sincerely hoped there was some sort of heating in this place.

He offered her a can of Coke.

"I need something hot. It's freezing in here." He shrugged and chucked the can back into the bag. "Maybe some tea?" she suggested.

His eyes gleamed with amusement behind the mask. But, to her surprise, he dragged out a spirit stove from a cupboard beneath the sink and lit it. Then he drew off some water from the large water container in a corner of the kitchen, filled a battered metal kettle, and put it on to heat.

Within a few minutes, Michelle found herself sipping hot tea with long-life milk, and eating a peanut butter sandwich. Nothing before had ever tasted quite as good.

"Thanks," she said. She hesitated. "I don't know your name." Didn't they say you should try to befriend your captors if you were kidnapped? That way, it made it tougher for them to harm you?

His response was a contemptuous grunt.

"Sorry. I thought it might be best to call you something." She gave a nervous laugh. "Pick a name, any name," she said, using the inflection of the television cartoon character.

He hesitated. "Dave," he said, at last.

"Okay, Dave. What am I doing here? Have I been kidnapped—or what?"

Their brief moment of rapport instantly evaporated. His hand went to the knife on his belt. "No questions," he shouted. "Or I tape your mouth shut again."

"Okay, okay. I'm sorry." She couldn't bear the thought of having that tape over her mouth again. She'd just have to try to pick up clues from what he did, but she sensed that he wasn't going to hurt her unless she did something stupid. For now she was so exhausted she felt she could just fall asleep sitting on the smelly old couch. The thought that it was probably a favorite nesting place for mice made her squirm.

"I'm really tired," she told Dave. "Is there a bed here?"

"You're sitting on it." He jerked his head at the couch.

"That's it?"

"Yup. I'll get the blankets from the car. Come outside where I can see you while I get them."

"Do I have to? I'm so cold." She wasn't putting it

on. Her teeth were chattering with the cold, raw dampness of the early morning.

She walked to the door. Dave put the spring latch on, so that the door would stay open, and allowed her to wait in the doorway. "Don't move from there," he warned her.

First, he carried in an armful of blankets and pillows and then made more trips to and from the car to bring in a couple of boxes of groceries and provisions. Finally, he brought in Michelle's carry-on bag and suitcase. She felt a rush of relief to know she'd have some more clothing with her, but she couldn't help, asking, "Am I here for a long stay?"

His eyes gave her a dark look, but he said nothing. He threw two of the pillows and a couple of blankets onto the couch beside her and then carried the grocery boxes into the kitchen.

The pillows were springy, with pristine white cotton covers. The blankets were dark green, made of a hundred percent wool, Michelle noticed from the label. She pressed her face against one of them. It was soft and smelled deliciously clean and fresh. She found the smell supremely comforting. Wrapping herself in the blanket, she stretched out on the couch, trying to ignore the broken springs digging into her side.

From the kitchen came the slamming of cupboard doors and occasional footsteps, but slowly, as the early morning light began creeping into the room, the sounds receded . . . and Michelle slept.

Chapter 21

When Michelle didn't come down for breakfast, Grace offered to go upstairs and wake her.

"Yes, please do," Eleanor said with icy calm. "It's almost nine o'clock. She told me yesterday she'd have to leave here by nine at the very latest, to get back to Fredericton in time to catch her plane to Winnipeg."

"Why on earth she couldn't stay one more day, and drive back with us this evening, I don't know," Grace said.

"I agree," Norman said. "Hard to believe one little gift store can't do without her for just one extra day."

Eleanor's hands twisted together in her lap. "Bob has been waiting for half an hour in case she wanted to leave a little earlier. And she's not even down yet. She'll have to travel without any breakfast."

She'd tried to maintain her composure ever since she'd woken early this morning and felt despair, like a gray pall, roll over her. The thought of losing her granddaughter, just when she'd found her, was unbearable.

Michelle hadn't come near her last night. Eleanor had been tempted to go to Michelle's room when she'd heard her come upstairs, but a strange lethargy had crept over her and she'd fallen asleep almost the moment she'd lain down.

At least here, in Prospect House, she could sleep without the memory of Griffon lying on her bed to haunt her.

But her sleep had not refreshed her at all. When Lauren had brought up her morning tea, Eleanor had asked her if Michelle was up, but Lauren said she hadn't seen her yet. Eleanor waited and waited for Michelle to come to her, but she never came. It was obvious that her granddaughter had been so disgusted by that terrible scene with Grace last night she hadn't wanted to see anyone this morning. And Eleanor was far too proud to knock on Michelle's door herself. Oh, no, the first move must come from Michelle.

She could hear Grace's footsteps slowly descending the stairs. When she came into the breakfast room she was holding a piece of paper in her hand. "Has anyone actually seen Michelle this morning?"

Only Norman, Lauren, and Larry were in the room with Eleanor. None of them had seen her.

"I should ask the kids."

"Most of them are still sleeping," Larry said, spreading some of Janet's homemade marmalade on his toast. "From the sound of it, they were all having a great time last night."

"Well, she's gone," Grace announced.

"Who?" Norman demanded.

"Michelle. She left this note on her bed."

"How can she have gone?" Norman said. "She didn't have a car."

"She called a taxi with her cell phone. All her things are gone from the room. She's gone, all right. Took a taxi back to Fredericton."

Eleanor felt as if all the blood was draining from her face. "Read her note to me, please."

Grace heaved a sigh and took her glasses from her pocket. " 'Sorry to leave without saying good-bye,' " she read. " 'I think it's best this way. Now I understand why my mother told me not to get in touch with her family. I've ordered a taxi to drive me to Fredericton. (Sorry I broke the rule about cell phones.) All the best, Michelle.' "

"Let me see." Eleanor held out her hand, trying to

still its tremor. Grace handed her the note. "How did she type it? I never heard a typewriter."

"I expect she has a laptop and portable printer, Mother," Norman said, seeming to anticipate the question. "She's a businesswoman, after all. I always take mine with me wherever I go."

"We're not all workaholics," Grace said, acid in her voice. "But you're right, it's a generic electronic printout."

Eleanor looked down at the message, its coldness accentuated by the perfection of the black letters on the crisp white paper. "She didn't even sign it by hand. Just printed her name."

"I feel that I'm to blame for this," Grace said. "I'm sorry, Mother. I had too much to drink last night. I guess Michelle decided we weren't the family she wanted, however well off we were." Grace bent to kiss her mother's cheek.

Eleanor put her hand up to Grace's cheek and pressed it. Then she turned away, slipping the note into her pocket. "Well, she's gone," she said after a minute or so had passed. "And that's that. What's on the cards today?"

"We've got a surprise for you," Grace said after exchanging glances with Larry and Norman. "We've booked a table for the Thanksgiving brunch at the Algonquin."

"But we've already had breakfast," Eleanor protested.

"We booked it for noon. We should all be ready to eat again by then."

Eleanor felt a pang close to her heart. "Michelle would really have enjoyed that. She didn't even see inside the hotel."

"That's not our fault, is it?" Norman said impatiently. "It was Michelle herself who chose to leave early without even saying good-bye."

Eleanor nodded. Disappointment was weighing her down, but she didn't want to show her children how much Michelle's sudden departure had affected her.

"I think I'll go back to my room for a while. Will you help me, Grace, dear?"

"Of course."

They all hovered anxiously over her as Grace helped her up from the dining-room chair. "No need to crowd about me," she said.

What was the line in that Monty Python film with the knights and the rabbits, which always made her laugh out loud? *I'm not dead yet.* That's what she wanted to shout at them all. *I'm not dead yet, you know.* But somehow, today, she just could not summon up enough energy to do even that.

"I'm fine now," she said to Grace when they reached the top of the stairs. "I can manage."

"I'll see you into your room."

"No. I can manage by myself, thank you." Eleanor stood with her hand on the doorknob. "I think I'll lie down for a little while."

"Good idea. Especially if we're going out for brunch."

"I'm not sure I want to."

"Of course you do. It will cheer you up."

How she hated it when Grace went into her rallying modes! "I'll see how I feel when I wake up. Make sure you call me by eleven." Eleanor turned the handle and opened her door. "That's what we should have done."

Grace looked startled. "What?"

"We should have arranged for someone to call Michelle this morning."

Grace gave a little sigh. "She said yesterday that she had an alarm clock. Stop worrying about her, Mother. She'll be fine."

"I hope so. Did she leave anything in her room?"

"I haven't had time to check. All I saw was the note."

"I hope she didn't forget anything."

"If she did, we can send it on to her. Come on. Let's get you lying down again. You look tired."

The kindness in her daughter's voice brought tears

to Eleanor's eyes. She averted her face. "Go on down," she muttered, and went into the room, closing the door behind her.

Grace stood staring at the door for several seconds. Then she heard the front door being flung open and Sophie shouted, "Anyone at home?"

Grace leaned over the railing. "Sssh! Your grand-mother's resting."

"Oops, sorry." Sophie came to the foot of the stairs. "Is she okay?"

Grace came downstairs and motioned to her daughter to come into the family room. "She's tired, that's all. And disappointed."

"About what?"

"Michelle."

"What about her?"

"She left this morning without even saying good-bye to your grandmother."

"Oh, bummer! How could she do that?"

Grace shrugged. "Who knows? I guess she didn't get what she'd hoped for, so she just upped and left."

"I heard there was some sort of family upset last night."

Grace felt the blood rush to her face. "Who said that?" she asked, her voice sharp.

"Lauren. She said you were a bit pissed and—"

"Do you have to talk like a foulmouthed teenager?" Grace paced to the window.

"Sorre-e-y. Just repeating what Lauren said. Is it true?"

"I don't know."

"You must know. You were there."

Grace suddenly felt tremendously weary. That episode last night had been a nightmare. She wouldn't mind going to bed herself and sleeping all day. "What did Lauren tell you?"

"Nothing. She just told me you'd said something to upset Grandmother, that was all. She told me it was old stuff that didn't matter, but that it had upset Michelle as well."

"I see." Grace sighed. "Perhaps that's why Michelle left without seeing anyone. Where are Jamie and Joel, by the way? Did they come with you?"

"No, they must still be sleeping, lazy bums. And Ramsey and Penny said they'd be getting up early to go for a long walk, so there was no need to wake them."

"I hope they're back in time for brunch at the hotel."

"The Algonquin?"

Grace nodded.

"Great. But after that we're leaving. We have to get back to Toronto tonight."

"Do you have to go so soon?" Grace couldn't hide her disappointment. She and her daughter so rarely had any time together.

Sophie grimaced. "Sorry. Let's face it, Mom, none of us really enjoys these family get-togethers, do we? It always brings out the worst in us. Apart from Dad, who's always unfailingly British and polite."

Grace gave a ghost of a smile. Perhaps it was for the best. The fewer people around at this time the better. At least, with Michelle gone, they'd crossed one major hurdle. Once the merger went through, the constant tension would ease and everything could get back to normal. Whatever normal was, she thought with a wry smile.

Chapter 22

$\sim$

Michelle became aware of the men's voices filtering through her sleep before she was fully awake. They were speaking so softly—a lighter voice and a dark-timbred one—she could barely hear them. She recognized neither voice. Keeping her eyes closed, she strained to hear what they were saying.

"She asleep?" asked the darker voice.

"Yeah. I checked a few minutes ago."

Michelle squirmed. She hated the thought of one of them bending and breathing over her while she was unconscious.

"She tied up?"

"I've taped one hand behind her."

"Only one? He said she should be tied up."

"She had to go to the john."

Dark Voice laughed. "Right."

"I've got to go. Watch her like a hawk. Here, I'll give you this."

"Nah, don't need it. Knife's too messy. Got this." Dark Voice tapped something metal, which sounded horribly like a gun. He had an accent, a hesitation on his *H*s, suggesting that English was not his first language. But, of course, that could be phony.

"Okay, but don't use it unless you have to." The lighter-voiced man sounded nervous. Michelle guessed now that this was Dave, speaking in a more normal voice. "Keep the fire going. It's friggin' freezing in here."

So that was why she'd felt the air in the cabin grow less chilly as the light increased earlier in the morning. She'd thought it was because it was warmer outside, but now that she was coming to her senses she could smell the wood smoke and hear the snap and crackle of logs in the stove.

The door crashed shut. Eyes still closed, she held her breath for a moment, wondering if she was on her own. Then she heard a movement in the room and knew that she was not. They weren't taking any chances. She lay there, trying to determine what to do next, but the gnawing in her stomach told her she had to eat pretty soon—or else. Also she needed to make another trip outside.

She became aware of the sound of breathing. She opened her eyes . . . and gave a startled yelp. A man much larger than Dave was standing right over her. He wore a red plaid shirt and his head and face were covered, as Dave's had been, with a black ski mask.

" 'Ow long you been awake?" he asked, suspicion edging his voice.

"I just woke up now. I heard the door close."

"Yeah. The other guy left."

"Dave?"

"Yeah, sure, Dave."

Michelle shrank from him, clutching the blanket around her neck. She hadn't liked Dave. She liked this guy even less. He smelled unwashed and his breath reeked of tobacco smoke. He was also tall with broad shoulders, very much larger than Dave.

"I need to go outside," she said, sitting up. Her head swam so sickeningly she was afraid she might throw up on the man's muddy shoes. Concentrating hard, she breathed in deeply through her nose.

"You dressed?"

"Yes."

"Okay. Let's go."

She threw off the blanket and stood up, then felt the room swing around her.

"What's wrong with you?"

She was cold. She felt like throwing up. Her neck and legs were stiff from her cramped position on the uncomfortable couch, and her right shoulder throbbed with pain. "I haven't had much sleep. My shoulder's hurting and—"

"Okay, lady. I get the picture. No talking or I tape your mouth."

"You asked me what was wrong. I was just—"

He shoved her hard in the back. "Shut up and get going."

Heart pounding, Michelle walked to the door ahead of him. She'd had the feeling that Dave was an amateur, that kidnapping people was some sort of game to him. This guy was for real. She shivered. If she was to keep herself and her baby unharmed, she'd have to be much more careful with him.

"Leave the door open," he said when they reached the outhouse.

She stared at him. "You must be kidding."

His hand clenched into a fist.

"I've got one hand taped behind me," she said, trying not to betray her growing fear of him. "You can stay right outside the door."

He hesitated, then grunted. Taking this as an affirmative, she stepped into the outhouse and closed the door. But all the time she was in there she was afraid he'd suddenly wrench the door open. She heard the flick of a lighter and when she came out, he was smoking a particularly foul-smelling cigarette, which looked as if it had been hand-rolled.

"Can I have some breakfast?" she asked him when they got inside the cabin again.

He shrugged. "Help yourself."

"Thanks." For a moment she thought he was going to leave her on her own in the kitchen. Perhaps give her time to find a knife and hide it somewhere in her clothing. But he followed her into the narrow galley, his dark eyes—topped by eyebrows like thick black caterpillars—watching every move.

She felt self-conscious, particularly as she was so

clumsy using her left hand. If he'd talked to her as Dave had, it would have eased the tension a little, but this guy was no talker.

"What's your name?" she asked as she tried to spread hard butter on the sliced bread.

"None of your business."

She shrugged. "Sorry. Dave told me his name."

"Good for Dave. You finished?"

"I have to get some juice and cereal."

She poured the orange juice into a paper cup and put some bran flakes into a cracked bowl. He reached for the carton of orange juice and drank directly from it. Her stomach revolted at the sight of his mouth on the same carton she'd used.

As there was no tray, and she had only one hand available, she had to make several trips into the living room. He made no effort to help her.

She found instant coffee, but now that she'd decided to give up drinking coffee, she'd have to get used to doing without caffeine. Further searching through the bags of groceries produced a box of herbal teas. Surprisingly thoughtful of her kidnappers, she thought. She made some black currant tea in a paper cup and carried it through, setting it down beside cereal, juice, and bread, which she'd also spread with honey, and then began to eat. It must be quite late. She was ravenously hungry.

Thank heavens they hadn't taken her watch away . . . yet. When the man turned away to fiddle with his portable radio, she dragged up her sleeve to glance at the time. It was almost ten-thirty.

He tuned into a country and western music station and sat on an old wooden rocking chair beside the stove, puffing on his cigarette, leaning forward every now and again to poke the logs into a blaze. When the radio announcer broke in after about five minutes of music, he spoke in French, which confirmed Michelle's guess that her kidnapper's first language wasn't English.

It was a welcome relief not to have his constant

gaze on her. This man scared her. She sensed that he meant business. She decided to have as little to do with him as possible, to avoid any kind of confrontation with him.

She took her time over her breakfast, knowing that there would be little else to do, other than eat and read, during the day. She was glad she'd packed a couple of new books—the Alice Munro and a biography of Auguste Rodin—in her suitcase. Eat, read . . . and think. There was something about this man being French-speaking that was worrying her, but she wanted to postpone the thinking part until later. The all-important thing for her baby was to keep herself comfortable physically and to try to relax as much as possible, although she was finding that increasingly hard as the silence and tension built inside the cabin.

She stood up. "I'd like to wash."

"Be my guest." He flung his cigarette stub into the fire.

"Where?"

"That's the only water." He jerked his head toward the kitchen.

"Is there another room?"

Another jerk of the head around the room. "This is it."

She had to boil several kettles of water on the spirit stove to get enough water to wash. It didn't stay warm for long. While she washed, he stood by the entrance to the kitchen, his mouth twisted into a smirk at her clumsy, one-handed attempts to wash in stages and stay covered at the same time. Tears of impotent rage stung her eyes as she scrubbed her teeth with bottled water. If Brian were here, she thought, he'd kill this guy with one karate chop. But Brian wasn't here. Brian hadn't even bothered to call her for Thanksgiving. She was on her own. No, not on her own. She was here with their baby and it was up to her to keep them both safe from all harm.

She read for most of the morning, but was always aware of her captor in the confined cabin, having to breathe the smoke from his foul cigarettes. Several times, she asked if she could go outside, so that she could breathe in the fresh air and escape from his looming presence and the incessant twang and whine of country music in the claustrophobic cabin.

Later, after a lunch of instant soup and a peanut butter sandwich, she lay down on the couch. Constantly aware of the man by the fire, she was afraid to sleep, but eventually her eyelids grew heavy and sleep overtook her.

She was in the middle of a dream about Bali, with gamelan music playing in the background as she and Brian walked hand in hand through a tropical garden of ginger and hibiscus, when the shrill ring of a cell phone, shocked her awake. She sat up with a start, to find her kidnapper speaking in French into the phone. Again, the sound of the language set off warning bells in her mind. What was it? Michelle's French was pretty good, but she found it hard to understand this man. He spoke rapidly, slurring his words together, but she did catch a few words. He seemed to be assuring someone that everything was okay. He used the actual word *okay* several times. He glanced up, saw that she was awake, and ended the conversation abruptly.

"Your boss?" she asked.

He shrugged and turned away.

Without asking, she got up and went to the kitchen to make herself more black currant tea. He followed her to the galley entrance and watched her, frowning.

"Tea?" she asked him, nervously seeking to establish some sort of rapport with him.

He shook his head.

"Coffee?"

His dark eyes avoided hers. "I'll do it," he said, his voice surly.

She wished she could get Dave back. Any chance of gaining this man's trust seemed fairly remote. And she knew that her only chance of escape was for her captor to let his guard down. She couldn't risk a physical confrontation. When she went back to the couch with her tea and two chocolate chip cookies, she knew she had to face the reality of her position and start working things out. She couldn't postpone it any longer.

The first question she asked herself was, naturally, who had kidnapped her? Was it just these two men? Had that been Dave on the phone, checking in to see if everything was *okay*? Or were they working for someone else, someone unknown? And if so, what was their object? Was it to kidnap the granddaughter of the Tyler Foods matriarch and hold her for a million-dollar ransom?

The questions came pouring into her mind. It was quite possible that she had been kidnapped for a ransom. Although she'd come to Fredericton unheralded, it wasn't a large town. Word could have got around fairly fast that Mrs. Tyler's long-lost granddaughter had come home.

That was it! Her heart pounded in her chest. Word *did* get around. Her half-brothers—hadn't she been warned about the Gaudry family? And they would speak French, wouldn't they? The possibility of her own father's sons kidnapping her for money was like a knife in the heart. But if they had kidnapped her, at least there was a better chance that she'd be found. Kidnapping was rare in Canada. New Brunswick wasn't densely populated. Once she was reported missing, the police would be scouring the entire province for her. Maybe someone would make the connection.

If she was reported missing. This returned her to the crux of the matter, of course. The other scenario she'd been avoiding ever since she'd been taken from the Tyler country home. Only last night she'd discovered that there was an urgent merger negotiation going on between Tyler Foods and some other conglomerate. A merger that Eleanor vehemently opposed. And Eleanor was the majority shareholder.

Was the fact that only a few hours separated her

discovery of this proposed merger and her kidnapping a mere coincidence or was there a more sinister explanation? If it was imperative for the family to get this merger through, would Norman and Grace—and even Stewart—be capable of going to such drastic lengths to ensure that she wouldn't be able to interfere, to support her grandmother in a stand against the rest of the family?

The iciness that crept over Michelle was not caused by the dying fire. Because if this was the case, and she had been kidnapped by her mother's family, not her father's, then not only was she in danger, but so was her grandmother. Either explanation sickened her, to think that her very own flesh and blood could be behind something like this. And if the Tylers were the ones responsible for her kidnapping, her disappearance would *not* have been reported to the police.

Panic swelled in her at the thought of being locked away in this remote cabin, without anyone even knowing she was gone.

Then reason returned. Of course someone would know. When she didn't turn up at Winnipeg airport this evening, Rebecca would surely call the Tylers to find out what had happened to her, wouldn't she? And once Becca knew she'd disappeared she'd get in touch with the police and they'd start a massive search for her, wouldn't they? Then Becca would call Brian's network in Minneapolis and tell them to track him down immediately. And once Brian knew the situation he'd be on the next plane out of Jakarta, wouldn't he?

Chapter 23

Rebecca stood near the foot of the down escalator in Winnipeg airport, waiting for Michelle to appear, but all that was left now were a few stragglers. Most of the people from the Toronto plane were waiting for their baggage at the carousel. No sign of Michelle.

"Damn!" Becca muttered. She'd left Paul and the kids at home watching a movie with pizza and popcorn to come out on a chilly evening to pick Michelle up . . . and she wasn't even on the plane.

She called Paul. "Did Michelle call?" She could hear three-year old Seth shouting "Hi, Mom!" in the background.

"No, she didn't call," Paul said. "Why? Wasn't she on the flight?"

"No," Becca said abruptly, feeling mad as hell, but also concerned. "It's unlike Michelle not to let me know."

"She may have missed her flight. The connector flight might have arrived late in Toronto. If so, she'll probably be on the last plane in from Toronto."

"Well, I won't be here. I'm not waiting another couple of hours. I'll check to make sure everyone's off the plane and then I'll come home."

"I said, no more pizza, Seth," Paul was yelling.

"Sounds like you're having fun. I'll let you go."

"Yeah, barrel of laughs here. Hurry on home, baby."

Becca laughed. "I'll wait a few more minutes and then give up."

"Sorry you had a wasted journey. See you."

She put the receiver back in its cradle, then went to ask the uniformed airport official if all the passengers were off the plane. She confirmed that they were. Becca then went to the airline counter and asked a woman who was busy filing her nails if she could check her computer to see if Michelle had been on the flight.

"Sorry. We can't give out that information," said the woman behind the counter, sounding like a taped message.

Becca swallowed her annoyance. "Then could you please have her paged for me?"

The woman released a heavy sigh. "The courtesy desk will do that for you."

Becca bit back the retort that she could do with using some courtesy herself and went to arrange the page. Then she returned to the baggage carousel area in case she'd somehow missed Michelle, but she definitely wasn't there.

Eventually, she left the airport, feeling furious with Michelle for not having called her to tell her she'd missed the plane. Fortunately the drive home to River Heights took less than twenty minutes, but it was enough time to cool her down. By the time she reached home she was more worried than annoyed.

Paul and the kids were still in the den watching *The Lion King* for what seemed like the tenth time. She poked her head in the door and grimaced at the mess. Pizza boxes open with dried-up pizza still in them. Juice glasses on the tables. Seth launched himself at her. "Any calls?" she asked Paul, hugging Seth close. Ruthie, who was curled up on her Dad's knee, demanded the same. Becca bent to give her rosy cheek a kiss. "Ugh! You're all sticky, Ruthie baby."

"No, only your mother. I told her where you were. She said she'd call you at the store in the morning."

Becca rolled her eyes. "That's all I need. I'll get a cloth for Ruthie, then I'm going to call the Tyler place to see what's happened to Michelle." She went to fetch a damp washcloth and towel.

"I'll do it. You go call the Tylers. Don't forget Fredericton's on Atlantic time, two hours ahead of us. It's twenty past eleven there."

"I don't care if it's three in the morning. I want to make sure Michelle's okay."

"Bet she decided to stay on," Paul said as he tried to get Ruthie to stop wriggling, so he could wipe her hands and face. "I thought going for just three days was a bit crazy, when she'd never met these people before."

"That's exactly why she didn't want to go for any longer than that. She wasn't sure how she'd get on with them."

"She's probably having such a great time living it up with her millionaire family she won't want to come home at all."

"Thanks. You really know how to cheer a girl up, don't you? I have an appointment with the pediatrician on Wednesday about Seth's ears. Michelle knows that."

"Go call her."

"Yeah, Mom," Seth said. "We're missing the movie."

"Okay, okay. I know when I'm not wanted."

She closed the den door and went into the kitchen to get the Tylers' number, which she'd stuck on the fridge door with a Franklin the Turtle magnet. When she punched in the number she got the Tylers' answering machine. She slammed the receiver down without leaving a message and dialed the number again. She did this four times. The last time, the telephone was picked up on the first ring and a man's voice said, "Yes?"

Becca explained who she was. "I was expecting Michelle home tonight, but she didn't arrive."

"She decided to stay on for a few more days." The man's voice was muffled, as if he had a blanket wrapped around his head.

"Sorry, I can't hear you very well. Did you say Michelle's staying on for a few more days?"

"Right."

"Can I speak to her?"

"She's asleep. It's eleven-thirty here."

"I know that," Becca said, growing more annoyed. "I'm her partner. I want to speak to her, please."

"Sorry." The voice was even more muffled than before. "She's at the cottage with Mrs. Tyler."

"I'll call her there. Give me the number."

"No phone at the cottage. Sorry." The line went dead and Becca knew he'd hung up on her.

The next morning, she opened up the store. She was late and in a foul mood. Her mother, who'd promised to pick up the kids from day care this afternoon, so she could stay late, had reneged on her promise, as she wanted to go out for dinner and a movie with a friend. The fact that she'd sniped at her mother, when she knew she had every right to do whatever she wanted without being burdened by commitments, made Becca feel guilty. And guilt always made her feel even more angry—at herself. She and her mother had compromised, as they usually did. She'd close the store early today and pick up the kids herself. Her mother would look after the store tomorrow, so Becca could take Seth to the doctor. But that made her feel even more furious with Michelle. Why the hell hadn't she called to say she was staying on in New Brunswick?

"I guess it's tough to think about slogging in a store when you're living in luxury," she muttered as she dragged out a particularly ugly pottery jug in a putrid shade of khaki from its protective wrapping. Good thing they were selling this particular artist on a consignment basis.

By the time Becca was closing the store at four o'clock, Michelle still hadn't called. She decided to call the Tylers again, this time to relay a message to Michelle, but although she called several times, no one answered, nor was there a machine pickup. Frowning, she glared down at the receiver, with its incessant ringing tone. It was almost as if whoever was there at the Tylers' house was trying to avoid speaking to her. Something weird was going on. If Michelle were there she'd say it wasn't like Becca to worry like this. But that was the problem, Michelle wasn't there. And she should be.

Chapter 24

⌒

Eleanor was relieved to be back in Tyler House. The bitter disappointment of Michelle's departure had left her feeling that her last hope of getting someone to help her had gone. She was utterly alone again. Indeed, it was worse than it had been before Michelle's visit. Seeing Carolyn's daughter for the first time and sensing the bond forming between them had given Eleanor a new zest for life, a feeling that there might be something positive in the future to look forward to. Then Michelle had crushed all the trust she had placed in her by taking off without even saying good-bye.

"Stop fretting about her, Mother," Grace said, as she was helping her up to her bedroom on Tuesday evening. "She's just not worth it. That's young people for you nowadays. Selfish and uncaring."

Eleanor wished Grace would be quiet. She needed all her energy to concentrate on getting enough breath to take each step one at a time. Her breathing was becoming even more labored nowadays.

"Really, Mother. You are so stubborn. Why won't you let us install a lift for you? It doesn't have to be a proper elevator. Just a stairlift would make such a difference."

"Oh, stop nagging me, Grace. The more you nag, the more I close my ears. You should know that by now."

As they approached the door to her bedroom, Eleanor tensed. She wished Janet were here to check the room, as she usually did before Eleanor went in, but she'd given Janet an extra two days off so that she could spend some time with her son, who was visiting from California. She was tempted to ask Grace to check for her, but resisted the urge. Displaying the least sign of weakness now could be fatal.

She could no longer trust any member of her family. All of them were suspect. Even those of the younger generation could be working with their parents on this. But the one person she'd invited here to give her help and support had let her down completely.

Grace went to the bed and drew her satin nightdress from its case beneath the pillow.

Eleanor reached out and took the nightdress from her. "I can undress myself, thank you. Anyway, I don't want to put it on yet."

"I thought you might like some help."

"No, thank you."

Grace drew in her breath. "No need to take it out on me, Mother. I'm not responsible for Michelle's behavior."

"Who said anything about Michelle?"

"I know she's hurt you by leaving that way, but—"

"I don't want to talk about Michelle."

"Okay. Oh, there is one thing I should tell you that's partly about Michelle."

"I don't—"

"I think you should know about this. Janet left a message to say that she'd forgotten to tell us that one of the Gaudry brothers phoned on Saturday night, asking for Michelle."

"The who?"

"Gaudry brothers. Michelle's half brother, I suppose he'd be."

Eleanor drew herself up. "Mike Gaudry's son? What on earth did he want?"

"Good question. Apparently he wanted to speak to Michelle. Or so he said. Janet said she wasn't here and he rang off."

"How did he know Michelle was here?"

Grace shrugged. "Who knows? You know Fredericton. Everyone knows everyone else's business here. Someone obviously told him Michelle was staying at Tyler House."

"Probably after money."

"Probably."

"No need for her to know he was calling. They'd be nothing but trouble."

"That's what I thought."

Eleanor turned away and struggled to reach behind to unzip her dress, but the damned arthritis in her arm stopped her from being able to get to the top of the zipper.

"Here, I'll do it." Grace unzipped the blue wool dress and held it so that Eleanor could slide her arms out of the sleeves. Then she helped her into her robe.

"Thank you, dear." Eleanor sighed. "Sometimes I feel as if all my clothes are designed to make things difficult for me."

"It's not easy, is it, with your arthritis? You should allow us to help you more."

Eleanor turned to face her. "And take away even more of my independence? I think not."

Grace's face flushed. "That's not what I meant. Honestly, Mother, you take everything I say the wrong way."

"And who's to blame for that?" Eleanor tied the belt of her robe. "Will you bring up my pot of tea as Janet's not here?"

Grace raised her neatly plucked eyebrows. "You mean you're letting me do something for you?"

Eleanor allowed herself to smile. "Touché." She sighed again. "I'm sorry. I don't mean to be a grouch, but it wasn't the greatest Thanksgiving, was it?"

"No, it wasn't," Grace admitted. "To be honest, I think we were all on edge with Michelle here. Not fair to her, really, but Carolyn and I never got along, as you know."

"That's no excuse for taking it out on her daughter, is it?"

"I suppose not." Grace hesitated. "Then I drank too much at the cottage and said things I shouldn't. I'm particularly sorry about that."

Eleanor felt a constriction about her heart. "I don't want to talk about it."

"No, I can understand that. I wanted to apologize, that's all."

"You did already. No need to mention it again."

Grace's mouth tightened. "Of course not," she said briskly. "I'll bring up your tea. Would you like a slice of Janet's lemon cake with it?"

"Two oatmeal cookies. That's all."

As the door closed behind Grace, Eleanor sank into the armchair by her desk. The tension between her and her daughter was growing worse. It was increasingly bad with all three of her children, but particularly so with Grace, who had more to do with her than the others. They'd been especially careful with her today. The younger members of the family had gone home, of course, but Norman had dropped in at lunchtime to see how she was doing and he and Stewart had arrived together in the evening after she'd eaten a light meal with Grace and Larry.

"Don't you two have your own homes to go to?" she'd asked them when they arrived without their wives. She'd keyed herself up, waiting for them to bring up the subject of the merger, but they held off, for a while, until Stewart began talking rather aimlessly about all the advantages it would bring to Tyler Foods.

"And line your own pockets, no doubt, as well," Eleanor had said. "I don't want to talk about it."

She leaned her head on her hand. How much easier it would be to give in, let them do what they wanted with the business. Even as she thought it, she could hear her husband's voice shouting in her brain, *You must be out of your mind. I left our business in your*

*care and now you're going to throw it away for the
sake of a few dollars?*

"I won't throw it away," Eleanor told him. "I gave
you my promise that I would never let anyone other
than family into the business and I've kept my
promise."

"Who on earth are you talking to, Mother?"

Grace's voice startled Eleanor. "Myself. A habit
you get into when you're old."

"Really?"

"No, it doesn't mean I'm going gaga, so you can
take that look off your face right now. Thank you for
the tea. Put it on my desk, please."

"If you'd like to have it in bed, I can put it on the
cart and roll it over beside you there."

"No, thank you. I have some papers to see to before
I go to bed."

"What sort of papers?"

"None of your business," Eleanor snapped. "Just
because I'm growing old doesn't mean you have to
know everything I do, you know."

Grace retreated. "Anything else I can do to help?"

"No." Eleanor switched on her desk lamp and
looked up, to see her daughter still hesitating in the
doorway. "You can kiss me good night, if you feel
like it," she said, her voice softening.

Grace came and kissed her on the cheek. "Good
night, Mother. Sleep well. If you want anything during
the night, give me a shout. I'll hear you down the
hall."

"I won't need anything, but . . . thank you, Grace.
And thank you for staying with me while Janet is
away. When is Larry going back to London?"

"Not until next month. He has to go to New York
and Los Angeles next week. It's wonderful having
him home."

"You get very lonely when he's away, don't you?"

Despite the subdued lighting Eleanor could see the
tide of pink rising in her daughter's face. "Sometimes."

"Why don't you travel with him more? Long separations aren't good for marriages, you know. I always made sure I went everywhere with Ramsey." She smiled. "Safer that way."

Grace stiffened. "I trust Larry implicitly."

"I'm sure you do, but it's a lonely life for you."

"I manage," Grace said through tight lips. She went to the door. "I'll pick up your tray in a while." She went out and closed the door.

Eleanor sat at her desk, thinking. A strange marriage, Grace and Larry's. It was easy to see that Grace adored him. Whenever they were together, she lit up like a two-hundred-watt lightbulb. She just couldn't hide her feelings. He was a handsome man with a great deal of charm. Still very attractive to women, Eleanor imagined. But as far as she could see, Larry seemed to return Grace's affection in his own inimitably English laconic style.

As she reached out for the Royal Doulton teapot, her fingers brushed against the telephone. Several times during the day she'd had the urge to call Michelle, but resisted it. Now that she was alone, the urge was stronger. Pride told her not to, that calling her granddaughter would make her seem weak, but her desire to know that Michelle had reached home safely overcame her pride. She looked up the number in her address book and dialed it. When she put the receiver to her ear, she thought she could hear a little rustling sound. Probably her imagination.

The phone rang four times and then she heard Michelle's voice. "You have reached Michelle and Brian. Please leave a message after the beep." It was only the answering machine, she realized, but just hearing Michelle's voice brought tears to her eyes. She hesitated . . . and then put the receiver back in its cradle. No point in leaving a message. She'd never call back. Silly to think she'd get her at home. She was probably with friends while her husband was away.

*   *   *

Grace looked at Norman as she carefully set the phone down on her father's desk. "She was calling Michelle. She got her answering machine."

"Did she leave a message?" Norman asked.

"No."

He nodded. "That's good."

"Just before I left her room, she talked about papers she had to deal with. For a moment I thought she was working on her will again, but I managed to get a glimpse of the papers on her desk and they seemed to be connected with one of her charity boards."

Norman shook his head. "She's so disappointed about Michelle leaving that she'll probably forget about changing her will."

"Let's hope so," Grace said.

Chapter 25

Michelle woke up in the early hours of Wednesday morning with a sore throat and stuffy nose. She ached all over. *That's all I need,* she thought, trying to drag the blankets over her and burrow down into them. Tears pricked her eyes. *Where the hell are you, Brian?*

The air in the cabin was stale, stinking of the man's foul cigarettes, which he'd smoked until after midnight last night. She tried not to cough, wanting him to think she was still asleep, in case he made another phone call. But when she drew in a breath she couldn't stop the impulse. She started coughing and couldn't stop.

He groaned in his sleep. Although it was still dark, she could hear him moving around in the sleeping bag he'd laid in front of the stove. He was probably a darn sight warmer there than she was.

She leaned down and poured some water from the bottle into a paper cup, and drank it down, hoping it would help stop the coughing, but it was too late. Cursing beneath his breath, he dragged himself out of the sleeping bag and stood up. Michelle lay back and closed her eyes. Although he wasn't a pretty sight at any time, this guy was particularly nauseating to look at first thing in the morning, dressed in his grubby undershirt and long johns.

She'd tried hard to keep her spirits up all day yesterday, but she was appalled by the thought of another day trapped in this wretched cabin with this brainless hulk. Although she guessed she was worth a lot more to him alive than dead, she'd discovered yesterday that he had a short fuse. When she'd asked him one too many questions, he'd unexpectedly grabbed her left arm and viciously twisted it behind her back. This was a guy who might lash out and really injure her and the baby, whatever the consequences might be to him, if she goaded him too much. She'd just have to be patient and wait until some means of escape presented itself.

The outside door crashed shut. She turned over on her side, with her back to the room, hoping to get back to sleep again, but her mind was hyper by now and she knew that sleep was impossible. All day yesterday she'd kept imagining the police turning up, bursting through the door. Even during the night, she'd kept waking up at every creak and squeak, hoping it was the Mounties coming to rescue her.

Surely by now Becca must have reported that she was missing. Over and over again, she'd tried to get into her friend's mind. Becca would have gone to Winnipeg airport on Monday evening, found she wasn't on the plane. Then she'd either go home and call the Tylers or call them from the airport, wouldn't she? And the Tylers would say . . . what? If she'd been kidnapped for ransom by strangers or by her half brothers, the Tylers would tell Becca that she'd disappeared from the cottage. But surely they'd have called the police themselves when they'd found her missing, wouldn't they? On the other hand, if . . .

Each time she'd gone through this process, Michelle had usually stopped right there, her mind going blank because she couldn't bear to consider it, but now she knew she *must* face the possibility. What if the Tylers had told Becca she was staying on with her grandmother for a few more days? What then? Becca would think it very odd that Michelle hadn't called herself to tell her, but she'd accept that it would be a normal thing to want to stay on with your newfound relatives for a few extra days. She certainly wouldn't think that those very relatives might have kidnapped her friend and be hiding her away in a remote cabin, would she?

That was the problem. No one in their right mind would even consider such a thing could happen. Brian might, but Brian seemed to have fallen off the edge of the earth.

Panic rushed over her like a tidal wave. *Don't even think such things,* she told herself. Indonesia was a dangerous place for foreign news correspondents at present. Only last week she'd head that one had been killed there. She broke out in a fine sweat. No! She must not think of that. She had a baby who needed his or her father to come home. Michelle willed her body to relax beneath the blanket. She must do an hour of tai chi today for exercise and relaxation and to keep her blood pressure down. *Please God keep Brian safe and tell him I need him to call Becca as soon as possible,* she prayed. But reason also told her that even Brian might believe that she was staying on for a few days at the cottage with her grandmother.

A spasm squeezed her heart. *And please God keep my grandmother safe.* She sincerely hoped that her kidnappers *were* strangers, in it strictly for the money. Then her grandmother would not be in any danger.

But what if no one paid the ransom money? What then?

The door swung open and slammed shut again. She opened her eyes, preparing herself for another very long day in captivity.

Brian had landed himself in the center of one of the hottest stories of the year. Dili, the capital of East Timor, was in flames, its people scattered. Students in Jakarta were rioting against foreign interference. He barely had time to sleep, throwing himself on whatever bed was offered him and crashing out, sometimes without even stripping off his clothes first.

When Dili shut down, he returned with his crew to Jakarta, but now the feeling toward foreign journalists was hostile, not welcoming. The crew set out the morning after they'd flown in to Jakarta, knowing that trouble was expected in the streets again. It didn't take long to find it. As they filmed a band of rampaging students turning over a jeep and setting fire to it, Brian could feel the intense heat from the burning metal. He struggled to breathe normally, despite the acrid smell of gasoline and burning rubber, while he tried to do a commentary into the hand mike. The angry crowd pressed in on them, arms flailing.

A man with a placard knocked the camera flying. Vince, the cameraman, cursed, then yelled as the crowd closed in on him when he tried to retrieve it. Brian started forward to protect him. Someone grabbed the microphone from his hand. People were shoving him from all sides, making it hard to stay on his feet. He tried to recover, grabbing hold of the shirt of the person nearest to him. Then he was slammed from behind. A blast of pain shot through his head. It seemed to explode into a million pieces until the pain gave way to a black void.

Chapter 26

When Eleanor awoke on Wednesday morning and sat up in bed, she felt totally disoriented. The room seemed to be swinging around her, as if she were on one of those flying chair rides at the fair she loved going on when she was young. What on earth was the matter with her? All these horrible things happening to her and she had no energy nowadays. It seemed such a long time since she'd felt well. If this was what old age was about, she didn't want any part of it!

But she wasn't going to give in to it, either. She swung her legs over the side of the bed and tried to stand, but again her head spun and she had to sit back down quickly, or she might fall.

"Grace," she called. When there was no response, she called again, "Grace!"

She heard hurried footsteps, but when the door opened it was Janet, not Grace, who came in. A wave of relief passed over Eleanor. "Oh, I am so glad to see you." If she'd been the hugging kind, she'd have held out her arms and hugged Janet.

Janet beamed. "Well, that's a lovely welcome. How have you been, Mrs. Tyler?"

Eleanor grimaced. "Not so good, Janet, but I'll survive. I'm feeling a bit light-headed this morning. Think I'll take breakfast in my room."

"Right. I didn't want to wake you. I thought you

probably needed your sleep after all the excitement of the holiday weekend."

"Yes." Eleanor didn't want to think about the holiday weekend at all, but the subject would have come up sooner or later. "Have you seen Grace this morning?"

"Yes. She and Mr. Larry went into the office about half an hour ago."

Eleanor moistened her dry lips. "Did she tell you?"

"About Miss Michelle?" Janet nodded. "A great shame. I must say I was surprised to hear she'd do such a thing. She seemed such a nice young woman."

"That's what I thought. Oh, well, you never know with people, do you?"

"That's right, you don't." Janet set out Eleanor's slippers and cashmere robe for her. "Will you have your usual soft-boiled egg and croissants this morning?"

She didn't feel like eating anything, but she supposed she must. "No croissants, just toast. I'm hoping I'll feel better after some breakfast."

"Shall I call Dr. Andrew, ask him to drop by?"

"No. Not yet, anyway. Let's see how I feel once I've eaten."

When her breakfast came, Eleanor could barely swallow the egg, but she did manage two half slices of toast and honey and two cups of tea. "I think I'll work up here today," she told Janet when she came to fetch the tray. She didn't like to admit that she was afraid of walking down the stairs in case she got dizzy and fell. Perhaps an elevator or a stairlift was a good idea, but if she got one it would be her decision, not her daughter's.

For almost two hours, she sat at her desk going over the figures Norman had prepared for her. Usually she found it easy to analyze charts and tables and financial reports, but today everything seemed to be in a haze, the figures dancing before her eyes. Maybe she needed new glasses. She must make an appointment for an eye exam. But bad eyes or not, she was sure there was some problem with the international figures. She made a mental note to speak to Norman about them next time she saw him.

At eleven o'clock, Janet brought her more tea and a blueberry muffin.

"Smells good," Eleanor told her, but she knew she wouldn't be able to eat it.

When Janet left the room again, Eleanor's mind drifted away from the Tyler Foods accounts and statements. She could hear Michelle's voice in her mind, telling her about her store and her partner. What was her name? Eleanor frowned, trying hard to remember. Rebecca, that was it. Rebecca. Becca for short. Unusual, that.

She reached for her address book. She seemed to remember that Michelle had given her a business card. Yes, there it was: SIMPLE PLEASURES GIFT STORE. For a long time she stared at the card, wondering what she should do. How would she feel if she called Michelle and she was cold and distant on the phone?

She drew herself up, sitting erect in her chair. She could deal with that if it happened. What she couldn't deal with was not knowing *why* Michelle had left without a word. Perhaps someone had upset her on Sunday night, made her feel she wasn't wanted. Grace hadn't been exactly welcoming, had she? And Sophie was a pain in the neck. Perhaps one of the younger people had got into a fight with Michelle, and coming after Grace's outburst, it had all been just too much for her.

She needed to *know*, that was all. Because, yes, as Janet had said, Michelle was a nice young woman and it just didn't seem in character for her to take off without saying good-bye.

When she dialed Michelle's home number she got the machine again. For a moment, she wondered if she should leave a message, but then decided she could call again and do that if she didn't get Michelle at the store. Heart pounding, she dialed the store number. The phone rang three times and then was picked up. "Hello," a woman's voice said. It wasn't Michelle.

"Is this the Simple Pleasures Gift Store?" Eleanor asked.

"Yes, that's right." The woman sounded rushed, as if she were busy with something else.

"Is this . . . Rebecca?"

"That's right. Who's this?"

"I'm looking for Michelle."

"Who isn't!"

What a rude young woman! "Is she there?" Eleanor asked.

"No, she's not. She's spending a few days with her family in New Brunswick."

A mantle of ice descended on Eleanor. "Rebecca— I'm sorry I don't know your surname. This is Eleanor Tyler, Michelle's grandmother."

"Oh, sorry, Mrs. Tyler. I didn't realize it was you. I can't tell you how glad I am to hear from you. Is Michelle there? I'd like to have a few words with her."

Eleanor took a deep breath to ease the heavy pounding of her heart. "But she's not here. She left our cottage early on Monday morning to go to the airport."

"Oh, my God." There was a long silence, then Becca said, "I was at Winnipeg airport Monday night to pick her up, like we'd arranged. She wasn't on the plane."

"Why didn't you call here? Someone would have told you she'd left New Brunswick."

"I did call. Whoever I spoke to said that Michelle had decided to stay on with her grandmother for a few more days."

"No, no, you must be mistaken. We all knew she'd left that morning to drive to Fredericton airport."

"How did you know?" Becca demanded.

"No need to shout at me."

"Sorry."

"We knew because Michelle left a note saying she'd gone."

"A note?"

"It was typed—computer printout."

"Well, I can tell you now that she never got here. I've been to the apartment. Her mail hasn't been picked up. I checked her messages. Nothing there."

Eleanor's hand pressed against her heart. "Dear God, what can have happened to her?"

"I don't know, but I'm sure as hell going to find out," Becca said grimly.

"I just don't understand about your call here. Who did you speak to? Was it a man or a woman?"

"Man. His voice sounded muffled. Now that I think about it, he could have been trying to disguise it."

"There's no one here who would lie to you like that." Eleanor's brain seemed to be swirling even faster. "I can't even think who was here that night. My sons, perhaps a couple of their sons, but—"

"I think you'd better call in the police, don't you?"

"Yes, yes, of course. I'll get Norman—my son—to deal with it right away. Dear God, what can have happened to her?"

"I hate to worry you, Mrs. Tyler, but it doesn't sound good."

Eleanor tried to pull herself together, but she was shaking so hard she could barely hold the receiver. "You're right. If anything terrible has happened, I shall never forgive myself for asking her here."

"You can't blame yourself. I'll try to get hold of Brian, her husband, if I can. He must be told. You get your son to contact the police. Will you keep in touch and let me know what's going on?"

"Of course I will."

"I'm going to close the store and go home." Becca gave Eleanor her home number. "You call me if you hear anything, anything at all, okay?"

"Yes."

"Try not to worry," Becca said. "Michelle's pretty tough. But . . . there is one thing you should be thinking about."

"What's that?"

"Who was the man I spoke to in your house? The one who told me she was staying on for a few days. You realize if you hadn't called me, neither of us would have known that Michelle was missing, would we?"

Eleanor held her breath for a moment. "That's true."

"Better watch your back," Becca said, and rang off.

Eleanor sat staring at the phone, her mind spinning. She started up and stumbled to the door. "Janet," she called. "Janet!" There was no reply. Had Janet gone out? She'd said something about going for groceries when she brought the tea.

Did that mean she was alone in the house? Eleanor thought of the man who'd lied to Becca. She had no reason to doubt Becca's story. Who could it have been? "Janet!" she shouted, her voice rising in her anxiety. She went out into the hall and then started down the stairs, but in her haste she missed a step. She felt her feet tangling in her robe, tried to grab the railing . . . and pitched forward, to land with a crash on the small landing at the curve of the staircase, six steps down.

Chapter 27

"No, the ankle's not broken. Looks like a bad sprain, though. I'm glad you didn't try to move her."

Eleanor felt as if there were a dozen voices swirling above her, the sound swelling and decreasing as she slipped in and out of consciousness.

She felt hands gently moving over her head. "She doesn't seem to have any head injury, but she'll probably have some bad bruising on her face and body." It was Andrew speaking. Janet must have called him when she found her.

She tried to move, then groaned as a pain darted through her shoulder and down her arm. "My arm hurts."

"Hello, there," Andrew said, his face looming above her. "Welcome back to the land of the living."

"What happened?"

"That's what we'd like to know. I guess you must have fallen from the top step to the landing."

"What on earth were you doing coming downstairs?" That was Janet's voice. "I thought we agreed you'd stay upstairs today."

Eleanor put a shaking hand to her head. "I can't remember . . ."

"No more questions," Andrew said. "Now that we know nothing's broken we must get you back to bed—"

"I wasn't in bed," Eleanor said indignantly. "I was

working at my desk." But something else had happened while she was working. *What* was it?

"We're going to pick you up and carry you upstairs," Andrew told her.

"I wish you luck. I probably weigh a ton."

"Hardly. I've told you before, you're underweight for your age and height. Norman and I will carry you." Andrew explained to Norman what he was to do.

Eleanor felt herself being lifted, and with Grace and Janet following behind, the two men carried her up the stairs and laid her on her bed. Janet fussed around her, covering her with the quilt and punching up pillows.

"Stop flapping around me like a flittering hen, Janet. I'm all right."

"I should never have left you alone like that. I should—"

"You should stop all that nonsense. It's giving me a headache."

Janet gave her a twisted little smile, which made Eleanor feel guilty, but she really could not stand being fussed over. All this time, Grace stood at the foot of the bed, watching, her face drained of color.

"You look as if you'd seen a ghost, Grace," Eleanor told her.

"When I saw you lying there I thought you were dead."

"For God's sake, Grace," Norman said. "What a thing to say."

"Sorry." Grace shook her head. "It was quite a shock. You're sure she's going to be okay?" she asked Andrew.

"Absolutely. I'll arrange for an X ray, but I think we can leave that until tomorrow," he told Eleanor, "so you can get some rest before having to go out again. Pity you don't have an elevator here."

"I keep telling her—"

"I intend to get some estimates for one," Eleanor said, glaring at Grace. "It would save Janet's poor old legs. She's had too many years of having to carry piles of linen and towels and trays up and down the stairs."

"Good idea," Andrew said. "You certainly won't be able to walk for a few days, but all being well, once the swelling goes down, it won't take too long to heal."

"Glad to hear it." Eleanor laid her head back on the pillow. She suddenly felt utterly exhausted. She wished they'd all go away and leave her alone. There was something she wanted to remember and couldn't. Something important. She frowned, trying to concentrate, but her head was pounding so hard she couldn't think. Could it have been something she'd found in the figures she'd been examining?

"My head hurts," she said in a low voice as Andrew was taking her pulse.

"I'll give you some Tylenol." He looked down at her, still holding her wrist.

"What?" she asked when he didn't say anything.

He shook his head and gave her a faint smile. "I know there's no point in telling you to take it easy, so I won't."

"Good."

Andrew addressed the others. "Would you mind waiting outside while I check her heart and examine her for bruising, please?"

The three of them left the room.

"Your heartbeat's accelerated again," he told Eleanor after he'd checked her, "but that's to be expected in the circumstances. I'm pretty sure you haven't broken any bones, but I still want to be sure by getting that ankle x-rayed. As for the bruising, we'll have to wait until tomorrow to see how bad it is."

He went into her bathroom to wash his hands. "Can I use your telephone to arrange for the X ray?" he asked when he came out again.

Telephone! Eleanor shot bolt upright in the bed. "Oh, my God! Michelle!"

Andrew's eyes widened. "What about Michelle?"

"Michelle," she said again, not able to say any

more. She started gasping for air. Her chest felt as if
it were being crushed by a massive weight.

Andrew rushed to her side. "Easy, easy," he told
her, his face alarmed. "Take a slow, deep breath." She
did so. "And another. Good. Another. That's better."

As her breathing quieted, tears filled her eyes and
slid down her cheeks. She seemed to have no control
over them.

"Easy, now," Andrew said. He took a handful of
tissues from the box on her bedside cabinet and gently
wiped her eyes. "Keep taking slow, deep breaths and
try to tell me what is troubling you. It's about Michelle, right?"

Eleanor nodded, tears still swimming in her eyes.

"She went back to Winnipeg without saying good-
bye, right?" Andrew prompted her.

"How did you know that?"

"Grace told me when I asked her if Michelle had
gone home yet."

Eleanor grabbed his arm. "She didn't go home."

"Yes, Eleanor, she did," Andrew said. "She left
on—"

"She never got home. *That's* why I fell. I called her
at home and then I called her store. Becca was there."

"Becca?" Andrew asked. "Oh, right. Michelle's
partner." She could feel his arm tense beneath her
clutching fingers.

"She said Michelle never came home."

"Are you sure of that? Maybe she went somewhere
else? Perhaps to meet her husband?"

"No. Becca was to meet her at the airport. She
never arrived." She fixed her gaze on his face. "I think
she's been kidnapped."

"Kidnapped?" He seemed bewildered, shocked.
"Why would someone kidnap Michelle?"

"For money, what else? Someone found out she was
here and thought she'd—"

"Has anyone contacted you about a ransom?"

"No but—"

"Who else knows about this?"

"Just me and Becca—and the kidnappers themselves. I remember it clearly now. As soon as I finished speaking to Michelle's friend, I rushed out and called for Janet. When she didn't answer I started to go downstairs. I must have tripped or caught my foot in my robe."

"Have you got Becca's number?"

"Michelle's business card is in my address book. Norman gave me one of those newfangled Palm organizer things for my birthday, but I'm still only halfway through transcribing everything into it. Much faster to open up a book and find an address or a phone number at a glance."

Andrew was already at her desk looking through her book. "I'll call her."

"No, you will not," Eleanor said in her haughtiest voice. "My son will deal with this, Dr. Lenzie, not you." She wasn't sure whom she could trust anymore, but she was determined to keep this in the family for as long as possible. She wasn't about to relinquish control to an outsider.

Andrew turned around and she saw now how drawn his face was. "I want to know Michelle's all right."

"I'd like to know that, too, but you won't hear it from her friend. I keep telling you. Michelle is not in Winnipeg. She didn't go home on Monday. She's missing. And the police must be notified right away." She flung back the quilt.

"Where do you think you're going? You stay in bed, or you'll be falling over again. Next time you could do yourself a worse injury. Absolutely no walking, understand?"

"Then please fetch my sons and daughter for me."

"Norman and Grace are right outside your door."

"Any sign of Stewart?"

"Not yet. I think he's been called, though."

"He's probably too busy to worry about his mother . . . or, more likely, too hungover to present himself. Please ask Grace and Norman to come in again. Not Janet."

"Okay." Andrew went to the door and called them in. Eleanor heard him ask Janet if she'd mind making some tea and bringing it up in about fifteen minutes. Tactful Andrew! she thought.

"Is there some problem?" Grace asked as she came into the room. She looked anxiously at Andrew and then her mother.

"Your mother certainly thinks so," he said, his expression grim. "She believes that—"

"Thank you, Andrew. I'm perfectly capable of speaking for myself." Eleanor told them about her conversation with Rebecca.

"You mean Michelle never went home?" Norman asked.

"I'm sure there's some logical explanation," Grace said. "This Becca person must have muddled the plane times. Or Michelle intended to meet her husband in New York or somewhere else and forgot to let her friend know."

"Don't be such an idiot, Grace." Eleanor glared at her. "We all know how you felt about Michelle."

"What's that supposed to mean?" Grace demanded.

"You wouldn't care if she lived or died, so long as I didn't leave money to her, right?"

Grace's face blanched. "I'm not even going to reply to that."

"Good. Because you know it's true. What do you think, Norman?"

"I think we should be very careful of our facts before we approach the police," he said slowly.

"Meanwhile, Michelle could be locked away somewhere, being abused or who knows what?"

Andrew's expression grew even tenser. "If she's been kidnapped, Mrs. Tyler, they will look after her well, so they can get their ransom."

"And how many kidnappers have killed their victims, despite getting the ransom, tell me that?"

"Before we all go overboard," Norman said, "let's cover all the logical possibilities first. I agree with you, Mother. We should start an investigation immediately, but you know how something like this would erupt like a volcano if even one person in the media got hold of it. I'll speak to Michelle's partner and ask her to keep it quiet until we've set our own security people onto it, okay?"

"If you think that's best, but I can't bear the thought of her being held captive and suffering—"

"I'm sure that's not the case," Grace said firmly. She was tempted to mention the call from the Gaudry brother, but figured she'd wait and see how things developed. "Let Norman deal with it." She turned to Andrew. "I take it we can rely on your discretion here?"

Andrew didn't respond.

"Andrew?" Grace's voice sharpened.

He nodded, then turned to put his stethoscope back in his leather bag.

Grace went to her mother's bed and took her hand. "Try not to worry. I'm sure Michelle's just fine, wherever she is."

Chapter 28

The car from the Bali Hyatt Hotel was waiting for Brian at Denpasar airport. As he settled back on the leather seat he took a deep breath, savoring the air-conditioned coolness, a welcome contrast to the steamy heat of the night outside.

He'd suffered only a slight concussion, but they'd all been pretty shaken up by the experience. The police had helped them out of the melee and escorted Brian to the nearest hospital to make sure he was okay. He'd ended up with nothing more serious than a pounding headache.

Brian immediately decided that a couple of days rest in Bali would be good for all of them and they'd managed to get an evening plane out of Jakarta. His crew had chosen to spend their first night on the island in Kuta, the brash, lively pub-and-club part of Bali. Vince—armed with his backup videocamera—promised to bring back some great video footage of Kuta nightlife, to contrast with the grim realities of Jakarta and East Timor. Brian had opted for a far quieter stay in the oceanside Bali Hyatt resort at Sanur.

As the car drew up before the hotel entrance, he swallowed a lump in his throat. The last time he was here Michelle had been with him. She'd been reluctant at first to fly halfway around the world for their honeymoon. "Trust me," he'd told her, and she had. When, after the long journey, she'd mounted the steps to the open-sided, bamboo-roofed foyer, and turned to him with shining eyes, saying only "Oh, Brian," he'd released a long pent-up sigh of relief, knowing that he'd chosen the right place.

The foyer was more like some vast ancient ceremonial meeting place than the center of a hotel. Deep-seated cane chairs with bright silk cushions were lit softly by lamps made of natural stone with silken shades. Here—and throughout the grounds of the hotel—were the small stone carvings of the gods that were ubiquitous to the island, always decorated with delicate floral offerings. The foyer was open to the sounds and warmth of the sultry night, the rustle of trees and sweet-scented plants that were always threatening to take over in the tropics. This potent combination of luxury and nature had a wonderfully sedating effect.

But as Brian entered his room, with its gleaming marble bathroom and king-size bed, he began to think that coming here without Michelle had been a big mistake. The place was filled with memories for him. His longing for her was a physical ache in his heart as well as his body.

"Hang on," he told the bellboy. He opened his duffel bag, hung up his last clean pair of tropical pants and a couple of shirts, and gave the rest of his clothes to the bellboy to be cleaned. "Tomorrow morning, as early as possible, please." Having handed him a couple of American dollars—more valuable than gold to the Indonesians, with the current low value of their rupiah—Brian slid open the glass door and went outside to the tiled sitting area. He sat down in the rattan chair and lit a clove-scented cigarette.

He never smoked at home, but somehow this part of the world—where everyone seemed to smoke—brought back his old craving. He could remember Michelle commenting on the bizarre sight of several men dressed in their brightest silk sarongs and turbans for a religious ceremony, hoisting the statue of one of their gods to their shoulders, nearly all of them with a cigarette hanging from their lips.

He switched on the overhead fan and sat in the rattan chair, stretching out his legs. Then he glanced at his watch. Just after midnight. Eleven in the morning central time in North America. Would Michelle be at the store yet? Of course she would. When he was away, she liked to fill up the time with work. Smiling, he closed his eyes, imagining her performing the mundane tasks of her usual morning routine, switching on the lights, making the coffee, watering the plants, checking for messages.

His heartbeat speeded up. Breathing in one last gust of clove smoke, he stubbed the cigarette into the ashtray on the rattan table and went back into the room to pick up the telephone receiver.

What a pleasure to be able to get a line immediately! he thought as the phone rang in his ear. The machine picked up and he heard Michelle's voice brightly telling him, "You've reached Simple Pleasures, the gift store for all ages and prices. Leave a message and we'll get back to you."

Brian thought it strange when no one picked up, but perhaps they were busy with customers. He left a message. "I love you, Mish. I'll call again in a few minutes. Soon be home." Then, longing to speak to her right away, he decided to try the apartment, in case she was there.

As he dialed their apartment number, he looked around the hotel room, taking in the delicate little touches that were so typically Balinesian—the pottery bowl of hibiscus blossom, yellow and orange, and the fruit basket containing small sweet tropical bananas and passion fruit.

The answering machine at the apartment clicked on and he heard Michelle's voice again, telling him to leave a message. "It's Brian, sweetheart." When no one picked up, he left his number, then said, "It's just past eleven o'clock Winnipeg time. I'll try the store again. Love you," and set the receiver back in its cradle.

His excitement at the thought of being able to speak

to Michelle at last was swiftly fading to disappointment at not being able to get her right away. Disappointment . . . and apprehension. *Don't be an idiot*, he told himself. *What could be wrong?* Michelle was busy at the store, that was all. Or she was out on some business matter.

When he called the store ten minutes later, the machine came on again. He crashed the receiver down in the middle of the message. Even if Michelle wasn't there, where the hell was Rebecca?

He opened his carry-on bag and got out his Palm organizer to look up Rebecca's home number and then dialed it. Becca's line was busy. Brian cursed. But at least that meant he might eventually get hold of someone other than a machine.

He dialed Becca again. This time, to his huge relief, she answered with a breathless "Yeah?"

"Hi, Becca. Brian here. I'm calling from—"

"Thank God! I tried to get you through the network, but they said you'd left Jakarta and—"

"What's wrong? Has something happened to Mish?"

"She's disappeared, Brian. I don't know where she is."

"What do you mean, *disappeared*?"

"If you'd quit yelling, I'll try to explain."

Brian sank onto the bed. "Sorry. Go ahead."

"I promised Michelle I'd pick her up at the airport Monday night. But when I went there she wasn't on the plane from Toronto."

"Maybe you'd got the wrong flight."

"Hallo-o," Becca said sarcastically. "Even if I had missed her, she'd be home by now, wouldn't she? But she isn't."

"Did you try her grandmother's house in Fredericton?"

"Yep. When I got home Monday night, I called to find out what had happened to her. Some guy told me she'd decided to stay on for a few more days."

"What guy?"

"I don't know. Wish I did."

"Was this at the Tyler place? In Fredericton?"

"Yeah. Would you please let me finish?"

"Sorry." Brian's heart was pounding hard.

"This guy, whoever he was, told me she was with her grandmother at the Tyler cottage. Apparently, there was no telephone there."

"So you didn't speak to Michelle."

"No. I couldn't call her, he said. I thought it was weird that she hadn't called me herself to let me know she was staying on. Surely there'd be a pay phone somewhere near the cottage."

"Mish took her cell phone with her."

"There you go. When she still hadn't called me since Monday I began to get pretty mad with her for leaving me high and dry without even a word."

Brian felt as if he were suffocating. "She wouldn't do that."

"I know, but apparently she *had* done it. I guessed she was so excited about being with her family she couldn't find the time to call."

For God's sake, get on with it, Brian wanted to yell, but he kept his mouth shut.

"Earlier this morning, I got this call from Eleanor Tyler, Michelle's grandmother."

I know who she is! Brian felt like shouting.

"According to her, Michelle left their cottage Monday morning without saying good-bye. Mrs. Tyler said she'd thought that was weird, but all Michelle's things were gone and there was a brief note, so she didn't think there was anything wrong."

"Let me get this straight. Mrs. Tyler thought Mish had left the cottage to go to Fredericton airport."

"That's what the note said."

"How was she going to get there?"

"She ordered a taxi of some sort."

"Has anyone found the driver of this taxi?"

"How the hell would I know?" Becca screamed

down the line. "I'm here in Winnipeg, trying to tell you all I know, but you keep frigging interrupting."

Brian dropped his head, releasing a heavy sigh. "God, Becca. Just give me the end part of all this. I can't take the suspense."

"There is no end part. Mrs. Tyler was supposed to get back to me with what's going on there, in Fredericton. She said she'd get her son to contact the police and then she'd call me back, but she didn't."

"Why?"

"I'm about to tell you. An hour ago, I got a call from Mrs. Tyler's doctor, who told me she'd had a slight accident and was resting. He wanted to know if I'd heard from Michelle, so I told him I hadn't. He sounded pretty worried about her."

"Why would Mrs. Tyler's doctor be worried? Never mind, don't bother with that now. Have you spoken to any other members of the Tyler family since then?"

"Yes. I was about to tell you. Just before you called me, I spoke to Michelle's uncle, Norman Tyler."

"And?"

"He was pretty cagey. Demanded to know who I was before he'd answer any questions, that sort of idiot. Sorry, Brian, I know they're Mish's relatives, but this guy really got to me. He didn't seem to give a damn about Michelle."

"He'll give a damn when I talk to him," Brian said, his jaw tightening.

"He said he was calling in his own security firm to deal with it."

"Not the police?"

"He doubted that they'd take on a missing persons case this early. You have to be missing much longer than this, he said."

"Bullshit. Where can I get hold of this guy?"

"I called him at Tyler Foods. He complained I'd pulled him out of an important meeting."

"Did he? Right. What's his number?"

As he was writing it down, Becca said, "When I called Tyler House again, I asked for Michelle's grandmother, but they told me she was still resting after the accident. Could the two be connected, do you think? Michelle's disappearance and her grandmother's accident?"

"Who knows?" At the moment, Brian only cared about Michelle, not her grandmother. "Did you try the airline?"

"Yes. They wouldn't give out any information. I've been going crazy, wondering if I should get in touch with the police here, or what. I can't tell you how glad I was to hear your voice."

"Give me the airline number." Becca read it out to him. "Any other numbers you called?"

"No, that's it," she said.

"Thanks, Becca. This gives me a start, at least."

"What could have happened to her?"

"God alone knows, but I'm sure as hell going to find out. Can you stay at home?"

"Yes, I thought that's what I'd do, in case she calls from somewhere."

"Right. Keep by the phone and try not to tie it up with any other calls."

"Is it difficult for you to call me from there?"

"Not at all. I'm in civilization again, at the Sanur Bali Hyatt." He gave her the number. "I'm filthy. Got to take a fast shower. Then I'll call Fredericton."

"Will you call me if you have any news? Anything at all, however insignificant?"

"Sure will. Don't worry. Mish could have been in a minor accident herself and be waiting in a hospital emergency room somewhere."

"That's what I thought. I suggested that to Norman Tyler."

"And?"

"He said he'd get his secretary to call the Fredericton hospitals for me."

"For you?" Brian exploded. "Doesn't *he* care about his niece?"

"Apparently not. Maybe you'll be able to get some action out of him."

"You'd better believe I will. Hang in there, Becca."

"You, too. Brian . . ."

"Yeah?"

"I'm so sorry."

"Nothing to be sorry about. You did all the right things."

"When I called the network in Minneapolis, they said they weren't able to get hold of you. Some riots in Jakarta. Of course, that got me even more worried, thinking—"

"I'm fine," Brian said, cutting her short. "You've been great. I'll get on to it now. If Mish calls you, let me know immediately, anytime. I'm going to sign off now, but I'll be in touch, I promise. Once I've spoken to a few people, I'm going to get a flight out of here as soon as I can. I wish it could be tonight, but that's not possible. It's after midnight here. Soon as I know when, I'll let you know."

"Can you do that? Get away, I mean? Won't the network want you to stay on?"

"I don't give a shit what they want. I'm outta here tomorrow. Must go. Thanks, Becca."

"Bye, Brian. Try not to worry. Maybe she'll call."

But as he set down the receiver, Brian knew in his heart that she wouldn't. If Michelle had been able to call she would have been in touch with Rebecca or Tyler House by now.

What could have happened to her? As he stood in the tiled shower stall beneath the pulsating water, his mind ran in all directions, trying to cover all the possibilities, but it was hard to conjecture until he had more facts to work on.

He wrapped himself in the thick terry-cloth robe and called room service to order a large pizza and six Bintang beers, preparing for a long night.

Setting himself up with the phone on a table at his side, he switched on the television, tuning into CNN with the sound turned off. As he dialed the Tyler Foods number Becca had given him, he tried to shake off that sense of foreboding that had been dogging

him since he'd made that first call to Tyler House,
when they'd told him Michelle was asleep. He'd felt
that something was off then. Now his suspicions had
been confirmed.

Chapter 29

~

Norman went home early on Thursday. So early, in fact, that he surprised Lauren, who was stretched out on the couch in the family room, watching Oprah. When she heard his key in the lock she jumped up, but in her haste to turn off the television, she dropped the remote, and Norman was standing in the doorway before she had time to find it.

"I didn't know you watched this junk," he said, crossing the room to switch off the television.

"Oprah isn't junk," she told him. "You're home extra early tonight. Anything wrong?" Her eyes widened. "Is your mother—"

"Apart from a sore ankle, my mother's fine." His gaze ran over her, taking in the jeans and sweatshirt.

Lauren's cheeks grew red. "I was about to take a shower and change. I was working out on the exercise bike."

"Good," he said absentmindedly. "What are we eating tonight?"

"I can order in a pizza, if you like."

He closed his eyes for a moment. "I wish you'd learn to cook."

Lauren's sapphire eyes glinted. "You didn't stipulate cooking when you asked me to marry you."

"Sorry, sweetheart. It's just that I've asked Grace and Larry—and Stewart—to come over. I thought we could have a dinner meeting."

"I've got a big casserole of Janet's chili in the

freezer. I can heat it up in the microwave. How would that do?"

"Perfect." He came to her then and put his arms around her, pulling her tightly against him. God, how young her body felt against his, young and firm. He buried his face in her sweet-smelling hair. "Sorry I'm being such a miserable bear."

She pulled away to look up into his face. "What's wrong, honey? Is it the merger?"

His body tensed and he frowned down at her. "You do remember that you mustn't mention the merger to *anyone*, don't you?"

"Of course I do," she said indignantly. "I'm not stupid, you know. You told me it mustn't go outside the family."

"Okay." He ran his hand through his hair. It still felt strange to feel hair there, after years of having only a few thin strands left. "Michelle's husband called me from Bali this afternoon. He's mad as hell."

"I'm not surprised. I'm sure you'd be the same if I'd disappeared the way Michelle has. He must be worried sick."

"He is."

"What did he say?"

"He wants me to call in the police right away."

"Oh. But you said you didn't want to do that, didn't you?"

"If I call in the police, it will get to the media, and that would be disastrous at the moment, with only nine days to go before the merger deadline."

"Did you tell him why you don't want to call in the police?"

"No, of course I didn't. He's a member of the media himself, isn't he?" Norman shook his head. Although he loved her, sometimes Lauren could be astonishingly . . . guileless. He'd thought "innocent" at first, but she was certainly no innocent in bed. Just the thought of her in bed made him come alive. He glanced at his watch. Quarter to five. No, there wasn't even time for a quickie. Grace had said she and Larry would be over by five.

Lauren flashed a sexy smile at him, as if she could read his mind. *Later*, her blue eyes promised. "I'll go get the chili out of the freezer."

"Thanks, sweetheart." Norman took off his suit jacket and flung himself down onto the couch, dragging off his tie. *God, what a mess!* he thought. This was all they needed at this crucially sensitive time: his mother falling down the stairs and Michelle's irate husband demanding they bring in the police and promising to make the Tyler family responsible for whatever had happened to his wife. All this because his mother had insisted on inviting Michelle for Thanksgiving. It was as if there were a curse on their family. His sister Carolyn's curse, perhaps?

As if conjured up by his brain from a deep underground vault somewhere, an image of Carolyn's face swam into his mind. The face of a sixteen-year-old child, pinched and defiant, as she defended her right not to be forced to have an abortion. He could hear his father's voice in his head, bellowing that she'd do what she was told, or else she could leave this house and never come back again.

Norman was still living at home then, a young man of twenty-four who'd recently completed his MBA, but he hadn't dared defy his father by supporting his younger sister. When, an hour later, he'd heard the front door crash behind his sister, something deep within him had stirred—pity, or perhaps envy? He'd hurriedly opened the window of his room on the third floor and called down to her. When she looked up, he threw down a book with eighty-five dollars inside, wrapped with an elastic band. It was all the cash he had. That was the very last time he'd seen Carolyn.

"Stewart's here," Lauren said. Norman jumped, startled by her voice intruding into his thoughts. "Sorry, were you asleep?" She put a tray of cheese and crackers and pickles on the coffee table.

"No, just thinking." He got up slowly, the old football injury still making his knee stiff when he sat for any length of time. Old age coming on, he thought, depression creeping over him as his gaze lingered on Lauren's lithe body.

Well, at least he was in better shape than Stewart, he thought, when his brother sidled in, his rust-colored sweater clinging to his protuberant stomach.

"What the hell's going on?" Stewart demanded belligerently.

"We need to talk."

"Thought we had already, on the phone." Stewart looked around. "I'll have a scotch, thanks."

"I'm not giving out drinks. It's imperative that everyone keeps a clear head. We've got a lot to work out."

Stewart turned and went to the door. "Then I'll get my own bottle, if I have to."

"For God's sake, Stewart, can't you go one hour without booze?"

"Sure, I can. I don't choose to do so, that's all."

Norman sighed and shook his head. "I don't know how Anna stands you."

"She has her faults, too."

Norman opened his mouth . . . but, determined not to undermine this meeting, kept his comment to himself. "What about a beer?"

"Moosehead?"

"Of course."

"Okay." Stewart sat in the leather armchair and swung his feet clad in comfortable Timberland shoes onto the footstool, while Norman fetched the beer. "How's Mother?" he asked when Norman set the pewter tankard on the table in front of him.

"Haven't you called her?"

"I saw her this afternoon. Any change since then?"

"None that I know of. Andrew said the bruising is pretty bad, but that was to be expected. He said he'd call Grace with the results of the X ray as soon as he gets them."

Their eyes met. "She could have broken her leg," Stewart said.

"Or her neck."

"Are you sure you didn't stretch a cord across the top stair?" Grinning, Stewart raised his eyebrows at Norman.

"That's not even one bit funny. What a bloody awful thing to say!"

Stewart shrugged and looked down into the tankard of beer.

"What's a bloody awful thing to say?"

Both men looked up to find Grace standing there.

"I can't believe you still do that, Gracie," Stewart said.

"What?" Grace demanded.

"Creep up on people so you can listen in to what they're saying."

"I wasn't doing that," Grace said, her face flushed with indignation. "The front door was open. Anyone could have walked in."

"Where's Larry?"

"Coming. We took separate cars this afternoon. I needed to go in to see how Mother was doing."

"How is she?"

"Shaken up. Her right side and both legs are very painful. It's a miracle she wasn't killed."

"That's what we were saying."

"Ah, now I understand." She sat down, crossing her still shapely legs. "Stewart was asking if you'd stretched a cord across the stairs."

"So you *did* listen in. Oh, no," Stewart said in a pseudo-female voice, "I never creep up on people to eavesdrop."

"Drop it, Stewart." Norman leaned forward. "This is serious, and you know it."

"You'd better believe it," Grace said. "We still haven't persuaded Mother to accept the merger and we've got only nine days left."

"Well, you've had more chances to be with her than we've had," Norman said. "She's weaker now since the fall. She might be willing to give in just to get us off her back."

"Did you speak to Douglas, as you promised?" Grace asked. "I thought you were going to ask him to arrange some sort of competency hearing."

"It can't be done in time," Norman said flatly. "Besides, you saw how he was over the will thing. Not sympathetic at all to our problem."

"So we have to do this without Douglas, right?" Grace's fingers twisted in and out of the strap of her leather handbag.

"It's safer that way. At least Douglas admitted that she hadn't signed any papers yet, so we know she hasn't changed her will. If this thing's going to go through, all three of us will have to lean on Mother."

Stewart took a drink from his tankard. "It's hard when she's so fragile. I hate to see her like this."

Grace rounded on him. "We all do. But in the end, she's going to benefit as well, isn't she?"

"Face it, Stewart," Norman said. "She's out of touch with the reality of the current business world. Has been for several years. The days of the family business are done. Look at what happened to the Eaton family. And now I hear that Bata Shoes is closing its factory in Canada."

"I suppose we could wait until Mother . . . goes." Stewart blinked rapidly.

"By then it would be too late. Do you want us to have to declare bankruptcy like the Eatons?"

"You know damn well I don't," Stewart said, his face reddening.

"Well, then. It's up to you to play your part, pull your weight." Norman shrugged. "Let's face it, Mother listens to you more than she does to Grace and me."

"She always did have her favorites," Grace declared.

Stewart rolled his eyes. "If you two are going to play the *Who's the favorite?* game I'm out of here."

"We're not, but—" Grace's comment was interrupted by the front doorbell ringing. Her face brightened and she sprang up from the couch. "That'll be Larry. I'll let him in."

"Wait," Norman said. "Lauren can let Larry in. Before he joins us, I want to know how much you've told him?"

"About the merger? Everything." Grace frowned. "I thought we'd agreed—"

"Yeah, yeah. We need Larry's input from an international aspect. Okay, then we can discuss that with him. But there's the other matter."

"What's that?"

"Michelle. What the hell are we going to do about Michelle's husband?"

"Who cares?"

"We all should. He's coming here as soon as he can get his flights arranged."

Chapter 30

~

The pile of logs against the house was noticeably decreasing. Every time Michelle went outside she checked it. The temperature had dropped considerably on Wednesday night, so that the Brute (as she'd taken to calling her captor in her mind) had to keep piling logs onto the fire all night to keep them from freezing.

"We need more logs," she told him Thursday morning when he was taking her to the outhouse. She paused to indicate the depleted pile.

"Get going," he muttered.

"What about more logs?" she asked again.

"We've got plenty logs," he told her.

"It was freezing cold during the night."

"I am not cold."

All right for you, buddy, sleeping in front of the fireplace, she wanted to say, but the Brute's uneven temper had taught her to be wary of antagonizing him.

When he opened the door to the outhouse, the stench gushed out at them. Michelle recoiled, trying to stifle the retching that rose in her throat. "That's disgusting. Don't you have some Pine-Sol or some other disinfectant?"

"Just get in," he told her, and shoved her inside.

She tried to hold her breath as she latched the door and turned to sit down. The wooden seat was mired with frost, so that by the time she stepped out into the blessedly fresh and frosty air, she was visibly shivering with the cold. In any other circumstances she might have enjoyed the crisp morning, the sight of the silver-coated tree branches, the mist hanging in the air, the crunch of leaves beneath her feet, but her fear of this man, of what was going to happen to her, tainted everything. She pretended that Brian was inside the cabin, making hot chocolate for her, grating dark bittersweet European chocolate on the frothy top. She was learning to use her imagination to lift her flagging spirits, determined to keep trying to send good vibes down the pipeline to her baby.

Although one arm was still bound behind her back, the Brute had reluctantly allowed her to switch arms when she told him she was losing the feeling in the fingers of her right hand. She tried to exercise as much as possible: usually one-armed tai chi, which relaxed her tensed muscles and helped her to breathe more easily.

She also tried to engage the Brute in conversation, hoping to find out where the cabin was, but this man was not a talker and questions made him angry. When she made breakfast for herself, she checked out the food situation. There were two cartons of long-life milk and a box and a half of cereal, but there was hardly any fruit left and the bread supply was dwindling fast, mainly because the Brute devoured three or more sandwiches at a time.

"We need some more groceries," she told him as she came out of the kitchen with her breakfast tray.

"Oh, yeah?" He grinned at her with nicotine-stained teeth. "You want I go leave you for 'alf a day to go to the store with my little grocery list? Nice try, lady."

She digested this information. Half a day. Her heart sank. Whatever half a day meant to him, to her it meant that they were deep in some wood or forest, reasonably far from civilization.

"We need bread, salad stuff, fresh fruit, and vegetables."

He grinned again. "You planning to stay a long time 'ere with me, no?"

"Not if I can help it," she said coldly. "But if you want to get a good ransom for me, you'll need to keep me healthy." As if to illustrate her point, she sneezed, almost dropping the tray.

He just looked at her with that sly look of his, his half-closed eyes peering from the ski mask he always wore, then gave a Gallic shrug, and walked past her into the kitchen.

Grabbing a handful of tissues, she sat down on the couch that was also her bed and pulled a blanket around her knees, staring down at the food on the tray. This cold, plus the nausea mixed with despair, were making her actively anti-food, but she knew that she must eat.

Had the kidnappers made a ransom demand yet? she wondered as she took a spoonful of her mushy Weetabix—the Brute had finished off the box of bran flakes last night. If whoever had kidnapped her had sent a demand, to whom had they sent it: Eleanor? No, not Eleanor. She felt a spasm around her heart. What was happening to her grandmother? Please God, keep her safe, she prayed. The kidnappers certainly couldn't go to Brian. Brian, the one person who would scour heaven and earth to find her, was far away in Indonesia, unaware of what had happened to her. A single tear dropped into the plastic bowl of milk and cereal.

Enough of that, she told herself. *Keep to the point.* Okay, the kidnappers—she preferred to think that they truly were kidnappers, even if it meant they might well be her half brothers—would probably have approached Norman Tyler, wouldn't they? Norman was the man holding the money bags. What was she worth to him? she wondered. Precious little, she guessed. Even if they hadn't actually planned this, Norman and his family would be glad of the chance to get rid of her. She was a threat to them.

Which brought her back once again to the chilling supposition that her mother's family, not some fortune-hunting hoodlums, was behind her kidnapping and would be perfectly able to cover up her absence for several days, at least, if not more.

No! She mustn't dwell on negative thoughts. Surely by now Becca would be demanding to talk to her. She knew Becca. She'd be furious that Michelle hadn't spoken to her in almost a week. Even if her abduction had been orchestrated by the family, Becca would have started asking questions by now.

Probably contacting Brian, Michelle thought with a sudden tidal wave of hope. Once Brian knew she was missing, he'd come racing back to Canada, determined to find her.

She picked up her mug of black currant tea, but it remained suspended in the air. All this, of course, depended on the premise that whoever had kidnapped her wanted her kept alive.

What if the whole object was to make her disappear . . . forever?

Surely, if that had been the case, she would have been killed immediately, she conjectured, striving to think positively. But she knew it was not necessarily so. Whoever they were, her kidnappers might be waiting to make sure of something before they killed her. Keeping their options open.

And although he hadn't physically hurt her . . . yet, Michelle sensed that the Brute was perfectly capable of carrying out any orders he was given. Even murder.

Michelle sat there, staring into space, her mug of herbal tea untouched and cooling fast.

Chapter 31

It had taken Brian more than thirty hours to get from Bali to Fredericton. He'd managed to get an executive seat on a flight out of Denpasar airport on Thursday afternoon, Bali time. Since then he'd been changing planes, racing to make tight connections, blarneying his way to the head of long lines, all to make sure he got to Fredericton as soon as possible. And throughout this time he'd silently prayed like he hadn't prayed since he was a kid of nine, when he'd asked the Holy Mother to intercede for him for a very special, very expensive pair of hockey skates for Christmas.

He managed to get an Air Canada flight out of Toronto, which landed him into Fredericton airport just before noon on Friday.

"Tyler House!" he barked at the cabdriver as he threw his bags into the backseat and settled into the front seat beside the driver. He'd entrusted Vince with all his precious videos to take back to Minneapolis, telling him to say he'd be in touch with the network as soon as he could. Too bad if Sam didn't understand. He scrabbled for the address of Tyler House in his pocket.

"I know where Tyler House is," the guy said. "You visiting the Tylers?" he asked, eyeing Brian with interest.

"Something like that," Brian replied. Normally he would have been happy to get into a conversation with the driver, but he didn't want to talk. "Sorry," he said, feeling he should explain. "I've been flying all night and day without any sleep."

"You from the States?"

"Right."

"Boston?"

"No, Minneapolis. But I've flown in from Asia."

"What part?"

"Indonesia." Big mistake, Brian thought as soon as the name escaped him. If he'd said *Bali* the guy probably wouldn't even have known it was part of Indonesia.

"Is that right? They've been having quite a time of it there, haven't they? Terrible things happening in East Timor and Prime Minister Chretien wanting to send in seven hundred troops and all we could find was two hundred because so many of our lads are already serving in Bosnia and Kosovo and Rwanda and God knows where. I tell you, if they don't put more money into the Canadian military soon, we'll have to be saying no to the United Nations, which wouldn't look too good for Canada, would it? And then there's the equipment they expect them to work with. Did you hear about the planes that had to turn back when . . ."

Brian let him drone on, trying to make appropriate responses at the right times, but his mind was entirely taken up with Michelle. *I'm on my way, Mish. I'll find you, wherever you are.*

"Come straight to my office," Norman Tyler had told him when Brian had called from Toronto to say he was on his way to Fredericton, but Brian was determined to see Michelle's grandmother before he saw anyone else. Whatever was going on, he sensed that he might get the most direct and credible answers to his questions from Eleanor Tyler.

When the cab swung into the driveway and pulled up outside Tyler House, Brian whistled silently. The old house and extensive grounds reeked of money.

"Keep the meter running, would you? I won't be staying long."

Leaving his bags in the cab, he ran up the steps and pressed the gleaming brass doorbell. He heard footsteps and then the door was opened by a stocky, elderly woman. "Yes?" she said with a hesitant smile.

"Hi," he said, smiling. "I'm Brian, Michelle's husband." He stepped inside before she could stop him.

"Who is it, Janet?" called a woman's voice.

Brian caught the flash of anxiety in Janet's eyes. "It's Michelle's husband, Mrs. Anderson."

Mrs. Anderson? Brian's eyes narrowed. When she appeared from the doorway on the right, he saw a thin, stylishly dressed woman of about fifty. He guessed she must be Michelle's aunt.

"Mr. Norton?" she said briskly, holding out her hand. "Grace Anderson, your wife's aunt." She shook hands like a man, a brief, solid handshake, but her body language was unwelcoming. She stood there, directly in front of him, blocking him from going any farther into the house. "My brother, Norman, is expecting you at his office."

Brian's temper soared, but he kept it hidden. "So he told me, but I wanted to see Michelle's grandmother first."

"I'm sorry, that's impossible. My mother's not well. She's under strict orders from her doctor to rest."

"I understand. I guess she's worried frantic about Michelle going missing."

"I imagine so."

God, what an icy bitch! He'd been prepared to play her game, but her coldness was getting to him, fast. "May I come in?" He brushed past her before she could say no. He turned to Janet, who was looking extremely uncomfortable. "Janet, I hope you won't mind, but I've had a hell of a journey halfway across the world. I'd give my right arm for a decent cup of coffee."

Her response to his smile and request was as he'd expected. "Of course." She hesitated, glancing at

Grace, and then said, "We're all worried sick about Miss Michelle."

"Thank you. That makes me feel very much better. But don't you worry. Now that I'm here, it won't be long before we find her, I promise you." He flashed a smile at her again, drawing her in as part of the "we."

With another glance at Grace, this time with a touch of defiance, Janet hurried away.

"You're not going to get rid of me," Brian told Grace, "so you might as well get used to having me around. I'm here to find my wife and I mean to do it quickly, before anything happens to her. Tell me," he added, before she had time to respond, "is there some special reason for your hostility toward me?"

She bridled visibly, the color rushing into her face. "I am not hostile, Mr. Norton. I merely object to people bulldozing their way into my mother's home."

"People?" he repeated in a soft voice. "Is that what I am to you? Just some nebulous person." He took a step closer to her, invading her space. "Your niece—my wife—has gone missing from this house," he said in a soft but menacing tone, "and no one seems to have done a frigging thing about it. But now I'm here and I'm going to find her, whatever it takes."

She stepped away from him, setting a distance between them. "There is no evidence that your wife has been abducted, Mr. Norton. No ransom demand."

"Nothing but the fact that no one has seen her since she left your house."

"Have you considered the possibility that she wanted to get away without someone being able to trace her?"

"By someone, I take it you mean me?"

"Look, Mr. Norton, it would be much better if you waited to discuss this with my brother. In fact, I'm going to call him now and tell him you're here. Have you booked a hotel room? Perhaps he can reach you there."

She turned away and was about to go through the

door on the right when a querulous voice from above said, "Who is it, Grace?"

Before Grace could reply, Brian moved to the foot of the stairs and saw an elderly woman peering over the railing. "It's Brian, Michelle's husband, Mrs. Tyler," he said, guessing that this was Michelle's grandmother. "I don't want to disturb you. Just wanted to let you know that I'm here and—"

Grace literally shoved him aside. "But you have disturbed her, Mr. Norton, and I must now ask you to leave this house and go to my brother's office, as arranged. My mother must not be—"

"How dare you, Grace Tyler!" The frail-looking woman had spirit, Brian thought, hiding a grin. "This is my granddaughter's husband. You will treat him as a member of the family, please. I can't come down, Brian, but I'd like you to come up and see me, once you've settled in."

"Settled in?" Grace said, her voice rising.

"Yes. Brian will be my guest while he's in Fredericton."

Brian was about to say that he'd prefer not to stay here, thank you very much, but kept his mouth shut. The best way to discover what was going on might well be to stay in Tyler House. After all, they could hardly move Mrs. Tyler out because he was there, could they? And he was sure that once he'd seen the police, Michelle's grandmother would be able to fill him in on what had happened here before Michelle disappeared.

"Do you understand me, Grace? Put Brian into Michelle's room."

"Whatever you say, Mother."

"Brian."

"Yes, Mrs. Tyler?"

"Once you're settled in, please ask Janet to bring you to see me."

"Thank you, I will."

"Where did you come from?"

"Today, you mean?"

"Yes. I take it you arrived in on the eleven o'clock flight from Toronto."

This woman was sharper than she appeared. "That's right. I flew from Bali."

"You must be exhausted. Have you had lunch yet?"

"Janet's getting me some coffee."

"Good. Grace will ask her to make up some sandwiches as well."

"Thank you." He didn't want to tell her he'd been stuffing himself with food on all his flights, to help pass the time.

"Michelle didn't tell me you were tall. My husband Ramsey was tall, too."

From behind, Brian heard Grace's grunt of exasperation. Apparently, her mother also heard it. "I'm going back to bed before my daughter explodes with an apoplectic fit."

"Thanks again, Mrs. Tyler," Brian called up to her.

"I'm so relieved you're here. I've been worried sick about Michelle."

Brian swallowed hard. "Me, too. See you later."

He sensed Grace's gimlet eyes piercing his back. He turned around. "Sorry about that."

"You're not bloody sorry about it at all. You barge your way in here without an invitation and smarm your way around Janet. Then you have the gall to wake my mother and get her out of her bed, when the doctor has ordered her not to get up because of the sedative medication she's on."

"Because of Michelle?"

"You may be an investigative journalist, Mr. Norton, but I'm not going to be interrogated by you in my own home. Please wait there in the hall until I call my brother."

"I have to pay the cabdriver and get my bags. Back in a minute." Before she could stop him, he went out the door and ran down the steps to the cab.

"Staying on here, are you?" the driver asked.

"I am." The driver got out. Brian hesitated, then drew out the photograph of Michelle he always kept in his wallet. "I'm looking for this woman. She's supposed to have taken a flight out of Fredericton on Monday morning. I don't suppose you happened to pick her up from here, did you?"

"Not Monday. I took the morning off to help my sister move house." The driver took the picture and looked at it. "Sorry. Never seen her. But I could show it to the other guys who do the airport route, if you like."

Brian hesitated, then he nodded. "Sure, that sounds good." He gave the driver his cell phone number. "Call me if you find anything out about her. Anything, okay?" He handed the driver one Canadian twenty-dollar bill. "That's for the fare." Then he gave him another. "That's for asking around about the photograph. Thanks."

The driver pocketed the money. "Want help with those?" he shouted to Brian, who was already taking his bags out of the backseat.

"No, I'm fine." Brian came to offer the driver his hand. "Thanks, buddy. Be sure to give me a call if you find anything, okay?"

The driver shook his hand. "I'll do that. And I'll drop the picture off next time I pass Tyler House. Good luck."

"Thanks. Looks like I'll need all I can get."

Grace met him on the porch. "Norman's on his way over."

"Great. That will save me having to waste time going to his office. Thanks, Grace." He grinned at her, ignoring her tight-lipped scowl.

She indicated the door to the family room down the hall and then left him to pour his own coffee. He sank onto the couch, glancing at the shelves of books, the fancy music system. So this was the place where Michelle's mother had grown up. Must have been hard for her to leave all this comfort behind. He thought of the cramped house in Chicago where he and his sisters and brother had grown up, and grinned. Better to be raised without money with his family than to be rich and have a sister like Grace.

A few minutes later, Janet brought in a plate of smoked salmon sandwiches, but she didn't stay to chat. Grace's orders, probably.

Although Brian ate a couple of the sandwiches, he didn't need any more food. What he'd really like now was a long hot shower to get the stale smell of airports and planes off him and then sleep for ten hours. He could probably get the shower—if they had showers in this old mansion—but he doubted he'd get the sleep for several more hours. Not that he thought he could sleep. He'd been wired ever since he'd left Bali. Sitting still on that first long flight had been agony. Thank God he'd managed to get an executive seat. With his long legs, it was always difficult to get comfortable, but he usually managed to sleep or to immerse himself in research material for the project he was on. This time, however, all he could think of was Michelle. His imagination ran riot, dwelling on the worst possible scenarios, so that he had to take a sleeping pill to stop himself from going berserk. Even then, when he dozed off, he was racked with nightmares of Michelle being dragged off by the student rioters in Jakarta and awoke, drenched in sweat, his heart racing. Better to stay awake, he'd decided, and put on the headphones to watch the movie, some ludicrous action pic with orchestrated violence that bore little resemblance to the real horrors of man's inhumanity to man that he'd seen only this week.

Now, as he reached out to pour himself another coffee into the small china cup, Brian's hands were shaking. Norman Tyler had better watch out. He felt like a ticking bomb, ready to explode at any minute.

When Norman walked in twenty minutes later, Brian recognized the type immediately. Mid-fifties, well groomed, expensive hair-job, even more expensive dark-gray suit. All affable bonhomie on the outside and manipulative on the inside. A politician to the core. Men like Norman Tyler made better politicians than businessmen in this end-of-the-century, technological era.

Norman held out his hand to shake Brian's and then clapped him on the shoulder. "Welcome to Fredericton. This your first visit to the Maritimes?" He pulled up the neatly creased trousers of his pin-striped suit and sat down in the chair opposite Brian.

Brian couldn't believe this guy. Here he was, frantic about his missing wife, and Tyler was making generic welcoming sounds. "Let's cut the crap, Tyler. I'm too tired to play games. I haven't slept since I spoke to you. What have you found out?"

Norman didn't blink, but his expression was wary. "Not much, I'm afraid. I've sent a man to St. Andrews, but he can't find any taxi drivers there who can recall picking her up from Prospect House, our summer home."

"That doesn't surprise me."

"Your wife could have walked into the town."

"Didn't you tell me on the phone that it was quite a long drive, never mind a walk, carrying her bags?"

"She might have hitched a ride."

"She might also have been abducted from the house and driven away."

"Oh, no, I doubt that very much. We would have heard. We have a security system at the main house."

"Were you all sleeping there?"

"No. Only my mother and Michelle, and my son, Ramsey and his wife. Grace and Larry were staying—"

"I take it he's Grace's husband."

"Yes. Sorry, I'd forgotten you didn't know about the family. Larry's coming over to meet you as soon as he can get away. Has to do his transatlantic calls in the morning, of course."

"Of course. What about Janet, was she there?"

"No. Janet always gets time off to be with her family after our Thanksgiving dinner."

"Which is on Saturday, right? Unusual that."

"Family tradition. We always have our turkey dinner on Saturday and then drive down to St. Andrews after the ten o'clock service on Thanksgiving Sunday."

"Did you know that I called here to speak to Michelle on Saturday?"

"No. Did you speak to her?"

"No. I was told she was sleeping."

"Sleeping? Did you call at night?"

"No, it would have been Saturday afternoon."

"Male or female? The person who answered the phone, I mean?"

"Male."

Norman shrugged. "Could have been one of several people. Ramsey or Eric, my sons, or Jamie, Grace's son, or Larry or Bob—"

"Who's Bob?"

"My mother's chauffeur cum general handyman. Lives in."

Brian made a mental note to speak to Bob. Norman glanced at his watch. He did it regularly, automatically. *Time is money*, Brian imagined him saying.

"So your wife was sleeping on Saturday afternoon. What significance has that?"

"Michelle never sleeps in the afternoon."

"For God's sake, man. I can see how worried you are, but you can't attach importance to such an insignificant little thing. She'd probably gone to her room to get away from the horde of Tylers and whoever answered the phone didn't want to disturb her. All I know is that I certainly didn't speak to you."

"I want you to find out who took that call."

"But we're talking about Saturday. Your wife didn't disappear until Monday morning."

"I want a detailed list of all that she did, and with whom, from the time she arrived on Friday until Monday morning."

"Very well." Norman didn't even try to hide his impatient sigh.

"Do you have a wife?"

"Yes, I do," Norman replied with a surprised expression. "Why do you ask?"

"I don't know anything about your relationship with your wife, but—"

Norman's eyes flashed with anger. "I love my wife very much."

"Then perhaps you might think about how you would feel if she'd suddenly disappeared into thin air and her own flesh and blood didn't seem to give a shit about her."

Norman's face reddened. "I'd be mad as hell."

Brian was surprised by his vehemence. He seemed to have struck a nerve. "Thank you. Now, perhaps, you will understand how I feel." He leaned forward, his hands on both knees. "Mr. Tyler, my wife came here to visit her mother's family, to spend Thanksgiving with them and her grandmother. While she's in the bosom of her family, so to speak, she disappears into the blue. Yet that family doesn't do a thing about it. They don't go to the police. They don't contact her husband or her business partner. How would you feel, if it were your wife?"

"Bloody awful," Norman muttered.

"Exactly. That's how I feel. Bloody awful. And my question is: Why? Why didn't you get the police in . . . I guess it would be the RCMP out of town, right?"

"They wouldn't investigate a missing person for at least forty-eight hours."

Brian gave him a quizzical look. "For the Tylers of Tyler Foods? Come on, boyo, let's get real here. If you'd called the local police sheriff—or whatever he's called, he'd have jumped through hoops for you."

Norman squirmed, but was saved from having to respond by the entrance of his sister and another man, tall, silver-haired, and languid, whom Norman introduced as Larry, Grace's husband. He and Brian shook hands.

"This is a rotten situation," Larry said immediately.

"It is," Brian agreed.

"I take it you haven't heard from Michelle?"

"I haven't spoken to Michelle since last Friday morning, the day she left to fly here. I called my network when I reached LA and she hasn't called there. Did you find her cell phone?"

"We found nothing," Grace said. "She took everything with her."

"I take it she wasn't planning to come back here, then? She took everything with her to your country house?"

"Apparently. As I said Michelle left nothing in her room." She lifted slim shoulders. "To be perfectly frank, we all thought that Michelle had deliberately left and gone somewhere other than home while you were in Indonesia." She flashed him a cold smile. "If you know what I mean."

"Oh, I know what you mean, all right," Brian said, anger forming a tight knot in his stomach.

"Hold on, Grace," Larry said in his English drawl. "That's a rather nasty presumption to throw at a man who's come halfway around the world to find his wife. I sat next to Michelle at the dinner table on Saturday. A charming woman I thought her."

Grace's eyes flared with something akin to jealousy. "Charming or not, that doesn't mean she didn't *want* to disappear, does it?"

"I suppose not, but—"

Brian stood up. He'd had enough talk. Now he wanted action. "I want to speak to Mrs. Tyler and to Janet."

Norman got to his feet. "I'm afraid that my mother—"

"If you don't let me speak to her I'm going to the police right away."

The three of them exchanged glances. "All right. As long as I can be there to prevent you upsetting her," Grace told him.

Brian nodded. "That's fine with me. If you'll excuse me now, I'd like to have a shower and get changed."

"I'll ask Janet to show you your room," Grace said.

"Thanks." Brian strode to the door and then turned again. "See you later, then," he told the two men who hadn't spoken a word since he'd told them he'd go to the police if they didn't let him see Michelle's grandmother.

What he hadn't told them, of course, was that as soon as he'd spoken to Janet and to Michelle's grandmother, his next move would be to go to the police anyway.

Chapter 32

—————

"**W**hy didn't you call her?"

That was how Eleanor Tyler greeted Brian when Grace took him to her room half an hour later. He felt better for having showered and changed into warmer clothes: chinos and the forest-green cableknit sweater Michelle had given him for his birthday, but he was still desperately in need of sleep and Eleanor's opening salvo startled him.

"Michelle? Why didn't I call Michelle, is that what you mean?"

"Of course I mean Michelle. Who did you think I meant? She was certain you would call her." Eleanor spoke as if each syllable were an effort. Her eyes were cloudy, unfocused, reminding him of people on Polynesian islands when they'd been drinking Kava. At first Brian thought Eleanor might have had too many drinks, but then he recalled Grace saying that her mother was under sedation. That must be quite a potent sedative!

At her bidding, he pulled up a chair and sat close beside her, while Grace was told to sit farther away. At first Eleanor had flatly told her she didn't want her there, but when Grace wouldn't budge, Eleanor merely glared at her and told her exactly where she was to sit. Brian could feel Grace's steely eyes boring into him from behind.

Eleanor sat, her knees wrapped in a blanket, in an armchair by the bay window with one foot propped on a footstool. Her silver hair was pulled severely back from her face, but nothing could take away from the fact that this was a strong and, yes, beautiful face. She reminded him of a recent picture he'd seen of Jane Goodall, the famous ethologist. Eleanor Tyler's face had the same classic bone structure.

"I did call Michelle, Mrs. Tyler," he told her.

"Here, at Tyler House?"

"Yes. On Saturday."

"Did you speak to her?"

"No, I was told that she was resting and couldn't be disturbed."

"How very odd. I know that she was longing to hear from you."

Brian felt guilt stab him like a dagger in the heart. "My cell phone wouldn't work in many of the areas I visited in Indonesia, and it was hard to get access to a phone."

"So I imagine," she said dryly. "To whom did you speak when you called here?"

"I've no idea. Your son said that, to his knowledge, it wasn't his brother, Stewart, and he certainly didn't take the call himself."

"It was a male voice, though."

"That's right."

She shook her head, as if trying to clear it. "Yet another mystery."

"Are there many mysteries, then?"

"Oh, yes, young man, there are, but I'm too tired to tell you all about them. But your wife knows. I told her all about my little dog and the cockroaches, and she was here when I saw Ramsey's ghost."

Whoa! What the heck was she on about now? Just when he'd thought she was eminently rational, despite the heavy sedation, Eleanor Tyler was going all Looney Tunes on him.

"I'm sure that Mr. Norton isn't interested in any of those things, Mother," Grace said hastily. He turned to look at her and she gave him a little shake of the head to warn him not to pursue her mother's ramblings.

He decided it might be better to include Grace in this discussion after all, and turned his chair toward her, although he addressed himself to Eleanor. "I wanted to ask you a few simple questions about Michelle."

"Ask away. We'll do anything we can to help you find her, won't we, Grace?"

"Naturally," was Grace's reply.

"Thank you. What I really need to know is what she did while she was here. Just a general rundown of her movements before you left for St. Andrews on Sunday."

Eleanor closed her eyes, obviously trying hard to remember, but it was Grace who replied. "Stewart picked her up from the airport and brought her here. We all met her—"

"When you say *we,* can you tell me who was here?"

"Me, Norman, Stewart, Mother, of course, and Janet."

"Not your husband or any of the younger members of the family?"

"No, they all arrived on Saturday. Larry, my husband, flew in from New York on Saturday morning and my daughter, Sophie arrived from Toronto with a friend. Most of the rest of the family live here, in Fredericton."

"Back to Friday, anything unusual happen?"

"Nothing, apart from your wife's arrival. Norman and I were here to meet her. She was given refreshments—it was after nine-thirty when she arrived—and then Janet showed her to her room upstairs."

"The same room I'm in now?"

"That's right. It's directly above this one."

"And Saturday?"

This time Eleanor answered before Grace could.

"Michelle went out and explored Fredericton. It was her only chance, as everything would be closed on Sunday and the holiday Monday."

"Where did she go, do you know?"

"She walked through the park to the Beaverbrook Art Gallery, had a snack at the hotel, and then did some shopping and—"

"What kind of shopping?"

"I know for certain that she bought something from Aitken's Pewter. I think she also went to the outdoor market and the loyalist cemetery."

"Did anyone go with her?"

"No, she was on her own," Grace replied. "We were all too busy getting everyone settled in and preparing for our Thanksgiving dinner."

"By everyone, I take it you mean your family?"

"That's right."

"No other visitors?"

"Only Mother's lawyer, Douglas Bradford."

Brian made a mental note of the name. "Was he here for dinner?"

"No," answered Eleanor, her voice curt. "He was here at my request."

He was immediately aware of a feeling of tension in the room that prickled the hair at the nape of his neck. What was so urgent that Eleanor had asked her lawyer to call on her the night of their family celebration?

"Was anyone else here from outside the family?"

"My daughter's so-called friend," Grace said, not even trying to hide her obvious dislike.

"Boyfriend?"

"Boy-toy friend, more like," said Eleanor with a chuckle, which made Grace clamp her lips together into a thin line. "Sophie must be at least five years older than him."

"For heaven's sake, Mother," Grace muttered, "what does it matter?"

"We're forgetting Andrew. He was here for dinner," Eleanor said.

"Andrew?"

"Yes, Mother's doctor, Andrew Lenzie."

"Your doctor had Thanksgiving dinner with you?"

"Andrew's the son of a dear school friend of mine and his father was also my husband's close friend." Eleanor pursed his lips. "But he's not the doctor his father was."

"Your wife and Andrew seemed to get on very well," Grace said.

Brian looked directly at her, catching her sly smile. "Oh?"

"So much so that they went out together after dinner."

Brian felt a spasm of anger. Did the wretched woman have to tell him with such relish? "Do you know where they went?"

Grace shrugged. "No idea. You'll have to ask Andrew."

"I will," Brian promised. "Do you know what time they came back?"

"They were back early, because that was the evening I saw Ramsey's ghost," Eleanor said, "and they were there. Of course, it wasn't really his ghost, but someone—"

"Mr. Norton is interested in Michelle's movements over the weekend, Mother, that's all. And I'm sorry to have to contradict you, but Michelle and Andrew went out *after* your little episode."

"Now, Sunday," Brian said, trying to ignore his baser instinct, which was clamoring to know what happened between this doctor and Michelle. It wasn't that he didn't trust her, but the thought of some other man having spent time with her, when she might be lying somewhere—No! He must not allow himself even to think that.

"Sunday we all went to the ten o'clock service at the cathedral," Grace said crisply. "Then Andrew drove Michelle back here."

Andrew again! Brian was prepared to hate the man even before he'd met him.

"Then we all took off for Prospect House," Eleanor said.

"That's your summer house, right?"

"Yes. We had our usual barbecue in the late afternoon. Then the young people drove to the Algonquin Hotel while we played some stupid board game."

"And Michelle?"

"She stayed with us," Eleanor said. For some reason, Grace's face went fiery red, as if she'd suddenly recalled something embarrassing, but whatever it was she didn't share it with him.

"Was the doctor with you?"

"Andrew? Oh, no. He was in Fredericton. He was going to his aunt's for Thanksgiving dinner on Monday."

"So . . . just your immediate family."

"Plus Sophie's dreadful boyfriend," Eleanor reminded him.

"Okay. Now we come to Monday morning." Brian's heart started pounding. "Tell me exactly what happened. Please don't leave anything out, however unimportant it might seem to you."

"Don't you want to take notes?" Grace's tone held a hint of sarcasm.

His eyes clashed with hers. "No, Mrs. Anderson. I'm used to retaining everything I'm told."

"He's a professional journalist," Eleanor reminded Grace. She turned back to Brian. "When Michelle didn't come down for breakfast I started to worry, because I knew she had to catch her plane and it's a fairly long drive to Fredericton from St. Andrews. Eventually, Grace went up to check on her and—"

"She wasn't in her room," Grace said. "There was nothing there except a note."

"Which you will want to see." Eleanor said. She opened her large leather handbag, took out a creased sheet of printed paper, and gave it to Brian.

Brian scanned the printed lines, reading them over and over again, trying to read between them. Each time, he stopped at the final line, jarred by it. As far as he could recall, he'd never known Michelle to sign off her letters with *All the best*. But then he hadn't read many of her letters, other than the many love letters or E-mails they'd exchanged. Other than to himself or her friends, with whom she was mainly on very affectionate terms, the only letters she wrote were business letters. For some reason, each time he read the note, that last line didn't sound right.

Grace held her hand out for the note, but he ignored her. "I'll keep this."

"Okay." Grace shrugged.

"For the police," Brian added. "Fingerprints. Your brother Norman told me he'd made inquiries, and as far as his people could discover, no known taxi driver picked her up at your summer home."

"That's right," Grace said.

"How was she planning to get back to Fredericton? I mean, before she disappeared, what was the plan?"

"My chauffeur, Bob, was going to drive her," Eleanor said.

"Bob?" Brian said sharply. "I didn't realize he was with you at St. Andrews."

"Yes, he comes down to help out with the barbecue and to do any repairs that might need doing to the cottage. The plan was that he would drive Michelle back to the airport. Mother was to drive back with us."

"How long has Bob worked for you?"

"He's been with the family for a long time," Eleanor said.

"More than twenty years," Grace said.

"And your brother told me that Janet was not there with you."

"That's right," Eleanor said. "Janet always spends a few days after Thanksgiving with her family in Fredericton."

"Oh!" Grace suddenly exclaimed. "That reminds me of the phone call Janet took on Saturday."

Brian swung around. "What phone call?"

"I'm not sure if it's of any importance or not, of course," Grace said, frowning.

"Well, don't keep it to yourself," Eleanor said impatiently. "What is it?"

"When we got back from St. Andrews, Janet said she'd forgotten to tell Michelle about a phone call that came in on Saturday night."

"A phone call for Michelle?" Brian asked.

"Yes. Apparently when Michelle was out with Andrew, one of the Gaudry brothers called for her."

"The Gaudry brothers," Eleanor repeated, frowning hard as if she was trying to access information in her befuddled brain. "Why wasn't I told about this call?"

Grace sighed impatiently. "You *were* told, Mother. You've just forgotten, that's all."

"Gaudry?" Brian said. "That was Michelle's father's name."

"That's right." Eleanor's breathing became labored. "He was the devil's spawn. Raped my daughter and—"

"Calm down, Mother. Besides, it wasn't rape. Carolyn was a willing participant."

"It was statutory rape. She was under the age of consent."

"That's all in the past," Brian reminded them. "What I'd like to know is who the Gaudry brothers are."

"Their father was Mike Gaudry," Grace said.

"Then they must be Michelle's half brothers, right?"

"I suppose so," Grace replied, not trying to hide the disdainful curl of her lip.

Brian frowned. "As far as I know Michelle's never been in touch with her father's family. I'd sure like to know why one of them was calling her. How did they know she was here?"

"That's what I was wondering," Grace said, her eyes gleaming.

"I aim to find out, but before I do I'd like to speak to Dr. Lenzie, if you'd give me his number."

Was it his imagination, or did he see a flash of anxiety in Grace's eyes? For some reason, Michelle's aunt seemed concerned about him meeting Andrew Lenzie. She stood up and led the way from the room, but when he was almost at the door, Eleanor called to him.

"Brian!"

He went back to her knowing that Grace was standing in the doorway watching them. "Yes, Mrs. Tyler."

Eleanor grasped his arm to draw him closer to her. He bent his head. "Don't leave me alone in the house with them," she whispered.

He tensed, wondering if Grace could hear the loud whisper. "You're safe here," he said soothingly. "No one's going to hurt you." Instinctively, he touched her hand, which was twisted with arthritis. The fingers clutched his convulsively.

"I'm afraid," she whispered. "I'm afraid for me and Michelle."

Brian held his breath for a moment.

"Everything all right?" Grace said, coming back into the room.

"Just fine," Brian replied. He gave Eleanor a reassuring smile and drew his hand from her clutching fingers. "I'll come and see you again," he promised her.

"What did she want?" Grace asked when he joined her in the hall.

"Only to tell me that she's worried about Michelle," Brian said.

"Aren't we all?" she said, but her words sounded hollow to Brian.

He walked past Grace to go downstairs again, but when he glanced down at his hand on the railing, he could still see the reddened imprint of Eleanor's fingers on his.

Chapter 33

W hen Brian spoke to Janet after he'd left Eleanor's room, she confirmed that one of the
Gaudry brothers had called on Saturday, but she
wasn't able to give him any fresh information about
Michelle's movements before she disappeared. Unlike
Grace, however, she did seem genuinely concerned
about Michelle's disappearance and confirmed that Eleanor had been distraught after she'd heard from
Rebecca.

"She fell down the small flight of stairs to the landing. I thought she was dead when I first saw her lying
there." Janet pressed a hand to her heart, her face
registering her anxiety as she relived the moment.

"She seems very heavily sedated," Brian said.

"Yes, she is. I hate to see her like that, but she's
been so terribly anxious about Michelle, it's probably
better for her."

Brian hesitated. He glanced around the large
kitchen, where they were sitting at the large pine
table, amicably drinking mugs of coffee. "She also
seemed—" He stopped, not able to gather his wits
into putting the question the right away, not wanting
to upset Janet. "Perhaps it's the medication, but she
seemed to go off into another world, talking about
mysteries and her dead dog . . ."

Janet heaved a sigh. "Oh, dear, not that again." She
shook her head. "She claims she saw the body of Griffon, her dog, on her bed one night. The dog had disap-

peared, you see, and she was very upset about it. We never did find out what happened to him. I think he must have been run over in the street, but she was certain she'd seen his body. It makes her very scared of sleeping in her bed, yet she won't sleep anywhere else."

"She spoke of other things."

Janet laid her arm on the table and leaned across to him. "She's imagining things, Mr. Norton," she said in a low voice. "The family's very upset about it. She was always so capable, mentally. She's been the backbone of Tyler Foods ever since her husband died."

"Did my wife know about this deterioration?"

"I think so. She said to me that she wished she'd come and visited her grandmother sooner."

Brian nodded. As far as he was concerned, he wished Michelle had never come to this bloody house at all, but he kept this feeling to himself. He pushed back his chair and stood up. "Thanks, Janet. You've been a real help. I've got to go and meet Mrs. Tyler's doctor at the Lord Beaverbrook Hotel. Is it far?"

"No, not at all, but you look really tired. Why don't you let Bob drive you?"

Brian was about to say that he'd rather walk, to keep himself awake, but decided to take advantage of this opportunity to talk to someone outside the immediate family who'd been at the summer house with them last weekend.

But he soon found that Bob was taciturn and given to answering questions in monosyllables. All Brian could get out of him, on the short ride to the hotel, was that he hadn't seen Miss Tyler since she went up to bed last Sunday. And he'd had to get up at the crack of dawn to be ready to drive her to Fredericton airport. Then she'd never come down from her room. "Course, they soon found out why, when Miss Grace went up and found the note she'd left," Bob told him. "Miss Grace said she must have printed it."

Brian turned halfway in his seat. "*Printed* it?" he repeated. Then he suddenly remembered he had the note in his pocket. He took it out and looked at it again. Yes, it was definitely a computer printout. Where the hell was his mind? He definitely needed to get some sleep . . . fast!

He didn't say anything more to Bob, but as he got out of the car, telling him he'd walk back, thanks, Brian reminded himself that—unless she'd changed her mind at the last minute, after he'd left for Indonesia—Michelle had told him she wasn't going to take her laptop, as she certainly wouldn't need it in New Brunswick and she knew that Brian couldn't E-mail her from anywhere but Jakarta or Bali. She was going to leave it with Becca, who'd wanted to try it out before she bought one for herself.

So how could she have left a printed note in her bedroom? he asked himself. He'd have to ask Becca whether Michelle had taken the lap-top or not, he thought as he pushed his way through the glass doors of the hotel.

Andrew Lenzie was sitting at the bar, as they'd arranged. He stood up and came forward to greet Brian, who'd told Andrew he was tall and "rangy-looking."

"You certainly are tall," Andrew said, holding out his hand.

"Useful. See me in a crowd," Brian said, but he didn't smile. He was leery of this man who'd spent time with his wife, and was also too tired for niceties. The doctor was of middle height with sandy hair and a pleasant, open face.

They shook hands and then sat down at the table. "What can I get you?" Andrew asked. He was drinking coffee and eating what looked like a seafood pasta. "Have you eaten?"

"To be honest, I can't remember." This time Brian did smile. "I've crossed so many time zones, I've probably eaten six breakfasts and five dinners. I'll have a coffee for now."

Andrew nodded to one of the servers. "Another coffee, Jim, and . . . How about a sandwich? You look sleep-deprived. Need some energy."

"Spoken like a true medical man. I'll have some of that pasta. Looks good."

"Good choice," Andrew said. "The seafood here is always fresh."

Brian eyed the man across from him. "You look a bit sleep-deprived yourself."

Fine lines of red appeared on Andrew's cheekbones. "I've been worried sick about Michelle ever since I heard she hadn't turned up in Winnipeg."

Brian admired his honesty. Andrew wasn't going to hide the fact that he'd liked Michelle. "Before we discuss my wife, can you tell me what's going on in that house?"

Andrew's eyes narrowed. "What do you mean?"

"There's something weird there. I can't put my finger on it exactly, but there's certainly a lot of antagonism between Mrs. Tyler and her daughter."

Andrew looked down at his dish of pasta. "Mrs. Tyler is getting older."

"And?" Brian said impatiently.

"And I guess her family is growing frustrated with her hold over the business."

Brian's heart skipped a beat. "It's a family-owned business, right?"

Andrew nodded.

"And Mrs. Tyler is the majority shareholder?"

"That's right." Andrew gave him a cautious smile. "It's an awkward situation."

"Is she going senile?" Brian asked bluntly.

"You know I can't discuss anything about her medical prognosis."

"She was talking about weird things to me. Dead dogs and cockroaches."

Andrew sighed. "Poor Eleanor."

"So you know about this stuff?"

"I'm her family doctor."

"Is she seeing a specialist?"

"You'll have to discuss that with her family, not me."

"From what I can see, they're all acting really weird,

as if they're hiding something. I mean, do they usually congregate at their mother's house? Don't they have homes of their own?"

"Can't leave the nest, I suppose." Andrew seemed reluctant to talk about the Tylers.

"It may be that I'm a bit weird myself from worry and lack of sleep, but I'm starting to wonder if Eleanor Tyler might have done something to Michelle and they're trying to cover it up."

Andrew looked startled. "Eleanor?" he repeated incredulously.

"Yeah, buddy. Eleanor. She could be off her rocker and the family's hiding what she's done. It would explain their strange reaction to Michelle's disappearance and to my obviously unwelcome arrival. For God's sake, man, they haven't even reported it to the police. What else am I to think?"

People were turning around to look at them and Brian realized that his voice had risen to the point of attracting attention.

Andrew grasped his arm. "Keep it down. This place is a hotbed of gossip."

"This bar, you mean?"

"The bar . . . and the town."

Brian leaned closer to him. "Another thing. She's dead scared of something."

"You mean Mrs. Tyler."

"Yep. Mrs. Tyler. She begged me not to leave her alone in the house."

Andrew's eyes widened. "Did anyone hear her say this to you?"

"Grace was at the bedroom door, but I don't think she could hear. What's going on, Lenzie? I can see that you know there's something."

Andrew bit his lip. "There's nothing concrete, but I must tell you that Eleanor would never ever harm Michelle. She was really excited about her visit. Michelle's disappearance has worried her so much that it's caused a marked deterioration in her mental health."

"She seems very heavily sedated."

"Necessary to keep her from crippling anxiety." Andrew looked at his watch. "I'm sorry, but I have a busy afternoon at the clinic."

"I plan to visit the local cop shop this afternoon. Anything you want to tell me about Michelle before I go?" Brian didn't even try to hide the menace in his voice.

Andrew shoved his plate of almost untouched pasta aside. "I liked your wife. We met only twice. We went for a walk on Saturday evening, when the atmosphere at Tyler House got too much for her, and had a cup of tea in the dining room, here. On Sunday morning, I drove her home from the service at the cathedral. We said good-bye. That was all."

Brian swallowed the lump in his throat. "Don't get me wrong. I trust my wife implicitly. If she was having a rotten visit with her family, I'm glad she had someone to enjoy an evening with." He leaned across the table. "But my wife has disappeared in mysterious circumstances and all her family can do is suggest, not very subtly, that she's run off with someone else."

Andrew lifted his head and laughed.

"What's so frigging funny?" Brian demanded.

"You could tell that she was head-over-heels about you," Andrew replied, his voice bitter. "And if you're so goddamned keen on her, why the hell were you thousands of miles away, when she was visiting her family for the very first time? One of the biggest moments in her life . . . and she had to face it alone."

"Good point." Brian closed his eyes for a moment. All of a sudden, they were aching unbearably.

Andrew shook his head. "Sorry. That was uncalled for. But I'm upset about this myself." He called for his bill and paid it with cash.

"I'd like to meet with you again," Brian said. His instincts told him he could trust Andrew.

Andrew shrugged and then stood up. "If you want, but I can't tell you anything more." He hesitated and then bent down, close to Brain's ear. "Except, keep your investigation close to home."

Brian looked up at him, startled. "Tyler House, you mean?"

But Andrew was already walking to the door, accompanied by greetings of "Hi, Doc" and "See you, Dr. L," from the servers and the patrons of the bar, leaving Brian staring down at his dish of seafood pasta.

Chapter 34

When Stewart received a call from Norman, telling him to come immediately to his office, he cursed to himself, knowing that meant he'd have to postpone his first drink of the day until later.

He made his way to the fifth-floor office that had once been his father's and went in without knocking. Grace and Larry were sitting on one of the Italian black leather couches and Norman stood by the large picture window, staring out at the broad stretch of river and the rolling hills beyond it.

"When's the funeral?" Stewart asked.

"That's not funny," Norman barked, turning around to confront him.

Stewart shrugged. "Sorry. Thought I'd try to lighten the mood."

"We're in deep trouble," Norman said. "I want to make sure we're all on the same wavelength here."

Stewart sank into a chair facing his brother's desk. "You mean, because of Michelle's husband?"

Norman glanced around the room, as cagey as ever about saying anything that could possibly be used against him. "There's too much going on," he said. "We have to get Mother's agreement before we can pull this thing off. And now we've got someone else breathing down our necks."

"Mother's falling apart," Grace said. "If we keep going, don't let anything sidetrack us, we won't even need her agreement to this deal."

Norman glared at his sister. "Isn't that just typical of you? Bulldoze in and to hell with the consequences. We don't want this deal to be tainted. It needs a delicate, diplomatic touch."

"Yours, I suppose you mean," Stewart said. "Meanwhile, it could get away from us if we don't grab it now."

Norman rounded on him. "You're getting interested a bit late, aren't you? We asked you to speak to Mother about it, to try to persuade her, but you did bloody nothing about it. Just waited for me and Grace to do the dirty work, so that you could keep your hands clean."

Grace sprang to her feet. "Well, I'm not about to wait around anymore. It's unfair that she holds all that power when she's going senile. If neither of you is willing to get her certified as being unfit to look after her own affairs, I certainly will."

Larry stood up and put his arm around her trembling shoulders, drawing her close against his side. "Calm down, darling. We must act together, as a team. You know that." He smiled at the others. "It's been a strain for all of you, I know, but there's only seven more days to go."

Norman leaned his hands on his massive desk. "Michelle's husband is asking questions."

"Well, that's understandable, isn't it?" Stewart said. "What's he like?"

"Good-looking man," Norman said. "Blunt, to the point; the way you'd expect an American investigative journalist to be. I imagine he'd use his Irish blarney to wheedle stuff out of other people, but between us, the gloves are off."

"I'm certainly not going to let the arrival of Michelle's husband stop me from going for the merger." Grace's chin stuck out defiantly.

"We have to work together," Larry reminded her. "If Norman and Stewart say do it diplomatically, then we must go along with that."

"It would look pretty bad if we backed down now,

at this point," Stewart said. "Make us the laughing-stock of the business world."

"For God's sake, Stewart," Norman said, "the business world knows nothing about this, so how would we be—"

"If we tell Grostig we're withdrawing, you can be sure it'll be the headline in the *Financial Post* the following morning. Our stock will plummet."

Larry sucked in his breath. "Sorry, Norman, but I think Stewart is right. You must go for it now."

"Then let Stewart bloody well persuade Mother to sign over her voting rights to him," Norman said belligerently.

"I'm sure I can get her to give it to me," Grace said.

"Then why haven't you damn well done so before now?" Norman demanded. "No, you just antagonize her and upset her." He turned on Stewart. "Will you do it?"

"I've tried before. You know that. Didn't work then. Why should it work now?"

"See what I mean?" Grace said in a shrill voice. "That's so typical of you, Stewart. All talk and no action."

"She's very frail," Stewart said. "Strange to see her that way, isn't it? Makes her seem more human, somehow." He glanced at the large oil portrait of his father that had hung on the wall of this office since time immemorial. "Okay, I'll give it a try."

"What about Michelle?" Grace asked.

Norman frowned. "What about her?" he demanded.

Grace lifted her shoulders. "I suggested to her husband that she'd run off with someone else."

"Well, he'll know it wasn't Andrew," Norman said with a wry smile. "He's meeting with him as we speak."

Grace's eyes widened. "With Andrew?"

"Yes. Norton called him and they arranged to meet at the hotel."

"Why didn't you tell me this?"

"I thought you knew. You were upstairs with Norton when he spoke to Mother."

"I knew he was going to speak to Andrew, but I had no idea he'd do it this quickly." Grace gave a shaky laugh. "He certainly is a fast worker. Punch drunk from lack of sleep, yet he keeps on going. Anyone know what he's going to do next?"

"Go to the police, I should think," Norman said. "If it were Lauren who was missing, that's what I'd do."

Chapter 35

~~~~~

Stewart hesitated outside his mother's bedroom door. Why had he allowed Grace to talk him into this? It had always been this way, of course. The others using him as a go-between to persuade his mother to do something; usually to intercede with their father for some punishment he'd imposed.

Grace had let him into the house. She seemed to have moved in permanently, using the excuse that their mother was ill, but Stewart knew that it was so that Grace could keep tabs on her, watch her every move, monitor every phone call. She was particularly worried about any contact Eleanor might try to have with Douglas.

Stewart raised his hand to knock on his mother's bedroom door, but then let it fall again. He'd felt like telling them to go to hell with the merger and the money. But, to Stewart, the money they'd each gain individually from the merger meant something far more important than power and prestige. It meant freedom. The ability to shake himself free from Tyler Foods forever. Each time he had to cross the threshold of that ugly brick and glass building, and look at the huge portrait of his father looming at him from the wall above the security desk, his stomach would clench into a knot, so that all he could think of was how soon he could take that first drink of the day.

Spurred on by the thought of cutting himself free

from the shackles of Tyler Foods, he knocked on the door.

"Come in," called Janet.

He went in, bearing the white-cap lace hydrangea plant before him like a peace offering. The room was dimly lit, so that he didn't see his mother at first. She was sitting in the alcove by the bay window, hidden by the high back of her chair. As he moved across the room, he recalled those boyhood days when he'd felt like some supplicant coming to the queen's private throne room. But now, as he came to stand before her, the queen seemed to have become diminished.

"She's sleeping," Janet whispered. "She won't sleep in her bed, so she sleeps here instead."

Stewart was appalled. How could his mother have deteriorated so fast? In only a few days, she seemed to have shrunk and her silver hair was thin and lifeless. "Is she eating anything?" he asked Janet in a low voice.

"Don't talk about me as if I'm not here." Stewart had to smile when he heard his mother's voice. At least her hearing was still sharp.

"We thought you were asleep," Janet said apologetically.

"Well, I'm not. Nice of you to come and see me at last, Stewart." Her tone was as biting as acid. She hadn't lost her sting, he was glad to see.

"I was here on Wednesday, but you were asleep."

"Stupid doctor filled me full of narcotics. Don't trust that Andrew. Never know what he's giving me." Eleanor peered at the plant. "What have you got there?"

"It's a hydrangea."

"A hydrangea house plant? What will they think of next!" She touched the fragile white florets. "It's very pretty. Thank you, dear." She put out a hand to him and he leaned down to kiss her cheek. "Move the other chair nearer and sit beside me."

"I'll do it," Janet said. She pushed the small armchair closer to Eleanor. "I must see how the dinner's coming along," she said, and left the room, closing the door behind her.

Stewart put the plant on the circular table in front of the window and then sat down.

"Do you have any news about Michelle?" Eleanor's expression changed from eager to resigned when Stewart shook his head.

"No, I'm sorry, I haven't," he said. "Where's her husband?"

"I made him go to bed. He was ready to collapse when he came back from the police station."

Stewart's heartbeat quickened. "So he did go to the police?"

"Of course he did. About time, too. I can't understand why you and Norman didn't call Gary Williams as soon as you knew Michelle had gone."

"I don't think it's in Fredericton's jurisdiction, Mother. It depends on where, exactly, Michelle disappeared."

Eleanor sighed. "That's what Gary told Brian. He said that as Michelle hasn't been seen since she went to bed at the cottage on Sunday night, that is probably the point where she can be said to have disappeared."

"That's what I thought. So . . . what's happening?"

"Gary's contacting the RCMP in St. Andrews and he said he's going to keep tabs on everything for me."

"For you?" Stewart said, trying to hide his smile.

"Of course. Who do you think sent Brian to Gary in the first place? After all, Michelle is my granddaughter. And your niece, too, I would remind you."

"You liked her, didn't you, Ma?"

Eleanor's hand clutched at Stewart's. "Don't speak of her as if she were dead. I told Brian before he went upstairs, we are going to find her. It's just a matter of time."

Stewart frowned. "You don't think she ran away with another man, do you?"

"Of course not," she said, her voice filled with scorn. "She's mad about Brian and he is about her.

Stupid man, can't get the wander bug out of his system. Time he grew up and settled down."

"Did you tell him that?"

"Yes, I did. Told him that as soon as he got Michelle home he should cherish her and make babies with her, and stop going off halfway around the world, leaving her on her own."

"What did he say?"

"Foolish man started weeping. That's when I sent him off to bed. I can't bear to see a strong man cry."

Stewart smiled.

"What's so funny?" Eleanor demanded.

Stewart shrugged. "You. Us. This whole ridiculous world."

"Very profound, Stewie."

Stewart had always hated it when she called him Stewie, but now it made him feel warm and safe. Suddenly he didn't want to do this anymore. His mother was worried enough as it was, without having him exerting more pressure on her. He looked at his watch. "I should go. Anna will be wondering where I am."

"Why did you come here?" Eleanor asked him.

Her question surprised him. "To see how you are, bring you flowers."

His mother breathed a long drawn-out sigh. "No. I want the truth. What are you here for?"

"You always could see through me, couldn't you?" She didn't reply, but kept looking at him with those all-seeing eyes of hers. Stewart smoothed down his navy-and-silver silk tie. "They want me to speak to you again about the merger."

"I guessed as much." She released another long sigh. "Earlier today, I was thinking about those international figures on the computer printout Norman gave me. I was checking them on the morning I fell down the stairs." Her forehead wrinkled. "How long ago was that?"

"Two days ago. You fell on Wednesday morning. This is Friday evening."

"The days all seem to be running together. It's those

wretched pills. They make me so woozy I can't think. Now what were we talking about? Oh, yes. The merger. The all-important, earth-shattering merger." She leaned forward. "Tell me, Stewart, what's so important about this merger? Other than what Norman has told me, of course. Why is it so important to you, for instance? You, Stewart Nathan Tyler; a man who has never shown much interest in Tyler Foods, but has always been happy to accept his highly inflated executive's salary."

"You want the truth?"

"Haven't I always wanted the truth? The problem is that my family has always been reluctant to give it to me."

"Perhaps because you would never listen to it." Stewart was even more surprised than Eleanor to hear himself say the words, but he didn't regret them. "You didn't always want to hear the truth, particularly when it involved something that you knew would upset Father. So you closed your ears."

She was breathing fast, her chest rising and falling rapidly. He was concerned that he'd said too much, but she drew in one long breath and her breathing quieted. "Well, well, well. If this is the time for truth, out with it. Your father is no longer here to do anything about it, is he?"

Instinctively, Stewart's gaze went to the portrait of his father on the bedroom wall, the penetrating eyes beneath heavy eyebrows looking directly at him, daring him to speak up.

"That's just a picture, Stewart. Nothing more." His mother leaned forward, placing her hand on his knee. "I loved your father. I always will love him. But I wasn't blind to his faults. When I came to him as a young bride, I thought he was like some Greek god, exciting, experienced, knowledgeable, but over the years I learned that he was also close-minded, ruthless, and a bigot. Worst of all, he had a strong streak of cruelty that made him pick on weaker creatures than himself, which meant you, our children. I am deeply

ashamed to say that I did not challenge his stated right
to deal with you as he thought fit. I should have. So,
yes, Stewart, for once, I would like the truth. Wait!"
She half rose in her chair, but then fell back. "I can't
do it. I want you to do it for me."

"What?"

"Take the picture down."

"Father's picture?"

"Yes, take it down from the wall."

"There's no need to go that far, Ma." Stewart gave
an embarrassed laugh. "I promise I won't lie to you."

"Take it down," she repeated, emphasizing each
word. "We have far too many portraits of your father
around us, as it is. Ramsey Tyler in the bedroom,
Ramsey Tyler in the study . . . Take it down!"

Not wanting to upset her, Stewart got up and lifted
the heavy portrait down from the wall.

"Now turn it around and lean it against the wall."

Stewart did as he was told. He looked up at the
place where the portrait had hung for many years. The
square of wallpaper was bright and fresh and new. "I
hadn't realized how pretty this wallpaper was. Look
at all the colors. I suppose the exposed walls must
have faded over the years."

Eleanor turned around. "I can't see too well, dear,
but I remember when I chose it your father said that
those flower sprigs would make it look like a Victorian
maid's bedroom."

It sounded so much like his father that Stewart had
to laugh. "But your choice prevailed."

"Your father agreed that when it came to the affairs
of the house, my choice was paramount."

Stewart sat down and squeezed her hand. "Not just
the house, I think. In the business, too, you were Father's wise adviser."

"You know, Stewart, you should try not to drink so
much, you can be very wise yourself when you're
sober." Before Stewart could recover from his surprise
at this broadside from his mother, she continued,
"Now, talking of business, let us come to the point

about the merger. I'm feeling very tired. It's been a stressful day, with Brian arriving and having to get the police involved in our affairs. Tell me why you think this merger with Bruneau's should go through."

Stewart plucked up courage, wishing that he'd had a couple of stiff drinks before he'd come to see her, but knowing she'd have bawled him out if she'd smelled booze on his breath. He hesitated and then waded in. "Because each of us will gain financially as independent shareholders. And I want enough money to get out of Tyler Foods for good."

"Do you really hate it that much?" she whispered.

"I dread each and every day that I have to go through those bloody doors. I wish I'd been sensible enough to pile up money in the bank, so I could eventually say 'Stuff it' and walk away, but I didn't, so I need the money to buy my freedom."

"I see." She was silent for a long time. "But Norman. What's in it for him? He has so much and, unlike you, has made wise investments."

"Norman doesn't want it for himself. He wants to see the company soar and become one of the biggest grocery businesses in the world of the twenty-first century, with him at the helm or a joint partnership. He doesn't care, as long as it's the best in the world."

"That's what his father would have wanted, too."

"Exactly. Father trained him well. Only I don't think Norman's quite as ruthless as Father was."

"We really are telling the truth today, aren't we?" his mother said. "Right, then. We come to Grace. What is her motivation?"

"There you have me. I'm not sure. She seems even more hell-bent on securing this merger than Norman, yet she has plenty of money."

"She certainly should have. With both she and Larry getting their money from Tyler's, they do extremely well financially."

"Exactly. Grace is nuts about Larry, of course. She'd do anything for him. But he seems just as crazy about her. Maybe it's because they spend so much time apart, but sometimes they act like a couple of lovesick teenagers together. Can't keep their hands off each other."

His mother's nose wrinkled. "I know. It's disgusting."

They looked at each other and burst out laughing. It was a long time since Stewart had shared a secret time like this with his mother. "You look better."

"You've given me a great deal to think about." She closed her eyes for a moment. "I'm feeling very tired now, though. Would you send Janet up to me?"

Stewart got up. "I want you to get well."

"So do I, dear. But more than anything, I want to know that Michelle is safe. I want to see her and her husband reunited. I'm terribly worried about her."

"I know that."

Eleanor gripped his hand. "Will you do something for me, Stewart dear?"

"Of course."

"I think you liked Michelle, didn't you?"

"Of course I did. I liked her for herself, but I liked her especially for being Carolyn's daughter."

Tears glistened in her eyes. "You and Carolyn were always pals. You were her special big brother."

Stewart swallowed hard. "I loved her. I wished I'd done more for her."

His mother's eyes closed and the tears rolled slowly down her cheeks. "I was her mother. How much more should I have done for her?"

Stewart couldn't recall the last time he'd seen his mother cry. He pulled some tissues from the box on the table and put them into her hand.

"Will you do all you can to help Brian find Michelle?" she asked when she'd pressed the tissues to her eyes. "You know everyone in this town and in St. Andrews. Your presence will open doors for him."

"From what I've heard of him, Brian doesn't need much help from anyone," Stewart said with a wry grin. "But, yes, I'll help him."

"Thank you, dear. And, Stewart . . ."

"Yes?"

"Putting your own selfish wishes aside—and disregarding what your brother and sister want—would this merger be a good thing for Tyler Foods, do you think?"

Stewart considered the question for a moment, then said, "Reluctantly, I must say it would be a good thing for Tyler's. Like you, I'd prefer the company to stay in the family, but it's not the way things work now. Even a highly successful company like McCain's is having to open up top executive positions to people from outside the family."

"Yes, but they're not merging with someone else, are they?"

"No, but they are one of the largest companies in the world. We could never hope to compete at that kind of level."

Eleanor nodded. "Thank you. You've been a great help." She sat there, thinking for a moment. "Tell me, Stewart. What would you think of me buying you out, taking over your shares in Tyler's, so you could be completely free of the company?"

Stewart stared at her.

She gave him an ironic smile. "I assure you I'd pay you a fair, competitive price."

Stewart was so surprised by her offer he couldn't think how to respond.

"No need to say anything about it now," Eleanor continued. "I just want you to think about it. But before I make any decisions I must speak to Norman. There's something about those figures that's bothering me and I can't put my finger on it. Maybe he'll be able to help me track it down."

"I think you should speak to him, anyway." He grinned at her. "Norman knows a lot more than I do about the business."

"You think I don't know that?" Smiling, she closed her eyes. "Now go away and send Janet to me."

Chapter 36

For the past two nights, the temperature had dropped to below freezing and the small log cabin wasn't even insulated. The Brute was now keeping the fire going during the day as well as night. Michelle counted the remaining logs each time she went outside. There were only fifteen left. At this rate, they had barely enough fuel for the next twenty-four hours. Her suggestion that he at least gather up some kindling to help eke out the log supply had not been well received. In fact, for a moment, she thought he was going to hit her. From that time on, she kept her mouth shut, except for essential requests.

She didn't feel well enough to exercise. She now had a sore chest and hacking cough to add to her other cold symptoms, without even cough drops to help. When she woke up coughing during the night, the Brute yelled at her to shut the hell up, he couldn't sleep with all that noise.

The days were beginning to run together, but Michelle was now secretly keeping a diary to give her something to occupy her mind. And to be able to recollect all that had happened to her, every little detail, so that when she got out of this hellhole she'd have a record. And she *was* going to get out, she kept telling herself. But, more and more, despair was taking over. Frequently, she'd pull the blankets over her head, seeking to escape into her memories of happy times she'd spent with Brian in Bali and Palau and

Europe. Or she'd talk to her mother in her mind, recalling her warning not to seek out her family, and wishing she'd heeded it.

Late on Friday afternoon, the Brute's cell phone rang. His usual monosyllabic conversation seemed more animated than usual. She caught a few more words other than his usual barked, "Okay." She noticed that he spoke in English this time. Usually he spoke French on his phone calls. Either way she couldn't hear what was going on, as most of the time he listened to his caller. Taking orders, obviously.

She watched him intently, waiting to see what he would do when the phone call was finished. Dressed in his greasy jeans jacket, he sat by the stone fireplace on the small footstool, its padding spilling out of the split vinyl cover.

When the call was over, he stood up. She could see his mouth grinning through the slit in the ski mask. "Party's over, lady," he said. "I'm outta here."

Heart pounding, Michelle threw back the blanket and stood up. "Did someone pay a ransom for me?"

"Oh, yeah, someone paid a ransom," he said with a mocking laugh. "Who'd pay anything for you?" He came closer, his sloe-dark eyes narrowing. "But you sure as hell owe me something for me being so nice to you."

She took an instinctive step back from him, but the couch was directly behind her. As he eyed her speculatively, her heart was galloping so fast she thought it would burst. This was what she'd been dreading throughout this interminable week.

Grinning, he reached for her and dragged her against him. She smelled tobacco and stale breath and then, before she could scream, his mouth was on hers, his body grinding against her. Lips tightly closed against his invasion, she fought him like a wild cat, trying to tear at his eyes with her nails, but she was hampered by the fact that she was one-handed, her left arm bound behind her back. *Please God, no!* she prayed, over and over. She felt his hand on her breast, squeezing. Adrenaline surged. Summoning up all her strength, she lifted her knee and caught him with full force in the crotch.

"Merde!" he yelled, and let her go. "Bitch!" He swung back his fist to strike her, but something stopped him.

She found her voice at last. "You bastard!" she yelled. "Touch me again and I'll kill you."

"Oh, yeah?" He came closer again, his eyes filled with menace. "With what? Don't worry, lady. I won't touch you again. You're not worth it." He pointed at her with one stubby index finger. "Don't move, or you'll be sorry." He went to the kitchen counter and came back with the roll of duct tape and the sharp knife the other man had used to cut her bonds. Dave. She wished with all her heart that she had Dave here now.

"What are you going to do?" she asked, the silence unbearable.

"Keep you quiet."

She shook her head and backed away again. "No, please no. Don't gag me."

"Why not? You've got a big mouth. Time to shut it. Should've done this before." He took hold of her free arm.

She shook him off and clapped her hand to her mouth. "I'm going to throw up," she said, and ran for the door.

"Oh, no, you don't," he said, trying to grab hold of her again, but she wasn't kidding. She just managed to get outside before she began retching beneath one of the maple saplings.

He turned away until she'd finished. The sky swung around her when she straightened up, so that she had to grab hold of the maple's thin trunk to steady herself. She wiped her right arm across her cold, clammy forehead.

"Finished?" he barked at her.

She nodded, tears perilously close, but she was determined not to let him see her cry. He shoved her ahead of him back into the cabin and then picked up the tape again.

"Please don't gag me," she begged. "If I throw up again I could choke to death. Then you'd be up for murder."

"You talk too much." He grabbed her arm, dragging it behind her back, and began taping her two hands together, winding the duct tape round and round her wrists.

"Where are you taking me?"

He held the knife point a few inches from her eyes. "I told you to shut your mouth." He shoved her down on the couch.

Fearing for her life, she kept quiet, watching him as he moved about the cabin, gathering all his belongings together, throwing them into a large, orange plastic garbage bag. Then he went to the door. Michelle stared at him. He opened the door. She suddenly realized what was happening. He was leaving her here, alone.

Panic swept over her. "You can't leave me like this," she yelled. "How can I do anything with my hands bound?"

"Sorry, lady. Time for me to go."

She got up, stumbling across the room, her balance affected by her bound arms. She stopped a couple of feet away from him. "I won't be able to eat or put logs in the stove. If you leave me tied up like this I could freeze or starve."

He gave that Gallic shrug, his shoulders high up to his ears. "So what!" he said, and spat at her feet. He opened the door, went outside and then slammed the door in her face. To her horror, she heard the grate of rusty metal as he shot the two outside bolts into place, imprisoning her inside the cabin.

Michelle had never seen his car or truck in the clearing outside the cabin, but he must have had a vehicle hidden nearby. She heard the sound of an engine turning over. The vehicle coughed and spluttered, then roared into life and slowly began moving away.

She stood listening by the door until she could hear nothing but the evening twitter and jabber of the birds, now her only companions.

Slowly, she turned and moved across the room to the hearth. She slumped into the old chair, which was draped with a grubby gray blanket. As the light gradually faded, she stared at the open top of the woodstove, watching the dying ashes of the fire.

When Michelle's captor reported in, he said he'd left Michelle at the cabin, as instructed, but he didn't mention he'd tied her up and locked her in. He'd collect his money from the spot they'd arranged, and then disappear. By the time anyone found her, he'd be hundreds of miles away, and she could be dead. Stupid bitch! If she'd been nice to him he'd have let her go free, since there was no way she could identify him. She could've walked through the forest until she got to the highway. It would be a long walk, but she could make it. Some passing vehicle would've picked her up there. Instead, she was tied up in that cabin deep in the forest, without being able to get food or heat, until someone found her.

If someone found her.

Chapter 37

~

The telephone was ringing far away in the distance. Although he was immersed in a deep sleep, Brian was awake in a moment. He checked his watch. Nine minutes past eight. He'd been asleep for almost three hours. Dragging on the terry-cloth robe Janet had given him, he stumbled to the door and ran down the two flights of stairs.

"Is that call for me?" he shouted from the bottom of the stairs, not caring who answered him, as long as someone did.

Larry came out of the family room. "Hello there. We thought you'd still be asleep."

"Was that phone call for me?" Brian asked again, not interested in exchanging pleasantries.

"As a matter of fact it was, but we didn't want to disturb you, knowing how tired—"

"Who was it?"

An almost imperceptible tightening around his mouth signaled Larry's annoyance, but he covered it with a smile. "Detective Inspector Williams."

"Did you get a number?"

"I believe Janet has it. She took the call. I'll get it for you."

"Thanks. I'll ask her myself. Sorry to disturb you."

Larry looked as if he wasn't quite sure how to take the apology. *Take it however you want, buddy,* Brian thought.

"She's in the kitchen," Larry said. "It's down the hall and—"

"Thanks, I'll find it." Brian padded away down the hall. What was it with this family and not calling people to the telephone?

Janet looked up from the sink when he came in. "You should have put your slippers on. Your feet will be cold on this tiled floor."

"After being in Indonesia, it's good to feel cold again."

"Is it a steamy heat?"

"It is. Saps the energy if you're not used to it."

"I wouldn't like that at all. Moderation in all things, that's what I like. I couldn't live in Manitoba, either, with its bitterly cold winters."

"Lots of sunshine, though. Mr. Anderson says you took a call for me."

"That's right. From Inspector Williams. Why don't you go into Mr. Tyler's study to make your call?"

"Sure. Could you be a sweetheart and get me a good strong mug of real coffee to wake me up?"

"Not decaffeinated? You've had a lot of coffee today, you know."

"Definitely not decaffeinated. I need a good jolt of caffeine to keep me awake."

"But won't you want to get back to sleep again?"

He grinned at her. "I've had my quota of sleep, Janet."

She gave him Williams's number, then led him to the study, which was dominated by another large oil portrait of Ramsey Tyler. Was there one of him in every room? As Brian sat at the desk and dialed the number, he felt those gimlet eyes boring into him. Somehow he didn't think he'd have liked Michelle's grandfather.

But he had liked the inspector as soon as he'd met him. Probably in his late forties, he was lean and balding, but brisk. A "let's get down to business right away" kind of man.

"We've been able to get hold of Pierre Gaudry,"

Gary told Brian when the call was put through to his office.

"Great! Where is he?"

"Here, in the station," Gary replied.

"That was fast."

"Can't take credit for it. He was in town for the weekend, staying with friends. We managed to track him down through his brother Marc in Miramichi. Can you come down?"

"Sure can. I'll be there in . . . let's say half an hour. Have to throw some clothes on."

"Janet Marlow said you were sleeping and weren't to be disturbed. I didn't want to push it, but I thought you'd want to talk to this guy."

"I do."

"Want one of my lads to pick you up?"

"I can get a cab."

"I'll drive you," said a voice from behind him. Brian swiveled around. "I'm Stewart Tyler," the man added, holding out his hand. "Sorry. I didn't mean to listen in."

Like hell you didn't, thought Brian as they shook hands. "Thanks. I'll rent a car in the morning."

"No need. It's Saturday tomorrow. I can drive you wherever you want to go."

Yeah. That way you can keep track of me for the family. Brian was sure that something strange was going on in this place and he wasn't about to be spied on by Michelle's other uncle. "I've got an offer of a ride. See you in half an hour," he told Gary and hung up.

"Police station, right?" Stewart said. "Any news of Michelle?" He sounded genuinely interested.

"Not specifically. But they've got Pierre Gaudry at the station."

Stewart whistled. "Do they think he's got something to do with her disappearance?"

"That's what I'm going to find out," Brian said grimly and bounded up the stairs. He threw on the clothes he'd changed into earlier and, ten minutes

later, was downstairs again. He found Stewart engaged
in a heated conversation, which sounded like a dis-
agreement, with Grace and Norman, but they all
clammed up as soon as he appeared at the door. Brian
realized he'd have to be more vigilant to catch everything that was going on in this place.

When they reached the police station, Stewart
stopped outside, but didn't get out of the car. Brian
had thought he might have a hassle about not wanting
Stewart to come in with him. "I'll pick you up when
you're finished," Stewart said. "Just give me a call at
the hotel." He jotted down his cell phone number and
handed his card to Brian.

"It's okay," Brian said. "I can walk back. It's closer
to the house than I remembered."

"Call me," Stewart insisted. "I'll be drinking coffee," he added with an engaging grin.

"Okay. Thanks."

When he asked for Inspector Williams, he was
shown into a small office with a table piled high with
papers. In their center, a chattering computer. Gary
Williams stood behind the desk. In front of the desk
was a young man in a black sweatshirt and faded
jeans, his long dark hair tied back in a ponytail.

"This is Pierre Gaudry," Gary said.

"Brian Norton." Brian held out his hand to the
young man, who appeared to be in his early twenties.

Pierre looked surprised, but shook his hand with an
embarrassed grin. "Guess we're related, sort of." He
spoke with a French accent.

Brian nodded. His face hardened. "You called my
wife when she arrived in Fredericton."

"That's right. But she wasn't there."

"You said you'd call back. Why didn't you?"

Pierre lifted his shoulders and turned his palms upward in the classic Gallic shrug. "I was with friends,
havin' a good time."

Gary intervened. "We've questioned his friends.
They confirm that he'd been with them since Sunday,
including Monday morning."

"Do you believe them?" Brian asked.

"Hey! That's not nice," Pierre said, his jaw jutting belligerently. "How'd you like it if I accused your friend of lying?"

Brian turned on him, so that Pierre took a step backward. "Look, pal. My wife's probably been kidnapped. She's been missing for almost a week. I don't feel like being nice."

Gary hastily intervened. "Okay, okay. Why don't we all sit down and discuss this amicably. Sit down, Pierre." He kicked a metal chair closer to the young man, who sat down on the edge of it. Then Gary turned to Brian, who reluctantly sat down on the remaining metal chair. "Pierre here tells me that he has never met your wife."

"What about his brother?" Brian asked.

"None of us has met her," Pierre said.

The inspector leaned back in his office chair, so that it squeaked in protest. "He told me he called Michelle after this friend of his told him Michelle was visiting at Tyler House."

Brian addressed himself directly to the openly sullen Pierre. "Why did you call her?"

" 'Cause she's my friggin' half sister. Me and Marc thought it would be cool to speak to her. That's all. How were we to know she'd been kidnapped?"

"That's the point," Brian said. "She wasn't kidnapped until after you called her."

Pierre turned to Gary. "Am I a suspect? 'Cause if I am, I want a lawyer before I answer any more questions. I know my rights."

"Can I ask him a couple of questions, off the record?" Brian asked Gary.

"It's up to him," Gary said.

"Okay. You can answer these questions, or not, as you wish," Brian told Pierre. "Understand?"

"Okay."

"I should explain that I'm a television news journalist." He gave Pierre a faint smile. "So I'm used to asking questions."

"Cool. I'm your man."

"Question number one. If Michelle had been at Tyler House when you called, what were you going to say to her?"

Pierre thought for a moment. "I'd probably have asked her to meet me somewhere to have a brew. Marc said he'd come in to town Sunday or Monday to meet her, if she wanted to."

It was so casual, so *real*, that Brian was taken aback. Usually, he would have expected kidnappers to have concocted some fancy story, but this was so lame, it might just be true.

"Course," Pierre added with a shrug, "she might not have wanted to meet us, after what our dad did to her."

"What was that?"

"I mean, he walked out on her when she was a tiny kid, didn't he? Left her mom." Pierre shook his head. "Still, she might've wanted to know something about him. We could tell her some tales," he added with a tight grin. "There's probably a lot more of us Gaudry kids hangin' around New Brunswick and Maine. Maybe even Nova Scotia."

Brian's heart turned over at the thought of Michelle and, yes, this kid, with their wastrel father. In his opinion, Michelle had been far better off being abandoned by him before she knew him. At least, she didn't have the hard cynicism about life this guy had.

"What's the other question?" Pierre asked.

"It's a tougher one. How well do you know this province?"

"That's it? That's your other question?"

"That's the first part of it."

"Pretty well. My dad was a lumber mill worker, but he never stuck to any job for more than a few months, so Mom and us moved around a lot."

"Okay. Then here's another question. It's a tougher one. If you wanted to hide someone away . . . say, out of town somewhere, where would you choose?"

This time Pierre's grin was a broad one, lighting up

his face. For a fleeting moment, Brian caught his likeness to Michelle. Then it was gone. But just that moment made him sincerely hope that the Gaudrys weren't involved in Michelle's disappearance. "As I said, my dad was a lumberman. Marc and me are foresters by trade. We know the woods and the forests of New Brunswick like they were our own backyard." His expression brightened. "You think Michelle's being kept prisoner in the woods somewhere? There's all kinds of old trappers' huts in the forest and the wilderness. Me and Marc used to—" He stopped short, aware of the police inspector's gaze on him. "Hey, me and Marc could help you look for her."

"We don't know where she is," Gary said. "But we aim to find out." He went to the door and called for the sergeant, who left his post at the front desk. "Have you typed up Mr. Gaudry's statement?"

"Yep. All done."

"Good. Get him to sign it and then he can be on his way." Gary turned to Pierre. "But Sergeant Steve McNab of the St. Andrews RCMP division wants to have a word with you as well, so leave a number where we can reach you, okay?"

"Okay." Pierre looked from Gary to Brian. "So you don't need our help to find Michelle?" His voice was filled with what sounded like disappointment.

"No, I don't think—"

"We might," Brian said, cutting in on Gary. "We could use any help we can get."

Pierre's face lit up. "Great. It'd be cool finding her. Sort of make up for what our dad did to her. I'll give you my cell phone number, okay?"

"Okay."

Pierre scribbled the number down on a piece of paper and handed it to Brian. "Hey, just think what a great story that'd be for a TV movie: brothers find kidnapped sister. Sounds cool, eh?"

Brian stared at him, stone-faced, unable to match his enthusiasm for Michelle's ordeal as a TV movie of the week.

"Sorry, man," Pierre said. Subdued, he followed the sergeant down the corridor.

"I don't think he has anything to do with her disappearance," Gary said, "but the RCMP will bring him and his brother in for further questioning and they'll put a tail on them, to make sure."

"What did you think of his suggestion about a trapper's hut in the forest?"

"It's a bit fanciful, I think. You saw how he clammed up when he remembered where he was. I guess they used to do some illegal trapping with their dad when he was alive. No, I doubt she's hidden in the wilderness. It's much easier to hide someone in the city."

"This city?" Brian said with raised eyebrows.

"No, not this one. We all know what's going on in Fredericton."

"I haven't been here more than a few hours, but that's the impression I got."

"And although quite a few people live there year round, St. Andrews is mainly a summer resort nowadays, so it'll be easy to do a check in that area."

"Any results on the note Michelle left?"

"It's a generic computer printout. Several fingerprints, but you told me it was handled by at least three people, including yourself."

"That's right. By the way, I called her partner about her lap-top. Michelle didn't take it with her."

"Figures," Williams said. "Someone else typed and printed it. Oh, one thing I wanted to tell you. Sergeant McNab tells me there was a report of what was called a fancy car speeding along the northbound road from St. Andrews early before dawn Monday morning. Apparently it almost knocked down a man who was going to fetch his cows for milking from his pasture across the road from his small farm. The RCMP almost missed the report, as it seemed so unimportant, but they're checking into it now."

"Was the man able to get a description of the car?"

"Fortunately, yes. He said it was a late model black Mercedes."

"What about a license plate?"

"No. It went by too fast. I don't want to get your hopes up. It's probably nothing. But you never know. Sometimes it's little things like a speeding car that can solve a case."

"Thanks." Brian summoned up a smile. "I need every ounce of encouragement I can get."

"What's strange is that there's been no ransom demand. Let's face it, the Tylers are a likely target for a kidnapping for ransom, but your wife's been missing for five days now and nothing's been heard."

"That's what bothers me." Brian turned his face away to study the large map of Fredericton on the wall. "I keep trying not to think about what might be happening to her, but I can't help wondering why no one's contacted the family."

"They're probably trying to decide what approach to make," the Inspector said.

Brian turned to meet the policeman's compassionate gaze head on. "Or she could be dead."

Chapter 38

For a while after the Brute had left, Michelle sat by the woodstove, overcome by despair. How was she going to feed herself and her baby? Keep them warm? "Brian, where are you?" she wailed.

Then, slowly, she staggered up, realizing that she must use the last remaining glimmer of light to find what resources were available to her. She went into the kitchen, to check out the food and water.

The box of bread was on the counter. Oh, God, there was only one bag of sliced bread left. The Brute had eaten the rest. And when she tried to get at it, she discovered how difficult it was to do so without her hands. She was forced to rip the plastic wrapping apart with her teeth to get a slice of bread out. Then she had to eat it from the grimy countertop, painstakingly picking it up with her teeth, taking a bite, dropping it, and then going through the whole process again, bite by bite.

Panic engulfed her. What if she couldn't eat enough to keep her baby healthy?

"Think!" she shouted. "Organize yourself!"

Cans of food were no good. She couldn't open them. On the other hand, she could tear cereal packets open with her teeth. And there was one box of cereal left.

Michelle surveyed the other open cartons of stuff. The box of crackers? Okay . . . teeth again. Fruit? One wrinkled McIntosh apple. Her gaze roamed around . . . and stopped at the large container of water. It was empty. And there were only two large plastic bottles of mineral water left. *Oh, my God,* she thought. How was she going to be able to get liquid into her? The bottled water had screw caps, but without her hands, there was no way to open them. She thought of films or television programs she'd seen about people with no arms—Christy Brown, the Irish writer, for instance—learning to type and do amazing things with their toes, but she doubted she could learn to do that in time to save herself from starvation or dehydration.

"If someone doesn't come and find me, I'm dead," she said, her voice sounding strangely hollow in the confines of the cabin. *And so was her baby!*

"No way," she shouted for her baby's benefit. "We're going to survive this, buster, you and me." She mustn't let her baby guess that she was starting to give up hope.

She'd have to attack the water problem right away. There were two pails stacked inside each other on the floor. She kicked them over and kept kicking them until they disengaged and rolled across the floor. The larger one was metal, the small, shallow one plastic. It looked fairly clean. "If I could open one of the water bottles and pour it into the plastic pail then I could kneel on the floor and lap water from it like a dog or cat."

Easier said than done. However hard she kicked at it, she couldn't dislodge the cap on the water bottle. Eventually, exhausted, she gave up, realizing that it was almost dark. "Blankets, blankets, blankets," she muttered as she gathered together all the blankets and the old quilt to keep herself warm through the night.

As total darkness descended, her spirits grew lower and lower. She sat hunched on the edge of the couch, listening to the scurries and squeaks of the woodland night, wondering if she would ever escape from this cabin that was now even more of a prison than before. As she sat there, utterly alone, every rustle and crack sounded horribly ominous. Although she was glad that the Brute had gone, she was still a prisoner, a victim of whoever or whatever roamed in the woods outside, only the wall of logs between her and the wilderness.

She awoke suddenly to the raucous screeching of a nearby owl. She had no idea of the time or of whether she had slept for half an hour or several hours. All she knew was that it was still dark. And as the darkness pressed in on her with claustrophobic intensity, negative thoughts descended on her.

If her kidnappers—hell, she might as well put a name to them now: Norman and Grace and Stewart and, possibly, their respective spouses, perhaps even their children—had intended to keep her until after the merger was signed, why had she been abandoned now, six or seven days from the deadline?

The only explanation that could possibly apply was that they'd beaten Eleanor down and managed to wrest her Tyler Foods stock from her. Or worse. Maybe Eleanor had had a stroke or died.

Appalled at this thought, Michelle jumped to her feet, knocking the pile of books, magazines, and old newspapers onto the floor with a clatter.

A clatter? Frowning, she gently slid her right foot through the pile of papers . . . and then stopped when she felt an object of about eight inches long beneath her foot.

The knife. The Brute had forgotten to take away the sharp knife he'd used to cut the duct tape.

Heart pounding, Michelle pushed the table back with her foot. Locating the knife again, she knelt down and bent backward, straining to pick up the knife with her fingertips. When that didn't work, she lay down on the floor, wriggling herself into the right position, so that her fingers were centered over the knife. Trying to avoid cutting her back, she struggled to get her fingers around the knife's handle.

Again and again and yet again, she thought she had it grasped between her fingers, only to have it slip away. Her wrists ached as she maneuvered her fingers back and forth.

Then suddenly she had it! Tightening her grip, she secured the knife's handle between her fingers. Slowly, carefully, trying to avoid cutting herself, she began rubbing the taped part of her wrists back and forth across the knife's keenly honed blade.

Chapter 39

~

On Saturday morning, Norman received a call from Martin Grostig, telling him that his accountants had found a discrepancy in Tyler Foods' international figures. He managed to cover his dismay by telling Grostig that it must be an internal error and he'd make sure that a new set of updated figures was E-mailed to him by Monday morning, but he could tell that Grostig was not impressed. From now on Grostig would be double-checking everything, suspicious that something questionable was going on.

That was the trouble; something questionable *was* going on, but exactly what wasn't clear yet. He was furious with Larry for having done such sloppy work on preparing the international figures. Damn the man; he was more interested in his sports cars and his bloody racehorse than in doing his job properly. It wasn't as if he didn't get paid well, either.

Norman felt as if his world was disintegrating around him. The merger, which had seemed such a superb opportunity, had caused a major upheaval in his family. His sister Grace was so totally obsessed with the idea of the merger that her behavior had become increasingly irrational, which was quite unlike her normal self. Stewart seemed to be drinking more and more, and working less and less. And in the middle of all this, Carolyn's daughter arrives on the scene, causing even more disruption, culminating in her disappearance. To cap it all, Michelle's husband was now front row and center at Tyler House, ingratiating himself with Eleanor and dragging in the police to sniff around and check into their private and corporate lives.

What in the world had he done to deserve all this? Even his beautiful Lauren was showing signs of rebellion. She'd told him last night that she wouldn't be coming with him to the private dinner ex-Premier Frank McKenna was hosting at the Hotel Beausejour next week, as she'd signed up for evening classes at the university, and she didn't want to miss the first class.

"You must be kidding!" he said, astonished by what appeared, in his eyes, to be a flagrant display of hostility on his wife's part. "Evening classes in what? Mascara application?" He meant it as a joke, but her icy fury silenced him. Before he had a chance to protest or apologize she stalked from the room, ran up to their bedroom, and—for the very first time in their marriage—locked the door against him, refusing to open it.

How could everything have gone so disastrously, so catastrophically wrong?

He felt like booking a one-way ticket to Tahiti or somewhere even more exotic, far away from the corporate world. Problem was, he couldn't stand the food in these places. There was nothing to equal a juicy Aberdeen Angus steak with a crispy, baked New Brunswick potato. Add fresh lobster from Grand Manan and he was in food heaven.

Wearily, he parked his car in the driveway of Tyler House, got out, and rang the bell. Janet opened the door and let him in. "My mother called me earlier," he told her. "Said she wanted me to come round." He gave Janet his coat. "How is she this morning?" he asked as she hung the coat in the closet down the hall.

Janet shook her head. "She won't eat anything. I'm really worried about her. Dr. Lenzie is upstairs with her now."

Damn! He didn't have time to wait. He glanced at his watch.

Janet knew the signs. "I'll go and tell Mrs. Tyler you're here."

"Thanks." There was a welcoming fire in the family room. He sat down in the chair close to the fire and started reading his *Globe and Mail*.

"Morning."

The voice startled Norman. He turned to find Brian standing watching him from the doorway. "Morning." Norman folded the business section of the newspaper and put it down.

"Please don't stop reading on my account."

Was it Norman's imagination or was there a hint of sarcasm in the man's voice? "Any news from the police?" he asked Brian.

"About your niece being kidnapped, you mean? How kind of you to ask."

Yes, definitely sarcasm. "I am interested, you know," Norman told him. "Interested and concerned."

"Sounds perfect, Mr. Tyler. You'd make a fine politician, so you would. I can see it now, can't you? *Mr. Tyler professed himself to be deeply concerned and very interested in the police investigation into his niece's disappearance.*"

Norman glared at Brian over his glasses. "Obviously there's no point in discussing it with you."

"In fact, there is. The police want you and your family to make yourselves available for questions some time this weekend."

"Questions?"

Brian nodded. "In deference to your mother, Detective Inspector Williams proposes that the entire Tyler family gathers here at Tyler House at a prearranged time to meet with him and Sergeant McNab of the RCMP."

"To hell with—"

"Or, failing that, he can have each member of the family come to the station separately for questioning. He also wants to question everyone who was in your cottage last Monday, which means all the younger people as well, I guess."

Arrogant bastard! Norman fought to control his temper. "Some of them aren't even here. Grace's daughter is in Toronto and my son Eric flew to Montreal last night and won't be back until tomorrow."

Brian shrugged. "Whoever's available." He took a notebook from his pocket, tore out a page, scribbled a number on it, and handed it to Norman. "That's Gary Williams's number. Call him to arrange a time. I'm driving down to St. Andrews to meet Sergeant McNab."

Norman heard his son's voice in the hall. Then Ramsey put his head around the door. "Hi, Dad."

"Hi. What are you doing here?"

"Checking on Gran. Ready, Brian?"

Ready, Brian? What was this? Had this guy taken everything over, including his son? Norman stood up. "Going somewhere?"

"I'm driving Brian down to the cottage. The RCMP want to check it over."

Rage flooded over Norman. "I don't recall giving anyone permission to let the police into Prospect House."

Ramsey looked surprised, but it was Brian who said, "Your mother gave us permission and the keys." He held them up, jingling them. "We should go," he said to Ramsey.

"Okay. Bye, Dad. See you later." Ramsey hesitated and then said, "I'll let you know what happens."

"Good of you." Norman turned his back on the two younger men.

"I think it's time we, as a family, got involved in finding Michelle," Ramsey added. It was a statement, made in a firm voice. Ramsey rarely made statements. He usually spoke to his father with deference, adding "Don't you think" and "If you think" to any discussion he had with him.

Norman didn't answer his son. How could he? He stared into the dying flames of the log fire. For years he'd tried to persuade his mother to put in one of those realistic gas fires, but she adamantly refused, telling him she liked real fires that smelled of pine or applewood, not gas.

"Norman?"

He turned. Andrew Lenzie stood in the doorway. "Come on in. How's Mother?" Norman asked.

"Not good. I'm concerned about her." Andrew rubbed his hand over his mouth.

"We're all concerned about her. Want a drink?"

Andrew shook his head. "No, thanks. Too early for me."

"Too early for me, as well. I just fancied one, for some reason. How about coffee?"

"Janet gave me a cup earlier." Andrew looked unsettled, as if he didn't know whether to stay or go. "Was that Michelle's husband I heard a moment ago?"

"Yes. Ramsey's driving him down to St. Andrews. The police want to go over the house there."

"Good. I'm glad they're covering everything. No other news about her?"

"Michelle? No, none that I know of. I seem to be the last to know what's going on," Norman added.

"I'm glad the police are involved," Andrew said.

"Are you? Why the hell should you care?" Norman demanded.

Andrew hesitated. "Because I liked Michelle." His expression darkened. "Because all of you, except Eleanor, treated her like shit." He was breathing fast now, his eyes flashing anger. "Because none of you seems to give a damn that she's been kidnapped or worse."

"Now, hold on. That's not true. What the hell's got into you, Lenzie?"

"A good question. Something that should have got into me a long time ago."

"Calm down, man. You must be working too hard."

"Working too hard and making too little money.

The story of most Canadian doctors' lives.'' Andrew's voice was filled with bitterness.

"I thought you loved your work, like your father and your grandfather before you."

"Oh, I do. I just get pissed off when people like you, driving their Jaguars and BMWs, expect us to heal you and your families, and deal with life and death on a daily basis, for money they wouldn't pay a checkout clerk."

"So you'd favor private medicine?"

"No, not at all. I favor being paid what we deserve. No more than that. Your son is ten years younger than I am, but he has his own splendid office in his daddy's business, his own house and cottage and Jaguar and 4X4. When I was his age, I was earning nothing or next to nothing while I undertook years of grueling medical training."

Norman shrugged. "Why do it then, when you hate it so much?"

"I don't hate it. That's the problem. It's the finest profession in the world, but sometimes I lose sight of that fact when I have to worry about support payments and custody battles and going home to an empty house."

Norman suddenly felt ashamed. "It must have been a tough time for you since you and Pam separated."

Andrew shrugged. "I can't blame her," he said, sinking into the nearest chair. "She was sick and tired of being left alone while I was working late every night, making calls, on the phone or at the hospital. Tired of not being able to go away for a proper holiday because I couldn't take more than a few days off at a time. Tired of having to watch every dollar, when wives of other professional men were able to go to Europe for three weeks or take winter breaks in the Caribbean."

"My God, Andrew, I've never heard you sound so bitter."

Andrew gave him a grim smile. "Must be having a bad day, eh?" He hesitated for a moment, and then said, "Norman, I have something to tell you. There's no way I can sugarcoat this, so I'll just jump right in. I have reason to believe that someone is"—he searched for the right words—"adjusting or adding to Eleanor's prescribed medication. It could be Eleanor herself. At first, that's what I thought was happening. It's a problem with many older people. And, as you know, Eleanor can be pretty obstinate at times. But now I'm not so sure. I'm going to order tests to see exactly what is going on."

Norman stared at him. "I thought you were arranging the tests for Alzheimer's, senile dementia."

A fine flush ran over Andrew's cheekbones. "I was asked to postpone those tests for the time being."

"What! Who the hell asked you to postpone the tests?"

"Your sister."

"Grace? But why?"

"You'll have to ask her."

"Why didn't you tell me this before?"

"I was told you had enough on your mind with some big business deal going on."

Norman couldn't believe his ears. "Grace actually told you that?"

Andrew nodded.

"And you . . . you just went along with her request, even though you thought there might be a problem?"

"On the contrary. I thought your mother was eminently competent for her age. At least, until these hallucinatory episodes began. If you remember, that was when we talked about getting tests done. But then Grace came to me and said that the family wanted to wait until later for the tests, because Eleanor was so upset by the possibility of having Alzheimer's."

"You should have come to me."

"I realize that now."

"What made you decide to tell me now?"

"Michelle's disappearance," Andrew said without hesitation. "I think the two are connected: Eleanor's visions and Michelle's abduction, or whatever it is.

There's something weird going on in this house, Norman. I don't know who's at the bottom of it, but if you don't find out pretty soon, I intend to go to the police with it." His eyes narrowed. "Of course, you could be the one who's involved."

Anger boiled up in Norman. He glared at Andrew. "No, I'm bloody well not."

"You were quick enough to want to have your mother declared incompetent," Andrew told him.

"That was because I thought she *was* incompetent."

"Oh, really? Strange that you hadn't said a thing about your concern earlier. I don't suppose it would have anything to do with this important business venture Grace was talking about."

Damn Grace, with her loose tongue! Norman leaned toward Andrew. "Look, Andrew, you're an old friend. I have to admit it's been difficult dealing with my mother recently. She's part of the pen-and-ink generation. We have to move into the cyberspace age."

"And she's the majority shareholder. That's the problem, isn't it?"

"To be perfectly honest, yes." Norman moistened his dry lips. "But this is strictly between you and me. If this got out, it could mean the end of Tyler Foods."

A slow smile spread across Andrew's face. "My God, what a perfect opportunity for blackmail. What would it be worth to you for me to keep quiet?"

Norman looked at him over his glasses. "Are you serious?"

Andrew stared at him. "You mean, do I want you to pay me for my silence?"

Norman nodded.

"You'd really do it, wouldn't you?" Andrew shook his head in amazement. "So that's how you operate, you big business guys."

"Nonsense, of course I didn't mean that," Norman blustered, hurriedly trying to recover himself.

"Come to think of it," Andrew continued, "Grace happened to mention the Tylers' generous gift each Christmas when she asked me to postpone the dementia tests. I must be very naive not to have realized she was talking about a bribe."

Norman wondered if anyone as bright as Andrew could be that naive, but he kept his thought to himself. They were in a sticky mess, and he desperately needed Dr. Andrew Lenzie to be on his side.

"Forget about that. If you believe that Mother had been taking more medication than she should—"

"Or less."

"Or less, then I want you to arrange tests for her immediately. We can fly her to Boston, if we have to. Just get them done quickly. My mother's health is paramount."

"There's no need to fly her anywhere. The tests can be done from blood samples."

Norman hesitated. "I don't want you to take this the wrong way, but can this be done discreetly? I mean, without involving the police?"

"It depends on what we find. And whether there is proof that someone other than Eleanor herself withheld, or administered more, medication."

"I'm going to do my best to find that out for myself. I'll start with Janet."

"That's good. But one word of warning. Don't make Janet the scapegoat."

"What the hell do you mean by that?"

"Think about it." Andrew got up. "I'll arrange for Eleanor to have samples taken first thing on Monday."

Andrew left the room without shaking Norman's hand. He was glad to get out of the house. He felt physically sick at the thought of how close he'd come to getting himself mired in this dirty situation at Tyler House. How much had he been influenced by Grace's silver tongue and assurance that the family's only concern was for their mother's health? Even now, he wondered about their involvement in their mother's hallucinations. Nothing in her previous medical history had suggested that she might be subject to mental disturbances of that kind. He wished with all his heart that he'd listened to his own instincts and tested Eleanor Tyler earlier. He'd allowed Grace's persuasion and his own sentimental aversion to the thought of Eleanor having dementia to sway him in the wrong direction.

And as he drove down Queen Street, the point that had been troubling Andrew ever since he'd suspected something was going on at Tyler House suddenly became clear. The Tylers—or some of them—*wanted* Eleanor to be suffering from dementia, so they could get power of attorney and take possession of her shares in the company. But Grace had asked him to postpone the tests not only because she knew they could be negative, but also because some of the blood tests would show if there was an imbalance or error in Eleanor's medication.

His hands tightened on the steering wheel. Had Michelle suspected something was going on? Had she actually found proof of it, and was that why she'd been kidnapped—or worse?

Andrew started trembling and found he couldn't stop. Mind spinning, he pulled over to the side of the road and stopped the car. Cursing aloud, he hit the steering wheel with his palms until they stung. If he'd followed his intuition and had those tests done—and they'd shown no signs of dementia—Michelle might be safely at home in Winnipeg now.

Should he go to the police with what he knew? That was the question. But what exactly did he know? What tangible proof did he have? Even if the blood tests showed that someone was abusing Eleanor's medication, how could he prove who it was? If he accused the entire Tyler family of plotting against her, and it was later found that they'd actually done nothing, he'd be drummed out of the town, relegated to practicing in the backwoods for the rest of his life.

Michelle had Brian to fight for her now, he thought, a taste as bitter as aloe in his mouth. If she was alive, Brian would find her. He wasn't about to risk his livelihood and reputation for mere conjecture. What was in his power, however, was to ensure that Eleanor Tyler received the best medical testing possible so that he would know exactly what was ailing her. That, at the very least, he owed to Eleanor—and to his mother, who had been Eleanor's close friend.

Chapter 40

Norman was about to go upstairs to see his mother when he heard the back storm door slam shut and then Larry's voice, followed by Grace's laughter. She always seemed to be laughing when Larry was around. When he was home, her life revolved around him. She glowed, drawing nurture from him like a plant from the sun. But when he went away again, she grew pale and wilted, although she tried to cover it with skillful makeup and an armor of impenetrable toughness.

As Norman stood there in the center of the family room, waiting for them to come in, everything suddenly came into focus, so that he saw it all with horrible clarity. "Oh, Gracie," he whispered. Feeling vaguely light-headed, he put out a hand, grabbing the back of the leather couch to steady himself.

"Hi," Grace said, appearing in the doorway. "We've been walking in the park. It's glorious out there today. Blue sky, sunshine . . ." Her face was rosy red and there were leaves in her hair, as if they'd been throwing them at each other. Larry beamed from behind her.

Norman's hands tightened into fists. "Come on in," he said, trying to keep his voice light, determined to remain in complete control of his feelings. "I need to talk to you."

"Sounds serious," Larry said. "We'll hang up our jackets first, okay?"

"And I'll make some tea," Grace added. "I'm

parched from all that running about." She laughed up into Larry's face. "You wretch, I've got leaves down my back."

Several minutes later, they both came back, Grace bearing a tray. "Want some tea, Norm?" she asked.

"No, thanks." He sat down, not wanting to loom over them, but then his anxiety got the better of him and he sprang up again. He threw a couple of logs on the fire, waited for the others to sit down with their tea, and then himself sat down.

"So . . . what's the problem this time?" Larry asked.

You are! Norman felt like replying. "That's what I'd like to know. I had a call from Grostig this morning. He's found a discrepancy in the international figures."

Larry looked surprised. "Oh, really?" He grimaced at Grace. "Always said I was bad at mathematics, didn't I?"

"This isn't a laughing matter. They've got their accountants checking it out. I'm asking you point-blank, Larry, is there anything I should be concerned about?" Norman looked from Larry to Grace. She was sitting on the edge of her seat, her hand gripping Larry's so that her knuckles shone like polished ivory. "Because if there is, I'd rather be forewarned, so that I can do some damage control before it's too late."

Larry gave an inane little laugh, but it was Grace who answered. "Of course, there's nothing wrong. Are you accusing Larry of something—"

"Come off it, darling." Larry drew his hand away from hers. "It won't take the accountants long before they find it." He looked straight at Norman. "Truth is, I had some bad losses at the races. Nothing that I can't redress," he added hastily, "but I've been taking . . . a little from the till to tide me over."

"You've been embezzling money from Tyler Foods' international division," Norman stated baldly. "Is that what you're saying?"

Grace sprang up. "For God's sake, Norman, don't be so judgmental. You sound exactly like Father."

"Maybe I do, but there's no point in wrapping something dirty up in clean linen, is there?"

Larry sighed and then rose to stand by his wife. "He's right, you know, sweetheart. I did tell you it would have been better to come to him when this first happened, didn't I?"

"If it hadn't been for this bloody merger," Grace cried, "he could have paid the money back, as he'd intended. But once the merger came up, we were forced to go all out in support of it, hoping that we could somehow make up the discrepancy with what we made personaly from the merger."

Norman turned on her. "And if you'd told me in the first place, we could have put the money back before the Bruneau Company found out. How could you have been so stupid?"

"Oh, and you, Mr. High-and-Mighty, you've never made any mistakes, have you? You marry that tart, Lauren, and spend thousands on her—"

"That's enough, Grace!" Larry's voice cut through the room. "I won't have you fighting with your brother when I'm the cause of this mess." His handsome face was ashen. For once, he looked fully his age. He turned to Norman. "What can we do?"

"*We* can do nothing. You're off the job, Anderson."

"You can't do that," Grace cried.

"Oh, yes, I can. You must be out of your mind if you think I'd ever let him get within a mile of Tyler Foods again. As it is, he may be responsible for blowing this merger. And I hold you responsible for aiding and abetting him. How could you do it, Gracie? How could you?" His voice cracking, Norman walked away from them, to gaze out the window at the broad expanse of lawn sweeping down to the river.

When he turned back, they still stood looking at him, Grace's arm thrust defiantly into Larry's in a statement of unity, her jaw jutting in the old belligerent way he knew so well. "What puzzles me," Norman said, "is why, when the merger was first proposed, you didn't oppose it, to avoid Larry's embezzlement being discovered?"

"Will you stop calling it that?" Grace said, eyes flashing. "I didn't fight it because I knew you'd smell a rat if I did."

"Our only hope," Larry said, "was to push the merger through, get our money, and pay the loan back."

"Loan?" Norman repeated through gritted teeth.

Larry gave an elegant shrug. "Whatever you like to call it. We had every intention of paying it back as soon as our share from the merger came through."

"After Grostig alerted me, I checked the figures myself. Did you really think that such a sum of money—yes, Larry, I know exactly how much it is!—would escape their accountants? And ours, once they were fully alerted to the problem?"

Larry gave a rueful smile. "We certainly hoped so."

"So you did everything in your power to push the merger through. Everything." Norman was looking directly at Grace now, fixing her with his gaze, so that she glanced away. Norman's voice dropped. "Even . . . adjusting Mother's medication to make it look as if she were going senile."

"Now hold on," Larry cried. "There's no way that—" His voice faltered as he saw Grace's defiant stance. "Grace?"

"I'm right, aren't I?" Norman said softly.

Grace glared at him. "You can't prove it."

"Can't I? This very morning I asked Andrew to have Mother tested to check on her medication."

Grace stood even more erect, head flung back. "Andrew probably made some error in prescribing for her. Or perhaps Janet mixed the doses up. She can be really scatterbrained, that woman. Or perhaps she did it on purpose."

"Why would Janet give Mother the wrong medication?"

"You never know. Perhaps she was fed up with Mother's high-handed ways. Perhaps she's going senile herself. I don't know." Grace waved her arms impatiently. "The most likely scenario is that Mother overmedicated herself. You know how forgetful she's getting." Grace's eyes locked with Norman's. "Impossible to prove who gave her what, really, isn't it?"

Larry was staring at her as if he'd never seen her before. "I can't believe you'd—"

"Shut your mouth, Larry darling."

"What about the other things?" Norman said. "They'll be easier to prove."

"What other things?"

"Griffon's body. And the thing with Father's so-called ghost." Norman's voice was iron hard. "Did you kill Mother's dog yourself or did Larry do that?"

Larry held up his hands. "Please, count me out on all this. I've no idea what you're talking about."

"However you did it, you needed more than just the two of you to carry it out and yet still be visible to everyone when it happened. That other person will be your weak link."

"Let's get this straight, Norman," Larry protested. "I know nothing about all this stuff with Eleanor you're talking about. If Grace did any of it, she did it without my knowledge."

Grace looked as if he'd turned around and suddenly punched her in the stomach. She said nothing, but her eyes were like dark, deep pools as she looked at her husband. Norman was torn by both pity and anger as he watched them. His eyes narrowed. "Was your son in on this, too?"

Grace gave a little start.

Norman felt sick. "Did Jamie set up the dead dog thing?" He saw Grace flinch and didn't wait for a reply. "Yes, of course he did. It was just the sort of thing Jamie would enjoy doing. Father's ghost, too, no doubt. How did he get in? Up the tree and through the window? Oh, how could I forget? Jamie is an expert at rock climbing, isn't he?"

Larry shrugged. "Your brother's got quite an imagination," he said to Grace, but he was chewing on the corner of his bottom lip.

Norman hadn't finished. There was one more matter he must deal with—the most troubling—before he could try to salvage something from this disaster. "What about Michelle?" he asked.

"What about her?" Grace countered after a pause.

"Did you kill her, too, as well as Mother's dog?"

"*Kill* her?" Grace looked genuinely amazed. Then she laughed in his face, but Larry became angry.

"Look, I can understand you feeling ticked off because of the money, but accusing people of murder is another thing entirely."

"Are you telling me that you haven't abducted Michelle or done something with her?"

"Why on earth would we do that?" Grace demanded.

"Because you were afraid she'd intervene in the merger. Because you didn't want her and Mother to become close so that Mother would change her will in Michelle's favor. Because you hated Carolyn. Perhaps all of the above."

Grace glared at him defiantly. "I don't know what happened to Michelle. What's more, I don't give a shit what happened to her, either."

Please God, let her be telling the truth, Norman prayed. The embezzlement and its cover up he could take. The medication part was far harder to accept, although he preferred to believe that Grace had never intended to cause permanent harm to their mother. But kidnapping, perhaps murder? That was something else. He could not, would not believe that his own flesh and blood was capable of something so horrific.

The telephone rang, saving him from having to respond to Grace. He picked up the portable phone from the corner table. "Yes?" he barked.

"Gary Williams here."

Norman felt the knot in his stomach squeeze tighter. At this moment, the policeman was the last person he wanted to talk to. He couldn't afford to let this go public. "Hi, Gary. What can I do for you?" he asked, trying to lighten his voice.

"I wanted to let you know that there's something going on with the Gaudry brothers. They've met up and are now driving north on One Two Six in Marc's truck. Looks suspicious."

"That's good news. You think they might lead us to Michelle?"

"It's possible. Wherever they go, we'll keep a tail on them."

"Could you let her husband know? He's driving down to St. Andrews—"

"Done that already. Got him on his cell phone. Okay, Mr. Tyler. We'll keep in touch."

"Thanks very much." Norman put the phone down.

"What was that about?" Larry asked.

"The Gaudry brothers are acting suspiciously. The police are tailing them."

"That's great news," Larry said with a broad grin. His arm slid around Grace's waist. "We're both ready to accept your apologies now for having suspected us of murdering your niece, aren't we, Grace?"

Norman waited for his sister to lambast him for having made such a preposterous accusation, but Grace merely nodded. For the briefest of moments, her eyes met Norman's. Then she turned her face away.

Norman's heart sank. The aversion of Grace's eyes from his was all he needed to tell him that he'd lost yet another sister forever.

Chapter 41

During the rest of Friday night and then at intervals throughout Saturday, Michelle kept working with the knife. Her hands were covered with little cuts where the blade had nicked her skin. She had to be very careful not to give herself a deep cut; the last thing she needed was to end up with a septic hand. At one point, she realized that it would be a while before she could throw a pot again. Tears filled her eyes as she thought of working at her potter's wheel, the clay oozing between her fingers.

Almost her entire day was spent in the same exhausting routine. An hour or so of lying flat, moving back and forth across the knife, striving to cut the tape from her wrists, alternating with a great deal of time spent in the kitchen trying to open the bottled water with her fingers. Finding a couple of individual packs of apple juice had been the highlight of her day. She managed to pierce one of them by standing with her back to the counter and poking at it with her nail, but her joy was muted when she knocked it over, and she was forced to lap the trickle of juice from the countertop like a cat. At this rate, she was likely to die of dehydration rather than starvation.

When, late on Saturday afternoon, she heard the raucous call of a pair of blue jays, she felt as if they were mocking her. "You'll never escape!" they seemed to be screeching. She longed to be outside with them, breathing in the fresh autumnal air, not the increasingly stale air in the cabin.

By the time darkness was closing in, she was exhausted from tension and the constant strain on her arms and shoulders. She lay down on the couch, burrowing into the nest of blankets, and allowed herself to wallow in despair. All day, she'd tried to keep up her spirits for the sake of her baby, telling herself— and the baby—they'd soon be free. Yet she didn't seem to be any further ahead in cutting off her bonds. At this rate she'd be found dead years later, a skeleton with duct tape still bound around its bony wrists.

Lying on her side, arms behind her, she felt like a trussed turkey. She was dreading the thought of another long dark night, without heat or light. She kept testing her bonds, trying to pull her wrists apart, but they seemed to be as tightly bound as ever.

All that work and nothing to show for it.

As the light faded, stealing slowly from the room, a feeling of hopelessness crept in on her. It was bitterly cold in the cabin. Teeth chattering, she tried to kick the blankets over her with her feet. "I love you, Buster," she whispered to her baby. "Brian, wherever you are, I'll always love you."

She lay there, trying hard to relax, breathing in the smells of years of wood ash from the stove and the old tar that had been used to bond the log walls of the cabin. Then she began to pray. She prayed to her mother. "I love you, Mom," she whispered. "I wish you were here with me." Then, rallying herself, "If you've got any spare angels up there, Mom, could you send me down a couple, please?" She even considered praying to her father, but decided that knowing what she knew about him, it would probably be a waste of time. She had to face reality. She was alone, utterly alone, and no one who cared about her knew where she was.

Shivering, she turned her face and buried it in the pillow.

*   *   *

She awoke suddenly, her heart pounding, not sure what had woken her. Probably another bout of coughing. It was still pitch-dark, but she wasn't sure if one or several hours had passed. For a moment, she lay still, listening, her heart drumming in her ears. Then she heard twigs snapping, men's low voices. Lifting her head from beneath the blankets, she saw the beam from a flashlight slide across the window.

Oh, God, this could be worse even than being left alone.

She struggled up to a sitting position on the couch and fixed her gaze on the door, straining to hear what they were saying. Then she realized they were speaking in French. Had the Brute returned, bringing a friend with him? It was difficult to hear the words, but she managed to understand a phrase or two.

". . . locked," one said.

"No one inside then . . ."

"Still, we can sleep here tonight." That she got quite clearly.

They were strangers. They didn't know she was in there. But what kind of men would they be? Would they rescue her . . . or attack her? Here she was, with bound wrists, like a lamb for the sacrifice. "God, help me, please," she managed to whisper as the rusty bolts were drawn back.

The door screeched open. Two figures stood in the doorway. The flashlight beam raked the room . . . and came to settle on her. She blinked in its blinding light and then almost jumped out of her skin when both men started yelling and laughing like hyenas.

"Bingo!" roared one of them and they both rushed at her.

Chapter 42

It took Michelle a few seconds to realize that the two young men were hugging her, not attacking her. And they were also yelling "Michelle!" at her.

"You are Michelle, yes?" one of them asked her, when he'd given her enough time to get her breath.

"Yes, I am." She was utterly, totally bewildered. Whenever she'd imagined the joy of being rescued, it had always been Brian or Andrew or the police, or even one of her uncles. Not two hefty young strangers smelling strongly of beer. "Who are you?"

"We're your brothers."

Brothers? She had no brothers.

"I'm Pierre. He's Marc," said the slighter man. "Our father was Michel Gaudry, same as yours."

"Oh, God!" Michelle started to laugh and then cry, and then laugh again. And then they were hugging again, and she was hugging them back. "I don't understand. How did you find me?"

"Wait. We have to cut that tape off you. Man, if I had the guy here who did this to you, I'd—"

"There's a knife on the floor," Michelle told him. "I've been trying to cut the tape off."

Pierre looked at her, shaking his head. "Turn around." She did so. With infinite care, he cut through the tape. When she felt the bond slacken and fall away, the relief was overwhelming. But so was the pain. As she tried to move her shoulders back into position for the first time in ages, agony shot through them. Groaning, she tried to circle them to ease the pain, but that only it made it worse.

"You'll need some heat," Marc said, gently touching her shoulder. "Who's the bastard who did this to you?"

"I don't know. They wore woolen masks that covered everything but their eyes and mouths. I'm dying for a drink. Could you pour me a glass of water? I couldn't get the water bottles open."

Pierre went to fetch her water while Marc stood there, staring at her. "Man, you're a cool one." Michelle took that as a compliment. "I'd have gone crazy locked in here in the dark."

Michelle shrugged, guessing she must look more in control than she felt. She winced again as she moved her shoulders. "I guess you do what you have to do to survive. You still haven't told me how you found me."

"When we heard you were missing, we took time off from work to go searching. We asked around the bars and checked a few old trappers' huts we knew about. Then someone in a bar at Miramichi told us about a drunk who'd been slinging money around like it was water last night. He was bragging 'bout a job he'd done and how he'd had this chick in a hut in the forest."

"Rotten liar! He didn't have me," Michelle protested.

"That's lucky for him or he would've had to answer to us."

Michelle wondered how much of this talk was sheer bravado, but somehow it was a comfort to think of having brothers who were prepared to defend her honor in the good old-fashioned way. Of course, she thought, at any other time but this, she might have burst out laughing at the very idea, but at the moment she was feeling vulnerable enough to appreciate it. It was a relief to know that she'd been wrong about them and that some members of her convoluted family cared about her.

She was about to drink the water Pierre brought her when a shout froze them all on the spot.

"Okay. This is Sergeant McNab of the RCMP. Drop any weapons you might have and come out with your hands on your heads."

"Oh, shit!" Marc whispered. "It's the cops."

Michelle stood up. "Don't move. I'll go. They won't shoot me."

"They might," Pierre whispered. "They could be ready to shoot as soon as we get to the door."

Michelle shook her head at them. She moved closer to the open doorway, but was careful to stay out of sight. "My name is Michelle Tyler," she shouted. "I'm safe."

Silence.

"My brothers are here with me," she yelled, her voice hoarse from lack of moisture. "They've just rescued me."

She could hear voices. Then she heard a single voice call her name, a voice that set her pulse wildly racing. *Brian?* No, Brian was in Indonesia. He couldn't possibly be here.

"Brian?" She rushed to the door before Marc and Pierre could stop her. Into the darkness she ran, to be suddenly blinded again, this time by searchlight beams.

"Michelle!" She was picked up bodily from the ground and swung around. Brian's arms were around her, crushing her against his body. Brian's lips were kissing every available inch of her face, her neck. Brian was here. She was safe.

"You sure you're okay, Mrs. Norton?" asked a tall man carrying a semiautomatic weapon.

"I'm fine," she managed to say. "I'm more than fine. Please don't hurt my brothers. They rescued me."

The policeman frowned. "You sure about that?"

"Oh, I'm sure, all right. They're not the men who kidnapped me."

"Let's go back into the cabin for now, shall we?"

She didn't want to. She didn't want to go inside

that ghastly place ever again, but with Brian's arm
supporting her, she went in, hoping that this would be
the very last time she'd have to step back into the
cabin that had been her prison for six days.

Chapter 43

⁓

Too exhausted even to ask questions, Michelle dozed all the way back to Fredericton. Each time she awoke, she'd find herself cradled in Brian's arm, her head cushioned against his shoulder, and murmuring something unintelligible, she'd fall asleep again.

When they reached Tyler House, she was surprised to find a group of family members waiting for her, even though it was past midnight. Ramsey and his wife, Penny, ran down the steps to greet her. Inside, in the hall, Norman and Lauren were waiting to welcome her. Lauren, openly weeping, gave her a hug. "Thank God, you're safe," she whispered.

Then there was Stewart and his wife. "Welcome home," Stewart said. He bent to kiss her cheek, then held his hand out to Brian. "Thanks for bringing her back." His mouth trembled and tears suddenly filled his eyes. "Old fool, aren't I?" he said with an embarrassed laugh.

Michelle shook her head. Her own heart was so full she couldn't speak. She hadn't expected anything like this. The reception bewildered her. Had she been wrong? Had the family not been involved in her abduction, after all? She looked up at Brian. Her bewilderment obviously showed on her face, for he put his arm around her and said, "Wait until we're alone. We can talk about it then."

She didn't want to talk about it. She wanted only to be alone with Brian, to feel him holding her tightly against him, and then to tell him about the baby. But it seemed she'd have to wait. Janet, too, was crying and Michelle hugged her and assured her she was fine, but very, very tired.

"You must be. But would you be able to come up and see Mrs. Tyler? Ever since we heard they'd found you, she's refused to sleep until she saw you."

"Of course I will." Michelle felt as if she were sleepwalking; people milling around, voices rising and falling, as she slept through this waking dream. "Is she all right, Janet? My grandmother, I mean."

"She will be once she sees you. Go up and see her. Then you must rest."

Michelle doubted she'd be allowed to rest yet. She turned to Brian. "Come with me."

"You bet I will. I won't let you out of my sight."

She still couldn't believe that Brian was there, his tanned face beaming at her. It was all part of the dream. What worried her most was that she might wake up and find herself back at the cabin, numb with the cold, bound and alone in the darkness.

They went upstairs together, to find Eleanor up and sitting in a chair, with Andrew standing beside her. As they entered, he stared across the room at Michelle for what seemed like an eternity.

Michelle broke the silence. "Hi, Andrew," she said quietly. "I'm back."

He gave her a faint smile. "Thank God for that." Then, as if he'd suddenly recollected where he was, he said, "I didn't want to leave Eleanor until you came up. Her blood pressure's sky-high, as it is."

Eleanor waved an impatient hand "Oh, you're such a worrywart, Andrew Lenzie. Go away now and leave me and my granddaughter together. I'll be fine."

"I think you will, now that you've actually seen her." Andrew came to join them in the doorway. He hesitated for a moment and then held out his hand to Michelle. "Welcome back. We've been worried sick about you."

She took his hand, very much aware of the sudden

tension in Brian's body. "Thank you, Andrew. I'm fine. I really am," she assured him, smiling. "Is Grandmother okay?"

He grimaced. "This has all been a severe shock to her system. Has Norman brought you up-to-date with everything that's happened here?"

Michelle shook her head. "I know nothing except what happened to me. Did you know it was my brothers who found me?"

"Yes. Brian called to tell us. From the car, I guess."

"No, from the cabin," Brian said. "The police wanted Michelle to show them over the place and tell them what had happened there."

"That must have been pretty grim for you both."

"You can say that again," Brian agreed.

"I don't ever want to see that place again." Michelle shuddered. "But I suppose I may have to."

"What are you people talking about over there?" Eleanor said, raising her voice. "Do you realize how rude it is to leave me out?"

"I'm so sorry." Michelle rushed across the room to her grandmother, kneeling down to put her arms about her. For the first time since she'd left the cabin, she allowed the pent-up tears to flow.

Her grandmother's head bent to hers. "I'm the one who's sorry," she whispered. "I feel so responsible for all that's happened to you."

"But you're not. How could you be?"

"It's my fault. If I hadn't been so stubborn over this merger this would never have happened."

Michelle was even more bewildered than before. Hadn't everyone from the family been there to greet her, as if they really cared about her? Suddenly she realized that not all of them had been there. Not Grace, not Larry, not their son. "Grace?" she whispered.

Her grandmother's lips thinned. "Larry had been cooking the books. Even worse, it looks as if my daughter has been giving me too much of my medication."

"We're not certain about that yet," said Andrew sternly from the doorway.

"Stop eavesdropping. In fact, you can go away and leave us alone. I always said he wasn't half as good a doctor as his father," she added to Michelle. "*He* would have guessed what was happening and put a stop to it."

Poor Andrew, Michelle thought. She glanced up at the door and saw that he'd gone, leaving Brian standing there by himself. She sincerely hoped that Andrew hadn't heard Eleanor's last remark.

"So the Gaudrys turned out to be not so bad, after all," Eleanor said. "Better than my own daughter to you."

"I wouldn't be here now without them."

"Of course, you would. We would have found you eventually."

Eventually might have been too late, Michelle thought, but she said nothing. There was no need for her grandmother to know the details of her ordeal. Particularly not now, when she knew that Grace and Larry must have been involved. How and when had they hired the two kidnappers and who else had been involved? she wondered. But questions like those could wait until later. What made her blood run cold was that Grace had been messing with her mother's medication. It didn't bear thinking about.

"Did the Gaudry boys come back here with you?" Eleanor asked.

"No, they went back to Marc's place at Miramichi. I'm going to call them tomorrow." There was no point in discussing her father's family with Eleanor. "I'm really tired," she said, standing up. "Would you mind if we caught up with everything tomorrow morning?"

"I'm tired myself. It's been a terrible time since you left us at St. Andrews. Not knowing where you were, what had happened to you . . ." Eleanor's hands trembled in her lap.

Michelle took hold of one hand and kissed it. "I'm safe now," she said firmly, "so you can stop worrying."

"Easier said than done. Grace might have to go to prison. Not that she doesn't deserve it, but she's still my daughter."

Michelle felt a spasm of pity. She hadn't had time to think about the repercussions. "Don't think about that now," she told her grandmother. "Get lots of rest. That's what I'm going to do."

Eleanor patted her hand. "I don't want you to go."

"I'm not going far."

"At least you've got your handsome husband to take care of you. I like your Brian."

"Even though he's an American?"

"I like Americans," Eleanor said indignantly. "Whoever said I didn't like them?" She crooked her finger at Brian. "Come here, Brian."

"Yes, ma'am." He came to stand beside her, leaning down to her.

"I'm greatly looking forward to a debate with you on the pros and cons of the American Revolution."

"I didn't know there were any cons about it," Brian said with a grin.

"Aha! That's just the kind of misinformation I want to discuss with you. Even you, a supposedly informed journalist, don't have all the facts. Have you read Kenneth Roberts's wonderful book *Oliver Wiswell*?"

"Can't say I have."

"Read it! It caused a huge storm of controversy when it was published in the forties. It'll make you rethink some of your ideas."

"I'm always open to new ideas. But not tonight," Brian said firmly.

"Definitely not tonight. You take your wife away and look after her. I hope you won't hold it against us."

"What?"

"What's happened to her. It grieves me to think that my own daughter hurt her so deeply." Tears swam in Eleanor's eyes. "Ramsey and I raised our children to worship money and power. Now we're reaping our own bitter harvest."

Michelle turned away, unable to bear her grandmother's grief when she herself felt so fragile.

"You mustn't take the blame," Brian told Eleanor. "I can see how much you care for Michelle."

"Then you won't stop her from coming back to visit me?"

"I won't. But I'll be coming with her next time, if you don't mind."

Michelle swallowed as she watched her grandmother's face light up again. *Brian Norton, I love you to pieces!* she told him silently.

"Good," her grandmother said. "Then we'll have lots of time to talk about your War of Independence."

"Good night, Mrs. Tyler."

"Good night, Brian. Look after her for me."

"I will."

"And please stay home with her more."

Michelle felt a cold knot in her stomach. Just when everything was going so well between them, her grandmother had to say something that jarred. She glanced up at Brian.

"I sure will," he said, the brilliance of his smile totally dispelling her anxiety.

As she watched them leave the room, hand in hand, Eleanor sank back in her chair. She was exhausted by all that had happened. Moreover, she was well aware that there was a great deal more stress to come before this was all over. But she had also sensed something else when Michelle had entered the room with Brian. There had been a glow, a softness about her as she leaned against her husband that had resonated with Eleanor.

As she recalled Janet's remarks about Michelle not eating very well and looking pale, her mouth slid into a slow smile. If she was right, another generation of Tylers was about to begin. But her instincts told her that when Carolyn's daughter and her husband raised their child, they'd be able to avoid the mistakes she and Ramsey had made.

*   *   *

Douglas Bradford was standing in the hall talking to Norman when Michelle came down with Brian.

"Who's that?" Brian asked.

"Eleanor's lawyer," Michelle just had time to say before Douglas came over to them. Norman withdrew down the hall, disappearing into the family room.

"I'm glad to see you safely returned," the lawyer told Michelle.

"Thank you." Michelle introduced him to Brian.

"This is a bad business. A very bad business," Douglas said, shaking hands with Brian. "I'd like to talk to you both in private. Not here, though." He glanced at the solid form of Sergeant McNab, who was talking in a low voice to Ramsey.

"Sorry, Mr. Bradford, not tonight," Brian said. "The only people Michelle is talking to, apart from me, are Sergeant McNab and Inspector Williams. Then we're both going to catch up with some much-needed sleep."

"I understand. But it's very important for the family, for Michelle's grandmother, that we do some damage control here, Mr. Norton. I must impress upon you the importance—"

"Nothing doing until tomorrow morning at the earliest. See you then."

Andrew appeared from the direction of the kitchen, holding a glass of water. "Need some help?"

"Please explain to Mr. Bradford here about the effects of trauma and shock on the system, would you?" Brian asked him. "I'm getting Michelle out of here."

Andrew glanced at Michelle and gave a little nod. "I'll be glad to. Soon as you're ready to leave, I'll drive you over to the hotel." He led Douglas away.

"We're staying in a hotel?" Michelle said.

"I had Andrew book us a room at the Lord Beaverbrook down the road. Hold on a minute. I'm going to ask Gary and McNab to meet us at the hotel, rather than having to speak to them here." Brian went to have a word with them and then returned to Michelle. "All done. Let's go."

Now Stewart came out into the hall. "Can I drive you anywhere?"

Brian looked at him with raised eyebrows. "I don't think so."

Stewart nodded. "You're right. I've been celebrating."

"That's nice."

"Not just Michelle's safe return." Stewart grinned at her. "Also my resignation from the company, effective today."

"You're leaving Tyler's?" Michelle was surprised.

"That's right. My mother's buying me out. My shares will give her even more clout when she's dealing with Norman."

"What's going to happen?" Michelle asked him.

"Who knows?" Stewart's grin broadened. "Who cares?"

"I do." Michelle glared at him. "It was because of this wretched merger deal that I was kidnapped and could have died."

"Sorry. That was tactless of me. I imagine things will be put on hold for now, with Grace and Larry under investigation."

Michelle shook her head. "How can you all be so casual about it after everything that's happened?" She turned blindly to Brian. "Let's get out of here."

Stewart grabbed her arm. "Don't be angry, Michelle. The rest of us hadn't a clue that Larry had his hand in the till or that Grace would go to such crazy extremes to cover it up."

Brian grasped Michelle's elbow and eased her away from Stewart. "This can wait until tomorrow. Say good night to everyone for us, please." Ignoring Stewart's protests, he guided Michelle out into the chill night air and opened the back door of Andrew's car. "Get in. I'll get Andrew."

"I think I'd rather wait outside. I need the fresh air."

Brian went back inside the house and came out almost immediately, followed by Andrew.

Michelle suddenly realized that she was shivering violently. Andrew took one look at her and bundled her into the backseat. "Keep her warm," he told Brian.

"I'm s-sorry," Michelle whispered, her teeth chattering.

"Nothing to be sorry about," Andrew said crisply, starting the engine. "You're suffering from exhaustion and shock, that's all. You'll be fine after a good night's sleep."

"And something to eat," Brian said.

"Nothing too heavy," Andrew warned.

"A bottle of wine?" Brian asked. Michelle was about to say "No alcohol," but then remembered that Brian didn't know yet.

"She's better without alcohol," Andrew said. "I'll give you a couple of sleeping pills, in case she has trouble sleeping."

Now Michelle understood Eleanor's annoyance at being discussed as if she wasn't there. "Don't talk about me as if . . ." She was so tired she couldn't find the right words and left the sentence hanging.

When they reached the hotel, Andrew went in with them, insisting on carrying their overnight bags.

"There's no need," Brian told him. "We'll be fine."

"I want to make sure you are."

When Brian had registered, they found the two policemen waiting in the foyer for them. Brian introduced Inspector Williams to Michelle. She looked warily at the lean-faced policeman.

"We've both got some questions for you, Mrs. Norton."

"Ms. Tyler," Brian corrected Gary.

"Mrs. Norton's fine," Michelle said.

"Before you go any further," Andrew said, "I have to tell you, as Michelle's interim physician, that she is not fit to answer questions tonight."

So that was why Andrew had come into the hotel. Michelle thanked him with her eyes.

"But it's imperative that we find out what happened as soon as possible," McNab protested.

"No questions," Andrew said firmly. "I'm sure it can wait until tomorrow morning."

Sergeant McNab heaved a sigh. "If her physician says no questions, then no questions it is. Fortunately you gave us a good deal of basic information at the cabin, Ms. Tyler."

"But we'll definitely need to speak to you again tomorrow," Inspector Williams said firmly.

"Means me having to drive back from St. Andrews," McNab grumbled.

"Not too early," Brian warned them. "Don't forget it's Sunday."

The sergeant sighed. "Okay. Tomorrow at eleven?" Everyone agreed.

"There's one thing I think you should know right away," the sergeant added as he was about to leave. "We were able to trace the speeding car."

"What speeding car?" Michelle asked.

"A car was reported to be seen speeding first from St. Andrews and then on the road to Miramichi. We now know that it was the car used to take you from the Tyler cottage to the cabin."

"Whose car was it?" Brian asked.

"The Mercedes convertible is registered in the name of James Anderson, Grace Anderson's son."

Michelle clapped her hand to her mouth. "Oh, my God!" Her first captor, Dave, was that offensive idiot Jamie, Grace and Larry's son. It figured.

"I take it that you've met James Anderson before?" Inspector Williams asked Michelle.

"Oh, yes," she said. "I've met him."

"Would you say that your first kidnapper's build resembled your cousin's?"

Cousin! She was sickened by the thought that someone so closely related to her could have done what Jamie did. Even more sickening was her aunt's involvement. She thought about "Dave" for a moment. "Yes, he and Jamie would be about the same height. But he disguised his voice with a phony French accent."

"I think you should know that, after being questioned, Jamie Anderson has confessed to his part in the whole thing, which won't help his parents' position, I'm afraid. Apparently it was all done to get you out of the way, because of some important business deal. They cobbled the idea together last Sunday night, after a family upset at Prospect House."

After Grace got drunk, Michelle thought, and Eleanor spilled the beans about the merger and the family's pressure on her. She was careful to say nothing to the police, knowing that this whole situation was going to prove very nasty.

"Your cousin claims that they had no intention of harming you in any way. They intended to keep you away from your grandmother and then release you as soon as this deal went through. We'll get more information from his parents tonight, no doubt," Gary said, his face grim. "I feel very sorry for Mrs. Tyler. Did you know that it was Larry Anderson who knocked you out at Prospect House?"

Michelle found it hard to imagine the elegant, charming Larry knocking someone out. She closed her eyes, swaying.

"I thought we'd agreed there'd be no questions," Andrew said belligerently.

"That wasn't a question," McNab said. "We thought she'd want to know."

"Thanks, Andrew. I'm okay," Michelle said. "But what about the other one?" she asked. "The guy who was with me for five days? I think his French accent was for real. And why did he leave so suddenly on Friday evening?"

"Apparently, once the Andersons knew your husband had contacted the police," Inspector Williams said, "they decided they'd better order the guy to let you go. They hoped that no one would be able to pin it on them, and that by the time you found your way back the deal would have been completed. But this guy—and, later, Jamie—couldn't keep his mouth shut."

Michelle shivered. "Although I was afraid, somehow I felt that Dave—Jamie called himself Dave—wouldn't really hurt me. But the second man terrified me. And he didn't let me go. He bound my hands together and locked me in. I could have died." She felt Brian's arm tighten around her waist.

"From the description we got from the men in the bar, we think we know who he is," Sergeant McNab said. "Your cousin's not so keen to give us information about him. Probably because there appears to be some kind of drug connection there. But if he confirms our suspicions, the guy has a long record of robbery and assault. To be honest, you were lucky to—"

"Okay." This time Brian stopped them. "Enough." He stepped in front of Michelle, physically blocking her from the two policemen.

They hurriedly said good night, promising to be back in the morning, and left to "Go back to the Andersons' house," as Williams told them, his face grim.

"Time for me to go, as well," Andrew said when the policemen had gone. He rubbed his hand across his mouth. "It's up to both of you, of course, but Eleanor has begged me to keep quiet about Grace's possible involvement in the medication thing. I think she feels her daughter's got enough on her plate with the kidnapping, without adding any more."

"But what about the hallucinations?" Michelle asked. "The dog and Ramsey's ghost . . ."

"Staged. After Norman confronted Grace, she broke down and told her mother that she and Larry—and Jamie, of course—had worked it all out to make Eleanor look as if she were going senile, so Grace could get power of attorney. I believe that Bob was also involved."

Michelle stared at him, eyes wide with horror. "How could she do such a thing to her mother?"

Andrew shook his head. "Takes all kinds. She cared only about her husband, no one else." He blinked and looked away. "I blame myself for not having realized what was going on."

Michelle couldn't find the right words to console him.

Andrew cleared his throat. "I'm going to take a break for a while. Maybe take my daughter to Disneyland, or something. Get some perspective on my life."

Michelle gave him a faint smile. "Sounds good."

"Thanks for everything," Brian said, holding out his hand to Andrew. "I'm putting an end to this now, before Michelle falls asleep on the foyer carpet."

"Good night. Oh, the sleeping pills." Andrew reached into his pocket and pulled out a small envelope. "One only tonight. The second one is for tomorrow, just in case."

"Thanks, but I won't need any sleeping pills," Michelle said. "I'm sleeping on my feet, as it is."

"Okay. See you around."

They stood watching him as he walked away. "That guy's sweet on you, isn't he?" Brian said.

Michelle's face flared. "I'm afraid so."

"Can't say I blame him." Brian put his arm around her, drawing her close to his side.

"He's lonely. Divorced. Missing his daughter."

"He'll be okay. Just needs to get his priorities straight, that's all."

Michelle glanced up at him.

"Like I do," Brian added softly.

"I've got something to tell you," she said to him when they'd stepped into the empty elevator and pressed the button for the third floor.

"In the circumstances, I should imagine you've got a lot of things to tell me, but they can wait until the morning."

"This can't."

"Sounds exciting. What is it?"

"Wait until we get into our room."

"Shall I order some food?"

"I couldn't eat a thing."

"Me neither."

They walked down the carpeted corridor to a large corner room with two picture windows. One overlooked the St. John River. From the other, they could see the impressive old legislative building, lit with floodlights. Directly below the window there was an ancient maple tree, the wind blowing through it, shaking down its russet leaves. Brian drew the green velvet curtains across both windows and switched on the small table lamps, creating a cozy atmosphere.

He held out his arms and Michelle came into them. "Home at last," she said, her face pressed into the green sweater she'd given him for his last birthday.

"This isn't home," he reminded her.

"Wherever you are is home to me."

He sat down on the couch, drawing her down beside him. "I've had a lot of time to think recently. Too much time. From now on, things are going to be very different."

"They sure are," she said, grinning up at him.

"Will you let me finish?"

Michelle shook her head. "Me first. Then you can say whatever you like. We're going to be a family."

"We are a fam—" Brian stopped, his eyes widening as he suddenly realized what she was telling him.

"I'm pregnant."

He sat back, mouth open, his face pale beneath the tan. "You're sure?"

"Oh, yes." She gave him a wry smile. "That hasn't helped this past week, I can tell you. Try being kidnapped and having morning sickness as well."

"I'd like to kill those bastards!" Brian said, but he couldn't stop grinning.

"Let's not worry about them now. So, what do you think?"

He crushed her against him. "I think you're the most wonderful person I—"

"People."

"What?"

"People. There's two of us now." She took his hand and pressed it again her stomach. "Our baby helped to keep me alive," she told him softly. "Every move I made, everything I did was in consideration of him or her. You know me. Impetuous me. Without the baby, I might have tried to make a run for it, done something physical, which might have worked, but also might have injured me or worse. Because of our baby, I had to use my brains instead of—"

"Your brawn. Right! Oh, sweetheart. I can't bear to think of—"

"Then don't. I'm fine."

"Are you sure?"

"Absolutely. As soon as we get back to Winnipeg I'll see an obstetrician."

"Does he know?"

"Who?"

"Your Dr. Andrew," he said. His jaw tensed. It was the first real sign of jealousy of Andrew she'd seen in Brian.

"Of course not! The only other person who knows is Becca." Michelle clapped her hand to her mouth. "Oh, no. I haven't called Becca yet. She must be sick with worry."

"I'll call her. You get undressed. I'll find your pajamas for you."

"Are you sure you're okay about the baby?"

"Okay? I'm over the moon about it—him—her."

"I cheated. I stopped taking the pill. That was wrong of me. It should have been our decision."

"It would have been if I hadn't been so blind and selfish all this time. But things are going to be different now, you'll see."

"Don't change too much."

"Compromise, right?"

"Right." Michelle grinned at him.

While he left a message on Rebecca's machine, telling her they'd call again in the morning, Michelle got into her pajamas and climbed into the king-size bed. Brian leaned over her to kiss her. She held her arms out to him. "Make love to me, Brian Norton," she murmured.

"I don't think—"

"Please. I want to be really, really close to you."

He held her close for a moment, then released her. "Okay. Give me a few moments and I'll be with you."

But when he came out of the bathroom, she was curled up on her left side, fast asleep. Brian turned out the lights and carefully got into bed beside her. Turning on his side, he put his right arm around her, lying close to her, spoon-fashion, his hand pressed gently against her stomach. And as his tense muscles began to relax, and he matched his breathing to hers, he started to plan the greatest adventure of all that lay ahead of them.